ISBN 978-1-943773-23-73 (eBook, 2nd edition)
ISBN 978-1-943773-24-4 (paperback, 2nd US edition)
ISBN 978-1-943773-43-5 (paperback, 2nd INTL edition)

Cover Design by Untold Designs Romance and Fantasy Covers
https://www.facebook.com/untolddesignscovers/

Copyediting by R.A. Weston
www.rawestoneditorial.com

I0579569

STAY UPDATED!

If you haven't heard anything from us in a while, it means you're
no longer on our list.

So if you'd like to get updates on our new releases (And we have a
lot of them!) please consider signing up here!

Newsletters not your thing? Consider joining our
exclusive Facebook Group!

We want to hear from you!
Write us at guinevere.libertad@gltomaswrites.com to discuss your fave stories by us! Comments, Suggestions, even requests what you'd like to see in our next publications!

Also, if you loved this book, please consider leaving a review. It really makes an authors day to read them and they're so, so helpful in determining if this is the sort of read for the next reader who may stumble across it. You can do so by clicking here. And remember no review is too short!

SUMMARY:

New to Providence, RI, **Naima Adewunmi** had every intention of fulfilling everything she left her New York borough for, finishing up her Bachelor's degree and finding a job while doing it.

She wasn't supposed to fall for **Timothy Ferreiro**, a smooth, slick talking, sexy specimen of a man, messy bedhead hair included, who also happens to be her new boss. From first wink she was under his spell, which wouldn't be a problem if there weren't one underlying issue: Tim's got a long distance girlfriend.

Drama unfolds in a tale of will they or won't they in this steamy office romance. Can two people in a messy game of attraction find themselves on the same page?

Same Page ends in a cliffhanger and is concluded with Next Chapter

CHAPTER ONE

Naima

Want to know the most important thing you learn living in the city?

Always wear flats to a job interview.

If you're walking block after block, there's no way your feet are *not* feel it in heels. I'd only been downtown once since I got to Providence, but I was so sure I'd be trekking this entire town twice before breaking a sweat. There was a reason people from New York never left New York. If you were cut out for it there, everywhere else seemed easy. That was my impression of Providence, Rhode Island.

I stopped by the Starbucks along the way. This part of town was already calling me. I wouldn't confuse it for Manhattan, but it was just as nice and a heck of a lot cleaner.

It was 9:37 by the time I arrived at my destination, and I was met by two open carts of newly released books, blue-rimmed glass doors, and an overhead sign in Roman cast metal letters.

SYMPOSIUM BOOKS

For an independent bookstore, it was impressive. Definitely outdoing some of the chain bookstores. This place had a dope cafe area, and since I was early, I decided to give my crying stomach a treat.

I sashayed over to the glass display, weaning a half-filled Grande Latte, regretting wearing a white button-up to my interview. I'd have to get something I wouldn't make a mess over. No easy task when you were hungry as hell.

Pastries, sandwiches, and all the best smelling foods your nose could think up sat behind the glass. I wanted to try everything, but I jumped back when a guy behind the counter came out of nowhere bearing greetings.

"Scare ya?" he said as his lips edged up into a smile. He was young. Early to mid-twenties. Average height. He wore a beanie, but from his facial hair and dark eyes, he was definitely brunette. Maybe white or Latino, but definitely cute. The apron he was wearing kind of killed it for me, though.

But still. Cute.

"What can I get for you today?"

I took a sip from my latte. I was still trying to figure out what I wanted. I always blamed it on the fact that I was Nigerian or just from the idea that I was from the city of a thousand cultures, but I loved me some food.

"If you tell me what you like, I might be able to suggest something for you."

He flashed a megawatt smile that made me wonder how many women had fallen victim to his charm. My eyes glossed over the menu. I couldn't decide without knowing my options, but I knew a toasted croissant wasn't going to cut it.

"Do you like spinach?" he asked, followed by a description of a sandwich that would've sounded blazin' if it wasn't served on onion bread. I hadn't brought any gum, so I made it known I'd have to pass.

"See now, you left out vital information. No onions, got it! But you like spinach, right?"

I nodded, smiling a little too hard. What can I say? I loved spinach.

"So we have a sandwich that has cheese, spinach, avocado with smoked salmon. It's made on pumpernickel bread. No lie. It goes down."

My face soured. "I don't know about that salmon, though. Same deal with the onions."

"But you like avocados, right?" he asked. I felt like he was going out of his way to be helpful, and I wasn't used to this type of service. But if I planned on working here, he was the prototype of the perfect employee. Wasn't really a people person, but I was definitely taking notes.

"Okay, we have a sandwich known as The Providence. It has spinach, avocados, and Swiss cheese on a flatbread. If Swiss is too rank for you, I could always substitute it for provolone. That one is a personal favorite."

The Providence it was.

He struggled with plastic gloves as I noticed him staring at my breasts. At least I thought it was my breasts.

"Not trying to be nosy or anything, but…did you get that coffee from here?"

I bit back a smile. I was caught red-handed. "No, I bought this from the Starbucks up the street."

Mr. Cutie sucked his teeth. "See, had you had come here first, it would've been a one-stop shop. For the record, we've got coffee, iced cappuccinos, macchiatos, lattes… Hot *annnd* cold. And I'll tell you what we have that Starbucks doesn't." He shot me a wink and pointed to himself. "Me."

I giggled. Mr. Cutie was definitely a pro at the art of flirting.

"Nah, I'm just playing. I like Starbucks, too. So are you a native or new to the city?"

Damn, was I that obvious?

"It's just I've never seen you before, and we get a lot of regulars more than anything."

I smiled. "New to the city."

He cocked an eyebrow, wearing a playful expression. "Here to stay or on vacation?"

The reality was, I honestly didn't know. I was here for school but only to finish my undergrad degree in modern languages. Two years from now, I had no idea where I'd end up.

"Don't know."

"Wait. You don't know if you're on vacation?" He joked.

"Give me a break, okay? It's like my second day here." I said as I stuck out my tongue.

"New York?"

I nodded. "How'd you know?"

He gave me a playful look that ended in a wink. I thanked the heavens that my dark brown skin hid my emotions, otherwise anyone would've seen me blushing right now. "I didn't. You just told me."

Cute and slick. Two of the deadliest combinations.

* * *

Timothy

The worst part about back-to-school week? That there was no busier week than this one.

The best part? The women. Back-to-school week brought in ladies from all over. I didn't know what it was about New York girls, but they were always the baddest.

Looks weren't everything, but if I was being honest with myself, she had *everything* I liked to look at. It'd suck if a girl like that didn't have the brains or the personality to back it up. Much like some of these Providence chicks I encountered daily.

Damn, am I seriously still thinking about her? Who was I

kidding? I was thinking about her ass. It wasn't some plastic-surgery-enhanced type shit, but it fit her athletic legs. Even when I wasn't necessarily attracted to a person, I was a sucker for ass and legs. But her, she was definitely someone from first glance who looked like she had the whole package. This is too distracting. My ass needed to get back to work.

I usually had another person working with me, running the register and cafe station while I unloaded my morning shipments in the back storage room. But with an unexpected callout, I was by myself until Katrina came in at eleven-thirty. And these perishables needed to go out, like, yesterday.

Heels clicked behind me, followed by a firm grip on my shoulder. I didn't need to turn around to know that it was Symposium's HR Manager Martha—or what we called her: "Kmart." Her full name was Martha Stewart, so she'd wore the moniker well.

"Morning, Timothy. Busy, isn't it?"

She wanted something. I just knew it. It was kind of *the thing* to have a nickname at Symposium. My slave name was "Timbaland," and while I was used to it, I hated it. So whenever someone called me by my real name, they wanted something.

"Got anybody else coming in?" she asked, worried.

Kmart reminded me of one of my boy's moms. She had a short curly afro and always wore fly ass pantsuits. Even though she was in her fifties, you knew by her demeanor she's one you would've had your eye on when she was young. Always the first one to start poppin' and lockin' at holiday parties when the soul train line formed.

That was what I loved about working here. Symposium stayed turnt up.

"Timothy, I hate to bother you. It's just I have an interviewee coming in today, and you know we have that second interview policy. I know you hate them, but if you just do me this one favor…"

She was right. I hated conducting interviews. I think I'd done twenty-three since my promotion three years ago to assistant manager for the cafe. I dreaded every last one of them.

Symposium had a policy where every applicant had to be interviewed by two managers to avoid bias. All it ever did was slow down my production. There was never a time I wasn't an hour behind after conducting one. Never.

I was a team player so I didn't plan on telling her no, but I had terms.

"You're gonna have to send me someone over here to help out."

She nodded. "Of course. You can have Mr. Rogers."

I shook my head, and looked at her like she was crazy. Jasper was my boy, but he was older and came up short when he didn't wear his reading glasses. I prided my department having

the least amount of shortages. Martha was trying to pull a fast one. Not today.

"Give me Rocketman and we have a deal."

Her eyes narrowed. "Ugh, okay. But as soon as Kandy Krush gets here, I need him back on the front end."

I couldn't wait for this interview to be over with. It was just the beginning of the week, but was it too much to get to leave on time?

* * *

Naima

I held out as long as I could before I took my phone out to check my messages.

Two that said: *Call Mom. Delete.*

My mom was new to texting, so her messages were hard to understand. Except for the ones scolding me to focus all my attention on school and not men. Or better yet, the ones contradicting those: *Are you going to wait until you are too old to get a husband?* Even reading them to myself, I could hear her accented English in my head. And that was just bad.

I was twenty-seven with no kids and not a care in the world. I wasn't wasting a thought on marriage. I was too busy trying to get the degree I should've gotten years ago. Which my mother reminded me on a regular basis.

Nigerian moms. You had to love them.

The legs of the chair screeched across from me, followed by the sound of a clearing of throat. He laid his apron down on the table and tucked in his lips, like he was trying to stop himself from laughing. It was the guy from the counter. Sans the apron. "Hi" was all I could muster and even then my voice cracked.

He sat down, scooting the chair close enough to rest his elbows on the table. I hope he left before this second interviewer got here. The last thing I needed was to be flirting while I was waiting on a job interview.

"See now, *you* didn't tell me you were here for an interview." His smile was sly, and close up, I noticed a mole on his left cheek. He wore a slim-fitted grey sweater and loose-fitting jeans that would have convinced me he was a cookie-cutter white boy had it not been for the Timbs on his feet and the diamond stud in his ear. Those told a different story.

He picked up the papers the first interviewer, Martha, left behind and rolled them into a cylinder. When he didn't get up, it dawned on me.

"Don't tell me *you're* the second interviewer?" I asked. Please say no.

"That would be me," he said, flashing me that smile again. "But it's Mr.Ferreiro if you're nasty."

That made me laugh, but I wished I hadn't. I had a snort to my laugh, and it was not cute.

"I'm the cafe assistant manager." He held out his hand for me to shake, and I couldn't help admiring his slender fingers. Maybe it was that "if you're nasty" comment. Keep your head in this interview, Naima. He unfolded the papers, reading over something. "You must be…Naima Adewunmi?"

I was impressed. He got it right on the first try. No one ever said my name right the first time.

#africangirlproblems

"So um…I'm pretty sure Martha asked all the preliminary questions. Availability, experience, all that good stuff. Did she ask you why you wanted to work here?"

Damn, did she? I was so busy trying to get this job, I was telling her whatever she wanted to hear. "No, I don't think so."

His brows rose. "You sure? Because you don't sound sure. For all I know, she could have asked you. By now your answer might be memorized and perfected."

I lifted my left hand and put my right hand over my chest. "I promise she didn't. Scout's Honor."

"Cool. So…" He dragged on the *O* like it was stuck to his tongue. "Why do you want to work here?"

Hmm… I'd found out about this job from my cousin Katrina. She, like me, was in school full time and understood how hard it was finding a job when you don't have a full-time schedule to dedicate to it. So a flexible job was a must. Oh, yeah, and that thirty percent textbook discount didn't hurt, but if I told him that, I was sure I wouldn't get the job.

I kept my answer simple. Translation: I lied my ass off. "I think I can really use my personality to engage customers. Customers like feeling human, and I'm good at striking up conversations about books." He peered at me with slit eyes, so I'm not sure he bought it.

"Attending RIC. Hmph, good school. Says here you graduated from College of Staten Island?" he asked, glancing over my application. "Is that where you're from?"

I nodded.

We spent the next few minutes arguing who was and wasn't

from Staten Island. He guessed right with most of the Wu-Tang Clan. Most of them were from Clifton, my hometown, but he lost all credibility when he tried to stick me with *all* the cats from *Jersey Shore*. Only Vinny was from SI; Pauly D was one of his.

"Sorry for getting off-topic."

I wasn't complaining. This was the most entertaining interview I'd had to date.

"Okay, so seeing how this is a bookstore, it just wouldn't feel right not asking you what your favorite book is. And please, I'm begging you, anything but *50 Shades of Grey* or *Twilight*. *Harry Potter* or anything Octavia Butler or Zane is, however, totally acceptable," he added with a laugh.

We went back and forth over our favorites, and I learned he was a nonfiction fan. I was never really into nonfiction, but he recommended Assata Shakur's autobiography, as well as some other memoirs about interesting folks you have to learn about outside of school. Even if I didn't get this job, I'd still look up his suggestions.

He pointed to a spot on the page and looked up at me. "It says here you were referred by an employee? Can I ask which one?"

I laughed. "Will it affect your decision?" He shook his head. "Katrina Okorocha," I said through a fake smile. My cousin was a little young and had a big mouth, so she wasn't always on everyone's friends list.

"Who—Kandy Krush?" he asked, his face beaming.

"Is that what you call her?"

"It's a Symposium thing. We're all like family here, so we have certain nicknames for each other. But honestly, KK is my girl. You were referred by the right person. She works really hard and *most* the customers love her."

Glad that didn't backfire on me.

The rest of the interview was smooth sailing. We talked mostly about hours and departments to the point where this job felt like a shoe-in.

"So…when do I start?" I teased. He laughed before he explained that he wasn't the one in charge of those matters.

"But if Martha liked you as much as I did…may the odds be ever in your favor," he said with a cheesy expression on his face.

"Ahh, *The Hunger Games*," I shot back.

"Yes, and if you hadn't known that, I may have just changed my mind about you… Sike. My ass just saw the movie. But anyways it was a pleasure meeting you, Naima. I hope to see you again soon." He shook my hand one last time before heading in the same direction Martha had disappeared to.

He had a cute little walk. Shit, he had a cute little everything. A part of me wanted this job just for the chance to see him again, but if I didn't get it, I might come back just to get his number.

CHAPTER TWO

Naima

What a waste of six hours.

Not only was apartment shopping mentally draining, it messed with you on a psychological level. After today, I wanted to shoot myself.

I figured catching an early-bird train to Providence might've allowed me to manage my time well and see as many places as possible. The plan was to visit four apartments in the first six hours, with a little time in between to fit in a light breakfast and lunch.

However, between transit and time wasters, I'd only seen two.

The first place was gorgeous. It was an apartment complex made up of a few buildings. Located downtown, it was in walking distance to the best route for transportation, as well as anywhere else I'd need to go, including work, if the fates were on my side.

My second appointment was supposed to be at ten-thirty, but between going over the process of applying and the leasing rules, I learned being a full-time student might be a problem. There was no way of knowing how much I'd take on my plate, and while it was nice, I decided against the place. I still toured it, but the minute I was out of sight, I crossed it from my list.

Shit would've been too expensive for me, anyway.

The next one required a short bus ride to Olneyville, and from first impression, things were heading south. It wasn't as conveniently located as the first place, which was understandable. But then the property manager showed up late, with a half-ass apology about traffic. By the time she got there, I'd been catcalled, hooted and hollered at, and rubbed the wrong way in just a mere half-hour.

I'm from Staten Island, so it's not like I wasn't used to the worst of the worst, but being a woman in a foreign place by myself? I'd entertain it for the price, but it didn't seem like the best idea.

I could've lived with the bars on the window and the fact that the apartment itself needed a paint job. But I had to put my foot down walking by a bottle of orange Cisco in the hallway.

I might have ignored it had it been in a bag. Hell, I might have given it a pass for a different flavor. But I had three stories involving orange Cisco, and none which were good.

Needless to say I would not be moving here.

I'd let Symposium know, that in order to take the job, I wouldn't be able to start until the last week in August, so it still left me time to look should today fall through.

Was it too much to ask for something cost-efficient, conveniently located, decent if not safe, with a roommate I can live with?

I grabbed a bite to eat before I hit up the next one. Figured, if I'm gonna be checking out bullshit, it might as well be on a full stomach.

* * *

The next place I'd found on an ad via Craigslist. Craigslist seemed a bit shady at times, but after exchanging a few replies, texts, and phone calls, I'd found the only legitimate place in my price range.

I was meeting up with a woman named Lisette. She sounded *kinda* Black over the phone. Not that it should matter. But it did seem like an easier transition from the latter.

I didn't officially have the job at Symposium, so I didn't bring it up when we talked, but I'd saved well enough to have the required security deposit and first and last month's rent, should it come up. Lisette planned to meet me at a public place, which was fine by me. I'd googled her so I could be sure to know what she looked like should a creep roll up claiming to live with her.

"Naima?" a stranger approaching asked.

She resembled Lisette a little, but her hair was different. Online, she looked darker, but in person, in-between races. Her pictures showed her having a teeny weeny afro, but in person, she had a platinum pixie cut with shaved sides.

"Lisette?"

She pointed to herself, replying with a, "That's me." We joked around a bit to break the ice. I was a little nervous meeting people for the first time, but she seemed cool—at least for a first impression. She offered to show me around, just to get a feel for the area.

"I thought it'd be better for you to see West End for yourself before you make a decision. Last girl who came to view the apartment said the place seemed fine, but then I got a text message about not feeling safe or whatever, so…"

I shot her a concerned look, one she appeared to see right through.

"She was a white girl…"

"See, you should've said that from the beginning!"

Lisette laughed as we moved on.

"The area's pretty diverse, but it is mostly Latino. As long as that doesn't bother you…"

I shrugged. Why would it? I spoke Spanish fluently, so I'd never encounter any language barriers. "It doesn't. I'm from NYC. Lots of different people over there."

West End was nice so far. It was summer, and neighborhoods were lit up, something I couldn't stand about the last neighborhood. It wasn't Martha's Vineyard, but for the price and location, it was nice. I could totally see myself living here.

"So what brings you to Providence?" Lisette asked.

I shrugged again, keeping pace with her. "Just school."

Hopefully that job, too, but who's counting? I was expecting a call today from their HR team about my future at Symposium. They told me I'd hear from them no matter what decision they made. I wished they'd called earlier, just in case Lisette asked, but so far? Nothing.

"What are you studying?"

"Modern languages."

"Oh. That's different."

If only she'd heard the way her voice sounded when she said it. Only a few months ago, my own parents had questioned my career path. "You want to study talking?" my mother had asked, as if it were that simple.

In a Nigerian family, it wasn't worth going to college if you weren't planning on studying law or medicine, but my mother didn't understand I was learning more than just speaking different languages. Linguistics required studying how people acquired their knowledge about language and how it varied, based on the way they communicate.

Most never consider why their voice pattern changes when asking a question or why we possess the knowledge of word order in the language we're fluent in. Maybe my folks worried about where the field would take me, but there were a number of career choices I could make when the time came.

"Are you going to school?" I asked before the moment was gone.

Lisette smirked, speaking through gritted teeth. "Third-year med. Reason why I'm tweaking. I've got that med school stress."

"Been there." Not that I was comparing community college to graduate school, but the longer you waited to go back, the harder it was, so I understood.

"Hope you like Dominican or Mexican food. Outside of franchises, that's, like, the main fast food places around."

"I'm not picky."

Through the thirty-minute walk around the area, I noticed we weren't that far from downtown. Providence was surprisingly small if it only took a half-hour to walk downtown. We weren't that far from Symposium. Even if the place didn't work out, maybe I'd find another cool spot. Everything was so close to each other.

"It's Tuesday. Mind if I hit up the farmer's market while we're down here?" Lisette asked, already heading there. I'd noticed the farmer's market before I'd gotten on the bus but hadn't had time to check it out. Seemed like a good time as any.

I took my own tour, allowing Lisette to shop in private. If she were anything like me, I hated people breathing down my neck while I shopped. I ignored the catcalls coming from the bus stops, honing my attention on the apples at the second stand as if it were the Cave of Wonders. Anything to keep my attention away from losers.

Lisette found me not too long after. She juggled a few items, making it over to a register. The clerk was a little rude. He rang up the stuff, but didn't bother even bagging.

"You guys don't have bags?" I asked nonchalantly.

Lisette covered her face, scooting opposite of me, as she pulled a felt square from her pocket. "This girl? She's not with me. I don't know her."

She unfolded the square to reveal a small canvas bag.

Confused, I followed her through the crowd as we created distance between us and the farmer's market.

"What was that all about?"

"Girl, were you trying to embarrass me? You don't ask for bags at a farmer's market. Are you crazy?" Lisette added through a forced smile.

I laughed. She couldn't be serious. "I'm just saying. You're paying all that money..."

But Lisette shook her head laughing. "Girl, you're a long way from New York. There's a bunch of cultural differences you might want to brush up one."

That was fair. I'd probably say the same thing to someone moving to my neck of the woods. But now I was curious. What others quirks might Lisette be referring to? What else might I have to learn?

* * *

We took the bus back to West End, and upon reaching the three-family apartment building, I immediately inspected the area. No bums, condoms or condom wrappers, and for the love of God, orange Cisco. So far, so good.

Lisette rustled through her purse to grab her keys and unlocked the door to my new potential place. It was cozy. It made the most of its lack of space.

"The kitchen's a little small, but if you don't on doing anything but cook in there, you should be straight."

No worries. It was a step up from the last place and worth it for the price. Lisette gave a small tour, which didn't take long. The kitchen and the living room mirrored each other. Lisette pointed to a closet in the hallway and opened it.

"One of the perks," she said, referring to the washer and dryer inside. I'd save trips to the laundromat should this work out.

"How much did you say you were looking for this place again?"

"425?"

Good. Was making sure the price hadn't miraculously increased since the last time we spoke. Lisette was pointing out the bathroom when the phone in my pocket began to ring and vibrate at the same time. Since I'd saved the number in my phone as "A chick need this job," I answered it right away.

"Hello?"

I recognized the voice on the other line. It was Martha Stewart, the first person who'd interviewed me.

"Hi. I hope you're doing well, Ms. Adewunmi."

It wasn't long until we were small-talking about the weather. That led into a conversation on how it'd taken her some time to sort through the slush pile of applicants, which was why it'd taken so long to call.

"I'm not sure if you've received any offers since your interview, but we'd like to open our employment opportunity to you. That is, if you're still interested."

My mouth dropped. Nothing came out. I patted my head, pulling at the root of my hair. "I can't wait to start. I'm just so happy to hear such good news. Thank you."

We spent the next few minutes discussing details of what I needed to do next, when I might start training, and what my schedule would be like. By the time I'd hung up, I'd forgotten where I was.

"So...I hear you got that job," Lisette said with a sarcastic cough.

"Yeah, well...I didn't want to tell you I didn't have one until I knew I didn't. I would have first, last, and a security deposit ready, though, so you wouldn't have to worry about that. Can I assume I'm in?" I prodded as Lisette's face lit up in a smile.

"I haven't even shown you the bedroom yet. I think I explained before..."

Lisette had mentioned in past correspondence that the space was so cheap because it was only one bedroom. I didn't mind sharing a space, as long as there was enough room for two people. When she opened the door, it reminded me most of a dorm room. Two twin beds, nightstands, and small dressers on both sides, only unlike the hallway, the room was heavily decorated.

West African art danced across the walls. There were masks, ornaments, paintings. She even collected figurines on her dressers. I picked one up, examining it in my hand. It was a regal Black woman, with a dress that could've easily been mistaken for a tail.

"Girl, what you know about Yemayá?" Lisette giggled, reaching for the figurine in my hand.

"I studied primitive art and anthropology when I was an undergrad. It didn't hurt that my grandmother was a Santería practitioner, too. How do you know Yemayá? Are you Brazilian? Cuban? Haitian?"

"Nigerian, actually." Lisette put her hand to her chest, pursed lips to match.

"Well, excuse me, Ms. International."

Yemayá was an important figure in Yoruba culture, faith, and myth and growing up with a Yoruba father, I knew more than the next person. Santería was just another way of acknowledging her. It was cool to see this. Most people demonized non-Christian cultures and belief systems.

"Look, I'm interested if you're trying to know."

"Good because, not that it should matter, but I was only interested in renting to students. Last roommate didn't work out. She paid rent on time but was highly inconsiderate on nights I needed to study."

So study time wouldn't be an issue. Lisette didn't waste any time showing me the closet space I'd have, where I could dump my dirty clothes, or any additional storage space I'd have should I need it. Everything seemed in perfect order until I saw the bag of weed sticking out of what I assumed to be her dresser.

"You smoke?" I asked.

Lisette shoved it deep into her dresser, as if embarrassed. "I'm sorry! If you have an issue with that, I get it. I won't do it in the house if that's the case. It's just...I'm in my third year in med school. Sometimes I need to take the edge off."

I opened the dresser and smelled the contents of the plastic bag. "I'm not judging. I indulge from time to time myself. I see you've got that haze, girl. At least when you do it, you do it right."

"If you don't have anywhere to be, we can blaze an L real quick."

"Shit, you don't have to ask me twice."

* * *

Whatever parts of this day that turned out to be shit were forgotten in a matter of minutes after lighting that bud. Sativa make shit feel so psychedelic. When you smoke with a person for the first time, it's a bonding experience. You learn things you would've never guessed about them from initial meeting.

"I'm no dictator. I know we have needs and shit, but please just let a chick know in advance if you're going to have someone over. The living room couch's a pullout. You look out, I'll look out."

I took a puff, inhaling the fruity aroma of the sativa plant. Each inhale got me closer to bliss. "I don't know about all that. Right now, all I'm worried about is work and school. But if you have a guy that comes around, let me know."

Lisette laughed, taking a hit from the joint, smiling.

"I mean, I think guys are cute, but women are more my thing. I hope that's not an issue."

She handed me the joint, and I puffed away. "No. I just feel stupid for assuming."

"Last chick thought I was always looking at her or something. Trust me when I saw this but she wasn't even that cute. I'm not attracted to every single girl on some predatory nonsense. Women kill me with that shit. Fuck outta here."

All I managed to do was crack up hysterically. Everything was funnier when you were smoking weed.

"Nah, but like I said. I'm just worried about me right now, and it's not a problem. Do your thing, girl."

Lisette got up, facing the mirror. "Damn, I'm looking fly as fuck, though. I'm 'bout to take a selfie."

I laughed. "You're stupid." I jumped in the background of Lisette taking pictures. I could already tell that the two of us were going to get along just fine.

CHAPTER THREE

Timothy

On some real shit. I hated early morning meetings. 7:30 a.m. was too damn early to be talking about books, adjustments to the schedules, and improvements that'd push sales for back-to-school season. The upside was the complimentary breakfast and coffee. It was served in the cafe for anyone who got here before all the savages got to it. Too bad for the rest, I was one of those savages.

Suckas...

My boy Angel came and headed straight toward the bagel table. His real name was Angel Ortiz, but we called him Du-Wop because it was his life mission to sing every song hitting the airwaves via the satellite radio the bookstore used. And don't let them play some bachata—it was over. None of us could rag on him, though. The dude had pipes.

"Sup, son?" he said with a full mouth, navigating the table behind me. We pumped fists as the cafe began filling up fellow employees.

Symposium wasn't like any other place to work. There were

no asshole bosses, beefs or cattiness. It wasn't even a place where all the older, younger, or people of different backgrounds cliqued up.

Most liked each other. Better yet, everyone talked to one another. I didn't mean to brag, but it was a straight place to work. Some of us had been here for years. Others decades. With exceptions for the summertime, turnover was low. It'd been months since they hired someone new. Imagine my delight when the new girl walked through the doors.

"Scoot in some," my girl Genesis said, taking a seat at a nearby table. I almost didn't hear her because I was too busy checking out new girl. Naima, was it? I shouldn't get used to her name since pretty soon we'd have to call her something else, but *my god* she was bad!

She was dark-skinned, reminding me a little of Kelly Rowland, but petite and curvier, with a whole lot of big, kinky hair pulled on top of her head in a high bun. When we first met, she'd looked uptight. Maybe even a little uncomfortable. Button-up, pencil skirt, flat-ironed hair.

But not today.

She wore a New York vibe that was dying to reveal itself. Confidence and attitude rolled into two door-knocker, name-plate earrings. Crazy, crazy sexy!

I was sandwiched between my girl Ruby Jiang-Cruz (notoriously known as Sailor Moon because she was always wearing her hair in those little meatball buns) and Bruce, better known as Rocketman, when Katrina yelled something across the room in a language no one else in the room spoke. It caught Naima's attention. It must have been a Nigerian dialect. I knew Katrina spoke Igbo.

"Ohhh, fresh blood. Tell your friend to come over here," Bruce said. He was wearing his crazy-ass, rhinestone-studded glasses, looking extra fly.

Wanna know why we called him Rocketman? Because he

looked like Elton John did in the seventies. He wore those glasses and sick polyester suits almost all the time. Shit, sometimes I think Bruce still thought it was the 70s.

Naima navigated a few serving tables and sat down at the table in front of me, next to Katrina, which was cool. It meant I could check her out without being obvious. Damn, she was fine.

"So what's your name, sweetie?" Ruby asked. It didn't surprise me that she was the first to be nosy. Ruby's sexuality was broad, more pan than anything, so we were always on the same wavelength, or at least when it came to women. She had a series of questions she referred to as the Santana-Lopez Test. It was her surefire way to tell if a girl swung her way or mine.

Told you everybody working at Symposium was nuts.

"Naima," she said. Bruce gasped, along with about eight other overdramatic people we worked with. We had rules around here.

"Jesus Christ, honey. We've got to get you out of that first name. Did anyone tell you about Symposium Law?"

Symposium Law was simple. In order to…*adapt* to Symposium culture, you had to take on a new name chosen by a single or several seasoned members of staff. You couldn't choose it, but you sure as had no choice but to live with it.

My dumb ass got mine for wearing Timbs to my job interview. I was seventeen and had no clue that people looked at what you wore down to your shoes. They liked me so they hired me, but the nickname stuck.

"See now this one," Naima said, pointing to me, "didn't tell me all that." So she remembered me. Nice.

When Martha and the floor manager Ravinder set up the PowerPoint screen, I knew this meeting was ready to get started.

I turned to the right and fought back a smile. While everyone was fixated on a dated, ten-minute customer service video, new girl had her eyes fixated on me. Damn.

If only I was single…

* * *

Naima

It was lunchtime and I was ready to crash. Back-to-school was a busy time for the store, and my voice was hoarse from answering so many questions. The master plan was to spend an entire half-hour resting my eyes, but when someone pulled up to the chair next to me, I peeked to see who it was.

Pursed lips followed by a crooked smile. It was the cutie from the cafe, Timothy.

"Long day?" he asked, assembling his sandwich to edible perfection. Now I was hungry. How much time did I have left? I rubbed my eyes to make sure I wasn't packing any crustballs. No crust. Good, I still looked cute.

"That seven-thirty meeting didn't really help," I said. "I probably got, like, three hours of sleep last night."

He lifted a brow, and I noticed how pretty his eyes were. They were as dark as mine, but it was the way he looked at me that made them seem different in color.

"Turnt up on a Tuesday," he said, taking a bite out of his sandwich. "That must be some New York shit."

If only it were that simple. People had this preconceived notion that New Yorkers partied all the time. Maybe in Manhattan. Maybe even in Brooklyn. But in the Shaolin where I was from? We were not where the party was at.

"I hope you don't mind that I sat with you. I have this thing where if someone else is in the room with me, I can't sit by myself."

He took off his beanie to reveal dark messy hair that didn't know if it wanted to stick up or lay flat. He was a real-life Danny Phantom. His hair smelled clean, like he'd just washed it, and made me want to be all up in his scalp. I loved guys who smelled good.

"Oh and guess what," he said, taking a sip from his iced coffee. "I come bearing breaking news. It took two and a half hours, but we finally decided what your prison name would be. Ready? … Staten Island."

Staten Island? It could've been worse. They could've given me something stupid like The Lion King because I'm African, which considering, I may have gotten off easy. The nickname system was new to me and would take some time getting used to. It was like *Roots* minus the whips and chains and dramatic background music.

"So um…Timothy. What's your nickname? Because I have yet to know it."

His mouth curved into something sinister that was a cross between "Like I'd tell you" and "you'd never let me live it down." Which was true. If it were something crazy like Woody Woodpecker, I'd probably fuck with him all year about it.

"I'll tell you but you have to promise not to laugh."

I nodded, not entirely sure I could keep that promise, but it's not like he knew that. He scooted in closer and cupped my ear with his hand.

"Damn, is it a secret?"

"Will you relax, Staten Island? I'm trying to tell you. You're getting all jumpy and shit. Relax, girl!"

How could I relax with his mouth this close to my ear? I kept thinking he was going to kiss me there, which at this point I wouldn't mind at all. His lips weren't as full as mine, but they were still fucking sexy.

"Okay, you ready?" he said with that sexy voice of his cupping my ear once more.

"Will you tell me already? Damn!"

He leaned in as close as he could without being out of line. "Don't laugh," he whispered. "But it's Timbaland."

Even if I had bolted my hands to my mouth, it wouldn't have

muffled the cries that erupted from my gut. To say I was on the floor rolling was an understatement.

Timothy took the last bite of his sandwich with a controlled amount of smugness in his expression.

"It wasn't that funny," he said through gritted teeth. After he told me how he'd gotten the nickname, I had to practically hold my stomach together to keep from heaving. Just goes to show you, first impressions were everything. A white boy named Timbaland was funny as shit. Maybe not as funny as I'd made it out to be but still. I was going to have a year's worth of jokes from this.

"*Anyways*," he interrupted. "You don't have to call me that if you don't want to. I'd actually prefer if you called me Timothy."

Like that would happen. If I was Staten Island, he was Timbaland. No exceptions!

"And why should I break Symposium Law and refer to you by your name when the latter sounds ten times more humiliating?"

"Well, because..."

He stood up, swaggering his way toward the break room door.

"I kind of like the way it sounds when you say my name," he added before an Asian girl (I think her name was Sailor Moon or Ruby or both) walked in with a younger blonde girl by her side.

"Ohhh," Ruby said, opening a bag of chips as she sat down across from me. "What'd I miss?"

The blonde girl sat down next to me. I glanced at the door to notice Timothy leaving. Rats.

Everything about him was loaded and indecipherable, but if his intention was to have me thinking about him for the rest of my shift...bravo. Mission accomplished.

CHAPTER FOUR

Timothy

Stop. Deep breath. Woosah. Reflect.

That was my routine each second week of the month. Can't believe it was my turn to do office duty again. Sitting down never brought on so much stress. Between making schedules, preparing sales reports, determining department inventory levels, I was always knee-deep in administrative shit I hated.

It was mandatory that each department manager rotate office duties, to keep each department sane, but it reminded me why I preferred the freedom of the cafe. All it was was food, coffee, and people. All this other stuff made my head hurt. The thing I liked the least?

Being a disciplinary figure to all non-managerial staff.

Most days I skated past it. I couldn't speak for other managers, but outside of seasonal staff, no one ever gave me much to worry about. Summertime and Christmas were the only real times I had to *act* like a manager.

Symposium was a fun place to work, but like any company trying to compete to sell products that were cheaper online, they had their own etiquette. Depending on the staff, most were lenient on the codes of conduct—*except* dress codes.

Knock, knock.

Before she entered the office, I had a good idea it'd be Genesis (also known as 2 Live Crew). She'd been working here almost fourteen months and, in the beginning, was about three votes away from carrying the alias Cinnamon Dominican. After a few ladies brought to our attention how sexist it was, 2 Live Crew was born.

She was always fun to work with, and had that type of personality to get everyone around her hyped. In retrospect, it suit her better. I rolled a chair over to the door to close it after she walked in. The issue at hand was obvious.

Certain customers had complained about the way she'd dressed. I hadn't seen her when she came in, but my eyes jumped out the sockets the minute I laid eyes on her.

"Damn Timbo, what's up? You call me in here?"

I bit my lip. I hated being bad cop. I was everyone's friend in this place, so it made that much harder for me. I leaned back in the swivel chair, pushing out air I'd been holding onto since she'd walked in the office.

"Girl, you've put me in a tight-ass predicament."

Her eyebrows met the center of her face, a sign she was clearly confused. Sitting at one of the round tables scattered across the office, her already *short* shorts rode up, disappearing under her shirt.

"2 Live, where are your clothes? I know it's hot but shit. This is not Cranston Street. We're at work."

Genesis adjusted the lower cuff of her shorts, begging it to cover more than it would. "What the fuck? Customers are complaining about me? That's some bullshit."

I kept getting lost in my train of thought over Genesis' legs. She wasn't too thick or skinny, but had a nice body. If she were new, I'd say it was an honest mistake. But she'd been here long enough to know what she was doing.

"2 Live, if those shorts were any shorter, I'd be eyeballing your lady parts. I can…" I searched for the right words to sound serious, but it was hard to look anything but goofy when people knew you. "…already see everything worth seeing. I'm not trying to be an asshole, but please tell me you have some pants or leggings hidden in your locker or something. Otherwise I have to send you home, and I really don't want to do that."

Genesis' mouth dropped. It was one of the few times she had nothing to say for longer than thirty seconds. "So…word, Timbaland? It's like that now? It's not like I'm carrying a duffle bag worth of sweats. Unless you 'bout to lend me some."

I'd planned on hitting up the court later with my friends, so I did happen to have some basketball shorts. As a last resort option, I threw the suggestion out there. We were way too understaffed to send people home.

When I did office duty, I typically spent most the shift there, so I carried most my stuff with me. Didn't see much daylight in here, and when I was ready to go, I didn't want to risk having to come back for anything.

"I'm going to help you this *one* time," I said, handing her the shorts from my bag.

She examined them, a look of disgust across her features. "Gross, I'm going to look frumpy as fuck. You don't have anything else?"

I shrugged. "It's either look frumpy or look broke. It's up to you."

Genesis rolled her eyes, releasing the most annoyed grunt her throat would allow. "I bet if this was a dude, nobody would be sayin' shit."

"It's not like I'm disagreeing with you. But in my defense, I can walk out here shirtless right now, and I know they won't be havin' it. You know how Symposium is with dress codes."

Genesis slapped her hands at her sides, finally caving in. Not to be a dog, but I was grateful for that one last look before she'd be walking around here like she got dressed in the dark. Sure Gen rocked it, but even Bruce got sent home back in his day for breaking the dress code with his larger-than-life style. At least he got to keep his glasses, though. It was a much deeper conversation to have in the future, but for now, I'd stick to working. Getting into trouble was better suited after work.

* * *

It was a little past nine, a subtle change in our summer hours. We closed later in the fall up until New Year's, when our volume of sales was highest. Even though I was happy to be leaving, I was anxious about Thursday. I wasn't allowed to make a work schedule based on personal preference, but with the new girl's availability, I'd be seeing more of her come Thursday.

Not that I was looking. It'd just be cool to vibe with a new personality. I don't know what it was with me and new people. I always had this aching urge to familiarize myself with folks I didn't know. Call it a vice.

Our common closers were working tonight. Katrina was my girl, but come end of the night, she'd look under every nook and crannie just to find a ride. Ruby was a hoofer and didn't mind taking the bus, but I had a favor to ask and it came at the risk of giving both of them excuses not to ride the bus. We'd already gotten an early night-before call out, and Ruby was the best bet compared to seasonal floaters.

"Hey, Timbo," Katrina flirted, closing any remaining distance between us. I knew it was coming, but I pushed away my skepticism to give her the benefit of the doubt. "You were going past Elmhurst tonight, right?" *Right.* Because Elmhurst was on my way even though I lived in the opposite direction. I admired her every attempts.

Ruby wasn't proud, but she normally waited for an offer or an opportunity to walk into someone's conversations. She was about to walk past me when I tugged at her elbow.

"Hold up, Sailor Moon, where you going?" I hadn't noticed the headphones until now, but she wore a dumbfounded look on her face.

"Can I help you, Timothy?"

I smiled my pearly whites, which I knew didn't work on her. She had a bullshit detector with a range of a thousand miles, and I was too close to hide detection. "You need a ride? I was about to drop off KK." I should've coached Katrina first because her face shot holes in my cover.

Ruby met her gaze to mine, suspicion pouring out her amber brown eyes. "Hmm…really? Because that sounds like a favor *laced* with the promise of a favor."

Damn, she didn't see past shit.

"Can I not just perform my duty as a gentleman, *a friend,* just to make sure you get home, okay?"

Ruby gave me a look over and swatted me away with her palm. "Boy, bye."

I followed her onto the retail floor, Katrina not far behind. "Okay, Sailor Moon, you got me. One of our *sea-bees* called out for an AM shift. I'd really appreciate it if you'd help out."

"Damn, you can't ask anyone else?"

"I'm asking you. Ruby, you're reliable. Don't say I don't look out come check time."

Ruby's lips pursed, looking between the two of us for a reply. "Okay, but I call shotgun, and you better not ask me for anything else this week."

"See, this is why you're my girl."

* * *

Whenever I gave rides, Katrina preferred getting dropped off first. If it was a car full of people, it was easier explaining to her Nigerian mother that she was just getting a ride home and not dating some foreign guy. Yes, she actually used foreign.

Most times the car was silent when it was just Ruby. She wasn't quiet, but she claimed I talked too much, so she preferred the radio. *She kids, she kids.*

I turned down the generic pop/R&B playing in the background, but she tried to turn it back up.

"What are you doing?"

"I can't want to talk to one of my dearest friends?"

"Tim, this is like the second favor you asked tonight. Are you trying to make me close, too?" Ruby was the Empress of Sarcasm, the one person at the job who got pleasure out of irking your nerves. She was known for having the best comebacks, snarky remarks, insults you don't know are insults until you're home and can't argue back.

"I just wanted your opinion on something."

She laughed, shaking her head toward the window. "We had this conversation a few days ago. Stop spitting that political or philosophical shit at me. I keep telling you, I'm not that deep."

I laughed, taking a left turn through downtown Providence. "Well, it's more like on someone, not something."

Ruby's eyes narrowed into a gaze of suspicion. "I think I know where this is going."

"Where is it going?"

"Like I can't tell. Don't play dumb. You're curious about Staten Island."

My mouth pinched into a grimace. It was obvious—she probably thought I was thirsty. It's not like I was interested in Naima romantically. She was a new face. Why do people always think the worst?

"You don't have to say it like that. I'm just curious. I can't be curious?"

"Well, what are you trying to know?"

I shrugged. "I don't know. Have you talked to her? What's your opinion on her?"

Ruby and I had this thing. She recognized my type instantly and would page the phrase **Public Announcement** over the intercom at work. "Well…she's pretty if that's what you're asking."

"Why does everything have to be about looks?" I asked, nonchalant. I didn't disagree. As a guy, looks physically attracted me. But Ruby knew me better than that. She knew I also liked being attracted to someone intellectually, psychologically, emotionally. Appearance was such small factor.

"You ask me what I think every time a new person gets hired. Hard to differentiate the masses." I trusted Ruby's eye for people. She was good at making accurate first impressions. It's not like I was expecting her to fall for Naima, too; she just had a better eye for women than I did.

"Well…" Ruby counted off each detail with her fingers. "She's nice. She's good with people. The other day some lady came in speaking something. She just talking talking to her, like bam, she may just be a human version of google translate. I can't really tell if she's fam or not…" A trait Ruby always wanted to know. Whether a person was part of the LGBTQIAP spectrum. "But she seems cool. I can't say I like a person I don't know. But from my first impression? I'd say cool."

That told me enough. I trusted her opinion. Naima seemed cool. Nothing would happen between us, but even so, I looked forward to Thursday morning.

CHAPTER FIVE

Timothy

I called this girl three times with no answer. I understood when things came up, but I wish she'd let me know. I cleared my whole schedule to have Skype sessions. Either she's late or texts me hours afterward to tell me she got caught up at work or something. A text beforehand would make shit a lot easier.

Sherri was my girlfriend of four years, and drove me freaking crazy the way she did things. We didn't have what you'd call a normal relationship. For the past two years, we did the long-distance thing. For anyone who's never been in a long-distance relationship, it takes so much energy to make it work. When you love someone, you're always a little ambitious that it *will* work.

My computer screen finally "rang," with the words "Sherri calling" scrolled across the screen. Late, but at least we'd get a chance to talk.

"Hey, babe, sorry I was late. I just got in," Sherri said somewhere off-screen.

"Hey," I replied back. She came into view when she sat down at her desk. The first thing I noticed was her naturally dark hair dyed a shocking shade of blonde. Don't get me wrong, my girlfriend fell in the category of skin colors that could pull off most hair colors, but I wasn't a fan.

"Wow, you dyed your hair," I said, trying to hide my disdain.

She saw right through me. "You don't like it?" she whined.

I bit my lip. "I don't know. It's different. If you like it, that's all that matters, babe."

She pouted her lip and pulled her thick curly hair into a ponytail. Pulled back, I guess it looked *kinda* cute.

We sat and small-talked for a bit until the topic of visiting each other came up. It was something we bumped heads on. I missed having her around, but it was always a hassle convincing her to take time off to come see me. She worked in a hospital, so it was rare when she used her vacation time to do anything but relax and chill at home. She hated leaving Texas because her folks had health problems and she was their only child. I understood the situation; it just felt like everything that held our relationship together was because of my effort. That's where things got frustrating.

"I can't come see you until next year, Sherbear"—yeah, we were just corny like that—"I already used up all my vacation time for the year, and I really can't afford to take a week off just to come back and be broke. Next year will be better anyways. It's, like, my fourth year as a member of managerial staff, so I should be getting an extra week off. But you know, if you change your mind and want to come here...the offer is always open."

I always put the option out there, but it was becoming ritual for me to expect the opposite. I usually caved in first and threw my pride aside just to come see her. That's how much I missed her.

"Te quiero, mi amor," she cooed on the other side of the screen. A smile crept up at the corners of my mouth, thinking of all the times Sherri seduced me with the promise of ending the night in Spanish. It was hard to stay mad at girls who could pillow talk in another language. My ass went fucking ape over that shit.

"You're mean," I said, taking a deep breath, trying to ignore the massive hard-on I got at the whisper of Spanish. Damn her.

She stuck out her tongue, knowing damn well she had me. There wasn't anything I could do about it. Another thing that sucks about being in a long-distance relationship—you're basically celibate. If you're a good boy. There was a shaky time in the beginning where I could have tried harder and we had our lion's share of problems, but these past eighteen months, I'd been practically a saint. The only thing that saw me naked was my mirror and that was just sad.

"Hey, papi, it's getting late. I have to get some sleep, okay? I got a really early shift in the morning, and I just know they're going to mandate me to work a double. I don't want to go to work looking like a zombie."

My lips pouted in disappointment. Guess it was just me and my hand tonight.

"Good night, beautiful," I said before disconnecting. I shut the top of my laptop and noticed the notification light blinking on my phone. I had four messages, all from Ruby. I'd conveniently saved her as Sailor Moon, but from time to time, she popped up as Ruby Woo.

Ranging from *"What's up, boss man?"* to *"I know yo ass ain't sleep."* Ruby definitely had the ability to get on my nerves through just a text. I loved her.

Me: *You're right, I'm not sleep. I'm hiding under your bed. Ha.*

Ruby Woo: *You know my dumb ass actually looked?*

Me: *Of course you did with your paranoid ass. Thinking everybody stalking you 'cuz of that last chick.*

Ruby's last girlfriend? Total stalker. Girl had to file a restraining order and everything.

Ruby Woo: *Speaking of stalking, guess who I found out has an IG? Type in NaijaNaima. Let's run a train stalk on her lol. Hold her* down, *Like her pictures, make that IG remember us *in my Breezy voice**

Me: *Yo you stupid. Rotfl. Imma see doh.*

I exited the text message box and rushed to my Instagram app to see what Ruby flapped her tongue about. I found her profile and let the pic lead me more places. The latest picture was at least a month old, but still, she was still fine. If I did the math right, she'd been here for a month, so her most recent photo was taken back home.

Ruby Woo: *You know you gonna be on some lurk status if you like and don't follow. Following now. Don't be a wuss.*

I hit the *follow* button and liked her most recent picture. Within seconds, she followed me back leaving a comment under my latest picture.

NaijaNaima: *Nice Picture. :)*

CHAPTER SIX

Naima

I clocked in late for my scheduled shift. A lecture ran longer than planned so I'd had to catch a later bus. Of course that one ran late, too. When I hit the floor, it felt like everyone was staring at me. I reported to the customer service desk to find out which department I'd be in and was met by Buzz Lightyear (I didn't know his real name), the floor manager.

Buzz was in his sixties, but with his smooth tawny complexion and sparkling hazel eyes, he looked twenty years younger. He looked so much like a Bollywood movie star, I was surprised his work name *wasn't* Bollywood. But he used to intern for NASA so the name Buzz Lightyear was fitting.

I approached him, nervous that he'd make a big deal out of my tardiness. But he assured me it wasn't a big deal, especially since I'd called to let someone know.

"I'm actually going to have you help out in the cafe today. They had a call out and could really use the help. Is that alright?"

It really wasn't, but what was I supposed to say? No? "Sure." He smiled. Even his smile was Bollywood-perfect.

"You can head over there now. They're waiting for you."

* * *

I ran into Emily, a teenage blonde girl who I learned real quick that, while she looked sweet on the outside, had a lot of spunk on the inside. I'd worked with her twice before, and she was mouthy, but reminded me of that one person you should have in your circle of friends who always told you the truth, whether or not it hurt your feelings. To sum it up, she was my kind of girl.

She was on her way out, so I must've been her replacement. Timothy approached me after scrubbing a nearby table with an apron in one hand and a smug smile on his face.

"Thanks for coming over. This is for you." He handed me the apron. "Since we handle food, you kind of have to wear one. It's more for us than anything, so we don't mess up our clothes. That and it actually makes us look like we're working," he said with a wink.

I put on the apron and followed him to the counter. He showed me how to work the registers and take orders until Ruby came in.

"Soon as Sailor Moon gets here, I have a special job for you, Staten Island. She'll be here in a bit, but it's about to get real busy."

So far, the orders had been just steady. How busy did he expect it to get?

"Honey, I'm home," Ruby said, putting on her apron as she reached in to lay a kiss on Timothy's cheek. Didn't they look friendly? For all I knew Timothy had a thing for Asian girls like most of the white boys I knew back home. If he did, I didn't stand a chance. Ruby and I couldn't be any more different in appearance. She didn't look East Asian. Or, at least, not only Asian. She had brown hair and an eye shape that made her appear racially ambiguous. With a last name like Cruz and Jiang, my only guess she was that she was Latina or Filipina. Browsing her Instagram timeline I had a strong lean towards the second. She'd had dozens of tagged pictures with #asiangirlsbelike, even when it wasn't necessary.

"Hey, girl." She directed toward me. I smiled and waved as she took my place as counter person.

"Sailor Moon, you got this? Me and Staten Island need to start setting up on the floor. You sure you don't need help?"

"Yea, I got it. GO!"

Timothy wasn't convinced. "You sure? Because it's almost seven. You know how this rush gets."

She gave him an annoyed look and shooed him away. "O-M-G, get out of here. Aggy ass!"

"Aggy? I thought I was bae."

She rolled her eyes and continued taking care of the small line that formed.

"*You*," he said, looking at me with those dark sexy eyes. "Can come with me."

I followed him to the dining area, careful not to linger too long on his ass. I didn't know if he had an ass, but his walk was reason enough to look. He seemed so confident.

"So here's the deal. We host a bunch of book clubs in the cafe. What I need your help with is arranging the tables, sorting out the seating, and putting up decorations. I'll probably need your help with serving, too. Doable?"

I nodded. Seemed simple enough. He gestured for me to help him push eight of the sixteen tables together, creating four rectangular tables.

"What's this club thing anyways?" I asked.

"Oh you ain't know?" He held up a sign he was seconds from hanging up, wearing a goofy smile.

Book Boyfriend Club

"Where women of all ages come down to debate about their favorite fantasy boyfriends."

Seriously? I couldn't believe there was a club dedicated to arguing about guys that weren't even real. Did people have nothing better to do?

"I see you're a skeptic, but these women come in twenty-five deep, order a ton of food and leave shitloads of tips. They're rowdy but a good bunch. I've got my own vices, so I try not to judge."

I mumbled something under my breath about being a huge *Supernatural* fan, and his face lit up.

"Wait, hold up. You like *Supernatural?*"

I didn't know whether to be defensive or just plain offended. The question came out like I couldn't possibly like anything other than "black" shit. But I didn't know him well, so I gave him the benefit of the doubt. I was this close to hitting him with a neck roll.

"Is that a problem?"

"Nah, it's just...you know what? We'll talk. We'll talk." He sounded sure of that.

More than once he scolded me on where the name plaques on the table should go. Supposedly Mrs. Grey couldn't dare be seated next to Mrs. Cullen and Mrs. Herondale had a fit if she wasn't sandwiched between her two besties, Mrs. Fuentes and Mrs. Sheridan. Turns out, their last meeting ended in a cupcake or two to the face. And to think, I'd be manning this station all night. Oh well. It beat being on the floor.

* * *

Timothy

$72.83. It averaged out to $24.27 each between the three of us. An unsaid rule? The one on serving duty got a little extra since the ladies weren't easy to deal with. We had a system. I made the food and drinks, Ruby held it down on the register, and Naima brought it out and took the orders. Naima did well on her first cafe shift. The way we worked, we'd managed to get the department cleaned up by 8:45. Time to go home.

"Timbo, you know I don't usually ask, but I need a ride." Ruby didn't live that far from me, but it was in the opposite direction from Upper South Providence where I lived.

"Only if you got that gas money," I joked. "You're really gonna do me like that, Tim?"

"*Do you like what?* I shared my lunch with you, got you out of the dreadful Book Boyfriend duties, and now you going for the hat trick. Trying to play me!"

I really was just joking. Ruby knew that, but it didn't mean I wasn't going to profit.

"I'm just playing. I got you if you buy me a milkshake. And not one of those small shits either. I want an extra-large with three toppings."

Ruby's eye twitched. She didn't have a better bargaining chip to hit me with. I'm sure she gave everyone she'd ever dated that same look when they tried to do some dumb shit. I hated to know what followed. Too scary.

"Okay," she said through a forced smile. Good because I had

an insane craving for a mint cookie ice cream milkshake but did not feel like running in Ben and Jerry's to get it.

"Let's go."

We ran into Naima on the way out, but she was too immersed in her phone to notice. I held the door open as both Naima and Ruby slipped by, and we parted in different directions. I had a monthly parking pass at one of the lots downtown so Ruby and I didn't have to walk far, but I didn't feel right. Was I really going to let the first chance to talk to Naima in an informal setting pass me by? What was I thinking?

Before she made it past Teriyaki and Korean house, I called out her name. "Hey, how are you getting home?"

She turned around but never stopped walking. "The bus," she shouted.

"Want a lift?" The street was damn near empty. The shouting just made us all look crazy.

"Depends. Am I gonna have to buy you a milkshake?" I was tempted to say something corny, but we weren't there yet. I didn't want to risk coming off as sexist. All the other girls I worked knew I was just one to blow smoke.

"Only if you help me eat it. Now, come on before this girl changes her mind. I want my shake!"

"Fine," she said as she changed her course, headed in our direction.

* * *

Ruby lived in Elmwood, a little off-course from West End, where I'd have to drop Naima off. I didn't mind the drive if it meant we could talk. Besides, Ruby complained the whole ride about how she was tired and how expensive that milkshake was. Hey, only the best for a friend.

"You work tomorrow?" Ruby asked, unbuckling her seatbelt. Naima and I answered simultaneously but with different answers. She worked; I didn't. Pretty sure it was my only day off.

"Guess I won't see you until Friday, then," she said with me in mind. "But I'll see you," she said to Naima. Naima smiled and waved goodbye as I caught Ruby mouthing the words *"totally straight"*. Santana-Lopez Test failed. "Let me see what my mama cooked in there."

"Bring me out a plate," I said before she slammed the door behind her. Next stop, Naima's place.

* * *

I sat parked for minutes before she finally decided to look at me from the backseat. "Are you waiting for someone? We're not moving?"

"Actually, I was counting on you to keep me company riding shotgun."

She grimaced. "Is it optional?"

It was, but I hated people sitting in the backseat when the front one was empty. I felt like a taxi driver. I brought my hands together and play-begged and pouted to her gain sympathy. It worked. Next thing I knew she was in the front.

"So where to?"

"Do you know how to get to West End from here?" She was talking to a Provy native. Nothing surprised me about Providence. I put the car in drive and took off into the streets.

West End wasn't far from Elmwood, but I was guilty of taking the long way. This was the first time I'd been alone with Naima since the day we met. Part of me wanted to get to know her as more than her coworker.

"Mind if I turn this down?" I lowered the volume. Not too low in case she wasn't in the talking mood. Here goes nothing.

"How are you liking RI so far? Go out yet?" Chances are she hadn't, but I figured I'd ask anyways.

"Go out, like partying? No, I'm not worried about partying. I didn't come to RI to party. I came here to study. I know, I know I'm whack."

I didn't think so. I'd been enrolled at University of Rhode Island for almost five years now and knew how important it was to take school seriously. I couldn't afford to take classes every semester. Bills too often came a knocking. I had to be selective which semesters I took, so I didn't waste money just to fail. I took more classes during the summertime when we were our slowest at the bookstore. But I was proud to say that this fall would be my last semester. Come May, I'd be a URI graduate.

"I still have two years left if I take the standard four classes a semester. But who knows, I might take some summer classes, too, when I go back to NY." So she was going back. Noted.

"I guess when you're not old enough to drink, what's the point of going out, right?" I said, joking.

She looked at me through slit eyes. "Boy don't make me slap you."

"I'm just playin'. I know you're in your twenties. I just don't know where you fall on the scale."

She laughed. "I'm twenty-seven." She was two years older than me. Nice.

"Take a left right here."

I pulled onto her street as she pointed me out to which house was hers. I couldn't stretch the car ride out long enough. Not without making it look like I was trying to kidnap her.

"Thanks for the ride, Timothy. I owe you for a milkshake next time I see you." She unbuckled her seatbelt. *It was now or never, Tim.*

"Actually…" I said, my hands circling the steering wheel. "I wouldn't mind just having your number instead. That is, if you'll give it to me."

She scrunched up her nose and pursed her lips. "Yeah, I can't do that."

Her reaction alone told me everything I needed to know. Either she didn't like me or she had a crazy-ass man, which only made sense if I was trying to get with her. But I wasn't, so it sucked. She smacked her forehead.

"I didn't mean it the way it came out. What I meant was, my phone plan right now really sucks, so I only use it to call family and stuff like that. I keep going over as it is. I really need a new plan."

"That's cool. I probably would done this crazy thing like call you. I know no one talks on the phone anymore but hey, I'm old fashioned." I smirked. She pursed her full lips to the side, drawing my eyes to stare at every direction she pointed them in. Her lips were…*fuck, let me stop*.

"Look, if we exchange numbers, texting is better for me since it's unlimited. Is that okay?" I nodded. In the next minute, she recited her phone number aloud and with a quick dial to hers, she had mine.

"So, since you don't accept phone calls, I don't know. You want to talk for a little bit? I'm not in a rush to go home." She nodded. Cool. I took a deep breathe.

"Can I be honest with you?"

"It depends. Do you plan on being insensitive, offensive, or demeaning?"

Damn, I wonder if she asked everyone questions like that or just me. Part of the pleasure of getting to know someone.

"You're from NY. Nothing anyone says should shock you."

She muttered under her breath and rolled her eyes. "You can be honest with me. But anytime someone starts out a sentence like that, you have to expect the worst."

Fair enough. I adjusted myself in the seat to face her and watched her do the same. Even in this dimly lit car, she was so fucking beautiful.

"I'm kind of bummed that we haven't had a real chance to talk since you started working here. I mean, unless it's intentional." I never knew if anyone personally found me annoying or abrasive. Naima got along with everyone at work just fine, but she seemed lacking when it came to me.

"It's not like we don't talk," she said as she chewed on her nails. "I acknowledge you when I see you." She did, but it was always work talk. *"Someone needs to know when the sale is over." "The toilet paper's low. Where do I go to restock it?"* I was dying to pick her brain, but opportunity never presented itself.

"It's never real conversations," I said with a shrug.

"What, like now?"

"Do you consider this a real conversation?"

She considered it a moment before she spoke. "Okay, so what would make this a real conversation?"

Just the question I wanted her to ask. I suggested we both admit something we've never admitted to another person. I didn't know anyone she knew and she didn't know anyone I did, so our secrets were safe with each other. I volunteered first as an act of trust and faith.

"I used to be a twin. My sister died of leukemia when we were five. Sometimes I miss her. Sometimes I barely remember her. Every year on my birthday, I visit her grave and talk to her. If she's listening." My mom didn't even know that I did that. As corny as it sounds, it made me feel less alone on my birthday. "Your turn."

Her lips tucked away, as her eyebrows met in the middle of her face. "Not sure I can top that." The point of the exercise wasn't to outdo each other but to discover something deep about one another. I wasn't the "what's your favorite color?" type. I had a feeling neither was she. She pulled at the strands of her long coily hair. Finally, she spoke.

"When I was nineteen, I got fired from my first-ever real, well-paying job. My mom was so proud of me that I didn't have the heart to tell her I got fired. I got a job at a clothing store and passed it off like I still worked there, but I'd feel horrible when she'd brag to her friends about how resourceful and intelligent I was. Meanwhile, I'm folding clothes and cleaning up messy dressing rooms." She went into this story about Nigerian mothers and their high expectations, and I couldn't help being a little grateful for my Portuguese mama. Not to say this wasn't the case for Naima, but my mother supported me no matter what I did. Either way, it was a cute story.

I checked the time on my phone. It was getting late. She laughed when she caught me. "Am I keeping you?"

"It's not that. I had some shit I needed to finish up for school. It's nothing exciting, but it has to get done." No lie, I really wanted to spend the whole night talking to her. She was dope company. It was always nicer to talk to someone in person than over the phone.

"Guess I'll see you at work, then?" she asked.

"Yes, indeed."

She gathered up her things and swore when her cell phone slipped through the side of her seat. I offered to help, sticking my hand down in the through the crack, but the tips of my fingers wouldn't reach so I told her to push the seat back and—*voila*— phone in hand. The passenger-side door clicked open, but Naima turned back. She'd probably forgotten something.

"Actually there is something else I haven't admitted to anyone."

Two confessions? The night just kept on giving.

"I'll tell you, but you have to close your eyes. I won't tell you with your judging eyes staring at me."

"Well, then, it must be good, because your ass is feeling guilty," I joked. The situation seemed silly, but I was dying to know. "And don't take forever either. Got me all closing my eyes and shit cause your guilty ass can't take the pressure—"

Pressure. Before I could finish, the pressure of thick, luscious lips showered mine. Her lips moved angry and possessive. Like my mouth performed only for her. She pulled away, traces of heat still lingering on my lips. Didn't see that coming.

"Confession: I've wanted to do that since the day that I met you."

Without saying anything else, she exited the car. She walked up her apartment stoop like she knew I was watching her, making sure she was switching extra-hard. Girl, I see you. She had me so fucked up, I probably wouldn't stop seeing her. What the fuck just happened?

Alerts from my phone pulled me out of my daze. Sigh. Two from Sherri.

Sherbear: *Guess you went to bed. Sleep well, baby. XOXO*

Me: *Miss you too. Besos*

I should probably leave out the part of me kissing another woman. It's not like it'd happen again. I wouldn't let it.

But I couldn't lie to myself. I really wanted it to.

CHAPTER SEVEN

Naima

I woke up to an upset mother standing over me, looking as if she were moments from unleashing terror. Not just any upset mother, either. When an Igbo woman asked something of you, there was no telling her no. There were no excuses to be made and definitely no sleeping in.

What she didn't seem to sympathize with, was the five hour bus ride I took to get into New York last night; not to mention the thirty plus minutes I waited at the ferry for someone to pick me up.

From last night to now, five hours of sleep was all I managed. Knowing my mother, she was just the kind of person to lecture me on how she raised a family, worked full time, took care of a house *and* had time for leisure activities all because she could function on four hours of sleep. I kid you not when I tell you I grew up with Wonder Woman for a mom. Nigerian women, they were ambitious like that.

"Ma, c'mon," I whined. "We don't have to be there until—" I picked up and glanced at my phone. "Eight 'o'clock, ma? We've got so much time. It's a wedding, you know no one in our family shows up on time for anything. Especially not Chizu and them. That girl would show up late for her own wedding." I said as I disappeared under the blanket.

"Naima, get up. I will not tell you again." She said in a dangerously calm voice. Notice how she said *tell* and not ask. My mother did not ask things of me. Asking implied that the choice was mine to make and often it wasn't.

She laid down a royal blue blouse and matching wrapper at the foot of my bed and warned how I better not keep her waiting. That was basically her way of saying,'I love the way you do my make-up, but I'd never tell you because then, you would get a big head about it.'

I was a pro at deciphering my mother's hidden language and foreign social cues, otherwise I would've grown up thinking my mother hated me. But nope, she loved me to pieces. That was just the odd way she showed affection. If she didn't insult me, nag or question my every decision *then* that would give me reason to worry. I climbed out of bed.

"Ugh, ma. Do you at least have the make-up kit you like downstairs?"

* * *

Top three reason I loved Nigerian get-togethers:

1. Aso-ebi
2. Finding *any* excuse to break out an Ichafu
3. #thegossip

For those of you unfamiliar with the first two terms, allow me to explain since it's hard to mention one without the other. See, we Nigerians(and Nigerian Americans like myself) are partial to a uniform look.

Aso ebi is a customary way we show solidarity or family line with the clothes that we wear to an event. Using matching or similar fabrics, we have dresses made to distinguish ourselves at a huge gathering that may or may not include solely family. Same color scheme is usually optional but our ensembles aren't marked complete without an Ichafu(Gele in my father's tongue) a sort of head wrap you wore to get all fancy.

I used to love watching my mother get all dressed up for a birthday party or baptism because her closet was filled with blouses and wrappers in nearly every color you could think of. I don't think we ever co-signed that rule that every woman should own a little black dress. For nothing major, black was just fine. But for the ultimate slayage, color was highly encouraged if not preferred.

All my cousins and aunties were decked out in matching royal blue, which complimented my own top and skirt. I wasn't a wedding person—in fact I avoided them like the plague. But everything about an Igbo wedding made western weddings look dull in comparison.

I remember my first western wedding. I kept asking myself how the bride could make her bridesmaids wear clothes so hideous. If I were the one spending the money, no woman would look anything less than incredible next to me. And that was assuming I was even thinking about marriage. I wasn't. But there was a certain man I couldn't stop thinking about since Thursday night.

Timothy. We'd texted a few times since our late night kiss but it was all pretty tame. Barely a mention between us. Maybe he hadn't felt anything when I kissed him, which, judging by the way he kissed me back, I couldn't understand why I was even asking myself that question. But ugh, not one *You have beautiful lips* text. No *I can't get you off my mind* text. Nothing.

That only left me feeling as though I'd done something wrong, or maybe he was just patiently waiting to run into me at work again. I didn't know what his deal was but was I wrong for feeling like there was chemistry between us?

"Naima, your mother tells me you moved away. Long Island, she says?" my aunt Adanma asked, interrupting my sudden drift from the world around me.

"Rhode Island." I corrected. My aunt Adanma was getting old and constantly mixed up locations. It didn't help that *Island* was at the end of every one of them. Most of my family in the States didn't know any places outside of the bouroughs, so Rhode Island could've been Laos and they wouldn't have known where it was.

"And school, what do you study there? You know Jason is completing his Master's degree. He is going to be an engineer." This was why I always made it my mission to avoid aunties. When I said I loved the gossip, I only meant when it wasn't about me.

Everyone knew what I was studying. They asked me every time they saw me; probably thinking my answer would change. In my family, it was never too late to change your mind to study science or medicine. Because I wasn't doing either, my name was often at the end of people's mentions.

"Auntie, you know I'm studying languages. I must've told you a million times now." The smile I forced my mouth to make feeling detached and disingenuous. She made this sound with her mouth that was a cross between a *heh* and an *umph*. With the flick of her wrist, her smile returned but not without a back handed compliment to go along with it.

"Oh well Naima, you've always been a beautiful girl. If that doesn't work out, you will have no issue finding a husband who's a doctor or lawyer. Don't wait too late my dear. What are you twenty-seven now?"

And here was where I needed to step away for a drink. When I caught my younger cousin Chiaka walking by, I took her hand, using this as my opportunity to exit my self out of the conversation.

"What did you say ma wanted…" I suggested, turning back ever so often just to ensure my aunt wasn't following us.

"Naima, what are you talking about? Get off me!" she shrugged me off joining some other young guests at a table nearby. I wanted to get this wedding over with but I did have to admit it was nice every once in a while seeing your family gathered up in one place. Just two months felt like years when you were as big on family as I was. What I needed to do was find my cousin Chizu and all the other bridesmaids.

"Nigh to the, E to the…" I started singing as I stood at the door of all my laughing cousins and even some familiar faces, as they joined in the memorable theme song we all knew and loved with my name replacing Moesha's. All you needed was to be around the girls you grew up with and suddenly you felt like a grade schooler again.

"Girl, look at you." I walked further in the room directing my words to my friend Erika who I'd known since the 5th grade. Not only did she tease me my whole existence for not being *regular* black as she called it, here she was decked out in full dress including a matching Ichafu like she was born to wear it. #HonoraryNaija

"Hey you want to give me and Naima a few minutes alone while she does my make-up for me." The bride called out to everyone in the room. When the room cleared out it was just me and Chizu standing there face to face.

Coral beads were woven in her braided hair and hung around her neck and wrists in the form of necklaces and bracelets, and her dress was astonishingly breathtaking. It was a cross between a traditional dress and a western gown. If I wasn't wearing a mountain worth of mascara, I would have shed a tear of how gorgeous she looked.

"I swear, I'm going to start charging you guys to do hair and make-up. You're only the ninth person who requested my services today." My cousin had damn near flawless medium brown skin, so my only objective was to bring out her eyes and make her lips pop with a bright pink.

"Stop acting like you don't love when someone asks you. I could've hired a professional and been done with this mess already. But here I am, waiting on your ass." She sneered.

"Says the woman who's about to get her damn face done for free." I teased. We engulfed each other in a bear hug, all the bickering somehow melting away in that one embrace. No matter how much we argued, I loved this girl like a sister.

For a good ten minutes, I took my time perfecting a dramatic eyelid before adding a requested wing of the eye. I stole a quick glance at my cell's screen to see who was blowing up my phone notifications.

It was a few people at the place I worked at leaving comments on my recent wedding photos but one comment had stuck out on a photo of me and my mother.

TimTbeau15: *Which one of you is the mother? You two are both beautiful.*

"Ohhhh, who has you smiling?" Caught right in the act.

"No one. Just a guy I work with commenting on my photos. It's not even that serious."

"Smiling hard for someone that's not even that serious," she mocked. Before I could fend her off, she grabbed my phone and was no doubt browsing through his profile of pictures.

"*Okay*, Naima. Naima went and scooped herself up an Italian. I'm not mad."

"Give me this damn phone." I snatched it out her hand. "And he's not Italian." Or at least based off what I knew he wasn't. I sort of had a love/hate relationship with Italian-American guys. I loved the way they looked but hated the way they acted. Staten Island had some of the most obnoxious ones you could ever meet and for that reason I'd convinced myself he was anything *but* Italian.

"So, what's the deal with this one?"

"*Are you not getting married?*"

"I'm asking for you, *stupid*. It's been a while since I've seen you with anyone and all my life I've had to hear about how damn pretty you were. It just doesn't make sense that every time I see you, you're single."

There was a difference between choosing to be single and desperately looking to be involved with someone. I was a firm believer in something that was meant for me would eventually find me if I was meant to have it. Until then, I wasn't in a rush to the finish line, not when there were so many things I wanted to accomplish before I reached that red tape.

Sure I was a slow at doing things but I did things in my own time, when *I* was ready to do them. Sometimes a man didn't fit into the grand scheme of things. Or at least not now they didn't.

"Eww, Chizu. Stop worrying about my shitty ass love life. You my love, are getting married. Can we instead focus on that today?" She swatted me away, her gaze shooting upward.

"At least tell me what the men are like up there. I know you have to be swimming in papis."

"Fine, I'll tell you. But only if you sit still while I paint your mouth. If you make me mess up and I have to start over, I'm not telling you a damn thing."

"Fine." She pouted. "But before I agree to that, just do me one last favor." I rolled my eyes.

"Girl, *what?*"

"Don't *girl what* me! You don't even know what I'm going to ask. *Anyways*. If you can sum up Mr.—"She once again took the phone from my hand, lingering on his open profile. "TimT-beau15 in two words, which ones would you choose?"

I didn't have to search long for that answer. I pulled out a brown lip liner from the kit sitting to the side of us as I prepared her lips for the base.

"Two words that describe Timothy? That would be charming and *very*."

* * *

I peeked in the living room to find my mother passed out on the couch. Despite us making it back over an hour ago, she still wore her festive gear from earlier. She hadn't even bothered to take off her head piece, proof that she must've been tired. My mother tied those things so tight, I couldn't wait to take mine off.

"Ma, wake up." I proceeded to untie and unravel her head piece, her short thick hair nearly flattened due to its tightness.

"Ma, sit up. I'm going to give you flat twists." I didn't want her to regret a much needed nap by waking up to hair she couldn't manage. "I looked around the house. Where are Ruben and Chiaka?"

Ruben was my step father but as long as I could remember back, a second father to me. He was sort of the pushover type. Nerdy, anxious to please and never missed a day in church. For those reasons, he was perfect for my mom.

He was the complete opposite of my own father, a Yoruba man. My dad was sort of the carefree type, a clash in culture for my mother and her perfectionist type nature. They'd only been together long enough to move here to the States, have me and then unfortunately divorce six years after. Ruben was a huge factor in why I didn't worry about my mom so much. While ten years older than her, as long as he was alive, I knew he'd take care of her.

"He took the little one to a film, I believe. Why didn't you go with them?" Same as her, I was exhausted after being out all day. Even being dowsed in freezing cold water couldn't have woken me up.

I led my mother up the steps, later helping her out of her skirt and blouse before she pushed me away scolding me on how she didn't need my help. She was my mom. No matter how much she'd tell me she didn't need me around; I always wanted to try to be there if I was able.

"So how is that place, so far, eh? And school, are you keeping up with your studies?" She mumbled, drowsy and in Igbo.

"Oh you'd like it, ma." I said hanging her two piece dress in her walk-in closet. "Why don't you, Ruben and Baba come visit in a few weeks after I'm done with mid-terms? We could go out or something. Or just you, Ruben and Chiaka. I know how you and Dad get when you haven't spoken in a while."

I turned around to find her passed out peacefully, tiptoeing my way to her bed as I laid a kiss on her forehead before seeing myself out.

* * *

Downstairs, I ran into both my stepfather and ten year-old cousin walking through the front door. "Oh, hey guys. I just helped mom in the bed so limit the noise, alright? You know how she gets when she doesn't get her thirteen plus hours before Sunday." I teased.

It was true. On the day before she praised, my mother needed her sleep. She liked to get up bright and early before what she'd always referred to as the Lord's Day. It didn't make much difference to me, but it did mean I'd have the house to myself for a few hours while they were at church. Sleeping in would be the only way I saw myself spending it.

"Good night people. I'm going to take my behind to bed. I had to be back before Monday, so I'm taking a late night bus out of here tomorrow." My stepfather embraced me in a hug before seeing me off to the room I stayed in when I visited home, my old bedroom.

I couldn't wait to lay back down. It seemed as if since I'd moved to Rhode Island, I hadn't remembered what eight hours of sleep felt like.

As I laid down on the mattress, a tiny voice in my head politely asked me to just go to sleep. Ignore the blinking light my phone was giving off. After all, I was tired, wasn't I? Nothing could be more important to me now than getting a full night's worth of sleep. Or so I thought.

Timothy: *Ahhh...she knows my number. I was beginning to think you saved it in your phone for show.*

My eyes widened at the timestamp and next to the message I didn't remember sending him almost four hours ago.

Me: *Hey you*

Hey you? I would never send a text like that to someone. Not only was it vague, it was plain corny. I had one drink tonight, clearly not enough liquor to send a drunk text.

Chizu: *Don't get mad Eema. Found that dude's number in your phone and texted him. I knew your scared ass wouldn't. Don't be mad. Luv you* 😙

This…ohhhh…I swear! This was the main reason I never told anyone anything. People could *not* mind own businesses. Now I had to text him back, otherwise he'd probably accuse me of phone tag.

Me: *You gave it to me remember?*

I bit my nails when I glanced at the time icon in the corner of the screen. 9:59.

Me: *Sorry for texting so late.*

Timothy: *NP. Got off work fifteen minutes ago. Still wired.*

Me: *Work tomorrow?*

Timothy: *Yea, early though. Isn't it obvious they hate me?*

Me: *Not trying to keep you up then. Better let you go.*

His next reply wasn't instant like the rest so I was bracing for a big fat yes.

Timothy: *Trying to get rid of me. I see...*

I laughed to myself, which in turn made me feel a little stupid. Even with just his text messages, his wit shined through.

Me: *No, not trying to get rid of you. Only trying to be considerate.*

Timothy: *And thanks for that. But I'm okay. I promise. Although, any text conversations that go beyond ten messages in a single session earns you a phone call.*

A brief second passed, as he texted back.

Timothy: *I know you're counting them...*

He read my thoughts like he was in the room with me. The last one marked ten. Oh, to hell with it. I dialed his number.

"Good evening." He said in a ghouly voice that could give one of those old time horror voice-over actors a run for their money. Was it weird that I liked that about him? He didn't take himself too seriously, something I found myself doing more and more as the years passed on.

"I like how you're so easy to make laugh. That trait is super rare nowadays. I warn you, once you get to know me better, you'll probably just think I'm a whack job. But I promise, I'm always someone who can make you laugh. I've been crowd tested." He joked.

"But enough about me and my many talents, talk to me. And before you say *'oh, you don't want to hear about how my day was'*, that's where you're wrong. I most certainly do. I've spent all day at work and I want to hear someone talk about something other than book signings and two-for-one deals. Plus, I want to know I'm talking to the right Naima. Judging by your Instagram feed, looks like you've got a doppleganger."

He was probably right about me being easy to make laugh. I practically cried hearing him say that. Yes, my mom and I looked alike but not young enough to be my doppleganger. At best, an older sister.

"Okay but if you fall asleep on me, next time I see you at work, there will be problems."

CHAPTER EIGHT

Naima

For some reason I envisioned Monday's shift going down a lot differently. Maybe I'd spend the afternoon leaving subtle cues with my eyes for Timothy's fine self to come on over. Perhaps I thought that getting all dolled up today would really mean something.

Sure, it was just a natural version of myself but a *polished* version of myself. I'd even straightened my hair, something out of laziness, I didn't often do. But even today, despite being straight, it had just enough body to put these tight jeans I was wearing to shame. There was something fierce about being able to flip your hair when you were trying to garner the attention from a certain someone. But surprise, surprise, Mr. Ferreiro was not working today.

All this effort I'd put in? All for nothing. I told myself that next time I planned on doing all this, I'd at least check the schedule ahead of time.

Tim and I spent all Saturday night talking on the phone—something in this day and age, I wasn't sure I was still capable of.

Conversations with me on the phone hardly went on beyond ten minutes, like he'd mentioned before no one really talks on the phone anymore. And yet…

He was so damn easy to talk to. Definitely one of those intellectual types that didn't believe there was such a thing of a stupid question. It was a shift in gears to converse with a man who asked me more than he talked. I pretty much knew a narcissist when I saw one but Timothy? He seemed different. Different was something I was becoming more attracted to, engaging with the people I'd met while working here. That *especially* included a girl called Sailor Moon.

"Hey, Staten Island. You got here at ten right?" Ruby approached me from behind. "You go on your lunch yet?" Even though she wore her signature meatball buns, she looked more Chun-Li and less Usagi Tsukino. But that was just me. Guess you really couldn't choose your nickname.

"Nope, but I'm just about ready to go."

"Cool, you wanna hit up something together?"

* * *

There was something odd about Sailor Moon that made her hard to describe. The girl was goofy, invasive, and a little mad scientist all in one, but I kind of dug that about her. She wasn't the kind of girl I'd chill with back home, but she was good company and I was glad to confess that she was becoming my closest friend in just a short time.

There were so many places downtown, we decided to hightail some place quick to fuel our appetite. We ordered two sandwiches and locked a spot by the glass window. This part of Westminster was always dead, but the occasional people that walked by were wrangled in our conversation like we were hired to randomly roast random strangers. No one was immune. Not even the cute ones. Speaking of cute ones…

"So what's the deal with you and Timothy?" From the outside looking in, Ruby and Tim looked close. If I wanted to know more about him without asking *"Is Tim available?"* I knew she was the one to ask. She nearly choked on her food, laughing so hard.

"Me and Tim? Ew... No. Just no. Don't get me wrong, it's not that he isn't cute. It's just, *gross.* I've known him since high school." She put her sandwich down and picked out a few pickle slices, which she laid on a napkin. She stabbed the slices with a fork, repeating the words *"I thought I said no pickles"* over and over again. Girl was a hoot.

"Plus, I'm not even his type."

So he has a type.

"He won't admit it out loud, claims he likes all types of women, but the only ones I've ever seen him actively pursue were, like, Black or Latina. Or a Black Latina, like his girlfriend now. But he's an equal opportunist I suppose."

And now it was time to choke on my food. Did she just say *girlfriend?*

"Hey, are you trying to get back? We literally have seven minutes left, and I always take super long walking back."

I grabbed my things. Side by side, we said goodbye to the restaurant. Whether we talked the whole way back, I couldn't tell you. Without liquor or bribing, I'd gotten Ruby to unload the detail that would have been helpful to know before I'd stuck my tongue down the guy's throat.

Timothy Ferreiro had a girlfriend. How could I ever show my face around him without feeling like a total slimeball?

* * *

Assisting customers at this place was always fairly easy. Assisting customers in my worst-versed language? That was hard. Portuguese wasn't a language I used often. In fact, I didn't use it at all. It wasn't like the months I'd spent in Montreal or the summer spent in Puerto Rico where I'd had time to fine tune my confidence for the languages. Portuguese was one I acquired through mainly compact disc lessons, films, and music. But try telling that to a Brazilian. *Just try.*

I'd managed to point them in the right direction of the books they were in search of, but only after mixing up a word or two, which they laughed off. Brazilians were friendly like that. All they appreciated was the effort.

"Girl you speak Portuguese, too? Oh, my nana would love you." I turned around to see Timothy looking sexy as hell in a white slim-fit Henley and loose-fit dark denim jeans. His beanie hung loosely off his head, and he was wearing clean Timbs. The best thing he wore? Definitely his smile. I ~~loved~~ hated that smile.

"And how do you know I'm speaking Portuguese?"

"C'mon, Staten Island," he sputtered. "I know Portuguese when I hear it. Last name's Ferreiro. I am Portuguese as fuck."

I knew he wasn't Italian. With his dark hair and eyes I could see where my cousin got mixed up but c'mon, I knew my stuff.

"So I know you speak Spanish and Igbo, right?"

"That would be correct. Along with French, Yoruba, and obviously English."

He smiled. "You don't understand how dope that is. A lot of us Neanderthals can barely speak one. So it's super-sexy that your brain can converse in six. When I'm in need of a translator, you'll be the first I hit up."

I'm going to ignore that he called me super-sexy and get back to shelving these returns. Besides, it wasn't like he was calling me super-sexy specifically. He was complimenting my brain.

I pushed my cart of books up and down the aisle, ignoring the fact he was watching me. He stood on the opposite side of the cart, charming me with those deep brown eyes. Rocking a little more facial hair than his usual, he looked ten times more attractive.

"You're only making it harder on yourself. Here, let me help."

He went on to organize the books by category, something I hadn't even considered since I wasn't familiar with the store layout.

"I think I'll find that much easier. What are you doing here anyways? Aren't you off?"

The new arrangement of my workload made it easier to spot the places for the books. Before I knew it, the only ones left were cookbooks.

"I had some stuff I had to pick up from one of my boys. He was going to meet me at the mall around five-ish. Figured I'd stop by and torture whoever was on." He picked up a fairly large book and read the title aloud as we walked through the aisles. "*Fast Track to the Race on Veganism*. Is that a word? I'm sure that's not a word." He turned to me, looking all coy and cute as if he didn't know he was. "Do you cook?"

My eyes widened as I shook my head. I couldn't *not* cook, but when you had a mom and dad who threw down in the kitchen, Egusi soup and Nkwobi never tasted quite as good when I made it. #americannigerianproblems

"Slowly getting there. Does your girlfriend cook?" I asked without thinking.

He laughed and placed the book on the shelf. "Does anyone cook anymore?" He picked up another book and flipped through the pages before turning to its back matter. "And no, she does not." He brought his lips into a thin line, making me feel like a total gossip for asking. I took a book off my cart and pretended to read it to give me an excuse *not* to look at him.

"I think I was talking to Sailor Moon about something— school, work, shit like that. Your name came up and she mentioned you had a girlfriend. I hope you don't think I was being nosy."

He shook his head. "Not at all."

"Soooo...were you going to tell me you had a girlfriend?" I asked without looking away from my book.

He pulled my book down, challenging me with his smile. "Depends. Were you going to ask me?"

My arms hung loosely at my sides. "To be honest, no, but then you asked me for my number—"

"And what? I sparked your interest?" he interrupted.

"Oh, please don't flatter yourself, *Tim-ba-land.* I thought…I don't know, that you were into me or something."

He leaned on a bookcase behind him. "Why? Because you're attractive?"

"Okay, don't try to play me." I attempted to push my cart away, but he stood in front of it, blocking its way.

"Listen. This is not to be taken the wrong way, but not every guy that's nice to you is trying to get in your pants. Just like every beautiful girl that smiles in my direction isn't begging for me to hit on her. I hate if you feel like I led you on that way. I just honestly wanted to know you better. You seem like cool people. Besides, when we talk, it's not like you ever ask me anything. It's always you answering my questions."

"Yeah, well, that shit changes *today*," I declared, pointing my index fingers downward.

"I figured, you're new to a city. I take it you don't have many friends yet. Here at Symposium, we take pride in being a cult —*ahem*—family of book enthusiasts. I was only trying to be your friend. That is, if you'll have me." He pressed his palm to his chest.

"Ugh." I brought the book back to my face. "I wish you would have at least told me before I humiliated myself by kissing you. Even over the phone would have been nice. That way, I wouldn't have to look at you."

He pried the book out of my hand and placed it in its rightful spot. That was my last one. Now I had to stretch out this last five minutes.

"Humiliated that you kissed me or humiliated that you liked kissing me?" he teased.

I really wished I still had that book in my hand. Would've been the perfect time to clock him with it.

"So I was going to ask since you're off at, like, four, right? You wanna hit up a movie or something? I won these advanced screening tickets to some horror flick that's claiming to be better than *Paranormal Activity*. It's the movie theater in the mall up the street. I was going to ask Ruby but poor thing be having nightmares. So what's up? Want to go?"

"Oh, so what, I'm like you're consolation prize?" I joked.

He licked his lips and did me the honor of returning the book cart to the front of the store, but left me one more thought.

"Believe me when I say this, Naima. *You* would never be someone's consolation prize."

Guess that extra time I'd spent on my looks paid off after all.

* * *

Timothy

So my business was out there. Why hadn't I mentioned having a girlfriend? Hadn't thought it was need-to-know. Relationships were supposed to be private. It was my personal choice not to bring it up in conversations. At least that's what I told myself when it came to Naima. She probably thought I was the scum of the earth. I feared anything I told her now would be read as a lie.

We took a left on Eddy Street as I mentally prepared for the longest walk of my life.

"You're so quiet all of a sudden." Of course she noticed. What could I say to get me out of this mess?

"Think so?"

But she was smarter than I was taking her for. "So Mr. 'Naima Never Asks Me About Myself.' Tell me about yourself."

I laughed. "That's not really a question, *is it?*"

She sighed, pausing long before responding. "Allow me to

paraphrase. What can you tell me about yourself?" She attempted to walk in the street on a green light, but I grabbed her hand and pulled her back. In RI, we actually waited for the light to turn red.

"Broad question...and vague. C'mon, Naima. You can do better than that." We crossed the street to see the mall a few ways up, which meant this conversation would be over soon.

"Okay, smart ass. What do you do for fun?"

"Ahh *Better*. I guess chill with my boys. Go out. Host marathons of my favorite *I Love Lucy* episodes. Kidnap coworkers. You know, the usual."

She laughed and shoved me off the sidewalk. She was probably one of those girls who beat boys up on the playground when they pulled her hair or proclaimed their sandbox love. Just the kind of girl I pestered when I was that age.

"You are something else."

I liked being something else. It beat being normal.

"I'm surprised you don't have your girl with you. What—is she meeting us there?"

Here it comes. The conversation I'd avoided since our last few moments at work. I wasn't in the mood to get into it, but she was someone I wanted as a friend, so lying wasn't an option.

"Yeah, that's not going to happen. My girl's not from RI. She lives in Texas. Dallas, to be exact."

Naima shot me a look of confusion. "What's that about?"

"She went to college here and moved back home after she got offered a job. It's not really a long story."

She went into asking all these questions that I didn't feel like answering. What's she look like? How long have you been together? What's her name, sign, Social Security number, credit score? Okay, so maybe that didn't happen, but it sure did feet like it.

"Listen, Naima. Is it possible we could talk about something other than this topic? It's a complicated subject for me."

"What makes it complicated?"

I sighed. "Clearly, you've never been in a long-distance relationship."

She sucked her teeth, making a face that reminded me of a kid when someone did something disgusting. "Uh, yeah, I used to date a guy from Queens."

"Yeah…" I paused. "I'm not talking boroughs away. I'm talking states, Staten Island. Like, in order to see your significant other you have to board a plane. For months all you get are really long phone calls, video chats, and maybe a package in the mail. You want to be impulsive, but this far away you can't be. The time you do spend together has to be calculated and planned like a vacation. It just doesn't replace actually being there."

"Damn," was all she mustered up to say. Exactly why I hated talking about it.

"So, Miss Staten Island. Where's your man at?" Not sure why I cared. I wasn't asking for myself, but it didn't hurt to know.

"My situation is less complicated. I don't have one."

I fought back the temptation to ask why, but it dawned on me. Not everyone is actually looking to be attached to someone. Smart people.

We walked up the steps to the mall's side entrance. "It's just in here." I held the door open for her, and she whisked past me.

It was a shame the circumstances weren't different. On a regular day, she was just the kind of girl I'd obsess over. Maybe even a part of me was obsessed now.

* * *

We trekked through the mall and reached the food court. We were an escalator ride away to the top floor where the movie theater in question was just a quick away from Dave and Buster's where my friend was meeting me. He owed me cash and asked me to meet him there to pick it up. I wasn't expecting all four of my boys to be there, plus my seven-year-old goddaughter, Brooklyn, trying to convince me to stay. That little girl had super-human, metaphysical powers. She could get me to do anything.

"Who shows up to Dave & Buster's to say hi but not stay? C'mon, Tim, stop being corny. Chill for a minute," my friend Marv objected.

I considered the invitation for a second. *No* would be the best answer. I wasn't trying to miss that movie. If I didn't see it today, I'd have to wait a whole three weeks to see it when it officially dropped. If I hadn't won the tickets, I wouldn't be here because I hated going to the movies. I was a total homebody. But I had Naima waiting outside in the lobby. I had to make this quick.

"Normally, I'd be down, but I've got one of my other friends with me and we were trying to catch a movie."

"Who? Ruby?" my friend KC asked. "Because she knows she can stop hiding like she's not invited."

"No," I said in a low voice. "This is a girl who just started at Symposium. I think she's a little shy. I don't want y'all to make her feel uncomfortable."

They all looked equally shocked that I would even suggest such a thing. Together, we were the Five Stooges. In high school, you could always count on us to be cracking jokes.

Brooklyn put her hands on her hips, looking too grown and too mean to be seven. Her hair was braided in intricate cornrows that rustled at the ends because of all the beads. She had the power to command a room, and I don't know why my friend Rick and her mom didn't enroll her in some arts school. She could totally be an actress.

I put my hands on my hips, imitating her stance, and tried hard to hide my smile. "Girl, why you looking all mad for? Haven't seen your Uncle Tim in two weeks and already you look like you wanna hang me. C'mere, girl." I picked her up and swung her around, planting a kiss on her cheek. Her giggles brought a joy out of me that reminded me why I loved her like she was mine.

"You're not going to stay?" she whined with the most adorable pouted lips. These guys fought dirty. Sending a child to do their bidding. Plain despicable.

"Just because you asked, babygirl, I'll stay. But first I have to ask my friend if it's okay with her, okay?" I placed her back on the ground, pointing in the direction of my friends before turning the corner. "Y'all dirty."

Naima was still standing outside, poised and patient, playing with her phone as I approached her. "Hey. I wanted to ask you, is it okay if we skip the movie and chill out here? My friends are giving me a hard time about taking the money and just leaving."

I expected a hard time, but she didn't give one. More easy-going than your average person.

"Problem is, I have zero cash on me. I don't know how much it'll cost to hit this place up."

"It's cool, Staten Island, I got you." But she insisted on paying me back when I took her home. I wasn't sweating it. Not like I didn't know where she worked.

"Let me introduce you to my friends."

* * *

Naima

I didn't know what to expect meeting Timothy's friends. What I got was an interesting mix of witty, charming, and equally geeky versions of himself. His friends were on a mission to make the new girl on the block laugh. His friend Marv had a bronze complexion, light brown eyes, perfect bone structure, and from his Español, I assumed *Dominicano*. Another by the name of Rick was what I'd describe as a young Michael Ealy, but his daughter was darker skinned like me and just the darn cutest. The other two in the group, Bobby and KC, were the epitome of smooth dark chocolate. I had to ask if they were Nigerian just to make sure they weren't fam because they were just that handsome. Was it legal for five guys in one group to be this fine?

Over dinner and five letdown rounds of *Deal or No Deal*, I learned that the five of them had been friends since high school. Three of them longer than that. All six of them were good company, and it didn't hurt that Brooklyn kept calling me out to tell me how pretty I was. *Kids didn't lie, man. Kids didn't lie.*

His friends were a good reflection of his character. All socially aware, all respectful, all good heads on their shoulders. NYC had been the wrong place when it came to dating. All of the most eligible bachelors worth having were right in this circle. It made zero sense that most of them were single.

Rick was the first to leave. He had to have his daughter home by ten, and after a few rounds and a battle to the death of *Hungry, Hungry Hippos*, Timothy decided that it was time for us to head out, too.

"Hey, Marv, did you drive with Bobby?"

"Nope. You know I don't do rides. Those two don't ever wanna go home."

"Cool if you give me and Naima a lift to mine?"

An elevator ride down to the parking lot chit chatting with Tim and his friend, Marv was pretty welcoming. Marv was one of his friends that was the most talkative (not to mention flirtiest and did I forget slickest?) and the closest one to Tim as far as personality went.

When we made it to his car, Marv gave me the front seat. Apparently whenever women rode in his car, it was mandatory for dudes to sit in the back. Timothy didn't argue, but he did kick the back of my seat like a bratty kid. So petty.

Lovesick *letras* in Spanish and the occasional *tresillo ritmo* I recognized as Reggaeton with the occasional Bachata balad poured through his loud speaker system. Bachata was always one of my favorite dances when I lived in Puerto Rico. Of course Puerto Ricans were always convinced they did it better than Dominicans but Bachata was just one of those dances you could not fuck up.

It took a few minutes to drive to Timothy's car, which did the trick of sobering us up. That guy listened to his music *loud*. "It was nice meeting you, Naima," he said with a wink. He was looking at my ass so that *definitely* meant these jeans were on point. I waved goodbye and followed Tim to his car.

"Let's get you home."

CHAPTER NINE

Naima

Timothy pulled up to my place and parked out in front. The clock read 11:32, but we both were a little amped and wide awake from earlier. "You want to come to the door with me? The cash I owe you is inside. Unless you have a curfew, *young man.*"

His eyes squinted with a hard smile. "Got jokes? No, Mrs. Parker, I do not have a curfew. Allow me walk you to your door." He unbuckled his seatbelt and met me on my side of his car. I let that Mrs. Parker comment slide, but trust me, it wasn't over.

Like a klutz, I always managed to trip when it was late at night. Timothy helped me up, but not without having a laugh and cutting on me.

"I have a roommate so try to be mindful," I said, fighting for the door to open.

A smile formed at the side of his mouth. "Is this an invitation?"

I wrestled with the wrong key three times, and it turned out that fourth time was a charm. "Don't tell me you're a vampire and need to be invited in first?"

He grinned. "No, but in all attempts to be polite…" The door swung open as he made his way past me. "I see you and I always have to do things the hard way." he added.

He plopped down on the couch and fiddled with his phone. I took this as the time to rummage through the kitchen in search of something drinkable to flush out the alcohol I had an hour ago. I found something better. A bag of Lisette's pre-rolled joints ripe for the taking. It was bananas how many of these things she had lying around the house. As long as I paid her back, her bud was my bud. That was what I called the start of a long friendship.

With a lit joint, I peeked back in the living room to check up on Timothy. "Hey, Tim, can I offer you something to eat…or drink?"

We'd eaten so much at dinner it didn't surprise me when he declined my offer. "I'll take a hit of that J, though," he said, gesturing for me to come over. He took a hit and passed it back. "Damn, this is that good shit. Let me find out you're growing."

I offered him another as I checked the bedroom to find it vacant. "Guess my roommate's not here," I said, walking back to the couch to collect my stash. I sat down next to him. He stretched his arms over the head of the couch, giving me enough preview of the insane V-shaped cut in his lower abdomen. It was a good thing I had this joint to my lips, otherwise I would've been drooling.

"Oh my god, I haven't blazed up in a minute. I'm feeling that shit ASAP." Seeing Timothy buzzed was the funniest thing. He was already super chill, but weed just made me floaty. I couldn't hold in a laugh to save my life.

"I swear your laugh is the cutest thing. It puts a smile on my face whenever I hear it."

"Oh, so you're trying to play me, is that it?"

"No," he said incredulously. "It's cute, y'know? In an 'Urkel meets I-boil-little-kids-in-a-cauldron' kind of way." He demonstrated how my laugh sounded to him, and I was appalled. I laughed nothing like that. Maybe the snorting was dead on, but that was about it.

His phone went off several times, probably flooded with messages. I had my guess who. He let out an arrogant snort as his thumbs flew across his phone's screen. I kept my distance on the other side of the couch. I had no desire to be nosy.

"Hmph. My boys…they're about to start an 'I love Naima' fan club. They *loved* you. All these texts. They're all about you."

"Oh, yeah? What are you telling them?" I reached over to his hands, play-trying to steal his phone. He pulled me onto his lap by my arm, and I lay sprawled across his knees.

"Being bad, girl. Might have to put you in a corner and spank you," he said, followed by a laugh.

I fought my way free, then kicked him in the side with my foot.

"I'm not telling them anything except that we're friends. At least, I think you're my friend. Are you my friend?"

It went without saying, but after tonight, how could he even question it? I secretly squeed when coincidentally we were on break together. My heart beat a little faster every time he touched me, and there was no way this guy would be in my house, helping me go through this blunt if he was not my friend.

"But really, though, since we're friends, can I be honest with you? Tell you what's on my mind from time to time? Without you freaking out?"

"You can tell me anything, but I can't promise not to go apeshit. It depends what it is."

He nodded in agreement and his phone away in his pocket. "Fair enough." He stretched his arm across the back of the couch, then patted the spot next to him. "I promise I don't bite."

I laid my head down on his arm, my head to the ceiling. His arm felt hard and tense, like he was flexing. Seeing how nice his stomach was, I gave him the benefit of the doubt.

"Okay, so ever since you kissed me that night, pretty much

every time I see you, I want to kiss you again. I spend an uncomfortable amount of time thinking about it. Especially at work."

My left brow rose as our faces met. "Yeah, Tim, definition of the word uncomfortable. Because face it, it's not like you're available."

His hand lifted, palm up. "But I'm not *not* available."

"You know what I mean." Not that I didn't think about kissing him. I did. But that didn't change that he had a girlfriend. If there was anything off-limits for me, that would be one of them.

"I just think about you, that's all. Did you like kissing me?" Was he really going to open this can of worms? "It's cool. You don't have to answer. Get up for a second. My arm's asleep." He brought his arm in and shook it out, then leaned toward the coffee table to take another hit of the blunt. He rested his elbows on his knees. I was going to regret this.

"Timothy, of course I liked kissing you. You're a very good kisser."

He laughed. "So just good, not great?"

Here we go. "First of all, who the hell says shit like, 'Oh, he was such a great kisser. Good thing he wasn't a *good* kisser'?" Being completely sarcastic. "It means the same shit, Tim."

He leaned back, resting his head in his hands. "It's really not but okay. Bet if I would have kissed your other lips, it'd call for a more thorough opinion."

I bit back my lip to keep from cheesing, but it was too late. I was grinning like a schoolgirl.

"Really? Timothy Ferreiro don't put it out there and let it hang like that if you aren't about that."

His lips curved into something sinister, an ambitious look in his eye. "*If I'm not about that?* Word? You really think I'm one of those guys who just says things just to say them?"

"I don't know, are you?"

He licked his lips, and I wanted to feel those lips, taste those lips, nibble on those lips. What the hell was Timothy doing to me?

"Are you going to let me?" The question wasn't was I going to let him. It was, once he was down there, would we stop at just that?

"Depends. Do you have something to prove?"

His laugh came out condescending this time. "Okay."

At first I thought he was getting up to leave, but then he kneeled down in front of me, trailing kisses on my stomach. His lips were tender, soft, yet hungry. He peeled off my pants, and I was thankful for a chance to catch my breath and center myself. What he was doing had already felt good, and he hadn't even really started.

He sketched kisses from my stomach to my panties and took great pleasure in watching me squirm. Asshole.

"Wait a sec." He pulled off his hat and laid it down next to me, his dark messy hair lolling in every direction. He winked. "Don't want that to get in the way."

I forced a smile. Could he stop with the teasing?

As if he read my mind, his lips found their way back to my pussy as he continued to tickle my clit through my panties. His brown eyes were focused, which only made me close mine. I could get lost in those eyes—or, worse, end up blurting something stupid. If I wanted this to last, my eyes were to remain shut. I was a sucker for seeing a guy's tongue at work, like a twelve-year-old schoolboy discovering porn for the first time.

His hands grazed my hips as he pulled down my panties. "Damn, girl. You keep it real nice."

As a reflex, I kicked him in the shoulder, but why lie? So not regretting that Brazilian wax a week ago. He grabbed both of my legs and pulled me closer to the couch's edge. "Now you tell me if I'm a great kisser."

His tongue separated my sensitive folds as he flicked underneath my clit to toy with me. His tongue was wet and warm and definitely knew its way around a vagina. He had this way of getting me close only to stop and build me up again. It was cruel, but shit did it feel good. I opened my eyes to get a glimpse of what he was doing. He never stopped, but I knew he was smiling. The tip of his tongue looped around happy spots, and even though I thought I'd be able to go another few minutes, he changed course with a flick of his tongue against my clit. Just the type of shit that got me off.

"Shit, Timothy, I'm gonna come," I cried, coming closer to ecstasy. He stretched my legs to my head and licked me until I couldn't take anymore. I pulled at his hair, spending that very last minute yelling obscenities until I reached my peak. Oh…my…god.

I caved into the couch, forgetting where I was. I only remembered when I felt kisses all along my pelvic bone. With his hand, he wiped his mouth and chin dry.

"Eating pussy makes me horny as hell. You and your sexy ass legs. Got me hard as shit." He rubbed the fronts of my thighs. Officially, this would be the last day I ever doubted Timothy Ferreiro. "Not sure you know what you started. What's up?"

I laughed. "You tell me what's up."

He stretched my right leg out and let it rest on his shoulder as he nibbled on my ankle. "If I'm being honest, I want to have sex. Do you want to have sex?"

I huffed. "With you? No!" It came out harsher than I meant it, but judging by his stark expression, I'd hurt his feelings.

He laughed. "You know, Naima, you're so fucked-up sometimes."

"I didn't mean it like that. I just meant…I won't do anything without a condom." That and the fact that he had a girlfriend. Not like I could forget that.

"Okay, well, if that's all you're worried about, I'll have you know that I never go into war without armor. I have rubbers."

If my looks were saying anything right now they'd be saying, *How convenient.*

He pinched my nose. "Relax, Naima. I'm a guy. I always have condoms on me. It's not that deep." So he carries condoms on him, big deal. It's not like he was counting on this to happen. Or was he? Was I? Now was the time to put a pause on things.

"Tim, you have a girlfriend. I'm not trying to get caught up in that drama."

He pursed his lips to one side. "Okay…you knew that I had a girlfriend a half-hour ago when you started riding my face, so sorry if that sounds a little…contrary."

"Tim, I'm sorry, you're just moving a little too fast for me."

He nodded with his tongue pressed into his cheek. "Okay." He picked up my panties and helped me put both my legs through. When he reached my hips, I pulled them the rest of the way. "Do you want your pants?"

"If you don't mind."

"Nope." He grabbed my pants off the floor and once again helped me slip them on. He put his hat back on and sat down next to me. "I have to be at work in the morning so…I guess I should head out."

And then it dawned on me. The reason why he was here in the first place. I owed him money.

"Hey, let me give you what I owe you first. Before I forget. Wanna follow me to my room?"

Behave yourself, Naima.

Those three words ran a mile a minute through my head as we walked in silence to my bedroom. Behave myself. How hard would it be to do that?

* * *

Timothy

I leaned against the opening to her bedroom door. Two perfectly made beds sat in opposite corners of the room separated by a nightstand. The room wasn't *that* small, but it was hard to imagine two grown women sharing it, probably killing each other over space. Her roommate must have been super laidback.

Naima kneeled down to reach for something underneath her bed and patted a spot on her mattress like she wanted me to sit. "You know you don't have to stand outside. You're not going to burst into flames by entering."

I didn't know about all that. By the way these ladies had the place looking, it looked like they were sacrificing virgins and shit. Candles, beads, sculptures of African deities. Definitely something you'd see on some Vodou movie set.

"My roommate's into Santería. They're just decorations."

I walked in and made myself comfortable on the foot of her bed. Seconds after typing numbers into a lockbox, she handed me forty-three dollars.

"This is bad timing. I like feel a prostitute."

She laughed and, in turn, made me laugh. Naima's laugh was wacky but drove me crazy. I tucked the money into my back pocket and was met with Naima kneeling down in front of me, rubbing her palms up and down the fronts of my legs.

"I hate to admit this, but you have me so fucking curious."

I suppose that was a step up from dissing me earlier, but I didn't blame her for how she felt. If it were me in the same situation, I wouldn't fuck a girl who had a man either. Yet there was something that drew me to Naima. I felt it. She felt it. We just vibed.

"I guess that can only be good, right?" I said, licking my lips. I interlocked my fingers in hers, and it was then I noticed how small her hands were.

"Look, this might not mean much, Naima, but I am really, really, *really* fucking attracted to you. I just want to be honest. Just in case you decide that being my friend is something you decide you still want to be. I won't ever disrespect you, but I can't pretend I don't feel a certain way when you're around."

If she was just a pretty face, it would've been easier to ignore. A lot my homegirls were sexy, but that didn't mean I was trying to cross that line with any of them. She was different. Relaxed, fun, intelligent, and didn't take herself too seriously. I could be myself around her. To me, there wasn't anything sexier.

"Okay," she said with hesitation. "If I'm being honest, there is something about you that goes beyond your physical appearance that attracts me to you. The only thing that's stopping me is that I've *never* been the type of girl to pursue another girl's man. It's just not my style."

That I respected. My situation wasn't simple—or, at least, not simple enough. The thought of making her uncomfortable made me not want to take it there at all. I liked being in her company. I didn't want that to change.

"I like you too much to fuck up our friendship over some shit neither one of us is really sure about. You're my girl more than anything. I just want us to be on the same page."

She leaned in and pressed her sexy lips against mine. "Well, I like you, too. Does that mean we're on the same page?"

She straddled me, our clothes finding her bedroom floor in a scuffle. Her hands glided over my chest, with a small comment about how pale I was adding humor to the moment. I wasn't ghastly white, but I could see how my skin up against her beautiful dark brown hue would make anyone look transparent.

"In case you haven't noticed, Naima, I am a white guy. Didn't you read the full disclosure?"

I drew kisses from her neck to her ear as she quivered in my arms. "Shut up." She leaned into kiss me, her hands raking through my loose hair.

"No, you shut up," I said as I flipped her on her back. "Unless you're telling me how you want it." Our pelvises pressed into each other, and the strength of her muscular legs wrapped around me only made me even harder. I wanted to feel her. But first, I wanted to make her whole body cry for it.

I peeled off her bra, my lips trailing light suctions along her collarbone and breasts as I felt her cave underneath me. Her heart beat faster the lower my lips traveled down her body.

"We meet again," I joked as I took off her barely there underwear and teased her lips apart with my tongue. I discovered fast how impatient she was. Once I did something she liked, she didn't want me to stop. But I was a tease. Once she was close, I switched it up to prolong the moment. *That* only drove her crazier.

Through gritted teeth and with a pull at my hair, she demanded my lips on hers. Naima had a bit of a yuck mouth, which was a turn on for me. It wasn't like I didn't love a modest woman, but a girl who could tell me what she wanted sexually was a rare find. No one thing worked on two girls, and I liked to be taught. Where was the fun in sex if I wasn't doing something that felt good? Closed mouths didn't get fed.

She reached over to my pants to grab the condoms I had stashed away in my pocket, all while never breaking contact with my lips. I thought about all the times I'd caught myself lingering on her body long enough to wonder what she looked like, tasted like, felt like. I was about to find out. I felt like the man.

I leaned up, not far from ripping that condom wrapper open, when her bedroom door met the wall in a thud. Naima, in a panic, reached for her clothes. I turned around to see a girl standing in the doorway. She covered her eyes, muttering apologies in both Spanish and English before Naima found her voice again to ask to give us ten minutes of privacy. It was awkward, but I was confused why Naima was freaking out. We were all adults here. It wasn't a big deal.

Her roommate closed the door, which left us to get back to business. I kissed her neck, ready and willing to resume what we had started. "Just so you know, I might need a little longer than ten minutes. Why didn't you tell her like thirty, thirty-five?"

She pushed me back, rejecting me mid-kiss. "That's because you're leaving Tim."

My brows met the middle of my face. "Seriously?" Two minutes ago we were all over each other, practically begging for this to happen, and now it was like her parents walked in on her or something. I tried to kiss her again but was met with a light shove. *Fuck.* "Naima, if you're embarrassed, we could head to my place."

I wasn't trying to be thirsty, but even on my best behavior, it'd been awhile since I let myself get this worked up over an actual person. Being faithful to a person had always been easy. I never prided myself on cheating, and while I couldn't say I never had, I always weighed the risks before I did. And being faithful when you saw your girlfriend a total of three times (four, if I was lucky) a year was a challenge. The human species had only five basic needs to feel alive.

To learn.

To eat.

To sleep.

To love.

To have sex.

I was barely living. I was going to go nuts if I didn't get some soon. Especially with the stress of this being my last semester.

"Maybe this is a sign," said Naima. "We should chill out for a second. I appreciate the offer, but now I have some stuff on my mind. Not sure if I'd be much fun."

She slipped back into her shirt and jeans while I located my shirt and pants on the floor. What was there to say to make this moment less awkward? "Are you okay?"

She nodded, but it was one of those *Of course I'm not okay* nods. The ones that required a second probing.

"And you'd tell me if you weren't, right?"

She smirked. "Yes, Timothy. I'm just in an analytic mood, that's all."

It was going to take more than two rounds of Twenty Questions to get it out of her. It was late, and she was eager for me to leave.

She walked me outside, saving me from taking the walk of shame by myself. When we finally made it to my car, I thought it wise to break the silence.

"So...guess I'll be seeing you?"

She faked a smile. An awkward, sheepish, guilty kind of smile. "I'm sure we'll see each other at work."

Obviously. A small voice inside told me to keep the moment right there, but I didn't want to leave on an awkward note. I pulled her in for a hug and kissed her on the cheek. "Don't be a stranger, girl. Text me." I fought the urge to kiss her as I strapped up in my seat. We said our goodbyes, and I made her promise to go back inside before starting up my car.

Don't be a stranger, I texted.

When she didn't text back right, I stuffed it in my pocket and took off toward home. I kept thinking about what she'd said earlier, about it being some kind of sign. But we couldn't undo what just happened. Didn't mean things had to be awkward. She was my friend, and if I could help it, I didn't want to lose her. So why couldn't I stop thinking about her?

It wasn't a crime to think about someone, right?

Maybe she was right. *No. She was definitely right.* We needed to take a step back. Things were moving too fast, too soon. I have a girl, who I love a whole fucking lot. Who means the world to me.

So why was I counting the days until I'd see Naima at work again?

I was beyond fucked.

CHAPTER TEN

Naima

Beep. Three in stock.

Beep. Eleven in stock.

Scanning inventory was boring just about the most boring thing I could find myself doing. It was that time to do a weekly sweep of the books out on display. To determine which books sold, which didn't sell, which would be replaced or returned. When you were in charge of non-fiction, memoirs, travel and cookbooks, it made the time go by that much slower.

When you were in YA, science fiction/fantasy, or romance, there was a skip in your step you couldn't fake. That area had the best covers, best atmosphere, and customers asking questions, let alone being the best place to waste time in.

I shouldn't complain. It was slow, and if I wasn't careful, I'd get sent home. Symposium anticipated a busier Thursday than this, so they were overstaffed. I needed my check to reflect that rent due, so even if I had to hide in the bathroom while they were looking to send people home, I'd do anything to stay.

Who was I kidding? I was really hiding from Timothy.

He was the manager on shift, and despite trying to be an adult about our recent dilemma, I was more comfortable hiding in a corner than facing him right now. I knew I couldn't avoid him forever. But another day would do.

When Timothy finally came into view, I made sure to surround myself with other employees. Genesis and Ruby were in a healthy chat, and it hadn't taken them long to accept me in their wave of nonsense. When Timothy approached, I was grateful he couldn't corner me.

He pointed between Ruby and Genesis, challenging which might be the first to volunteer to clock out first. "2 Live, you want to go home?"

"Nope!"

"Sailor Moon, you trying to go home?"

"Yup!" Ruby said without hesitation. She'd clocked in over thirty hours so far, so she wouldn't miss anything leaving early. With Ruby out the way, one by one, Timothy barked instructions for all of us to follow.

"Ruby, you can clock out. Genesis, you can stay on the floor. Naima, can you help out Katrina in the cafe?"

Even though I nodded my confirmation, I did my best to hide my anxiety. Of course he put me in *his* department.

I should've prepared myself regardless, but I wasn't ready for a confrontation. I should've known better. If I was going to put myself in that situation, the least I could do was prepare myself for "the talk."

"I probably won't need you there the entire night, but just in case it gets busy, I don't want KK over there by herself."

"Okay." Before Tim could make another remark, I made my way over to the cafe. My only desire was to appear as unaffected by our hookup as possible. It'd be easy around Katrina. We made a good team that had nothing to do with work.

"You're here tonight?" she asked out of habit.

"I guess," I replied in a flat voice. I tried smiling, but it didn't come off as genuine, not that Katrina noticed.

"It's about time Tim sent someone over here to help me. I'm bored out my mind by myself. Time always flies by when you're here."

If Katrina was right about anything, time flew with the two of us together. Both our mothers were Nigerian and Igbo at that, so exchanging family jokes, inside work banter, and pop culture, an hour in the cafe department felt like ten minutes.

The fun was short-lived. I knew there'd come a time Timothy and I might cross paths, but I was hoping at the very least it wouldn't be until the end of the night, when it'd be unavoidable at the time clock. Tim stalked behind the counter, waiting for both of us to finish taking care of the customers waiting for us.

"Kay. Kay..." he dragged, extending the sound of it with a devilish grin.

"No," Katrina said, despite him never having asked the question.

"*No?*" Tim held out both arms, his tension showing in his face, neck, and shoulders.

"Every time you try and butter me up with some compliment or line, it's always to convince me you want me to do heavy lifting. I keep telling you I'm a cashier, Tim. Not a damn dispatcher. So you can go ahead with that."

I had no clue what they were talking about, but I hoped Tim wouldn't ask me to do it either.

"It'd only be for a little while. I wanted to close out by seven, but there's no one else to help me."

Katrina's eyes widened, and one hand went to her hip, the other pointing in the direction of the floor. "Genesis ain't doing shit but walking around. Why don't you ask her? Or Naima. She's here, too, y'know? I'm not the only person on tonight."

If only Katrina knew how much trouble she was putting me in by merely just suggesting it. This was why you didn't mess with people you worked with. When Timothy looked in my direction, I knew what he was about to ask.

"Naima, would you mind helping me with dispatching? It's just some stuff for the pantry and refrigerator. With help, it'd probably only take an hour or so," Timothy said, as he held his palms together in a prayer-like clap. "You can even take your break after you're done. You don't have to ask anyone."

I slipped my hands into my pockets and nodded. "Okay, I guess."

Timothy didn't waste any time leading me from the pantry to the receiving dock, advising me to replace my apron with a back brace. He claimed I might not need it. He'd take the heavier ones and leave me with lighter items, but for my safety, I took one anyway. No wonder Katrina hated receiving. The braces alone didn't fit a real human being. I barely got it buttoned past my boobs.

The truck sat at the dock untouched, and I followed Tim's instructions. For each item, I had to scan it in for inventory purposes. If a box or bag was marked P, it was meant for pantry. If marked R, refrigerator. Simple enough. To make things easier, I took a mini-dolly, loaded my items after each scan, and reveled in not having to go back and forth the way Tim was forced to.

"By the way, if you have a minute afterward, I wanted to talk to you about something. If you didn't mind."

I nodded, but of course I minded. What was I going to say if I couldn't get out of it?

The only positive side about dispatching was that, outside of that exchange, he didn't mention anything while the work was going down. Should I prolong this, to give myself time to think? Or should I work quickly just to get it over with? By seven-thirty, it was high time for that break Tim mentioned me taking, but we were so close to completion, I stuck it out. I was sweating my tail off by the time I returned the back brace to its rightful hook on the wall.

"Hey, Naima. Thanks a lot for helping out. It would've taken twice as long without you, so I appreciate it," Tim said as he loaded the last box into the refrigerator.

I was so close to the pantry door. So close to freedom.

Tim conveniently blocked the exit. "Now that we're all set, think I could borrow your ear for a second?"

"What? *Now?*" I asked, pretending confusion when there was none.

Timothy held his palms out like he came in peace. "Just for a second."

I rubbed the back of my ear and shrugged. "*Okay?*"

"Naima, are you avoiding me?"

"How can I avoid you? We work together," I tittered back, trying not to give off my emotions.

Timothy crossed his arms across his chest, then slung them against his sides. "We've worked together three days this week, and this is the first time we've actually spoken together out of all of them. If KK wouldn't have turned down helping me, we would've gone an entire week without speaking."

"If that's all you're worried about, we're cool. Nobody's avoiding each other. We're just in different departments most times. We're supposed to be working." I joked, hoping to draw away from the tension.

"Naima, listen. I'm not trying to make you uncomfortable. I just want you and me to be good. I don't want things to be awkward between us."

I shook my head with conviction and added, "It's not." Then I excused myself from the room. Not as bad as I anticipated, but still...not my best moment.

* * *

Timothy

We didn't encounter each other again until the end of the night. I wanted it to be all in my head, but things weren't that simple. I liked Naima. I wanted to be her friend. Most times I wanted it to be more, but I was okay with exchanging inside jokes at the time clock.

I'd crossed a line. That much was clear. But it didn't mean we had to continue on this way. I wasn't going to deny I was attracted to Naima, but I was mature enough to keep it to myself. I didn't want her workdays to be filled with avoiding my company.

"Timothy, can you give me a ride? I only have, like, eight minutes to catch my bus," Katrina whined as I zipped my hoodie to my chest. I smiled. Katrina was about to get the business.

"Katrina, I'm confused. Yesterday I was your boo. Today? I ask you for a favor, and you pretend the shit wasn't good last night," I teased. Katrina was always bold enough to ask for a ride not more than a moment after dissing me, so it was a running joke around Symposium.

"Timmy, please! You know my back isn't good. I'm not cut out for all that dispatching stuff. You never ask Naima or Genesis with their skinny asses."

At the sound of her name, Naima crept into view, attention divided between Katrina and her cell phone.

"Just for that, I hope you miss it. Ha!"

Naima snickered, even though it seemed rather friendly. I was split between going straight home or going out the way for Katrina and Naima. Naima hadn't officially asked, but I wasn't going to offer one a ride without the other. Both lived in separate directions, so it might even give us a better chance at figuring us out.

"Look, I'm about to be Mr. Nice Guy. I'll do you guys this *one* favor, but only because Katrina is looking like a sick bunny and shit. Plus, you're not too far from me," I said, facing Naima. She rounded her shoulders, clearly uncomfortable.

"I don't mind taking the bus. But if you were going to drop Katrina off anyway, I guess I'll take it. Do you mind taking me home first? I have an important class in the morning."

It stabbed like a knife, but we'd put ourselves in the situation, so there was bound to a level of awkwardness and fear between us.

"Hoe, don't you live in West End? I'm right off 44. He'd basically be dropping you off just to come back."

"KK, it's cool. Girl's got school. You know when it's you and Ruby, you know you're ready to go home."

At least the car ride was quick. Confusing, but swift. It might've been instinct or maybe because they were talking in front of me, but Katrina and Naima spent most of the car ride speaking Igbo. It sounded more like gossip, so it wasn't likely I was brought up in conversation, but you had to wonder. When we finally arrived at Naima's stoop, she blew a kiss at Katrina and shot me a passive wave. By then, I knew it wasn't in my head. We weren't okay. Not by a long shot.

* * *

I loved Fridays. Getting paid was the obvious reason, with start of the weekend not far behind. It was also a sign for busier days at Symposium.

For reasons unknown, Friday was the one day of the week employees came to show their Sunday best as they picked up their checks. Whether it be fresh, fly, funky, or fancy, if a person wasn't scheduled, you could bet they'd come in looking like they *didn't* work at Symposium.

Bruce was a fan favorite. You could count on him to show up in his nuevo seventies-style suit, glitter shades, and boa, like it was coming back in style. He was wrong for it, considering he had direct deposit, but he was well aware that, regardless, we expected a show. He always had one.

Angel reminded me the most of my sense of style. Casual, but round the way. Fitted, clean watch, team jersey, jeans and Timbs. Even if he wasn't about to be a few c-notes richer, I'm sure he got a lot of love on the way here alone.

I rarely participated. It sucked working most Fridays.

When I caught wind of Genesis, it was that time again. She always came by in one of those body-clinging dresses that made her look thicker than she was. We always ~~joked~~ flirted when we saw each other in street clothes, and today wasn't about to be different. I rolled up to her as she checked her name on the new schedule, chanting the bridge of "Rump Shaker," our inside joke.

"Tim, who did the schedule? I forgot to tell you I can't work Thursday. I have concert tickets for that day."

"Well, why are you telling me?" A drawback of being cool with your friends at work? They wanted you to bend over backwards for them. Genesis thought she was in charge of her own schedule, expecting it to be changed at a drop's notice. What made it worse was that we were so cool. It was hard telling people no. "2 Live, you take this friendship too far."

Genesis tugged at my sleeve, forcing me to listen to her plea of why it was necessary for her not to work. She didn't make a good argument, but she got an A for effort.

"I'm not asking you to take it off the schedule. I'd switch hours with anyone scheduled that day."

"You'd have to find someone willing to work it, then come to Martha, me, or Ravinder after they agree to it. I can't do the heavy lifting for you."

Genesis stepped on her tiptoes, studying the schedule once more, pointing to random spots on the page.

"There's Katrina's Saturday or Naima's Sunday."

I pointed to myself, unsure why she kept referring to me. "Don't tell me! Ask them!"

It's amazing how whenever a person is mentioned, they show up out of nowhere. Naima roamed the backroom hallway, her check in hand. She didn't work today or tomorrow, and no one trusted getting their schedule read to them over the phone, so it was clear why she was back here.

"Staten Island, switch my Thursday for your Sunday!" Genesis said in a fit of excitement.

Naima's eyes bugged out a bit as she processed the request. "Hi to you, too, 2 Live."

"Hi, girl, just tell this fool you'll switch with me for Thursday. I have concert tickets, and I need to go! You wouldn't even have to work the weekend, so you should." Genesis managed to say all in one breath. She always had a way of spinning things so they sounded like *your* idea, even when it benefitted her most.

"I guess?" Naima said, almost as a question.

"See, Timbaland, I already found a replacement. That's how quick I work. Is it cool now?"

"Yeah, after you fill out the form," I added. I was not about to get in trouble off a verbal agreement. Genesis met Naima in a bear hug, and by Naima's jilted reaction, she still seemed like she was processing the exchange. After Genesis walked off, Naima took out her phone to snapshot her schedule.

She wasn't any different from anyone else picking up their check. She showed up in a knee-length dress and heels that peeked out from underneath a trench coat. All her nails were painted a blue that didn't match anything she had on, but diverted any attention from her outfit to her hands and feet.

"What are you all dressed up for?" I asked in the most casual tone I could manage.

Naima's eyes darted to a dozen other things before they came back to me. "Well…I'm not trying to brag, but my parents are coming up to celebrate the grades I got for midterms."

"Congratulations." I even meant it, too.

Naima rolled her eyes, but not at me. "It should be interesting. My mom, stepfather *and* my biological dad are all going to be there. It's been years, but they still don't know how to be civil with each other. Who knows how things are going to go."

"Good luck anyway. Hopefully the sight of all those A's is enough to forget bad blood."

Naima laughed, but I'd be lying if I said it sounded genuine. We passed on awkward goodbyes, parting ways not long afterward. I thought it'd be easier after we confronted each other, but nothing was easy. Not when it came to her.

* * *

Dinner alone on a Friday night. Things could be worse, but they used to be a lot less lonely before Sherri moved back to Texas. Sure we'd argue in the kitchen all the time. She wasn't the best chef, nor was she good at cleaning up after herself when she cooked. But all those wasted moments upset were some of our happier times. She lived seventeen hundred miles away. It was too far to be anything more than…far.

Sometimes I missed her. Sometimes I didn't. Sometimes she was all I thought about. Other times? She never crossed my mind.

I hated the distance. Until we had a better solution, our relationship consisted of a few trips a year and a few daily Skype chats. I was a homebody, but who really wanted to be a *lonely* homebody?

Mom: *Randomly texting I love you. Ma says I love you too.*

I smiled at the gesture. It never took much for the momma bears in my life to raise my spirits. I rushed a sloppy text back, detailing the same. Three other texts followed. One from my boy Rick. Another from Ruby Woo. But what I didn't expect came from the following.

Naima: *Wyd*

Was it a joke? A setup? A test? In the short amount of time we'd know each other, we'd grown close and then quickly grown apart. I'd tried, but most of my attempts to repair the friendship only ended in awkwardness.

I held my breath. Take your time. *Consider the least personal message to type back*, I kept amping myself to reply.

Me: *Nothing. Hbu.*

I expected a little time to go between replies, but receiving an instant one made me giddy.

Naima: *Stressed.*

She'd mentioned something about a night with her family coming up at work. Must not have gone well. Figured divorced folks would put aside their differences for special events but then again, mine never did.

Me: *Assuming it didn't go well?*

Naima: *It was ok. Could use a friend tho*

I was reluctant. Anything I texted at this point could get me in trouble. What did she have in mind? "Use" could mean talk, text, listen—all things I was equally prepared for.

Me: *Here if you need an ear. My number is useful.*

Naima: *Easier to articulate in person*

I was more nervous than I'd been since meeting her. What might she have in store that she couldn't articulate in a text?

Naima: *I'd drive around, meet up or hang. Up to you.*

Me: *I can pick you up if you want.*

Naima: *Ok*

Me: *Can roll up in 20.*

* * *

Naima with a story to tell was an interesting woman to be around. My only experience with discussing Nigerian parents was with Katrina, but Naima was a much better storyteller. She knew how to sell it with humor. I held onto my stomach, dying of laughter, trying to navigate the steering wheel with the best of my ability.

It was so bad I had to park close to the sidewalk. It was hard driving with no place in mind, and with all of Naima's stories, it was safer to park.

"Maybe we should just chill at your place. I hate to be the reason you're wasting all this gas."

I scratched the back of my neck before I came up with an answer. My sides hurt of exhaustion from laughing so hard, but I managed to respond without causing suspicion. "I'm not trying to make you uncomfortable. I kinda live alone, so…yeah."

Naima curved her lips to the side. "Ruby always talks about you having a banging surround system and flat screen, and I'm offended you've never offered to show me."

"Oh, yeah? What else does Ruby say about me?" Remind me to aggrevate the hell out of Ruby when I saw her. She caused a domino effect of arguments, and she wasn't even in the car. Talk of TV, shows, and Netflix opened up a debate worthy of the presidential candidate election.

Turns out Naima was a *huge* Supernatural fan, as were all the ladies at work, with exceptions for Bruce. The show was entertaining, but it definitely wasn't horror on cable networks at its best. Between back and forth of what was *Supernatural*'s best season, we ended back at my place for a bloodbath.

Naima didn't know what she was in for. I lived for horror. And now that mainstream was catching up to me, there were plenty sources worth mentioning that were scarier than *Supernatural*.

"What is your tolerance level? What can't you stomach?" I asked as a precaution. It surprised me Naima was even here, willing to go for a binge watch of the scariest shit on television.

"I can handle anything," she said with confidence, but I had something in store for her that would shake that attitude.

"Don't get cocky now. This won't be two swole Texan models slinging guns."

She shrugged me off, traveling from my small kitchen to my

living room. She hugged the couch before taking a seat, as I roamed in the fridge for a drink.

"I can appreciate a good slasher piece. Or something edgier. As long as you don't mind me screaming at the screen when I'm irritated."

"So you're one of *those* horror viewers." The ones who yell at the screen, barking out orders they assume they'd be resourceful enough to know if the time came. Nothing but talk. I couldn't imagine anything being funnier than Naima's storytelling, but watching scary shit with her seemed a decent way to test the theory.

"I'm one of *those* horror fans," she repeated back. "You have a nice place by the way. That Symposium check must be worth it because mine usually isn't."

Naima draped her jacket on the end of the couch arm, so I hung it up on the coat rack near the door. "You hungry? You probably ate with your folks, but I've got snacks. As long as you're not on some live right shit."

Naima dropped her head over the back of the couch, facing her gaze on me. "Got any popcorn or chips?"

"I may have chips." Of course I had chips. I needed to spoil my goddaughter with something when I watched her.

"I'm not picky with flavor, but if they're salty, I will be needing something to drink to go with it." She added, sitting up right back on the couch. I inspected the fridge again to see what was left.

"Damn. I'm starting to think it says grocery store over my kitchen. All these requests." Naima laughed, drawing me in with her laughter. "I have apple juice, lemonade, or iced tea. There's water too."

"Iced tea."

I took out the iced tea and laid it on the counter. Jogging over to the cubbies holding my controller, I turned on the system and TV and brought both with me. Pouring a plate of chips and cup of iced tea for the guest, navigating my PlayStation's screen to the Netflix app.

"Milady's chips and iced tea." I handed them to Naima over the couch. Scrolling through my lists of queued shows, I joined her.

"You're not eating?"

"Nah. Trying to keep that diet clean past seven-thirty," I joked, patting my stomach.

"So you're trying to plumpen me up so I can't fit in my jeans?" she fired back.

All I did was laugh. The view from here said she was fitting her jeans just fine. Maybe a little too fine. But the argument was cute. Definitely lightened the mood for what was to come.

"Can you eat and watch? Hope this isn't going to be what it's like the whole time with you." Even though I was only playing. She didn't watch many of the horror shows on TV, and I always said *American Horror Story* would make a horror fan out of anybody. I did my best educating her on its anthology format and history, but it was clear she'd learn more from watching. I may have been a few seasons in, but I invited a good binge rewatch every now and then. Especially with an *AHS* virgin.

By the first ten minutes, Naima's eyes were bulged out, show-casing a combination of her confusion, fear, or shock. But it was the last five minutes that always got to a newbie. Ah, the days.

"You all right over there?"

"Yes, stupid. Just play the next episode!"

And she wasn't lying. By episode two, it was a continuous banter of *"What is he doing?"*; *"These people are stupid, they keep going in that house"*; or my personal favorite *"Oh my god"* in more than one language I could understand.

"Does this woman know that wasn't her man?"

"Naima, can you just watch?"

I must admit that all I needed was a little dose of my favorite shows. It didn't hurt that I wasn't watching them alone, but with company, you didn't realize how fast the time flew when you had to drive someone home. It was almost ten o'clock by the time we were five episodes in. I was having fun, watching her anticipate each suspenseful music change through the peephole of her fingers, but I felt obligated to get her home at a decent hour.

"We're making good time for a few hours, but let me know if you're trying to go home. It's going to be be safe. It's not going anywhere."

"What episode are we on?"

In four hours, we'd managed to watch all but four episodes, so I did want to throw the offer out there. "We might as well try and finish it. I don't think I've ever been able to stop watching stupid people. All that murder and meaningless sex in one sitting while being completely terrified. I have to know how it ends."

"Whoa! Where is that coming from?"

Naima pointed to the screen, screeching her assessment of the show so far. "This girl didn't even know that dude. It didn't even occur to her to ask questions!"

"First of all, she assumed it was her husband, so basically that scene was rape, so scenes like that don't count. But if you're gonna watch it, you have to watch it until the end when the plot figures itself out better."

"I counted three sexual violations, a blow job, some lesbian action, and too much stuff to count. Assuming we're throwing out all that nonconsensual stuff, there's still a lot of crazy shit going on. I'm almost afraid to see if the season finale is going to have this much meaningless sex."

"Aw, come on Naima. There's no such thing as meaningless sex."

Naima rolled her eyes, and laid her cup and plate on the coffee table. "I hope you're not about to get all philosophical on me."

"*Really?* That's how you see me?"

"I'm just saying. Everything with you has to be a sonnet, deep words of wisdom, when everything really isn't that deep."

"I apologize for earning that reputation."

"It's cool, Tim. I'm not running into a whole bunch of people dropping knowledge at the water fountain at work. But some people aren't as complicated as you think they are. All sex having meaning? Sometimes it's nothing more than wanting to get a nut off."

"But that's a meaning. Granted, sex is not always an elegant meaning. Most times it's about feeling good. Other times, you're so frustrated. Like I'm so mad at this person, the only thing I can do without getting arrested is fucking their brains out. Or it can bring out confusion. Feelings. Ones you don't always know are there, but complicate things." Okay, *now* I was getting too personal.

"So you going down on me? What meaning did that have?" she said in a sarcastic tone, meant to provoke.

I wasn't prepared for the question, and rubbing the back of my neck probably hadn't sold my last argument. But she asked. Would she be able to take my honesty?

"I don't know what it meant for you, but for me...I don't know."

"Okay, Mr. All Sex Has Meaning."

"If you want a real answer, it was about making you feel good. Making you think about me. It may not have meant the same to you, but that's what it was for me."

"So if we would've had sex, what would that have meant?"

"It would've meant whatever we wanted it to mean. But we didn't. Maybe that's a good thing. Things have seemed so complicated between us. I just don't want..." Searching for the words that would get my point across but not offend was hard as fuck. "I'm just happy we're cool. I just want to go back to being the type of friends who have fun. Give each other rides. Bury dead bodies together. Be each other's alibis."

Naima hit my shoulder and joined me in series of cackles neither of us was able to hold in at this point.

"And they make each other laugh. I just can't do the awkwardness. You already know my situation, as complicated as it is. I can only respect your choice. It's not exactly a bad one."

I pressed play. We might be able to fit in one more before I got too tired to drive. Next thing I knew, the soft feel of her full lips made contact with my mouth, as we alternated biting and sucking on each other's lower lip.

Then I remembered where I was, and I stopped myself. "Wait a second, Naima. We should stop. I don't want you to think we have to do anything we can't walk back from." I pushed myself an extra inch away from her and rubbed my forehead, trying to make sense of things. "Don't get me wrong. I want this. But I'm a big boy. It's not going to hurt my feelings if you don't want that kind of friendship."

Before I could finish, she leaned into kiss me again. So this was really about to happen. She pressed her body up against mine, and I was more willing than ever to pull her closer. If she didn't want to, she'd stop. Any minute now…

With minimal effort, we managed to wrestle our way to my bedroom. I'm sure I stubbed my toe once or twice, but I was drowning in Naima's lips too much to notice. Lips that tasted my lips, my tongue, my neck, sending shivers straight from each point of contact.

In painfully long swipes, everything from Naima's shirt and pants to my Providence Bruins team jersey fell to the floor. Laying eyes upon Naima's barely covered body again, I was reminded of the athletic build I'd come to love. Taunt stomach, strong legs, firm behind, all stared at me from a matching pink panty and bra set.

She was trying to drive me crazy as she crawled down to my stomach, leaving the lingering imprint of lips from my midsection to my pelvic bone. Her fiery gaze ignited a spark in me I wasn't even sure was real. I was so ready to be inside her. I didn't know how long I could stand it. I tried sitting up, but Naima wasn't having it.

She pushed me back onto the bed as my belt became undone with each of her traveling fingers, moving as...slow...as...possible.

I'd earned it. For all the teasing I'd done in the past. I grit my teeth at every kiss, lick, or warm blow against my skin. When my zipper was completely undone, all of me pressed hard against the crotch of my jeans. I tried not to seem too excited, but I wasn't exactly selling it. All the blood in my body rushed to my groin. Soon my pants were history as she helped me slip out of each leg and onto the floor.

Naima leaned in, kissing my inner thighs and legs. It wasn't long before the sweet pressure of her tongue traced the outside of my boxers. With precise calculation, Naima pushed the head of my cock out of the fly.

"Do you want me to lick it?" she said in a coy, seductive manner. I was so ready to blow, I didn't know what to do with it.

"Girl, you are about to give me a heart attack talking like that." The rasp only highlighted my breathlessness. Light, feathery licks stroked the shaft of my cock. My toes curled each time she reached the head, but it wasn't until the warmth of her mouth devoured me whole that I let out the breath I'd been holding this entire time.

"You are teasing the shit out of me. *Fucking hell, Naima.*"

She laughed, and the hum of her mouth sent my body into overdrive. My body took turns relaxing and tensing as her head bobbed up and down all over me. I held both sides of her face and pumped my dick in and out of her mouth, watching her reaction to having her face fucked.

Her lips curled in as I slowed my pace down to make it comfortable for her. She locked eyes with mine, a glossed-over stare revealing longing and desire. I didn't want to get lost in my own pleasure for too long, so I leaned up and guided her face and lips to mine. "C'mere" I said as I guided her to sit opposite of my body. That beautiful pussy I'd gotten to taste once before was now right above me, hidden by pink panties.

Peeling them to the side, I ran my tongue on the outside of her other lips and blew on the remnants of slickness my tongue left behind. Her inner thighs tensed up around me, and I took it as the perfect time to flick and tease, to make her want it more. The scent she gave off drove my senses crazy. I was going to have fun making her squirm. I couldn't wait to taste her.

Her mouth teased my dick on the opposite side, but it was just to give a proper lube for a stroke down. It was all about her right now as I plunged my tongue between her luscious pussy lips, pulling her body closer to my face. A breathy gasp escaped her mouth as my tongue explored her sweet, delectable folds, alternating between flicking her clit and licking up and down her entire pussy.

The sounds of her illicit moans echoed through the quiet room as Naima centered her hands on the bed and jiggled up and down on my tongue to ride my face. I loved hearing her tell me how to eat it, if I liked it when she fucked my face, how too much of me was going to make her cum all over me. I smacked her ass and felt a twinge in my dick when she told me to smack it harder.

Spreading my tongue all over her nether regions, I took no mercy at her foolish attempts to separate her body from my tongue. Her thighs shook, and she dragged her pussy all over my face. A loud swear left her mouth, and I collapsed back on the bed and waited for her to crawl over toward me.

"Did you come, baby?"

She bit her lip and answered in a breathy, "Fuck yeah." I got the box of condoms in my dresser, ripped open a wrapper, and tugged my boxers all the way off. I slipped on the condom as I watched Naima sinfully slip out her underwear and bra, ready for what our bodies were about to do.

"Bend over."

It was good that I had a little restraint. Otherwise, watching Naima get on her knees and arch her back and ass toward me would've made me bust right then and there all over her. But I held myself back and stood behind her, over the bed. Slowly, I slid inside, feeling every inch of her warmth as I slipped deeper.

I grabbed a handful of her waist and gave her body a few hard thrusts, to make sure she felt me. "Damn, girl. You're so fucking wet," was all I managed to get out as I watched my pelvis and balls smack up against her ass.

"I'm about to show you how to fuck me." Naima backed up her body back and forth on my dick. My visual sensories couldn't stand it. I smacked that ass of hers, but it only made her go faster. She was about to make me come with her dirty mouth, asking if I could repeat what she was doing and handle her. I took the initiative, moving my hands from her waist to her behind, thrusting in and out of her the way she liked it.

As an added bonus, I spread her thighs apart, gently rubbing her clit while I plunged deep into her body. That tough girl attitude melted away, her voice cracking in an uncontrollable wave of moaning. It wasn't until then that the dialogue took a 180, and now all her dirty words consisted of me busting at the sight of me fucking her right. I'd held it too long. Four minutes left of consistent thrusting, and my dick turned into a living dynamite.

My body exploded upon impact, throbbing, deep, strong spasms that tensed at my groin. I pulled out of her, collapsing on the bed, totally forgetting to throw away the condom as I sat in a thin sheet of sweat. "That was fucking amazing, Naima."

A light guffaw left her throat, but the moment she reached for her clothes, I sensed a change in the air. "You all right?"

"Yeah. I'm good."

I sat up the minute she pulled her shirt over her head. Reaching for my boxers, I started to get dressed myself. "You sure?"

"Yes, Timothy." She attempted a fake smile. "But do you think you can drive me home now?"

* * *

The drive back to Naima's place drew question marks. For someone who wasn't shy, there hadn't been much to say most of the car ride. Outside of changing the radio station from time to time, there hadn't been much interaction at all. I didn't want things to take a turn for the worst. I wanted someone who'd talk to me.

"Please don't act all shy now. Talk to me. Tell me what you're thinking. What you're feeling. Tell me something…" I trailed off, hoping for the best.

"I don't know what I'm thinking or feeling. I'm just…thinking and feeling." It was better than hearing nothing. There was still a guard up, so I knew it wasn't all there was to say. I cut the engine and took the key out the ignition to take away my distractions.

"Here's what I'm thinking and feeling. Naima, when I'm with you, everything is with you. There aren't thoughts or body parts or words for anyone else. I don't deserve any part of you, but I want you. I want to be with you. But if making love is what turns things sour for us, I'm prepared to take things however you'd like to take them. You call the shots here. Nothing happens unless you want it to."

Naima rolled her neck from one side to the other, tapping her nails across the door handle. By the time she was ready to speak, five minutes had gone by. I didn't know what to think.

"Everything is confusing right now. I thought what happened was what I wanted, but now I'm not as sure. I think I just need a moment of clarity. Think things through more. I don't think I can solidify everything I'm feeling in the course of a car ride."

I nodded, soaking in all her words. She got out as my engine roared back to life with one turn. I waited for her to go inside before I drove off, just to make sure she got in okay.

Then my phone went off in my pocket.

Naima: *Gotta finish those eps. So we can get to season 2* 😇

A smile formed at the corner of my lips as I texted back.

Me: *For sure.*

CHAPTER ELEVEN

Timothy

Our Skype session was going over sixty-three minutes. Were we really talking that long? Was it her or me who called? Had I asked her how her parents were doing? I think so. But then again, I really couldn't remember. My mouth moved, but my brain wasn't one hundred percent functional. What was wrong with me today?

"Did you hear what I said, Tim?" Sherri said on the other side of the screen. Just like that, my brain was working again. Back here in the conversation. Back here to reality.

"Sorry, Sherri. I'm just out of it today. Just a lot of things happening with work and school. Everything's got me tired." Between the repeated rubs to my face and the pinching of the skin on my neck, I prayed I didn't look as guilty as I felt. "If it makes you feel any better, your trip is just three months away." Three months felt like an eternity when the lover inside you sat bottled up for months at a time. The old-me had been fun, affectionate, spontaneous. This current-me was an android that lived for work and school. Oh, and Netflix.

"I wish there was a way to see you sooner," I said, hoping that she'd get the hint and surprise me. All I ever got was a, "We'll see each other soon," which made me wonder why I'd even bothered mentioning it in the first place. Sherri's parents were in Dallas. Sherri's home was in Dallas. Sherri's life…was in Dallas. The only way I could see this thing working was if I sacrificed and made that move.

Sometimes I asked myself why it had to be me making all the sacrifices. Why did it have to be me? I know I wasn't perfect, but I loved her. I really tried to make this thing work. Because the more work I put into it, the less time I worried about the real reason my mind couldn't focus.

Naima. I was thinking about Naima.

"Tim? Are you sure you're up to talking?" Sherri asked, snapping me out of my trance. My phone rang, and I answered, looking for any excuse to cut this Skype chat short. I didn't care who it was; all I knew was I was tired of having this conversation. I wanted out.

"Okay, well, you look busy, Tim. I'm going to let you go." And with that she ended our session.

* * *

When my friends Rick and KC called, looking for a way to waste the next two hours sweating away at the gym, I happily obliged. It'd been a few days since I'd done any real lifting, and too much was on my mind to just be home alone. There were a lot of things to consider since my little talk with Naima. We'd seen each other off and on at work, and while I'd been her ride most days, we still hadn't gotten into the intricacies of our last heavy conversation.

She needed time and I was ready to give her that, but it was nerve-wracking waiting around for her answer. I needed to unwind. To forget. What I needed was 275 pounds of pure iron.

Five reps of a new weight and already my mind was in another place.

"Damn, Tim, you're in beast mode today. Straight up murdering these reps," KC said. He was the one who was the most built out of all of us. All the guy had to do was look at a weight and—*bam*—fifteen pounds of lean muscle added to his frame. We all fuckin' hated him for that.

"Well, I've got a lot on my mind. This shit is keeping me from drowning in it."

Questions formed behind their inquisitive eyes, and I prepared myself for what I'd say if they asked. They could never *not* ask. We weren't the types to shrug things off and not see what was up. Hell, I didn't know how anyone functioned that way.

"Everything okay, man?" Rick asked and there I unloaded.

My best friends knew me well. They knew that I lived and breathed for Sherri, but they'd also gotten the impression that Naima was something special. Something that had taken almost a year for my girl to do had only taken Naima one night at Dave & Buster's and that was win over my friends.

Sherri took a while to open up, which was hard because I was the complete opposite. I was gregarious, adaptable, and off the cuff. The reason why Naima and I got along so well was we were similar in ways that mattered most to me. And lately, she'd been the one I looked forward to seeing on the regular. I felt like shit even admitting that.

"Damn, maybe if you hadn't slept with her…" KC started.

I shot my friend an evil eye, asking myself if he was capable of telling me something I didn't already know. What's done was done. It wasn't like I could go back.

"She is bad, though. Like, damn, I about to ask if you could hook a brotha up, but I know the sistas all of a sudden sweating y'all light-skinned cats. Like, what the fuck?"

Just like him to make fun of a serious dilemma. Not gonna lie. It worked. Rick and I were dying.

Once Rick had caught his breath, we got back to the subject at hand. "I want to tell you just break up with Sherri. But damn that's four years..."

"I know. I love her, y'know? A lot. I'd never consider it unless it were in person and I could fully explain myself. But ending my relations over something that's not definite? It just seems dumb."

"You mean dumber than cheating in the first place?"

"KC, see that's why no one tells you shit, because you stay with the judgement. Less than a year ago, you were right here where I was. And I just listened. Supported. Offered advice. Which you didn't take, by the way."

"Yeah and my girl left me, so what you sayin'?"

I shrugged him off and directed my attention toward Rick, the sensible one. But all he did was give me a paraphrased version of what KC just said. Men could not give other men advice on girl problems they just didn't have. This was the time to hit up Ruby. I took out my phone to shoot her a text to find one unread message waiting in my inbox from Naima.

I want to be with you too...

* * *

Naima

I hadn't heard from Timothy since I'd found the nerve to send him that impulsive text. I had zero clue what I'd been thinking, but I'd had some time to consider his words and couldn't fight the feeling. Timothy made me all warm inside, made feel like I had a real friend. I'd had it with others, but it was different with him. He provoked me. Challenged me. Made me view things in different ways. And I liked that. I needed that. I just had to remind myself that it was all in good fun. Besides, I wasn't looking for something serious. Not with school and work in the way. But it was nice to have someone to call when things had the potential to become stressful. And it didn't hurt that he was a god in bed.

Lisette and I spent the night helping each other through wash day, eating junk food and parked in front of the TV for the latest episode of *Empire*. This girl was quick with the flat twists, and I swore my hair looked a whole nicer with the extra two hands I had at my disposal. One of the things I'd instantly liked about Lisette was how similar we were when it came to kicking back and fully engaging with our favorite TV shows.

Translation: We were both loud as hell and didn't give each other shit about it.

A text came in from Timothy. A part of me was afraid to open it. The other part? Anxious as hell. What if he was texting that not only did he *not* want to be with me, but didn't want to be associated with me? It had taken him so long to text back, the last thing I was expecting was good news.

I excused myself from the living room couch, phone in hand, getting ready to mentally break if it said something ego-crushing like, *Forget what I said, Naima. Do me a favor and fuck off.* But it didn't. What it said was better. Better than I'd anticipated.

We both have the next two days off. No plans. Full tank of gas. No set destination. Wanna get lost?

* * *

Tim had been driving for hours, until sleep could no longer be denied. I knew we'd driven into Massachusetts and eventually past Boston, but I'd expressed a little shock when we hit the New Hampshire state line.

"We are stopping in New Hampshire."

There was no objection there. I even volunteered to google the closest spots nearby. "Any prerequisites? Conditions?"

"No Motel 6s. No Holiday Inns. And not to sound uppity but

preferably something with at least a three-and-a-half-star rating. Work your magic, find something good."

I pulled up a Residence Inn that was only seven minutes away and somewhat generous on the pockets. Plus they offered free Wi-Fi and breakfast. From the pictures, the place looked pretty sweet.

"I have to warn you. I'm the type to go out of town, then spend the whole time there chilling at a hotel. If you're trying to do something, speak your mind or forever hold your peace," he said as he crashed on what looked to be an amazingly soft king-sized bed.

I'd never been anywhere in New England, and outside of NYC, the only other place I'd ever been to that wasn't for educational purposes was Nigeria and it was almost always to visit family. Never a vacation. Sure, this was just a weekend getaway, but that's exactly what I had planned on the schedule—to get away.

We both stripped down to our underwear, me in just a tank top and matching boyshorts and him in a sexy pair of black boxer-briefs as he patiently waited for me to secure my pineap-ple-ed hair in a silk scarf before he wrapped his arms around me and tangled my legs in his.

"Good-night, Naima."

I shifted around to return the words, but he was so knocked out from the drive, he was already snoring.

* * *

I got up early to get a head start on my hair. Tim didn't take long to wake up after me. Guess he too was excited to get a start on the day. I stood at the mirror, fluffing and separating my curls, and from the corner of my eye, I saw Tim playing with a camera that looked like it shot stills but it is was obvious he was shooting video. "What are you doing?"

"Documenting," he said with a wink.

"Documenting what?"

"Just a weekend diary of what happens when two crazy kids explore unknown territories for the first time. Don't worry, you can help me name it."

I pushed him away, laughing. My hair wasn't finished, and already I'd let this fool get me on camera.

"C'mon, Naima. By the time you finish, it's gonna be Wednesday. I'm trying to eat."

I only had three more curls to separate. Next we were off to breakfast. One less thing to do before we went into town to explore.

During breakfast we spent the whole time asking each other things we didn't know. He was most interested in my parents' cultures—one Igbo, the other Yoruba. Most thought that when you were Nigerian that you were just that, Nigerian. But there were so many ethnic groups in my parent's home country that saying you were Nigerian didn't always encompass the cultures you were made up of. Only other Nigerians spotted the difference, but it was fun explaining to him what it was like growing up with three cultures.

Language came up, as well as what brought me to my decision to study linguistics. My questions had more or less to do with what kind of music and movies he'd grown up loving. For some reason, it didn't surprise me at all to learn that he loved Tyrese and Anita Baker. He threw me for a curveball when he confessed his love for *Beetlejuice*. He'd even wanted to marry Winona Ryder. That she jumpstarted his interest in weird girls. I don't know what that said about me but it was interesting to be around someone who didn't have common interests most men had.

"You down to explore?" he said, standing up from the table.

He insisted I drive for a while as he claimed he couldn't trust me to be in control of the diary footage, but I knew a part of him was exhausted from the drive here. I took his keys argument-free and with a smile. I'd always secretly hated driving, but it was a chance to discover a new city with my choice at what we did first. Who could beat those odds?

Timothy narrated over his little diary while I looked around. I let the excitement of a new place get the best of me. Being from New York City, I appreciated the feel of a clean town not overrun by overflowing population. Everything had a vintage look to it but felt new at the same time. Fresh brick buildings, near empty roads, and almost no chain outlets or restaurants in site. A wave of urgency rushed over me when I saw something up ahead that looked like it'd be our first stop.

I looked over to Timothy, secretly hoping he wouldn't object to the idea, but all he did was join me in laughter. Our first stop of the day? A traveling carnival.

Timothy

"Naima, please don't tell me you've never had fried Oreos."

Her lips twisted to the side, and it was right there I decided she had lived a sheltered, unfulfilling life back in Staten Island. Who hasn't had fried Oreos? I walked up to a vendor and ordered half a dozen. Once you tried one, best believe you'd want another, and as predicted, she took one bite and loaded up on three more. I had to tackle her for the last two but eventually gave in. Sharing was caring and low carbs kept this stomach hard.

We went on ride after ride, even the corny-ass baby ones, but it was weird how everything I did with Naima was a little less corny. We always made the most of situations, and I couldn't remember the last time I'd had this much fun with a person. Where was a woman this amazing years ago when I needed her?

We stood in front of a massive tent adorned in alternating

yellow and red stripes, trying to figure out how to capture a picture that featured both of us. We'd never been to a real-life carnival like the ones you saw in the movies. We were ready for clowns, elephants, lion tamers, whatever the hell was in that shit. After a string of unsuccessful selfies, I was ready to hit up the tent before it got crazy crowded. Naima, however, wanted her picture.

"Play along," she said as she walked up to two complete strangers. "Excuse me, sir," she began in an amazingly convincing English accent. "D'ya think you could take a photo of us in front of the tent?"

The eyes of the couple lit up, immediately intrigued as they warmed up to Naima.

"Oh my god, I just love your accent," the woman replied. While I wasn't the type to come out my ass and attach ignorant stereotypes to certain people, I had to admit these two were probably the whitest folks I'd ever met. The way they talked, the way they dressed, even the way the simplest thing excited them. It didn't surprise me that they were from Vermont. I don't even think of anything but white people when I think of Vermont.

"And where are you two from?"

"You mean us?" Naima said, smiling wide and adding more umph in her performance. "Oh, love, we're from London—"

She'd said play along.

"No, she's from London. I'm from Manchester. She's just taking the piss," I said in my best impression of Ringo Starr. Don't ask me why Ringo Starr. I just loved the way he talked.

"How wonderful! What brings you two here?"

I pulled Naima in close to me and wrapped my arms around her waist. "We're newlyweds. We've been on our honeymoon since yesterday." I kissed her cheek as the couple congratulated us on our fake union and both agreed that now was a better time than any to snap a few photos.

"Thanks so much!" Naima said in her regular accent. I think

the two were in such awe of her that they didn't even realize she'd fucked up. I kept the show going until we were inside and out of their sight.

"Girl, how are you going start the charade and forget midway? It's a good thing I was there. You almost blew that one."

She pushed me off to the side, confessing the honeymoon bit was what threw her off her game.

"I could've dealt with the Manchester act and I was kind of on board with the newlyweds shit, but Tim, the honeymoon? Kind of pushing it. I wanted to laugh so damn bad."

That was the thing with Naima—she brought the liveliness out of me. The part of me I'd thought was gone. With her, I wanted to be silly, I wanted to be stupid, I wanted to bring laughs.

I'd spent all week stressed out and on edge, worrying about this and that and everything in between. Naima had made me forget a week's worth of problems in one afternoon.

"Shall we?" I took her hand, and together we anticipated what waited for us behind that tent.

* * *

When we arrived back at the hotel, we were just coming down from the excitement of the ongoings of the carnival's main event. What goes on in those tents, stays in those tents. That's how live that shit was.

"Aw, man, I don't know how tomorrow can top today. Today was...today was just *today*." She walked over to the dresser, taking off her boots and thick scarf. Even doing some of the most everyday things, she was beautiful and expressed it in every move she made.

"Are you fuckin' filming me, Timothy?" She rushed over to grab my camera but lost to my quick reflexes and skill.

"Don't worry. You look amazing on screen, I promise."

She sauntered off into the bathroom, returning five minutes later, hair partly scarfed with only the top peeking out. Fully clothed, she collapsed on the bed.

"Thanks for inviting me to come on this little road trip, Tim. I had...I'm having so much fun."

"No, thank you."

"For what? Coming? Here's what I would've did this week-end..." She paused for dramatic effect. "...*nothing*."

"No, I mean for getting me. Vibing with me. Choosing to deal with me, despite the rocky terms."

She narrowed her eyes and bobbed her head from side to side. She looked ridiculous, but it brought the humor out of an otherwise dreary moment. She caught me off-guard when she snatched my beloved camera out of my hands. Well played, Staten Island. Well played.

She pointed the camera at me. "So tell me, Timothy Ferreiro. If you were to watch this video a year from now, what would you want past-Timothy to take from this day?"

I laughed. I hated being put on the spot and hated more being filmed while doing so. If it was one of those capsule "homages," I'd better be sure to give myself some good advice. This would be on the record.

I considered my statement, conjuring up something wise and relevant to any time period in my life. "This is speaking to future-me, right?" Off-screen she nodded, giving me the confidence to go ahead.

"I'd tell him...get over yourself and just be happy. No matter what's going on in your life, fuck it! By now, you'll be a proud college graduate. Even if it took you almost six years and I'm pretty sure you'll remind your bosses of that promotion they promised you, once you got that B.A. and hmm...

"Nothing that you're going through today has to be a problem right now. I can't stress this enough, but, Future-Me, don't hold onto old stuff. Let that shit go. Trust me, shit for you right now, it's not that bad."

I hoped I wouldn't be dealing with the same shit a year from now. The very idea made me consider getting my act together.

She turned the camera on herself, but from the screen of the camera, she wasn't aiming it right. I offered to capture her at her greatness as I proposed the same question.

"What do you want future Naima to take from today?"

She pondered away, thinking long and hard before providing the simplest but honest-to-god answer.

"Just be happy, I'd tell her. Find a way to be happy."

CHAPTER TWELVE

Naima

A date with cheap gelato, old web series' I'd never started, and my down blanket was how I planned spending the rest of my day after my last class. The end of the semester was nearing, and I was more anxious than ever about passing. I wanted my mind off things. When Timothy called asking if I would be willing to cover Angel's call out, I figured what could take my mind off things better than work?

Plus it'd be a chance to see him. I knew we'd be working, but I was still grinning hard over our New Hampshire trip. It hadn't been a clear sign of the road to come, but it had made me feel at the very least good about us.

No one should be this excited about going to work, but that was the beauty of a work crush. You liked being there, even when you weren't scheduled to.

There were only short moments we shared glances or walked by each other just enough not to bring attention to us. Tim was in his department, and I was on the floor, so it was unlikely we'd get to go on break together. There weren't many ways that wouldn't look obvious. For some reason, no one was convinced we were *just* friends.

We were. Then we weren't. We weren't dating…or were we? What I did know? We were complicated. Nothing got my mind off things more than trying to understand us.

I was so engrossed in thought, it took Ravinder tapping me on the shoulder to snap out of it.

Time for that break.

One glance over at the cafe proved I was on my own for now. Tim and Katrina were backed up as it was. I had snacks I didn't want to share anyway.

Genesis, Ruby, and Emily were deep in conversation as I entered the break room. Emily didn't work past nine on school nights, so it was rare when she was here toward closing hours. The chatter died down until there was no talking at all, and I was met with the discomfort of a painfully silent room.

"I hope you all didn't end your conversation because of me," I said, opening the break room fridge and popping a cold burrito in the microwave.

"Why, Staten Island. We were just talking about you," Ruby said in a creepy deadpan voice. The sound of chair legs scraping against the floor filled the absence of silence. "Dinner's done. Have a seat."

The microwave timer beeped, and I opened the door, inspecting how much of the paper towel was stuck to the tortilla skin. I turned around to be met by three employees wearing the eeriest expressions they could manage as they waited for me to sit down in between Ruby and Genesis. Ruby's eyes were slit with accusation.

"What?"

Ruby pushed her chair closer to the table, flipping through a folder of paperwork. "Staten Island," she said, shaking her head, repeating my moniker over and over again. "Interesting fact. You have now worked here a total of four months. Yet we can find no record chronicling your initiation."

I pieced together remnants of the many times Tim had steered me away from death traps or practical jokes set out for me by employees.

It was an unofficial tradition, definitely not something in the employee manual or codes of conduct, but you weren't a real part of the family until someone played a prank on you before your first year was up. I wasn't above it, but if it was going to happen, I at least wanted to expect it.

"There's no video. No written documentation, no audio—"

"Oh, so it's just a requirement for you all to keep files or something?" I interrupted. Damn, was it that serious?

Ruby gave me a sinister smile that didn't match the silliness in her face. Seemed more meant for a dude twirling his mustache at the train tracks. She folded her hands in her lap, while Genesis slid the folder away and Emily tried to intimidate me with a major stare down.

"It matters not that there are files," Ruby said, finished by a fake cynical laugh too tacky for a horror movie.

"This is how you're all spending your breaks? You're whack," I pointed out.

They all stood up to go at different times. Ruby was the last to leave, making sure to up her creep factor before disappearing in the hallway. "Trust us, Staten Island. It's coming. It won't be today. It won't be tomorrow. It probably won't be while I'm on break either. But it's coming. *Fear the initiation.*"

* * *

It was a full car before Tim made it to the time clock. I felt a wee bit responsible. They'd only asked because it had become habitual for Tim to drive me home, even though I'd convinced everyone it'd only been for the promise of gas money. He should start a carpool because half of us who relied on public transportation didn't even take the bus anymore.

Since he wouldn't say no anyway because he was thae type of guy who'd take everybody if one person asked, he might as well bank. I rode shotgun while Genesis, Katrina, and Ruby spread themselves in the confinement of the backseat.

"Y'all got it feeling like a clown car in here. So I don't want to hear any requests on who I'm dropping off first or what you're all trying to listen to on the radio. All requests will be denied," Tim joked as he pulled out the parking lot.

"So, Ms. Naima. I would've asked you earlier, but at break we had much more pressing issues to discuss," Ruby said, leaning over the backseat, dangling a folded piece of paper in my direction.

"I swear to god this better not be all that stupid shit you all were threatening me with at the job—"

Ruby unfolded the paper and leaned on the shoulder of my chair. "Does it look like it? I asked Katrina and Gen, but they're afraid they're going to be around skinny chicks making fun of them."

"Well, I get enough of chicks like you at work," Genesis barked from the backseat. "Watch someone write a blog post on xoJane about how I probably wished I was skinny. Fuck that."

"I was originally going to go with my partner," Ruby went on, "but seeing that we broke up and I can't get a refund, I'm asking around. I might not even go if I have to go by myself."

I inspected the folded paper. It was a redeemable voucher for a dance class meant to expire in a month.

"Pole class? What makes you think I'd want to do that?"

It was as if Timothy heard there was a winning lottery ticket on the ground. The tires to his car screeched, and everyone lurched forward. Ruby shot Timothy an *Are you crazy?* look and rushed to put her seatbelt on.

"My bad, y'all. I just heard pole class. If Naima ain't biting, I'll go."

Ruby took the voucher from my hands and sat back. "After that fiasco, I'm not even sure I want to be in a car with you."

I wasn't sure I'd be any good. Pole dancing *looked* fun, but I knew it required a lot of experience I didn't have. But there were two things I stood to get out of it. A chance to hang out with Ruby because I liked having other friends who weren't Tim. And if I learned a thing or two, maybe I'd be able to surprise Tim with a lap dance one of these days.

"Sure. I'll go."

Ruby's big brown eyes widened at the confirmation. "You will? You know it's tomorrow right? One in the afternoon. If you need me to, I can meet up at your place so we can bus it together."

Hmm...that would mean Tim would have to take me home before then. I couldn't decline now, it'd look suspicious.

"Sounds good."

Timothy gave me a glance over, so I knew he was thinking the same thing.

Genesis was the first drop-off of the night, but a planned "fake" trip to the gas station ensured I'd get dropped off last.

* * *

My legs quivered as Tim attempted to calm them by holding them closed. His tongue traced circles against the hood of my clit, and my body had him right where I wanted him as I lifted my hips and rubbed my body up against his mouth.

"Just keep doing that, baby," I cried as I grinded his face all over me. The built-up tension in my body relaxed in a dozen waves of relief as I let out something between a laugh and a moan.

When Tim repositioned himself on the bed, I made sure to slip the condom on with enough space to account for the mess.

Crawling onto his lap, I took my time sliding him in and out of me as he begged me to keep going.

"You have to drop me off before the morning," I said in a weighted breath. His hands met the back of my behind as I slid up and down along his length slowly and purposefully.

As my body pushed down on him, I rotated against his hips, giving him a show, but rubbing myself in all the right places.

"Didn't you have tomorrow off? I figured we..." Tim's eyebrows creased toward the center of his face, followed by a gaping groan. "...could do *this*...for as long as possible."

I slowed my pace to keep him wanting more. To keep me wanting more. "I just don't want her to show up while you're dropping me off. People are in our business enough at work. Plus, it sounds like fun. I'll even give you a little lap dance if I learn a thing or two." I giggled, as he held onto my hips and pumped inside of me, and I held onto the bed for leverage. A series of swears soon followed, and I fainted into the open space next to him.

"Okay. But only because I want to see that lap dance."

* * *

The pole burn was real. The things your friends didn't mention before they invited you to a workout class? That they were three times better than they led on. The surprise 10 a.m. visit from Ruby should've been a foreshadowing of things to come. I hadn't gotten home until four in the morning, so it had left little time in between to get a fulfilled sleep. I didn't press too long or argue. It was half my fault after all.

Between the binge on holiday-flavored lattes and donuts, I zapped away any energy a class like this would have had on me. The warm-up was ridiculous. It was a beginners' course, so the only time I worked up a sweat was before the after-pole instruction. But with all the yoga moves and flexibility it required, Ruby had definitely been holding out.

I used to dance a little, nothing to brag about, was all I thought about during her timed, three-minute headstand. Without the wall, I would've joined the trickles of sweat from my forehead on the floor. The class was small, but some of the girls literally walked on air. Now I knew why exotic dancers had the possibility to make so much. Just learning how to walk in proper form around the pole was a challenge.

I tried to come prepared, but walking around in my underwear was not an option. I still managed to gain decent footing in shorts, knee socks, and a tank top. The hardest part was on my feet and hands. I didn't know Ruby had it in her to master the pointed-toe walk dubbed the Jessica Rabbit Butt Swivel by the instructor, but it was clear why, after a short discussion after class, most of the girls came alone.

"You're so bold. I'd never be able to come with a friend. I'd be too embarrassed if I messed up," one girl said, as if there'd ever been a time of her life when she hadn't flown in circles around the pole.

After an extensive google search, I forced Ruby to stop at a drugstore to stock up on Epsom salt and an anti-swelling cream to soothe the friction. We headed back to my place and decided to screw the whole thing off by ordering pizza.

"Thanks for not telling me you knew what you were doing."

Ruby's eyebrows creased as she took a huge bite of pizza. "I sucked, too. A year or two of ballet and hip hop doesn't make me an expert."

"See, you didn't tell me you *had* all that. I went in thinking we were both virgins," I joked, attempting not to drop pizza oil into my foot bath. It wasn't exactly the time of my life. I'm pretty sure Tim wouldn't be impressed with palm and foot burns, but I wouldn't have considered a pole class if Ruby hadn't asked me. I wondered about all the things I'd missed out on by not saying yes in the past.

"Where you guys coming from?" Lisette said, throwing her keys on the counter. She'd met Ruby briefly before we left, but hadn't stayed long for conversation. I don't know if my mind played tricks on me or my eyes just wanted to see it, but there was some major body language signals between Lisette and Ruby.

"Just a beginner pole class. Nothing extraordinary," Ruby said before inviting her to join us for pizza.

Tim: *How was the pole class?*

Of course Timothy wasn't about to let today go without asking.

Me: *Might have to get a raincheck on that lap dance*

Timothy: *Damn. It wore you out like that?*

Me: *Different experience. I'll have to show you sometime.*

"Are you not feeling the idea?" Lisette asked, taking me out the zone.

I was so busy texting, I forgot where I was. "Huh?"

"I was just asking if you wanted to catch a movie playing at the mall." Between the bus ride to Cranston Street and home, I wasn't looking forward to more walking, especially with swollen feet.

"I don't know. I doubt my feet can handle that much walking."

"This is why you stalk people at work. I'm about to ask Tim if he wants to hook us up with a ride."

I did my best not to betray the sinking of my stomach. I kept forgetting how close they were.

"He texted me back. He's down if we'll chip in for parking. Is it still a no?"

I agreed to it before it looked too suspicious. It'd be cool hanging with the girls I was most close to, but I also wasn't mad at being able to chill with Tim, while not coming off like a date. It was a slippery slope, but having Ruby as a mutual friend had its advantages.

CHAPTER THIRTEEN

Naima

I looked forward to the day when I could put in a request for another department. It was so quiet in the travel, reference, and cookbook sections that every once and awhile I had to pretend to take a bathroom break. Ruby, Genesis, and Emily were so damn giggly over in YA and science fiction. There was no damn way they passed the whole time working. The roar of laughter and gossip neared as Ruby and Emily approached me with wide smiles and a matching bounce in their steps. They were up to no good.

"Hey, Staten Island, you trying to vote on our little 'list'?" Ruby asked. She felt the need for animated quotation marks.

"List? What kind of list?" It was a slow day for me, but if the people over in the better departments had enough time to cultivate lists, it must have been dead.

"Yeah, so, shh…don't tell anyone. This is *technically* objectification, but we're making a ranking list of all the guys who work at Symposium. Solely based on artificial reasons like looks, body, height, and all that other good stuff. This thing is going around the whole store until we get everyone in on it to participate. You don't even have to rank everyone—just your absolute favorites and what not."

I swore Ruby was relentless when it came to getting me to admit I had a thing for Timothy. She was my girl and everything, but if Timothy hadn't told her anything, then I wasn't about to.

"Sorry to break it to you guys, but I don't have a work crush."

Emily rolled in the conversation being her usual snarky self. For a girl barely a hundred and ten pounds who hadn't yet celebrated her eighteenth birthday, the native Bostonian just loved to have the last word. "Keeping telling yourself that, Staten Island, but I see the way you look at Timbaland and I see the way he looks at you. Something is going on there, something is going on…" She ended in a surefire tone and slits for eyes. "Plus the two of you look cute together. Why not just own it?"

Ruby handed a printout sheet of what looked like a copy of the original. It was an elaborate list of all who identified as male at Symposium, as well as a long list of superlatives like best eyes, sexiest hair, and biggest flirt. They must have been working on it for a while because this thing looked too detailed to conjure up just three hours into a shift.

"I should also mention that results are anonymous." She winked. "So no one will ever know who you voted for or how you rated them."

So she claimed.

It was a fun way to waste the next few hours, so I figured what the hell. I grabbed a pen and started bubbling in a few answers.

* * *

Genesis strolled over with a worried look in her eyes. "Hey, Staten Island, you got that list from earlier?" Off and on I'd been working on it, but it had already been an hour and I still hadn't handed it in. Scoring people on their looks was harder than it looked. I was going to need until the end of the day to give it more consideration.

"I do, but I'm not done," I said holding it out for her to see.

She lowered my hands and pulled me into a corner that was free of crowds. "Okay, well, you have to hide that shit. They're busting operation. Trying to write up everyone involved since a snitch couldn't keep their mouth shut. Swallow it, shred it, do what you have to do, just don't let them catch you with it."

I stuffed it in my bra (the safest thing for anything if you asked me) just before Martha approached me, asking of my involvement. I played dumb. It was bad enough that finals week had me working only three days, the last thing I needed was to get written up and possibly lose more money. My answers would never see the light of day, and that was perfectly fine by me.

* * *

Timothy

The week of finals had everyone uptight. It was one of our lowest-performing weeks of the year, so everyone around here was either grumpy because they were cutting hours or antsy depending on the required workload the last few exams entailed. I was so glad this was my last semester. I didn't want to look at another book for a year unless it was a work of fiction.

"Hey, Tim, you in here?" Naima shut the pantry door behind her. I felt like I hadn't seen her all week. We were both swamped with studying and mutually understood that doing well trumped sleepovers or get-togethers, but seeing her brought a smile out of me. I abandoned unloading some boxes for a chance to get lost in her scent again.

"Damn, girl, where have you been hiding?"

"Today was technically my last day for the semester. I am so happy to say that I'm done with that place for another two months. Screw you for this being your last semester."

I pulled her closer to me, laying a light kiss on her full lips. "Screw me? *You promise?*" I wasn't even trying to be funny, I meant that.

Laughter poured from Naima's mouth as she slapped one of her hands across my chest. "You're so stupid."

I led her to a corner where we wouldn't be readily visible should someone come in looking for one of us. By my definition, we weren't a secret, but already folks had speculated that she and I were hooking up and it wasn't anyone's business. We got along. We were super-tight. Whose problem was it but ours what we were doing behind closed doors?

"We can be like Fitz and Olivia, The Pantry version." That time I'd meant to be stupid. I knew how much she loved that show, and given that we were surrounded by rows and rows of cannolis and cupcakes, I'd found a little humor in it myself. "So… what's this I hear about some list?"

She dismissed it with a distancing shrug. "Nothing really, just something stupid everyone decided to compile out of boredom. I'm sure by now all the butt-hurt boys are gossiping about it, trying to say how we're demeaning you guys. *Ugh!* I wish I would have never been a part of it."

Boredom drove people around here to do some crazy things. In fact, that's how the whole initiation concept got started, out of complete, utter boredom. My lips curled into a smile, suddenly anxious to know how well I scored amongst these women I called friends. "So where did I fare?"

"Are you seriously asking me that?"

"Well, I'm sure you guys had already tallied up the votes before you all got caught. I don't see why I can't know how I did." It wasn't even that serious how I did. I didn't care about that. My curiosity came from how Naima rated me. If roles were reversed, she would have made my top spot. She was more than a work flow. What we had was a thing. A very natural, mystifying, yet very complicated thing that wouldn't go away no matter how hard I fought it. I only wondered if she felt the same.

"Boy, get up off of me."

I threatened not to move until she told me.

"Tim, everyone's going to wonder where I went. C'mon now, let me go."

"What do you mean everyone's going to wonder where you went? You're off remember? Look all you have to do is tell me how I ranked according to you and you can be on your merry way."

"This conversation is over!" She slipped under my arms and blew a weak air-kiss when she got to the door. Genesis made an announcement over the intercom that any available manager was needed at the front registers. I suppose that meant me. "*See!* You're needed at the front registers?" she said with her tongue stuck out like a little brat.

"Hey, before you leave, are you coming over? Waiting for me? What am I doing later?" I was really asking if she was spending the night.

"I'm off now. I wanted to head home real quick. I'll grab my stuff and meet you back here if you want."

I tossed her a set of my keys. By now it was becoming ritual for her to meet me at my house when she got off early. Plus I liked not having to drive way across town since it was out of the way. "Cool. I'll meet you later."

We walked out together, ignoring the fact that Emily had hit us with a smug smile. It pained people here not to be able to confirm who was hooking up and who wasn't. For now we were just buddies. That's all anyone needed to know.

* * *

I wrestled with my keys to open the door and let out a sigh of relief that I was home after a long-ass day. Naima had gotten off at six and wasn't going to wait three hours for me, so we'd made plans to meet up at my house much later. I knew she was here because I hadn't left the bathroom light on. The door was open, so it was probably okay to invade. But just in case I whistled through the hallway to let her know she wasn't alone. She was straightening her kinky curls into sleek, straight tresses that cascaded down her back. Number one reason to love women with curly hair—they could go from coily to straight and look like a whole other person.

She donned a tank top and sweats that looked a little tight on her but made her ass look amazing. I creeped up from behind and ran my hands along her hips, butt, and thighs.

"Damn, girl, your ass looks huge in these pants...wait, hold up. These are mine." No wonder they looked tight. "Okay, new rule. These are the only pants you're allowed to wear around me. No leggings or denim. Just these."

She playfully pushed me away as she sectioned out the last few sections of her mane to un-kink.

"Let me know when you're done in here. I wanted to take a shower and brush my teeth. Someone at work let me try some of this stinky tofu entrée—or at least that's what they said it was. Now I can't shake the feeling like my breath stinks."

"I take it you've eaten already?" she asked.

"Nope. But I'm about start something right now. Mind fish?" I asked, heading straight toward the kitchen.

"I'm about to be done in here so you can pretty much take your time. I just have to clean up and the bathroom's all yours."

I unloaded some groceries I'd purchased on my way home, admiring how everything looked so remarkably edible even before I set things up. "Do me a favor while I'm in the shower? Slice these onions up for me."

There was never a better way to end a night than an episode of *iZombie*, a full stomach, and some private time between the sheets. A part of me sympathized. Naima had spent the whole time she was here flat-ironing her hair and already the roots looked lifted. It was worth it, though. Those squeezes on those last few strokes would be something I'd remember for days.

She got up and searched for her bra that in a horny, carnal frenzy I'd thrown on the other side on the floor. Why were women in such a rush to put their clothes back on after sex? A lot of us just wanted to look at you. Appreciate you. Remind ourselves how lucky we were to be a spectator to your greatness. But we couldn't do that when women made it a thing to get fully dressed before we could steal a glance. *Just why?*

She searched the bed for her panties, but I pulled her on top of me, bounding her arms with my embrace.

"You are so annoying, you know that?"

I leaned in to kiss her, but all she did was back away from my man-of-steel hold. I ran my tongue up the side of her face. She hated that, but that's why I did it. I always got the reaction I wanted.

"Eww…you are *so* nasty."

"That's funny. Just twenty minutes ago when I used my tongue on you, the words *nasty* and *Timothy* came out of your mouth, but it damn sure didn't sound like an insult."

She hit me repeatedly with one of the pillows, but it wasn't hard because she was too busy laughing.

"Chill," I said, taking a pillow to the face. I was just about to declare war on the battlefront, but a moment from our earlier conversation had been on my mind all day.

That list fiasco. I didn't know why I was sweating it, but it ate away at me.

I'd found out from Ruby that, out of fifteen people, I'd ranked number two. I wasn't a person of pure vanity and I knew wasn't the only good-looking guy at Symposium, but knowing Naima had a hand in the fun, it was killing me to know how I did on *her* list. Call me shallow. Call me aggy. Call me anything you wanted, but the suspense was killing me. I wanted to know where I stood with Naima. Something about us felt like more than a friendship and obviously more than sex. I loved being with her. The same way I felt about Sherri every time we reunited. It was such a complex situation, but I prayed it worked itself out when the time came. I was selfish, but both feelings made me happy.

"So you know what I'm going to ask you right?"

She released an exasperated sigh and threw the comforter over her head. "Timothy, why does it matter? It was just for fun."

"C'mon," I huffed as I struggled to pull the comforter away from her. She had some serious robot grip. "I just wanna know who your top ten was. Or at least your top five. You don't have to say it in the exact order. It can be random."

"Why is it so important?"

It was simple. I wanted to know who else we worked with that activated her lady parts so I could put their behinds on the morning shifts while Naima and I burned the midnight oil. Maybe I was kidding...*maybe*.

She sat up in the bed with a look of defeat. Persistence paid off. "Okay, since you want to know so damn bad, here it goes. I didn't have a top ten. Hell, I didn't even have a top three. You want to know how you scored on my list? I didn't have anyone else. You were my only one."

"*Really?*" I said with an ounce of shock in my voice.

"Yup."

She got up and rustled through her duffle bag, pulling out a scarf, a comb, and a brush. Guess that hair was getting wrapped up tonight. It gave me a few minutes alone to think about what it was I was actually doing with Naima. The stakes were getting high, and eventually someone would get hurt. I wanted to give

Naima what I *thought* she wanted—all of me. But that couldn't happen with everything being so open-ended with Sherri. Naima deserved better than me, and I was selfish for keeping things the way they were. This wasn't just a game anymore but a live, breathing organism that dared call itself a dependency.

You were my only one, she told me. I wanted so bad to say the same for the both of us.

CHAPTER FOURTEEN

Naima

Katrina spoke the magic words. In five minutes, the store would be closing, so that announcement over the intercom encouraged customers to bring their current purchases to the front.

I was at the main registers today, as opposed to my usual floor placement. I'd never missed the floor more than I did now. Customers ignored every warning until it was time to cash out your draw. I'd been scheduled for ten, but had been hoping for an early nine-thirty.

Twelve customers lined up out of nowhere, and since I was the only one up there, it took me twenty minutes to clear them out. When it was time to cash out my drawer, Emily and Katrina informed me that, with their meticulous teamwork, there would be nothing left to do but clock out. Looked like I'd be getting my wish.

If I was lucky, Tim wouldn't be a damn taxi service tonight, and given all the nasty texts we'd exchanged throughout our shift, a girl was super-horny. Please let these people find their own way home tonight. *Please*!

Genesis and Emily battled each other (including bum-rushing me, an innocent bystander) to the time clock in a race on who could clock out first.

"Damn, ladies. It's not like the time clock is going anywhere," I said as I watched Genesis win the war. She skipped away, giggling and triumphant. Sometimes I felt like the sanest person at this job. Everyone was so hyper.

"Just because you get there first, doesn't mean you get to cut the first slice," Emily said, adding a stuck-out tongue.

I was so ready to go that I hadn't noticed why everyone was so antsy. Folks who weren't working tonight walked past me to the cafe.

"Damn, what, are the checks coming early or something?" I asked, but everyone ignored me. I took that as a clue to follow and ask questions when I got there.

There were a few people setting up the tables with festive decorations. Ruby walked up to me and handed me a bulky cloth banner. "Hey, Staten Island. You and Butter Cookie can be in charge of the sign."

Sign? What sign? What the hell was all the fuss over? I glanced at the table in front of me to see an oversized cake with two lit candles resembling a "2" and a "6." I unfolded the banner, raeding the words off to myself.

Was it…Timothy's birthday?

"Girl, don't look so confused. It's not like you didn't already know," Genesis said with a roll of her neck and hand on her hip.

"Rocketman, Du-wop, you guys know you have to be the manpower today. Make sure Tim doesn't try and run off," Ravinder said, strapping on a party hat.

Bruce and Angel stood posted by the pantry door, waiting patiently for Timothy to walk out. Ravinder and Martha took turns pulling a bag load of wrapped presents out of a huge sack and strategically placed them on the tables in a decorative fashion.

How could I not have known?

Timothy walked out the pantry, throwing up his arms in a fit once he realized what was happening.

"*Oh, hell no.*" He attempted to duck back in the pantry but was caught by Bruce and Angel. They dragged him to the tables and parked his butt in a seat. I could tell he wasn't thrilled. He took a deep breath and rubbed his face in aggravation.

"Something was telling me. My *spidey* sense was tingling. '*Timothy don't go to work today*,' it said. '*Take a day off. Call out. You work at a god damn zoo*,' it said. But *no*, here I am, amongst all this madness."

"Look at Timmy whining over here like a baby. Getting mad over a little birthday party," Bruce chimed in. So it really was a birthday party for Timothy. Why hadn't he told me?

"I told y'all. *Individually.* Don't plan anything for my birthday. But here you all are, wearing these goofy-ass hats with a waste of party favors and birthday cake."

"Why do you think we do it?" Ruby said, getting him equipped with a pointed party hat. "We're running out of ways to torture you."

"You guys know how I hate birthdays."

Genesis sat down next to him, scooting a few wrapped gifts in front of where he sat. "Yeah, but I'm sure a situation changes when presents are involved."

He smiled devilishly. "Well, things change a little bit when presents are involved."

I sat in the chair across from him, feeling a tad left out that I was the only one who hadn't known. I'd been dealing with the guy for nearly five months now. How could I be the last to know?

"You're probably not gonna find one from me, Tim. This is all a surprise. I had no idea it was your birthday."

Timothy gave me this look that was a bottled version of embarrassment and sympathy. "So why was Staten Island the only one not in on this?" he asked to lighten the mood, but there wasn't anything that could change my mood. Not without making me look dumber than I felt.

"If she had known, she probably would've run off and just told you," Ruby said. "And we couldn't have that. Not with that tight little coalition yoy twol got going on there."

He laughed. "Damn, I can't help out a friend?"

If only I could find the humor.

"You didn't help out any of us!" Emily argued, but the spat drowned out under thirty-three people in unison singing him "Happy Birthday." Once the singing stopped, the song "Rumpshaker" played loudly over the store's satellite radio as everyone from Genesis to Bruce lined up next to him and shook their asses in his face. The whole thing would have been hilarious if I hadn't been in such a sour mood.

"Why? Just why?" he cried, jerking his hands above his head. He looked miserable, but his mood switched from annoyed to happy when he reached to open his first gift. He held a book in his hand, examining it from front to back as he reveled in his prize. "*Journey to Washington* by Daniel K. Inouye? Good choice, good choice." Another wrapped gift fell victim to his hands, the simple brown wrapping paper falling to the floor.

"*The Mark of Noba*?" he asked out of confusion. "Yo, who bought me a young adult book?" He looked around the room, but no one seemed to want to fess up. Guess no one here was going to admit to their YA addictions.

"Let me hit up my Goodreads app." He took out his phone and read along the tags associated with it. Actually sounded kind of interesting. "Let's see. Time travel. Science fiction. Portal fantasy. *Interracial*? Ruby, this is all you. *But* I do think it's dope that a hot girl is on the cover. Could the guy have been brunette, though? Guess it could be a hit or miss."

He pulled another book out of a bag, ignoring the bright tissue paper that kept it company. "*Book of Amazing History*? I'm telling you, if this is just some fabricated American history, whoever bought it can have that one back." He placed it on the table. There was a smaller gift he took his time opening in attempts not to break it. "Oh, wow," he said sarcastically. "A bookmark. Cheap. So it must be from Rocketman."

Bruce bowed, satisfied that folks knew him so well.

The rest of the gifts ranged from DVDs to gift cards and even a gift certificate for some birthday sex. That one I couldn't ignore, especially since Mr. Rogers was the giver of such a gift, with his old ass.

"Y'all gonna cut this cake or what? Because my bus leaves in like thirty minutes, so y'all are going to have to wrap this up," Katrina said.

Tim took his time blowing out the two candles, and piece by piece of his cake was quickly demolished. I picked at it, but the smooth blend of rich German chocolate and moist sinful layers ensured I'd at least be wrapping this one to-go.

Without Tim's help, the rest of us who'd stuck around to clean up had the cafe spotless like a surprise party hadn't happened fifteen minutes ago.

"So am I taking you home?" His code for *Are you sleeping over?*

"Sure. Just give me a minute."

"I'll give you two."

* * *

A twelve-minute drive to my house felt like a day and a half. Aside from the tired excuse I gave Timothy about how I needed to head home to ensure Lisette hadn't left the stove on, I hadn't said a word to him. When he parked, I thought I'd go the whole night without him asking about my shift in mood.

"You're so quiet tonight. I hope it wasn't because of the freak show at work. Because I didn't ask for any of that."

How could I say yes without sounding like a bitter stepchild? I couldn't admit to being put off that it was his birthday, yet I'd known nothing about it. It's not like we were together-together, but how could he not tell me something important like that?

I crossed my arms in front of my chest, trying hard not to let my real feelings shine through. "Tim, how come I didn't know it was your birthday?"

His eyes widened, bewildered I'd even ask. "Because it's not my birthday. It's actually not until next week."

My mouth dropped. Was he even going to tell me? "Seriously?"

"If you had known, what would you have done differently?"

I didn't have an answer, but it would have saved me the trouble of looking like a complete idiot. I was so out of the loop.

"Naima, based on how long we've known each other, I didn't want it to be so much pressure. Especially because celebrating my birthday has always been a disaster. I don't have one good memory where things just happened the way they were supposed to. People at Symposium, they have nothing better to do than to waste all this money on cheesy birthday parties. Trust me. When it's time to celebrate yours, you'll find out."

It was more than just a birthday. His birthday. My birthday. The problem was I didn't know about it. But what did I expect from a relationship that wasn't clearly defined?

"Naima, just so you know, birthdays aren't important to me. The time we spend together, that is. It's really not that big of deal."

"Apparently we give this impression to everyone that we tell each other everything,"

"We do tell each other everything."

"Obviously not birthdays," I snapped back.

He unbuckled his seatbelt and turned to me. "Okay, so when is your birthday?"

"July twenty-sixth."

His eyebrows shot up as he pointed toward me. "Ah, but what year?"

This was getting on my nerves. "Timothy, you held my application in your hands. I told you how old I was the first time you drove me home. Once that information leaves, it's classified. You don't get the runback." Timothy had this running joke that I was a cougar in cub's clothing. I was only two years older, but he loved teasing me about it.

"See, you won't tell me," he smirked.

I had half a mind to get out the car and leave his behind sitting here.

"Guess we're just on some friend shit," I said. "I don't even know when your birthday is, and it's not like we go on any real dates or anything. I'm cool with things between us, just don't throw me any curveballs. Keep it real with me." I picked at my nails, waiting for him to respond, but all he did was stare at me with those sad brown eyes.

"Naima…" He paused. "Naima, you know it's not just about the sex with you, right? I shouldn't have to tell you, but you do know that, don't you?"

I rolled my eyes as my head rattled from side to side. What was I supposed to know? All I knew was how I felt right now; the rest was unimportant. After all, why would you share your birthday with someone you didn't care about?

"Naima, I work with you. I wouldn't try to play you like that—"

"So what, if we didn't work together, you'd play me like that?" It was a poor choice of words but maybe with a little truth in them. As long as we worked together, things would be cool. What would happen if we didn't? Would it be that easy to cast me off? All these crazy things kept popping into my head one by one, and if I didn't get out of this car soon, I was going to explode.

"C'mon, Naima. That's not what I meant." He tickled one of my hands free and interlaced his fingers in mine. "I like you, Naima." He brought my hand to his lips, laying a kiss along my fingers. "I mean, I really like you. I'm not sure what there is I could do to prove that we're not just friends with benefits. At least, to me we're not."

I looked out the window, calculating just how long it'd take me to make a quick getaway. That was, if I didn't trip on my way up the staircase. Damn that staircase.

"So is it an official date you want? That's all? We can do that. Seems redundant since we do stuff all the time."

I turned to face him for the first time tonight not caring at all how clueless I looked. "Huh?" Good job, Naima. Good job.

"So this is how it's going to go. I'm going to take you out. We're going to have fun. I'm going to drop you off back here, and in all efforts to appear like the perfect gentleman, I'm going to avoid kissing you. But only at first. The magic happens when you let me walk you to your door." Tim was always so corny, but a part of me adored that about him. I wanted to laugh so hard.

"And *then*, when we get to your door, I'm going to sneak in a kiss. You know, because I'm slick like that. I may even throw in a horny grope, followed by a 'Can I come upstairs?' You're welcome to counter me with, 'I'm not that kind of girl. I don't get down like that on the first date.'" He made a pathetic attempt at a woman's voice. I didn't know who he was trying to emulate because it sure as hell wasn't me. I most certainly got down like that if everything felt right about the moment at hand.

Imagine dating a guy for twelve weeks only to find out he was terrible in bed. I'd been in too many situations like that to count. If the chance presented itself to assess what I was working with before things got too deep, the only other place to go was up at that point. Or, at least, that was what prior experience taught me.

"You're not working Saturday, right?"

I just loved how he could recite my schedule at the drop of a dime. *Stalker*. "No…"

"Then that's when we're going."

"Are you for real?"

"*Very*. I already know where I'm going to take you, too. It'll be outside so I suggest you dress warm. You know it'll be cold out. And before I let you go, you probably already know this because you're basically a Provy native now, but there's not much to do here in the winter time. I want you to have an open mind."

"Of course I have an open mind, dummy. I'm talking to you, aren't I?" I stuck out my tongue as he comically pouted his lips.

"Okay, I see it's Attack on Timothy Day. So I'm going to let you go." He reached in to kiss me, like he always did before he dropped me off. This time it went on for longer than the usual peck on the lips, blooming intensity surging between us.

"What about that stove you said Lisette left on?" he said through lips that had only one mission. To get me over to his house tonight.

"Yeah, on second thought, I think I may have left something at your place." I just barely took the time to let the words come out. His teeth came in contact with my lips with just enough bite that turned pain into pleasure.

"Cool, let me turn around so you can get that…"

* * *

Timothy

We were to meet up at Starbucks a little past six. It was already 6:23, and Naima wasn't here. I was the first one to arrive on scene, but judging from all the check-ins, it was going to be a full house. The tour guide of the group glanced down at his clipboard, probably to see who else was on his list. Then he made an announcement.

"Okay, guys. We're still waiting on one more person…"

"My date!" I interrupted. "She'll be here. Just let me text her really quick. She may have gotten stuck in traffic or something." I knew I should have picked her up, but she'd insisted on meeting me here. I took out my phone and sent a quick *"Where are you? XD"* text. Almost immediately I heard back from her.

Naima: *I'm @ Starbucks. Waiting on you.*

Me: *There's no way you're waiting on me b/c I've been here 20 minutes*

Five seconds later. A picture message. I opened it up. It was of the view from inside of Starbucks but not this one. The one on Thayer. The one closer to the job. *Fuck.*

I slapped my forehead, realizing that I'd never been clear about which to meet at. She was almost a mile away.

Me: *Fuck. My bad. I meant the one on Angell St. Hurry up and walk down.*

"You guys she'll be here any minute. She just got the Starbucks mixed up. It's my fault. I didn't make it clear. She said she's on her way. I apologize everyone."

A sense of relief washed over me when she finally came into view, coffee in hand. Her hair was out, a sort of thick, wild madness I rarely got to see, but I liked it when she wore it that way. It was nice.

She looked around, confused on what'd take place in the next few minutes. "Damn, my bad. I didn't know all these people were waiting on me. Sorry, everybody!" she announced loudly. I took her hand and we walked with everyone outside.

"You didn't tell me this was some group thing," she whispered.

I shushed her. The tour guide was talking, and I didn't want to miss anything.

"Naima, my friend, you are about to embark on a journey so uniquely Rhode Island, you may never be the same again. I present to you a *ghost tour*." And yes, I ended it with spooky sounds and spirit fingers.

Naima was such a huge fan of the supernatural (the show included), and after just five months, I'd already leaned her on all the scary stuff in my playlist. If anyone could have an appreciation for this stuff, it was her.

"Did they just say H.P. Lovecraft was born here?" she asked.

I tapped her nose. "See? You're already learning something new."

"Nothing new about the dude being a full-blown bigot, though," she added.

I shrugged unable to find a way to debate. "Hey, no one's saying the guy was perfect."

"FYI, Tim. This is probably the corniest thing I've ever done but…" She sighed deeply. "You know me so well. I'm loving it!"

We trailed behind the group in awe of the second stop at Brown University and finally to a pit stop between Benefit Street. The tour guide did the honor of passing around a few photos of paranormal activity in the form of orbs and glyphs. Naima held onto it for longer than most before offering it to me.

"Nah, I'm good." I'd already seen it before so it was more for her than me. We broke free from the group to take pictures on her phone, and not long after we grabbed a bite to eat at some upscale steakhouse. A simple way to end the night, but nice all the same.

* * *

Naima

There was a way his dark eyes praised me when I stood before him in my barely theres. My muscular legs that he loved so much shivered at the way it felt for his lips to cover every inch of them. He never missed a spot, and my sanity commended him for it.

A mix of firm, gentle touches awakened an ocean of pleasure that didn't feel legal as he spent a good time torturing me with his skillful tongue. I wanted him inside me. So bad I could barely stand it.

"Fuck me," I commanded.

Without debate, he reeled me by my hips, burying his cock deep inside me.

Timothy possessed an artistry when it came to making love. He didn't try to play dictator—he looked, listened, learned how my body reacted to his. There was no race to the finish line, no contest on how many times he could bring me there in one session. He just wanted me open. Free of all worry and stress so that we could enjoy the passion that flowed between us. Because of that, I took my sweet time soaking in his every inch, savoring his every thrust.

He guided my hand to my slippery center, requesting I please myself while he fucked me, because he was a man of visuals and nothing turned him on more than watching me have fun with myself.

"You look so hot when you do that!" he said, his voice heavy and breathless.

I brought my busy fingers to my mouth, taking pleasure in my taste as a low groan escaped his sexy lips.

He hooked his arms around my legs, filing me deeper with each stroke. I couldn't hold back the obscenities that left my mouth when I was this close to bliss. I had the tongue of a sailor, something he loved and hated about me. He unlocked his arm on one of my legs and placed his palm across my mouth.

"Mmm…shut up, Naima," he said with a smile. "When you talk like that, you make me wanna come. With your nasty ass."

I wanted him to come. To be the reason he did. So I didn't stop, not until the quake stirring inside me shattered into one hundred pieces, rendering me unable to function. His speed decreased, giving a few good pushes before he came, too.

"Damn, girl. I needed that," he muttered as he kissed my fore-head. He rolled off me and tossed the condom in the trash. "Aww, man. I'm so fuckin' thirsty. You want something while I'm up?" He stepped inside some clean basketball shorts and rubbed his forehead and scalp down with a towel. A bare chest with messy hair. That was Tim at his sexiest. Damn him and his little effort.

"When I get back, you want to get started on *American Horror Story: Freak Show*? I'm telling you, this season, I only caught a glimpse of the first episode, but I already know I can't get through that intro again. Shit is crazy."

I had no issue with lounging about in the nude, but I really wanted to hop in that shower. Call me a clean freak, but Tim had the tendency to wake me up in the middle of the night for another go at the stable. I felt better when I was squeaky clean and ready for my close up.

A knock and the sound of the door opening startled me. It was only Tim, but still. The bathroom sink flushed on, resulting in a quick change of temperature. From the vigorous scrubbing heard behind the curtain, my guess was Tim was brushing his teeth.

"Hey, I wanted you to know that I'm going to be leaving town in a couple of days," he said, his mouth full of foam from the toothpaste. "I didn't want you to freak out or be mad at me. It's why I didn't want to make a big deal about my birthday."

"Okay? Why would I be mad at you?"

He gargled mouthwash, delaying his answer until he spit into the sink. "Because I'm going to be gone for three days, but between layover and wait time, it'll be more like five. I bought the plane ticket over the summer, and because my dumb ass didn't purchase insurance on it, I couldn't alter or cancel it without losing money. Just letting you know the deal."

"So you planned a vacation over the summer. I'm not sweating it. Where are you headed?" I let the last bit of suds wash down the drain and shut off the water as he said something that stopped me right in my tracks.

"...Texas."

I steadied my breathing, trying to remain calm as I reached for my towel. He was leaning on the bathroom counter as if waiting for my reaction to go bat-shit crazy. It's not like I didn't know he was still in a relationship. We spent so much time together, but he rarely talked about it...about her. Hearing him talk about leaving gave me a huge dose of a pill called reality.

He still had a girlfriend.

"Okay."

His forehead wrinkled as he bit the inside of his cheek. I wanted to avoid the subject. Wanted to watch the damn TV show like we'd planned. If I talked about him leaving, I'd only make myself feel like shit, and I didn't want to feel like shit. Besides, the way I felt now was worse than feeling like shit.

He placed his arms around me, laying a gentle kiss on my shoulder. Maybe we didn't have to say it in words, but this trip was going to change us. For the worse or for the better? That we wouldn't know.

CHAPTER FIFTEEN

Naima

Timothy nudged me awake, kneeling down at the side of his bed. He'd been up at least an hour, getting ready to leave. Getting ready to spend the next few days with the girl he was serious about.

I was confused by the way I felt about Timothy. I didn't know if it was love. But it wasn't nothing. I wanted so bad for this to be *just* a really good friendship, but it was too late for that. Five months too late.

"Hey." I rolled over to meet his eyes, all sleepy yet focused. "I was just telling you that Rick is here to drop me off at the airport." I rubbed my eyes, hoping the exhaustion would mask how much it sucked to see him go.

"You look so cute," he said with a chuckle and kissed my forehead. "It's early, but I didn't want to leave without saying goodbye. My other set of keys is sitting on the kitchen counter, so if you don't mind, just lock up when you leave. Unless you're trying to chill here until I get back. Just don't have any house parties. Or at least wait until I get back." He smirked.

"I'll get up in a minute…"

"No, take your time, beautiful, just letting you know." He leaned in to kiss me on the nose. "I'll call you when I get there, so make sure you answer, okay?"

I nodded, only half-listening. It was a little after five in the morning, so I was too sleepy to be fully coherent.

"See you when I get back." He made his way to his bedroom door and grabbed his suitcase handle as he rolled it into the next room. Not long after, the front door slammed shut and Timothy was gone.

* * *

Another night of *Dawn of the Dead*. That's what we called slow nights at the job. It was so damn quiet that nearly half of us scheduled had already been sent home. It was just me, Emily, and Ruby left behind with five massively stuffed carts filled with returns. We were *not* pleased.

My phone went off with notification after notification. There were so few of us around, but I still found time to take it out to sift through new messages. Two missed calls from Tim. One from Mom. My text message thread was getting ridiculous. I'd had eight texts since the last time I'd looked at it. The first I opened was from Lisette, worried if I was okay since I'd missed our weekly *HTGAWM* bond session. Another one from KK asking if we could swap shifts. The last six came from Timothy and included a photo he'd snapped of me just moments before he left.

Got you while you weren't looking. Bastard.

The others ranged from "*Miss you already*" to "*Shoot me a text when you're not busy.*" I was seconds away from replying when Emily and Ruby rolled up behind me, complaining about how fast I was working (or, rather, not working) and how they wanted to go home.

Emily bragged about finishing two carts on her own, and Ruby was just about finished with the one she had. That left just my nearly full one, along with another filled with only stuffed animals and figurines. Emily grabbed a large stack from my cart, moving with impeccable speed in her trendy black moto boots to put those books where they needed to be. Less than five minutes later, she came back to stake claim on my full cart.

"Damn, girl, save some!" I said, not really meaning it. She could put this stuff back if she wanted to. I had a stack of text messages I was debating replying to or not. I'd probably just put the books anywhere. I had too much on my mind.

"Oh, no, Staten Island, I'm bringing it back. There were just a few books I saw on my way that I should've brought the first time. After that, it's all yours." She disappeared across the store, leaving me and Ruby to sort out the last cart.

"Soooo, you talk to him?" she asked out of the blue.

Damn, did I have *I miss Timothy* written all over my face? "Sailor Moon, how many times do I have to tell you people? I don't like Tim like that."

Ruby squinted and nodded like she wasn't buying it. "Okay…" I had a feeling that wasn't the end of it. "So you do know that I'm cool with both of you. Like both of you are what I'd consider to be best friends. You know that, right?"

Cue in the cynical explanation…*now*.

"So tell me why just three weeks ago I caught my dearest, closest friends confirming my suspicions by swapping spit in the pantry? Talk about hot, Staten Island. I mean, I hope the sex is as hot as your makeout sessions."

"You've known for three weeks and you let me sit up there and lie to you every time you asked like I thought I was getting over?"

"Three weeks? Try when you started working here. I've always known you guys were hooking up. I didn't need to walk in on you to prove it. So…Are you guys serious?"

Were we serious? Probably not. Sometimes yes. Or maybe I only wanted for us to be. I had to remind myself where he was right now. With his girlfriend of four years. Celebrating his birthday with his girlfriend of four years. Most likely sleeping next to and with his girlfriend of four years. When I thought about it that way, maybe we'd never really been serious.

"Do you like him, Naima?"

I nodded sheepishly. It was hard to look her in the eye with how foolish I felt.

"Normally, I'd tell someone to fuck that guy, he's probably just using you. But I've known Tim for a long time. I've known how he's felt about you for a long time. This isn't an ideal situation, but I do think if he felt the need to step outside his relationship, it's probably because he feels really close to you. He's not the type of guy to do that otherwise. Only advice to you, don't give too much of what you can't get back. Timothy's my boy and everything, but you're too cute to be worried about some guy."

Emily walked back up with the cart halfway empty. The girl went to town. "Look, I have some stuff I haven't even started for school yet, so before you say something smart, I did half your cart because I'm trying to go home."

Since she'd been so generous, there was no reason I couldn't do the rest. It was my department after all.

"Why, yes, Staten Island. Please do. Take the load off me." she said in a spooky, *Children of the Corn* sort of way that made me want to avoid her for the rest of the night. She also kept staring at me with those scary ice-blue eyes of hers. Girl was just creepy.

I knew something was up when her eyes met Ruby's. It still didn't dawn on me when they broke into an eruption of laughter.

"What the hell is so funny?" I tried to lift my hands off the cart, but they were stuck. Stuck. I mean, literally stuck. Like one false move and I'd be walking away with three layers less skin. Emily held up a bottle of Super Glue, and it became obvious why she'd been so helpful.

"You stupid bitches!" I cried, but they didn't hear me. They were too busy taking out their phones, eager to get my long-awaited initiation on film.

I crouched. I ducked. But there was no way to hide from the both of them. Not while I was glued to the cart.

"I told you I was out for blood, Staten Island. Where's your sidekick to save you this time huh?"

I guess I had this coming. But damn, did they have to get all in my face, though?

"C'mon, Staten Island, me and Sailor Moon will help you off this thing, but first you have to say the magic words."

I swallowed my pride, wanting desperately to have use of my hands without losing skin in the process. Ruby pointed her phone in my direction as I looked into the camera and spoke through gritted teeth. "My name is Staten Island, and I…survived initiation.

* * *

The spring semester wasn't playing games. With just two classes in the week and another two at the end, I'd already had what was a week's worth of assignments from last term. And all this stuff was due next week. Thank god for distractions like *Angry Birds*. How had I ever procrastinated before without it?

An incoming call came in, and being the clumsy moron I was, I accidently hit answer. I had no choice but to take it, otherwise it would look like I was screening his calls. FYI: I was.

"Hey, Miss Lady," Tim said. It was real nice hearing his voice, but the feeling didn't last long. He was seventeen hundred miles away from me…in Texas…with his girlfriend. I looked at my laptop's calendar. Today was February second. Tim's official birthday.

"Happy Birthday, Tim."

"Why thank you." I was sure he was smiling on the other end. "What are *you* up to?"

There wasn't anything I could say that would make me feel better. The whole situation made me all bitter and grouchy. "Nothing much. Just debating on whether I should end my life now or wait until the workload gets crazier…"

"That's right. The new semester started back up. No offense, but I have no desire to be you right now."

Sigh. Neither did I. "So why are you calling me?" The question came out rude, but it was too late to switch it up now.

"Isn't it obvious? I miss you. You and your cold-ass feet. No lie, it is so hot down here."

"Guess you had a free second to sneak away from your little honeymoon weekend." That one definitely came out snarky, and this time I meant it.

"Naima, don't be mean."

Who was being mean? I was just being honest. It made little sense he was calling me when he was supposed to be away with the Mrs. I was surviving here by myself. Just like I always would.

"First of all, no one has to sneak around to call you. I called you twice yesterday, but you didn't pick up."

And I probably wouldn't have picked up this time if my dumbass hadn't been playing *Angry Birds* and let my finger slip on the answer button. "I was at work." Not a lie.

"You weren't on the schedule for Tuesday."

"Yeah, well, I switched with KK."

"Oh." The other end went quiet. So quiet I was sure he'd hung up on me. "Naima, are you mad at me?"

Mad? I wasn't mad. That implied I had the right and reason to be mad. I'd known what I was getting into, and yet I'd still chosen to enter my own confusing little relationship with him. Mad didn't encompass how I felt.

"Why would I be mad at you?"

He paused. "I don't know. You're just not your usual self around me."

Now I was annoyed. "C'mon, Tim, I have no valid reason to be mad at you. You are not my man." There. I'd said it. And it only managed to suck the life out of the conversation.

"You're so mad at me. I can tell."

"Oh, *puh-leaze*, Tim. No one is mad at you."

"Okay. So do you miss me?"

The question came as a shock considering where he was right now. I did miss him, but the thought of him knowing everything that had happened had chained him to my heart was too much to give. Ruby told me don't give too much of what you can't get back. No man should have that kind of power over you. But he did and I feared what he'd do if he knew it.

"No," I lied.

"So you don't miss me?"

"Nope." Another lie.

"Naima, you're such a liar. You know how I know? Because I miss you like crazy."

I had no interest in ruining his trip with my sudden change in attitude, so I offered to let him go. It was more for me than anything. I didn't feel like talking.

"Wait, Naima, before you hang up, I wanted to talk to you about something. Thing is, I'd rather not get into it over the phone. Can we talk about it more when I'm home? Or am I just going to get mean Naima who's mad at me?"

I took a deep breath to center myself. *Don't be mad, Naima. Don't be jealous. Just get a friggin' hold of yourself.*

"Yeah, we can do that."

"We can do what?" he challenged.

"Talk more about it when you get home."

Silence traveled through the phone waves before he took the plunge and spoke. "Promise?"

"Yes, Timothy, I promise. Now go enjoy your trip."

"Bye, beautiful," he added after I wished him another happy birthday.

Incoming multimedia message from Timothy Ferreiro popped up after I hung up. I opened it to find a photo of Timothy with his lips puckered out like they were moments from coming through the screen. A simple *"Miss you"* was captioned beneath as my stomach sank into oblivion. What were we going to talk about when he got back? I wasn't looking forward to any conversation that ended with a broken heart or ego.

I kept telling myself that Tim had all the power, but it was me who carried all the pieces to the puzzle. If I carried on, I'd never be able to put myself back together. I knew what I had to do now.

I had to end things with Timothy.

CHAPTER SIXTEEN

Timothy

I'd called Naima nearly ten times since I landed and probably texted her more than that. I'd hoped to see her before work, but it looked like she was either avoiding me or had her phone off. I texted once more.

Working later. Was hoping to see you before then but I guess I'll just see you there.

I left out *"I miss you"* this time. How many times was I going to say it to not hear back from her? She knew I missed her. But I didn't know whether she missed me. I didn't have time to wait on a reply, so I hopped in the shower and got ready for work.

First day back and already I had a lists of tasks that required my attention. Apparently I'd come back just in time to do next month's schedule. I wonder how *that* had happened?

Damn everyone with their fucked-up availability. *Damn them all to hell.*

Genesis walked by the office, which I assumed was to clock out for the day. The sound of punching numbers in the time clock could be heard inches away.

"2 Live, are you out?" I said, typing away on the computer's keyboard.

"Yes, sir."

"See you tomorrow."

She peeked her head inside the office. "Hey, Timbo, are you doing schedules?"

"That I am," I said, entranced with the graphs, names, and numbers looking back at me from the monitor's screen.

"Good because I'm going to need Wednesday off."

This time I peeled my eyes away from the screen. "Did you put in a request for it?" I asked, knowing damn well she hadn't.

"No," she whined. "But damn, Tim, you can't just *not* schedule me on Wednesday? If you do, I'm just going to call out."

I worked Wednesday night, so I couldn't have that. Not on a day where she was scheduled in my department. I slid her over a pen and stack of Post-it notes, promising to hook her up this one time. She wanted weekdays off and I needed her on weekends anyway. That's what I called a fair trade.

"You got it, dude," I said in my best Michelle Tanner impression.

She laughed and hit me over the shoulder with her beanie and put it back on her head. "See you tomorrow."

The next half-hour was uneventful. I wasted away with office tasks at hand. I needed a break or something to recharge my battery. I was literally running on E.

A knock on the door made me spin around in my chair, and my lips formed into a smile. Naima looked surprised to see me, but she was just the jolt I needed. I missed me some her.

"Oh. I thought Kmart would be here."

"You look like you've seen a ghost," I joked.

"Not a ghost, just you," she threw back.

I sensed a little tension, but I wasn't sweating it. I'd missed her that much.

She tried to leave with a quick hi-and-goodbye, but I beat her

to the exit, carefully closing the door behind us. I held her hands
and leaned in to kiss her on the cheek.

"C'mon, Naima, talk to me. Why don't you look happy to
see me?"

She rolled her eyes, tossing her hand backward into the door.
"Tim, I'm just late is all. It's not even that serious. I should head to
the floor."

My shoulders slumped as I let a frown take over. I'd spent five
days thinking about her. Wasn't exactly the reunion I'd been
expecting.

"Okay. Then hit me up on break."

She nodded without elaboration. With a peck on the lips, I
saw her off with a small "see ya then," ignoring that foreboding
feeling. Something seriously wrong was brewing between us. It
was up to me to change that.

* * *

Naima

Why had I turned off my phone this morning? If I hadn't, I
would've known I'd see Timothy a full day ahead. I'd thought he
was coming back tomorrow. I'd thought it'd be easy—rundown
of why things weren't working, ending things on a high note.
That was how I'd mapped it out in my head.

In my head, it was organized. In my head, it was foolproof. So
why did seeing him in person make it so hard to say the words? I
liked him. I wanted to be around him. Maybe more than I should
have. But the longer I dragged things out, the harder it would be
to bounce back from it. As much as I hated to admit it, Timothy
had a certain power over me. It was now or never. I needed to
take that power back.

"Damn, girl, it's almost six. When are you going on break?"
Tim surprised me in an aisle. Great. Now I couldn't even plan

how to end things in peace. Why had I thought hooking up with someone I worked with was a good idea?

"Yeah…I already went," I said sheepishly.

His eyebrows shot up, holding in what looked like confusion and shock. He, however, spoke with control and calmness in his voice. "Okay. So what happened to hitting me up when you went on break? I figured we could go to lunch together, talk…I don't know. Catch up."

Truth was, come lunch time, I hadn't even tried to look for him. In fact, I'd spent my whole day ducking and dodging him every chance I had. I tried to come up with the best excuse time would allow on why I hadn't felt like talking.

"You just looked busy when I was ready. I didn't want to wait."

"Okay well, did you want a ride home tonight or were you going to do that by yourself, too?"

I let out an exasperated sigh. He was onto me. Why had I thought I could spend my day pretending I wasn't ignoring him? It was better to accept his invitation to get this out of the way. But it had to be away from work. Away from people. Or else it wouldn't get better, it'd only get worse.

"Sure. You can give me a ride home."

* * *

No one talked for the first five minutes of the drive to my house. If he wasn't going to talk, I wasn't going to either. What was there to say? He'd come back in a chipper mood after spending a week in paradise with his *actual* girlfriend. That gave me a lot to think about.

I broke my vow of silence when he missed the exit, taking me god knows where. "Hey, you know you missed the exit, right?"

He didn't turn to me, didn't acknowledge my words, didn't even blink. He kept driving until, five exits later, he pulled into an empty parking lot and chose a spot in the center to park.

"Timothy, what the fuck?"

"You're never going to talk to me if you can just get out and walk inside your apartment. So we're here. Nowhere near home. And now we are going to talk, *falou*?"

The chance to tell Timothy how it was going to be from now on was here. I couldn't handle this friends-with-benefits package. Not anymore than I could stand sleeping with someone who wasn't single. This was the time to call it quits. So why did I want so badly to pull him into the backseat and show him how much I missed him. He did not have me thinking straight. More than enough reason to end it before I got my feelings hurt.

"Naima, why have you been blowing me off this whole week?"

"Tim, stop exaggerating."

He laughed. "Exaggerating? Okay…" He pulled out his cell phone, and for a second, I thought it was some rude mess when he dialed a number in front of me. Then my phone rang in his familiar, assigned ringtone. "So that is your number?" he said like a smart ass. "Because the twenty-four times I texted you on top of the thirteen times I called you, I was thinking that maybe you changed your number or something. *But nope*, your phone works just fine. It must've been me you didn't want to talk to."

"It's not that. I just…I just needed some space." I pinched the bridge of my nose, feeling a little exhausted that I was losing the upper hand in the conversation.

"Space? From me? You mean the five days we haven't seen each other or do you mean something else?"

Before I could stop myself, I blurted out the one thing I couldn't take back. "I don't want to do this anymore, Tim. It's too hard."

He adjusted his seat, giving himself room to lean back in his chair. He ran his fingers through his hair, silent, wearing a look of stress that aged him ten years.

"I knew I shouldn't have gone."

But I needed him to. Him being gone had helped me see the

situation for what it really was. I was a side chick, a mistress, a homewrecker. There was no other way around it.

"Naima, I don't know what to say to you to make you see things the way I see them. You're not a side chick. It's never been that way with you. If it was, I wouldn't even care that you were mad at me. I would've been like 'fuck it.'"

"Did you have your fun in Texas?" I played with the ends of my newly flat-ironed hair.

"I did."

I needed to get to the question I really wanted to ask before I lost the nerve. "Did you have sex?"

He took in one deep breath. "I don't want to lie to you, Naima. Once."

There it was. The answer I needed to hear.

Tears welled up in my eyes. Not wanting Timothy to see he'd gotten the best of me, I stepped out of the car and took off. A car door slammed shut soon after.

"Things got emotional. Just let me explain what happened..." he said, trailing after me.

With no clue of where I was, I kept walking. I had zero desire to hear all the details of his little getaway with his girlfriend.

"Naima, would you just let me explain?" He caught up and grabbed my arm. I shoved him away, this time unable to hide the tears streaming down my face.

"Why, Timothy? You don't owe me anything. You and I are not together. We're just friends. I know that now. I let your ass inside my head. I let myself think that it was always more than it was, and that's *my fault.* I just can't do this anymore, Tim. I can't." I stormed off, hoping this was the end of it, but no, he stood firm on my coattails.

"Naima, would you get in the car please?"

"I'm good. I'll walk home." It was a crappy plan, but anything was better than the alternative.

"Naima, I get it. You don't want anything to do with me right now, but there's no way I'm leaving you out here by yourself. You're too far from home. It'd take you hours. You can sit in the backseat or even the trunk if that's what you want to do, but you're not walking. I'll only follow you if you do."

I didn't have a choice. Both included Timothy, and the ride was a helluva lot safer. I sat in the backseat, gathering all my things from the passenger side. It was a rude gesture, but I didn't care. I just wanted to go home.

He pulled up to my house, and I moved faster than I ever had before trying to get out of his car. One look in his eye and I knew I'd reconsider. Right now, I needed to be by myself, let this whole thing sink in.

I struggled with my keys to open the door. The moment I stepped inside, I collapsed to the floor. I don't know how long I sat there and cried. Twenty minutes? Maybe longer? My phone buzzed with a text message alert, and I slid across the screen to see Timothy's picture next to the thread of new messages.

Tim: *So that's it? You're not even gonna talk to me?*

It took a few minutes for me to text something back. I wasn't trying to appear petty. It was best to keep it simple.

Me: What's there to talk about? This thing we have is over. Might as well get on with our lives.

I turned my phone off and headed for Lisette's weed stash. I wanted to feel far away. Most of all, I wanted to feel numb.

CHAPTER SEVENTEEN

Timothy

What was the shittiest thing about working with someone you spent the last couple of months falling for? Knowing every second of every minute, she spent a huge portion of her time avoiding you. I'd had a good three weeks trying to get her to see my side of things, but I suppose I shouldn't have been surprised that I was getting the cold shoulder.

What could I have done differently? Should I have lied? Sure, it would have been easier to lie. I can't say the thought hadn't crossed my mind. But the thing about lies was they eventually became harder to remember as time went on. The way I felt about her, lying never seemed like a reasonable option. To build something on lies...that was like asking for things to blow up in your face. In the end, I was left feeling like she'd never give me the right opportunity to explain myself, but that didn't mean I had given up on her. On us.

I just wanted things to be the way they were before I left. I wasn't sure how to bring our situation back to that. Fuck, I couldn't wait to get off. Five more minutes and I was out of this place. Early for a change. Six o'clock may not have been early to some but I was so used to seeing the sun come down. Six was efficient enough.

"Hey Tim, you coming back downtown later? We were all going to go ice skating after work." Because the rink closed in March, every fourth Sunday of February it was sort of a tradition to go skating at the Providence Rink just a few blocks up in the center of Downtown. If I were in any other mood I would have been all for it, but I just didn't have the spirit for socializing.

"Nah, Sailor Moon. I'm think it's going to be a pass for me. I'm not trying to come back once I get out of here. I'm just trying to chill once get I get home." She held her arms up in defeat.

"All about breaking tradition over a ten minute drive. Okay. But if a certain someone was hoping to run into a certain someone, I just got a text from that certain someone and she's totally going to be there later on tonight."

At that I tried not to flinch but judging my Ruby's expression, I wasn't doing a good job. I'd always had a feeling Ruby knew more than she let on. She like me, was good friends with Naima. In fact, when Ruby wasn't with me, she was often with her. Without knowing for sure if Naima ever let it slip that we were intimate, any time she hinted at it I played dumb.

"Not sure what you mean." She took my arm and pulled me into the pantry, deciding somewhere in the cramped corner was a more than an optimal spot to grill me.

"Okay so I've tried ignoring this as long as my curiosity would allow me to but—what's the deal with you and Naima right now?" I shrugged. "Nothing really. Unless you've heard something different." For all I knew Naima confided in her everything about our relationship but I wasn't falling for a trap. If she was ignorant, I planned to keep it that way.

"So you're saying around your birthday the two of you are attached at the hip, then you leave for Texas for a week and the two of you are barely talking. What about that is nothing really?"

I took a deep breath, pressing the back of my head on the wall I was leaning on.

"Ruby, it's complicated. So…so complicated." She folded her arms across her chest as her face contorted to match her analytic mood.

"You know, I figured as much. You're like, not your usual obnoxious self and her—well she's walking around like," she paused. "Like she just got her heart broken." Knowing I was the reason for it just made me feel worse. There goes going home with the intention to zone out. I wouldn't be able to sleep until I at least figured out what's going on with her. But fuck, I looked like shit.

"Look umm…I'm going to head home and come back. I have to see if Angel is around to give me a haircut or something. I'm looking rough as fuck. Do me a favor. Would you leave out that I'm coming if she asks you? I want a chance to talk to her out of work but I know if she knows I'll be there she may not show."

Her hand rested on my shoulder. "Even if you don't get a chance to hash things out, it'll be fun. But for what it's worth, Naima digs you. Present tense not past. She just needs some time to figure out what's right for her but I promise, she'll come around."

* * *

I pulled up to Angel's apartment complex a few minutes shy of 6:30. Like all the other times he'd taken time out of his schedule to fit me in for a quick line up, I was going to owe him one. Seeing how this was a *major* emergency, it was worth the heavy price tag over my head.

As my friend he never charged me, not even when I'd go see him at the barbershop he worked at when he wasn't working at our mutual place of employment. However, he did came up with creative ways for me to return the favor. If I didn't need this haircut.

I waited for him in the front lobby as he met me at the door to let me in. "What's good?" he said as he gave me dap and patted me on the shoulder. "Just getting ready for this whole work thing. You going?"

I followed him up two flights of stairs and went through a thick brown door that led to his apartment's floor. "Yea, I was trying to. Soon as I help my mom out, I was going to hang for a little bit."

One of the things I admired about Angel was how dedicated he was at caring for his mother. The kid was young, younger than me and when he wasn't working one of his two jobs and actually had time for a life, he was over here being a good son to an ailing parent. Definitely in line for world's greatest human being. According to my list that is.

We entered his apartment passing the dozens of framed photos on the walls of the hallway that led to his kitchen. I swear, every time I came here, there were at least five current photos of a handful of his family members acting as some sort of timeline of how much they'd grown.

Not a lot of people I knew still hung up framed photos in 2016 but I guess tracking memories was never a bad thing.

"Hey, don't laugh but..." I slipped my hat off to reveal my untamed, unshaped cut from a good few weeks of ignoring that something needed to be done to it. I had one of those asymmetrical haircuts that required an insane amount of maintenance, which was why I hadn't let this hat leave my head for weeks. Angel jumped back in horror.

"Damn, Tim. Are you going through some shit or something because this isn't like you. I mean, I know it's been a few weeks but damn, I wasn't ready for all that." Out came a forced laugh from me but considering how late I'd waited to get cleaned up, what did I expect?

"C'mon man. Stop staring and fix my shit. Damn. And before you object, I will be helping myself to some of these plantains, too." On the counter near the stove sat a plate of freshly fried plantains, and they were good. Damn.

"Cool, so what do you want? Same as before? Or maybe you want it to fall to the other side this time?" I sat down at a chair he pulled out from the kitchen table where he then drapped a barber's cape over my torso, securing a clasp at the back of my neck.

"You think it's long enough to switch where the length hangs?" He shrugged. "Yea, maybe. But it's not going to be as long as it was before when it hung to the left. It'll be more subtle."

"That's cool. Trying to do something different anyways." I said, the buzzing sound of the clippers drowning out the Spanish language programs playing from the living room. Even if my night didn't go according to plan, the least I could do was try.

I'd make a lot of sacrifices this past month and if she let me, I was ready to invest more in what I had with Naima. This thing we had, I didn't want it to be over.

* * *

"Hey, you made it." Ruby and Genesis embraced me for a hug. "Yea, and you're lucky I came back too. It's cold as hell out here." I looked amongst the gathering of fellow employees that were already here and just arriving. From the look of things, Naima was a no-show.

"Don't worry, she sent me a text ten minutes ago. She's coming. Looking sexy by the way. About time you did something about that hair." I hooked my arm around her neck and planted a sloppy kiss on her right cheek. The girl got on my nerves on a regular but it was hard to deny that she was one of my closest friends. Every one needed someone like her in their lives. She just got me.

"Yea, well everything I learned about being sexy I learned from you, sunshine. Now let me whip some of your asses on this rink real quick." I'd played hockey for years before I discovered basketball. Because of that, I was a decent enough skater.

The girl behind the counter handed me a pair of black skates and after a quick lace up, I was on the ice showing these ladies how it was done. It was a challenge standing up in these things when you had klutzes like Genesis and Emily colliding into you every chance they got. But I was enjoying myself too much to fully comprehend that my ass would be feeling it in the morning.

Besides, I'd already spotted Naima in the clearing. I'd have my shot to confront her once and for all about the weight I'd been carrying since coming back from my trip. Whether she were willing to hear me out was something I wouldn't know unless I tried again.

"Hey Tim." Ruby skated alongside me, crashing into me hard enough to cause a mishap for anyone *but* me. Lucky for her, I handled myself on these skates. Silently, I debated waiting for Naima to join us all on the ice before I approached her but my nerves got the better of me—I couldn't wait.

Just as I was headed toward the end of the rink, the sight of someone wrapping their arms around her caused me to brake. African-American for sure, or at least by first impression. I wasn't bitter, so I could at least admit that he was conventionally attractive. He leaned into kiss her, and at that moment something inside me shut down.

My muscles stiffened making it, for the second I stood there, that much harder to move. That was it. The motivation I needed to bring this night to an end. I didn't have the craving often but I needed a smoke—*bad*. Aware in my sudden shift in mood, Ruby caught up to me as I skated over to Ravinder.

"Hey, Buzz, do you have any loosies?"

He answered with a no as he tried to steady himself. "Ask Rocketman. I think he might have some."

With graceful ease, I glided over to Bruce. "Hey, Rocketman, let me get a loosie."

He pulled out a carton of cigarettes from his back pocket, then frowned at the crushed box. "All this falling on my ass. Is menthol okay?"

Can one really be picky when you were asking for something you didn't need? "Yeah, man, that's cool."

He handed me a smoke and offered me his lighter. When I told him I wasn't coming back he said it was okay to give it to him when I saw him next. Ruby and I skated past Naima and her date as we both headed to the rental counter to exchange our skates back for boots. The counter girl telling us if we checked out now, we'd have to pay again to skate.

"Yea, that's okay, we're not coming back. Thanks, though."

Without saying much to each other, we made our way through the tunnel that out looked Washington Street and I lit up my smoke, letting the mix of menthol and tobacco navigate its way through my lungs. It was strange how smoking had a calming effect on me. Even stranger that I didn't find it as addictive as many who had found it hard to quit after that first puff. Maybe I had a load of will power, but lighting up was always a social thing for me. Like drinking or blazing up. I needed people around me to do it, otherwise I didn't give it much thought.

"I'm sorry, Tim. I didn't know." Ruby said in defeat.

"Ruby, it's cool. All that time I had her feeling like a side piece, what more do I deserve, right?" Given all the times I'd tried to convince her she wasn't just a sexual conquest, there was no doubt in my mind she'd ever felt anything otherwise. I wasn't even that to her. I was nothing. At least I knew where I stood now.

"Maybe she's just trying to make you jealous."

"Well bravo, it's working." I sharply stated. I quickly apologized for snapping at Ruby. She didn't take it personally but I did feel bad for taking my hurt feelings out on her.

"I broke up with Sherri." I said to no one particular as I smoked my last puff before flicking it on the ground. Ruby's mouth dropped, surprised by the news.

"Wow."

"But you know what? I'm done. Done with Naima, done with this whole getting her to forgive me bit. She's over me. I'm not going to chase some girl who doesn't want me." And yet she wasn't just some girl. She was the one I had chosen. All these past weeks she'd been all I ever thought about, only to find out she wasn't even worried about me. Like these past five months hadn't mattered. Ruby didn't bullshit me by telling me something she knew probably wouldn't happen, so I appreciated not having the *"Everything's going to be okay"* talk. It would have only made me more irritated.

"Hey, let's get out of here, Tim." She worked her arm around my waist and together we walked around for a bit, the night air biting, before heading back to my car.

CHAPTER EIGHTEEN

Timothy

The last few weeks had left me exhausted. Putting all your energy in keeping a level head was finally catching up with me but life went on. Or at least that's what I'd kept telling myself. We were like strangers. Maybe even more distant than that. She kept her distance and if I could help it, I kept mine. I wasn't sure how long this would go on for but I only had to last until the end of spring.

Come summertime I'd be free of her presence, if even for a little while. That was the time I looked forward to. Until then there was going to be this negative air between us. When I thought about it, the only thing keeping it negative was not addressing it at all. And that was not going to happen.

Some days didn't feel like work at all, others, made the time just drag. And tonight was one of those nights that was supposed to run smoothly. No shipments. Limited staff but slow, like most Tuesdays were. But the moment Angel came from his break to find me in the pantry loading up for the night, I predicted my once peaceful night would soon come to a halt.

"Hey Tim. I've got a family emergency, you think I could leave early? It's just some shit with my mom and no one else can get off to be with her. I know I have three more hours but--" And here was where the favor I owed him came in handy. I couldn't tell him no--especially not in an emergency. But it'd left me with a hard decision. One I didn't feel like asking of someone. With Angel gone there were only two people to consider convincing to stay and one was one I wasn't looking forward to begging, though the likelihood of her saying yes was higher.

"Go, go. See about your mom. Hit me up later to tell me how she's doing."

"I hate doing you like this. I know it's just me and two other people." I shook my head.

"Yea but it's slow. We'll be alright. Go on. Matter of fact, I'm going to have to punch you out anyways, so let me just do that so you can get out of here." We walked through the store and to the back office where the time clock was situated. Martha was in the office closing with me so I peeked in to explain Angel's situation.

"It's cool. I've got the cafe pretty much cleaned up. I can help the girls on the floor if something else happens. I'll get a cash til if I have to." The look she gave me was high on the nervous scale and if it wasn't for the fact that she was conducting a phone conversation while talking to me, she would have expressed her concern in far more words. She covered her palm over the phone's receiver.

"That's a good backup plan but since Butter Cookie's at the registers and it's a school night, you can't ask her to stay. See if Staten Island will stay until ten if need be. She's supposed to get off at eight and since Du-wop's got to get out of here, it's better to be safe than sorry." I took a steady breath. "Yea I'll ask her. But if she says no, I got you."

"Make her say yes, Timbaland. It's not like you're not good at convincing women to do something." *Right.* If this woman only knew.

My fingers dashed off a twelve digit key code overriding

Angel's punch out to reflect the earlier time. "Alright, you're good. Take care of your mom."

He said a quick goodbye to Martha and jogged to the front of the store. I gestured to Martha that I was on my way to the front as she gave me a quick nod and hurried back to her phone conversation.

The place was nearly empty mind a few customers scouraging the aisles, while two other sat on a bench browsing through the magazines. Naima was hard to miss with her brightly colored kente print scarf tied in a sort of regal way on top of her head. She was sorting through a cart of books and placed a handful of them on a display table in the center of two aisles. *Stop dragging your feet, Timothy.*

"Hey, umm Staten Island. You think you can stay until nine-thirty, ten? Du-wop had to leave early." I said passively. She considered the request for a moment, most likely aware I wouldn't have asked her if she wasn't my only option. Her hands disappeared in her back pockets as she looked off to the side and nodded.

"Yea, I mean I guess I can stay. Would I be able to call my ride first about the change in time?"

"Yup." I said as I headed back over to my station to finish cleaning up. That wasn't so hard, was it?

* * *

Thank god it was slow. With my help I had us out at nine-thirty, and with all this tension brewing inside of me; I couldn't wait to go outside to have a cigarette. I wished Martha a goodnight as she finished cashing out the draw Naima had to take out. so that Emily could be off the registers at eight-thirty. I made my way out the front exit, the night air brisk as the snow crunched under my boots with every step. My icy breath was seconds from forming small icicles on the tip of my lips, a brief reminder of how cold it got in Providence came late winter.

March looked like it wasn't letting up anytime soon with the snowfall, which was why I couldn't wait until spring. I had about enough of shoveling my car free from snow and I wouldn't miss these icy ass roads. I lit up my cigarette and took a deep inhale. The entrance door lightly slammed behind me and from the corner of my eye, Naima stood next to me a few inches away from the curb. I went in the direction of my car, not willing to share the space. If she hadn't called me out on it, I would've went straight to my car without saying anything. It felt petty not at least not finishing my smoke first.

"Don't mind me, I'm just standing here. I don't own the sidewalk. You don't have to leave because I'm standing here with you." I stayed put.

"You know, I didn't know you smoked."

"I don't really. Just kind of bum one off someone when I'm bored or stressed out." I flicked the remainder of it in the pile of snow in front of me. Though I'd only gotten through half of it; I didn't feel like smoking anymore. She took a few steps towards me and stopped.

"So how long are we going to do this for? You know? Go on avoiding each other?"

"Staten Island, for me it's hard to avoid you. But I am giving you that space you asked for. How is that working out?" I said, not intending for it to sound nearly as salty leaving my mouth.

"On second thought, I think I'm going to just stand over there. It's obvious talking to you has been a mistake on my behalf. For some dumb reason, I thought that you'd moved on from this already."

"Like you have?" She balled her hands into fists spinning away in a huff only to turn back around to lay into me.

"Oh for the love of—you know what Tim? Fuck you. So I started dating someone else. Big deal. It's not like you don't have someone. What was I supposed to do? Sit back and continue being someone's second string? It was already bad enough I caught feelings for you—"

"I broke up with Sherri." I blurted out, frustrated before I could stop myself.

"You...you what?"

"My second to last day in Dallas." Her gaze went distant and for the moment she stood there, she stayed silent in order to gather what she planned on saying next.

"Tim, why didn't you tell me?"

"Because you never even gave me a chance to. You just blew me off and I tried to understand. I hurt you, I get that. But dammit Naima. I wanted to be with you. I ended my relationship because I wanted to be with you. I loved you. I love you." I said the words out loud, admitting to her what I'd felt for months now. But it was too late to worry about what could've happened. Things were already broken. Even if she had been open to fixing it; I wasn't.

Feelings aside, I wanted away from the angst, away from the drama our relationship both caused each other. If everything happened for a reason, I had to trust that our separation was for a good one.

"Tim, I know I haven't been the best person to deal with, but you telling me this," She paused. "Damn it, this would have changed everything."

"Well, Naima. I guess we'll never know, will we?" With my lips I pointed to the car that pulled up, recognizing the guy she'd brought to the skating two weeks ago in the driver's seat.

"Your ride's here." I gestured a small salute as she reluctantly opened the passenger side door and took one last pained breath before she averted her eyes to the ground.

My thoughts recalled a book of love quotes I caught myself reading while trying my damndest to rush the hell out of here.

The greatest pain that came with love is loving someone you can't have.

Whoever said it, they were right.

* * *

Thanks so much for making it all the way to the end of part one of Timothy and Naima's story! We so hope you devoured it! Before you go, we'd love if you could leave a few short words of what you thought of Same Page!

Follow this link to review and tell others what you thought. Again, thank you for your purchase and be sure to flip through the end pages to discover more addictive reads from G.L. Tomas.

Happy Reading!

G.L. Tomas is a twin writing duo and lover of all things blerdy, fearless and fun. When they're not spending their time crafting swoon-worthy heroes, they're battling alien forces in other worlds but occasionally take days off in search mom and pop spots that make amazing pasteles and tostones fried to perfection.

They host salsa lessons and book boyfriend auditions in their secret headquarters located in Connecticut.

Head over to our Official website @ GLTomaswrites.com There we have a list of our upcoming titles and you can purchase our paperbacks directly, along with other swag!

Tim and Naima aren't over … Or are they? Stay tuned for their story to continue in *Next Chapter*.

Jump on over to our official Bookish Friends to Lovers Pinterest board to see our fantasy casts and dream-ups of the characters!

Sign up for G.L. Tomas' newsletter.

You'll get exclusives, such as book release updates, chances to win or earn free swag, access to well thought-out book lists, and opportunities to save on books before anyone else!

Don't forget to connect with us on Bookbub and our

exclusive Facebook Group! And be sure to send us an email to talk books and about your fave characters! Drop us a line at guinevere.libertad@gltomaswrites.com

If you liked reading *Same Page* as much as we did writing it, please consider leaving a review! Reviews are a huge part of how other readers discover and judge a book. It may seem like such a small gesture but it's a small gesture that goes a long way and makes the book you loved come up in more also bought searches and has the chance to be featured in consumer newsletters.

Just a quick "I loved this book" is praise enough and encourages your favorite writers to churn out that next favorite read. So don't be shy, if you enjoyed reading, a review would mean the world for a relatively new book! You can do so by clicking here!

Evan Cattaneo was used to getting what he wanted.

The successful career. **Check.**

The Penthouse apartment overlooking the city. **Check.**

Let's not forget the drop-dead gorgeous girlfriend. **Triple Check.**

Only now, being in the relationship of his dreams, he discovers one slight problem that puts a dent in his plans for the future. His girlfriend Luz doesn't see herself getting hitched.

Forcing Evan to confront their differences and understand their conflicting ideas.

The Engagement Plan.

A trip across the country, some much-needed therapy and their ability to work together as a couple fit into that neat little package. Only the closer he comes to uncovering the truth behind her reasons, he learns a devastating secret that will affect the state of their once happy union.

<u>Pre-order now!</u>

AVAILABLE FOR PRE-ORDER: MELT FOR YOU

BOOK TWO OF THE KINKY MATCHMAKER SERIES

*L*eomie Coutard was looking to create a fresh start. New place, new job prospects, the task she's yet to conquer? Her non-existent love life. Considering her unique taste, sadly, not just any guy would do.

SHE MET the man of her dreams presenting at a kink conference a year ago, but being oceans apart forced their two-week long connection to come to an end. Or did it?

DAMIEN KARAGIANNIS COULDN'T BELIEVE his luck. Settling into a different country and a new practice left him less time to meet people, let alone date. Through a wicked twist of fate, he not only gets the chance to reconnect to his budding Dominant stranger through matchmaker Mistress Alice she ends up being a part of his surgical team.

LEOMIE CAN'T GET the intimidatingly sexy surgeon out of her system. Damien craves that soft command he once explored. Their undeniable passion will have them breaking all their rules for each other.

MELT For You is a steamy May/December romance that features a gentle Domme with an appetite for masochism and an arrogant yet romantic male submissive who wants nothing but to make her wishes come true. It is BWWM with no cheating and a guaranteed HEA. If Dominance and submission aren't your style, sit this one out. If you like a little kink, let this Alpha submissive melt his way into your heart!

<u>Pre-order now!</u>

<u>Pre-order now!</u>

LA GEEKETTE

Une nouvelle de Déjouer le système

Brenna Aubrey

Traduit par Suzanne Voogd

SILVER GRIFFON ASSOCIATES
ORANGE, CA, USA

Design de la couverture :(c) Sarah Hansen, Okay Creations

Traduction française : S. Voogd
Révision française : Valérie Dubar

ISBN 978-1-940951-49-2
Silver Griffon Associates
P.O. Box 7383
Orange, CA 92863
www.BrennaAubrey.fr

Celui-ci est pour les merveilleux membres du Brenna Aubrey Book Group sur Facebook. Pour tous les moments géniaux que nous avons passés ensemble et pour votre amour de cette histoire en particulier.

Prologue :
Je veux un nouveau jeu !

Remarque : le texte suivant doit être chanté sur l'air de 'I Want a New Drug' de Huey Lewis and the News

J'veux un nouveau jeu. Un jeu qui m'ennuie pas.

Un jeu qui m'énerve pas ni me traite comme un objet !

J'veux un nouveau jeu... qui ne rend pas malade.

Qui file des sensations.

Qui semble super réel.

Qui me fait me sentir...

Bref, vous avez compris... et maintenant vous avez la chanson de Huey Lewis and the News dans la tête. Joyeuse journée nostalgie à vous aussi !

Alors, quelqu'un a-t-il entendu parler de nouveaux jeux à l'horizon ?

J'en ai jusque là des FPS, particulièrement ceux qui sont très orientés pour les hommes ou bien ceux qui ont des filles en mini shorts, et je pense devenir folle si je dois farmer plus de minerai dans Skyrim.

J'ai romancé ma route à travers Dragon Age et j'ai bricolé partout dans Azeroth. Qu'y a-t-il d'autre ?

Je veux un nouveau jeu !

Cela fait un moment et je dois trouver des nouveaux mondes à explorer. Une nouvelle vie et de nouvelles civilisations. C'est ma mission pour les cinq ans à venir !

J'ai un peu d'espoir, cependant. Mon colocataire a réussi à obtenir un compte bêta pour un tout nouveau MMORPG, Dragon Epoch. Il peut inviter une seule personne à le rejoindre. Devinez qui lui a forcé la main a gagné le concours de colocataire la plus charmante ?

*Exactement. Moi !*Danse de Snoopy**

J'ai un nouveau jeu !

*Je dois admettre qu'après avoir étudié les visuels préliminaires, je suis un peu inquiète. Oui, mes chères lectrices, les visuels montrent les redoutables bikinis en cotte de mailles style lingerie... car rien ne dit 'guerrière hardcore' mieux qu'un soutien-gorge push-up à la Victoria's Secret dans vos teintes préférées d'inox, bronze ou chrome brillant. *Lever les yeux au ciel ici**

J'espère que le jeu se rattrapera par un bon contenu. Une geekette qui se respecte peut pardonner beaucoup de choses si on lui présente un bon jeu bien charnu dans lequel elle peut enfoncer ses crocs pointus !

Oui, les garçons, pas besoin d'avoir recours à vos blagues sur les filles et à vos idées sexistes. Les défenseurs des droits masculins peuvent s'abstenir ! Les filles peuvent être tout aussi enragées concernant leur game play que ceux qui ont les trucs qui pendent entre les jambes.

En parlant de ça, quand les garçons qui conçoivent ces jeux vont-ils se lasser de soulager leur frustration sexuelle en parsemant chaque jeu de femelles à moitié nues ? Quand verrons-nous des vêtements pour femmes plus équitables ? Ou bien... donnez-nous simplement l'équivalent en nudité masculine. Puis-je s il vous plaît avoir un guerrier viking qui part à la guerre avec ses abdos huilés et son cul ferme à peine couvert d'un petit pagne ? Ou peut-être que cette délicieuse virilité se destine à rester cachée pour toujours sous un plastron et une braguette. Vers quoi une geekette hardcore doit-elle se tourner pour se rincer l'œil virtuellement ?

Veuillez me renseigner. Et tant que vous y êtes, trouvez des développeurs de jeux qui ont des vies sexuelles normales et saines afin qu'ils aient moins tendance à afficher leurs fantasmes à l'écran. Ou même, OMG ! engagez une femme. Sinon, faites davantage correspondre les fantasmes aux miens. Muchas gracias et thank you very much !

Voilà, c'est ici que vous l'avez appris en premier. Geekette fera le bêta d'un nouveau jeu, Dragon Epoch, et je vous tiens au courant ASAP. Je me sacrifie afin que vous n'ayez pas besoin de le faire, et ne vous inquiétez pas, Mesdames, je ne ferai aucune concession, sauf si le jeu l'exige, bien sûr !

Chapitre Un :
Un tout nouveau monde

JE LUS LA CLAUSE DE NON-DIVULGATION EN DIAGONALE, cherchant les failles qui pourraient me permettre d'écrire sur le jeu. Pour une NDA, celle-ci était courte et claire…

Non-divulgation à la con. Les bêta-testeurs devaient toujours en accepter les termes, mais j'étais certaine de pouvoir contourner suffisamment la lettre de la loi pour intriguer mes lecteurs. D'accord, cela m'interdisait de discuter des mécaniques de jeux, d'objets dans le jeu et de révéler des secrets sur les quêtes. *Des détails, rien de plus.*

Après avoir signé électroniquement et envoyé le document, je relus la dernière partie de mon article de blog le plus récent, je fis quelques modifications, puis j'appuyai sur le bouton 'envoyer'. Il n'était pas facile de produire quotidiennement un nouveau contenu, mais cela valait la peine. Mon lectorat augmentait tous les jours, d'autant plus depuis que j'avais commencé à parler de Dragon Epoch.

Je n'étais pas la *seule* personne à être enthousiaste au sujet de ce jeu !

Mon regard se posa sur mon livre de cours abandonné dans un coin de mon bureau. Tout ce travail du blog de jeux vidéo ne gênait pas mes études, pour l'instant. Mais le nouveau jeu en plus du travail à l'hôpital que je venais de commencer le mois dernier m'inquiétait. Quel effet allait avoir Dragon Epoch sur la dilatation du temps ? Allait-il aspirer des heures de ma vie en un clin d'œil ? *Danger, Will Robinson* !

C'était une bonne chose que je n'ai aucune vie sociale. J'avais bien quelques connaissances dans le groupe de révisions en prépa médecine, mais quand nous étions ensemble, nous parlions de terminologie médicale, nous nous plaignions des examens à venir et nous discutions des meilleures stratégies pour gonfler nos CV pour l'École de Médecine.

Juste après avoir posté sur mon blog, l'écran de mon ordinateur craqua : des lignes et des vagues couvrirent l'écran. Je tapai sur le côté de l'écran monolithique. *Bon sang !* Il ne pouvait pas se casser maintenant. Pas alors que ce délicieux nouveau jeu se profilait à l'horizon.

Et à présent que les revenus de mon blog augmentaient – apparemment, c'était un effet secondaire des articles réguliers –, ceci était comme un deuxième travail. Cela pouvait en valoir la peine. Un jour.

Cependant, je me doutais que si je calculais exactement combien je gagnais, cela reviendrait à quelques centimes par heure. En fait, beaucoup moins que le travail d'aide-soignante.

Mais je le faisais pour mon amour de l'écriture et des discussions autour de mon passe-temps préféré : le jeu vidéo !

Au moins, écrire le blog était amusant. Pour l'instant. Je pouvais planifier l'avenir plus tard.

Juste au moment où je tapai sur mon clavier, la porte d'entrée s'ouvrit et claqua une seconde plus tard. Mon colocataire entra à temps pour voir la fin de ma crise de colère. Il fronça les sourcils en regardant la scène.

— Que se passe-t-il, Mia ?

Il jeta son sac à dos sur le canapé dont j'allais devoir le retirer quelques heures plus tard, probablement. Mon colocataire, Heath Bowman, n'était pas quelqu'un de très rangé. En vérité, c'était un porc. Mais c'était mon frère d'une autre mère, et je le tolérais. Et comme toute sœur l'aurait fait, je râlais contre lui. Souvent.

— Tu as besoin d'un nouvel écran, dit-il. En fait, tu as besoin d'un nouvel ordi, mais ce n'est pas le sujet.

— Waouh, quel merveilleux travail de déduction, Sherlock .

Je m'adossai contre ma chaise, croisant les bras et le dévisageant de haut en bas. Heath était aussi grand, puissant et pâle qu'un ancien Viking. Il était beau, bien que je n'avais jamais pensé à lui de cette façon. C'était une bonne chose, car il se trouvait qu'il était aussi homo que j'étais hétéro.

— Si je demande un rappel quand tu te produis sur scène, tu chies dans ton froc ?

Il leva les sourcils.

— Tu es bien bougonne aujourd'hui.

Je me frottai la nuque.

— Je n'ai pas très bien dormi la nuit dernière et je me suis endormie en cours de littérature ce matin. La prof m'a dénoncée. C'était gênant.

Il plissa le front.

— Pourquoi cette nouvelle phase d'insomnies ? C'est la troisième fois en quinze jours.

Je haussai les épaules.

— Je n'en sais rien. Sûrement le stress des examens.

Ouais, le redouté examen d'entrée en médecine... j'essayais de rester calme. J'étudiais au moins une heure par jour, mais à mesure que la date approchait, mon angoisse semblait monter sur l'échelle de l'anxiété.

La méditation. Il fallait que je commence la méditation pendant tout le temps libre que j'avais. Puisque les médicaments ne semblaient pas être une option viable, de toute façon.

— Tu stresses pour rien. Tu as des mois pour te préparer. Et tu apprends par osmose.

Je souris.

— Jaloux.

Il haussa les épaules. Heath n'avait jamais été très scolaire. Particulièrement pour les examens. C'était pour cela qu'il s'était inscrit dans un centre universitaire et qu'il avait déjà fini pendant que j'étais à la fac d'à côté, Chapman. Après ça, il s'était trouvé un chouette travail dans la conception de sites internet. Un travail qui lui permettait souvent de travailler chez lui.

Heath hocha la tête en direction de mon écran pénible.

— Je viens de recevoir un bonus pour avoir terminé le renouvellement du site internet de Harrison et Fils avec un mois d'avance. Je vais l'utiliser pour m'acheter un super nouvel écran et une carte vidéo, afin de pouvoir profiter de Dragon Epoch dans toute sa gloire. Je te donnerai le vieux. Et puis, plus personne n'utilise ces gros écrans cathodiques. Ils sont merdiques et prennent bien trop de place. Cet ordinateur sort tout droit du jurassique.

Je bondis de ma chaise et je passai les bras autour de son cou, l'embrassant sur la joue. Comme d'habitude, il fit la grimace requise, celle où il semblait avoir avalé un citron très acide. Heath, mon très cher ami, ne changeait pas. Il n'avait pas beaucoup changé au cours des presque dix années que je le connaissais.

— Tu es génial, mon ami. Merci.

— Eh bien, quand tu seras un médecin riche et célèbre, tu pourras me rembourser.

Je ricanai.

— C'est ce que je ferai. Des conseils médicaux gratuits à vie.

Il leva les yeux au ciel.

— Supeeeer...

Puis il disparut dans sa chambre. Le sac à dos fut évidemment abandonné et oublié jusqu'à ce que je m'assoie accidentellement dessus quelques heures plus tard.

En effet. Il ne changeait pas...

Par exemple, il tenait toujours ses promesses, et donc quelques jours plus tard seulement, Heath ramena son nouvel écran à la maison. Et, tout aussi vite, il démonta mon PC afin que cette vieille chose se remette à fonctionner.

— Bon sang, j'ai l'impression de faire une fouille archéologique, souffla-t-il en réarrangeant les cartes à l'intérieur.

Il attrapa la bombe d'air comprimé et il se mit à souffler dans les entrailles de – d'accord, je vais l'admettre à contrecœur – mon PC antique. Lorsqu'il souffla l'air froid à l'intérieur, d'immenses nuages de poussière s'élevèrent.

Brian, le petit-ami de Heath, était assis près de là et il agita les mains devant son visage en toussant de façon exagérée.

— Eh bien, quelqu'un a besoin d'apprendre à mieux faire le ménage, gronda-t-il en me jetant un regard prétentieux.

Je sentis la chaleur monter dans mes joues et mon front, une chaleur corrosive. Pourtant, je fis comme d'habitude et je me mordis la langue.

Si cette expression était prise au sens littéral et non figuré, j'aurais déjà coupé ma langue en deux !

— Tout le monde a de la poussière dans son unité centrale, rétorqua Heath pour me défendre. Le commentaire sur les fouilles archéologiques, c'était à cause de l'ancienneté de cette technologie. Toute droite sortie de la civilisation atlante de *Stargate.* Je m'attends presque à ce qu'elle ouvre un passage vers un autre monde.

Pour souligner la différence entre ma tolérance aux plaisanteries de Heath et les remarques désobligeantes de Brian, je ris.

— Tu adores les défis. Tu as toujours aimé ça.

— *Toujours aimé ça,* répéta Brian d'un ton désagréable et en faisant des guillemets avec les doigts d'un air exagéré. Vous ne vous connaissez pas depuis assez longtemps pour affirmer quelque chose de ce genre.

Je me mordis la lèvre.

— Je crois que se connaître la moitié de sa vie, ça compte.

Brian fronça les sourcils.

— Tu ne sais pas calculer.

Mon visage se remit à brûler. Heath, qui était absorbé par sa tâche – du moins, c'était ce que je pensais – leva la tête.

— Quelle importance ? aboya-t-il.

Brian ne répondit pas, se contentant de hausser les épaules et de lever les yeux au ciel. Il se leva de l'accoudoir du canapé où il était assis et il attrapa son sac de cours.

— Faut que j'y aille. À plus.

Heath se raidit lorsque Brian se dirigea tout droit vers la porte et qu'il partit sans baiser d'au revoir et sans le moindre mot gentil.

J'écarquillai les yeux, mais je ne dis rien et au bout de quelques minutes Heath s'était remis au travail. Je fronçai les sourcils en le regardant, me demandant ce qu'il se passait entre eux. Allais-je oser dire à quel point la façon dont Brian le traitait me déplaisait ?

Des marques de dents sur ma langue. C'était tout ce que j'allais avoir…

Au bout de dix autres minutes, il se redressa, s'essuyant théâtralement le front du dos de la main.

— Et voilà… l'exposition miraculeuse de mes talents en paléontologie informatique.

Je frappai dans les mains, surexcitée.

— Merci !

Il hocha brièvement la tête pour montrer qu'il avait vu ma gratitude, mais il pensait manifestement à autre chose. Peut-être à l'insolence de Brian un peu plus tôt. Je m'éclaircis la gorge.

— Alors… on se connecte sur le nouveau bêta ce soir, n'est-ce pas ? demandai-je en levant un sourcil.

Heath m'observa du coin de l'œil avant de se lever et de partir à la cuisine. D'après l'odeur, il avait préparé plus de café. Je fronçai les sourcils en le suivant. Il se passait vraiment quelque chose, c'était visible à la tension dans ses épaules et à sa posture raide.

— Vous ne vous entendez plus tous les deux ? demandai-je doucement.

Il poussa un long soupir et il haussa les épaules, mais il garda le dos tourné vers moi en continuant de préparer sa tasse de café.

Encore du silence entre nous. Je m'appuyai contre le comptoir et je croisai les bras en essayant de résister à l'envie de casser du sucre sur le dos du petit crétin. Brian semblait prendre plaisir à torturer mon meilleur ami et cela faisait ressortir mon côté ourse protectrice.

Ils sortaient ensemble depuis environ six mois et c'était houleux dès le début. Mais comme Brian était le premier petit-ami stable de Heath depuis une longue série d'amourettes, j'avais été ravie pour lui... au début. Puis j'avais commencé à voir les doutes s'entasser à chaque demande de diva que Brian imposait à Heath. Ils se disputaient beaucoup, mais Heath était amoureux et bien décidé à ce que cela fonctionne.

Je détestais – je haïssais – voir mon ami souffrir.

— C'était quoi, cette fois ? demandai-je.

Heath haussa les épaules et se tourna vers moi.

— Il veut un plus grand engagement de ma part.

Je poussai un soupir.

— Cela fait des mois que vous vous voyez exclusivement. Que veut-il d'autre ? Le mariage ?

Il grinça des dents, mais il ne répondit pas.

Je ricanai. C'était peut-être ça.

— Vas-y, mais tu seras tout seul, mon vieux. Je ne me marierai jamais.

Il leva la carafe de café devant moi comme pour me demander si j'en voulais. Je secouai la tête.

— C'est effectivement ce que tu as dit. Tu seras une nonne sans le côté religieux.

Je fis la grimace, mais je ne dis rien, attendant qu'il réponde à la question. Il passa la main dans ses cheveux blonds et il soupira.

— Il veut que nous vivions ensemble.

J'attendis une seconde qu'il continue. Deux secondes. On se regarda dans les yeux. Je haussai les épaules.

— Pourquoi ne lui demandes-tu pas d'emménager ici, dans ce cas ?

— Seuls. Juste nous deux.

Une autre seconde, gênante et poisseuse, cette fois-ci. Je détournai le regard. Que devais-je dire ? C'était évidemment son droit de vivre avec Brian – seul – s'il le voulait.

Mes mains tenaient mes bras juste au-dessus des coudes et je serrai plus fort. J'essayai de ne pas montrer à quel point j'avais mal, mais je ne pus m'empêcher de le ressentir. Je déglutis avant de parler.

— D'accord, alors.

Pendant qu'il buvait sa tasse, sa posture devint encore plus tendue, sans doute en se souvenant du conflit.

— Je lui ai dit qu'il n'y avait pas moyen. Je ne vais pas te jeter à la rue. Il a piqué une crise et affirmé que tu comptais plus pour moi que lui.

D'accord. Cela expliquait la dose supplémentaire de méchanceté cet après-midi.

J'avais très vite eu l'impression que Brian ne m'aimait pas. Je ne prétendais pas être la personne la plus appréciable qui soit, mais son comportement avait surtout ressemblé à de la jalousie. Ce qui était ridicule. Heith et moi nous n'avions pas de frères et sœurs en dehors de ce que nous étions l'un pour l'autre. Heath était cent pour cent gay et il ne s'intéresserait jamais à moi en dehors de l'amitié, ce qui me convenait tout à fait. Mais Brian était jaloux du temps que Heath passait avec moi au lieu de lui. Je me demandai en silence si ce type avait d'autres intérêts ou d'autres loisirs en dehors du fait de sortir avec Heath. Apparemment pas.

J'avais le cœur lourd et je sentis une légère pique de trahison à l'idée que Heath puisse envisager cela, mais je pris sur moi et je le libérai.

— Eh bien, tu n'as pas nécessairement besoin de me jeter à la rue, tu sais. Je peux trouver un appartement pour moi, si tu veux partager celui-ci avec lui.

Il secoua vigoureusement la tête et il reposa la tasse de café.

— Non. Tu pourrais rester ici. Je pensais m'acheter un appartement de toute façon. J'ai fait des économies et les prix de l'immobilier ne sont pas du tout mauvais en ce moment.

Je lus entre les lignes : Brian n'avait pas approuvé notre appartement. Je courbai le dos, déprimée à l'idée de vivre ici sans Heath. Nous avions vécu ensemble depuis notre première année de lycée.

À l'âge de quinze ans, il avait fait son *coming out* à ses parents, et son père l'avait jeté de la maison. Ma mère lui avait ouvert les bras et il était devenu un hôte permanent du B&B de la famille. Après le lycée, nous avions tous deux déménagé à Orange County, et il avait été mon colocataire pendant les trois années passées.

J'essayai de ne pas paraître aussi désespérée et vide que je me sentais.

— Je ne pourrais pas me permettre de vivre ici toute seule et je ne sais pas à qui je pourrais demander d'emménager. Reste et je trouverai quelque chose. Peut-être une chambre universitaire près de la fac.

Heath pinça si fort les lèvres ensemble que celles-ci blanchirent.

— Je déteste vraiment ça.

Moi aussi... mais je ne voulais pas du tout le faire choisir entre son petit-ami et moi.

— Je ne vais pas être la raison de tes problèmes avec Brian, d'accord ? Il n'y a pas de soucis. Tout ce que je demande, c'est que tu me laisses un peu de temps pour trouver quelque chose.

Je levai la tête vers lui, déplaçant mon poids afin de m'appuyer contre le comptoir.

— Se calmera-t-il si tu lui dis que je cherche et que j'ai une date de déménagement ? Disons dans un ou deux mois ?

— Pas moins de deux mois. Et si tu as besoin de plus...

Je secouai catégoriquement la tête.

— Je n'ai pas besoin de plus. Ça ira. Appelle-le et fais-lui savoir que nous y travaillons.

Heath hocha la tête, mais il ne parut pas ravi. Et bien que je déteste voir mon meilleur ami dans une relation compliquée, je ne pouvais nier l'autosatisfaction que je ressentais à avoir évité, à l'âge mûr de vingt et un ans, les tenants et les aboutissants des relations romantiques. J'avais appris à mes dépens et à un très jeune âge que les relations amoureuses n'étaient absolument pas faites pour moi !

Beurk. Il était temps de changer de sujet.

— Alors, en ce qui concerne le bêta de ce nouveau jeu... dis-je en agitant les sourcils.

Heath sourit, visiblement soulagé.

— Ouais ? Il a l'air énorme, hein ? Les dessins. La bande-annonce... de super dragons. Des quêtes dynamiques. Je pense que je suis mort et que je me suis rendu au paradis des geeks. Ou que c'est pour bientôt.

J'acquiesçai.

— On dirait que cela pourrait devenir addictif. Tu me promets que nous nous connecterons ce soir ? Je crois que mon ordinateur possède les caractéristiques minimales pour le faire tourner si j'éteins tous les effets supplémentaires.

— *Tout juste, monsieur*, dit-il en imitant l'accent de Scotty dans Star Trek. Les processeurs ne peuvent pas en supporter davantage, capitaine !

— Eh bien, c'est tout ce que j'ai. Et puisque je suis ta gameuse qui déchire préférée…

Il attrapa la tasse sur le comptoir et il se remit à boire.

— Tu ne serais même pas accro aux jeux vidéo sans moi…

— Espèce de *dealer*, dis-je en pointant un doigt sur son grand torse.

Il me sourit.

— Droguée. Je ne suis pas celui qui a passé vingt-quatre heures sans arrêter sur Dragon Age. Ça, c'était toi, poupée.

Je poussai un soupir rêveur en me souvenant avec tendresse de ce merveilleux jeu.

— Oh, Alistair…

Heath posa sa tasse de café et ramassa son téléphone. En inspirant profondément, il se mit à envoyer un texto à Brian.

— D'accord, rendez-vous est pris. Toi et moi, ce soir. Brian sera apaisé et il travaille ce soir, de toute façon.

— Mmm, c'est bon à savoir, dis-je en me tournant pour quitter la cuisine.

J'avais réussi à ne pas lever les yeux au ciel à cause de Brian la catastrophe tant que je n'avais pas tourné le dos à Heath.

Tout juste, monsieur…

Chapitre Deux : Lorsqu'Eloisa rencontra FallenOne

LA SOIREE DONNA L'OCCASION TANT ATTENDUE DE BETA-tester le nouveau jeu Dragon Epoch. Enfin un jeu immersif auquel je pouvais jouer après des mois d'attente durant lesquels j'avais rejoué à de vieux jeux. Malgré les visuels, qui montraient des mannequins en petite tenue peintes sous la forme d'elfes agiles avec de grands seins défiant toute gravité, il semblait prometteur. Je fis donc craquer mes articulations – de façon figurée – et je m'assis devant mon clavier, prête à *pwn* ce jeu.

— Waouh, regarde ces graphismes, dit Heath depuis son bureau pendant qu'il examinait le paysage fantastique sur son écran haute définition tout neuf.

Je luttai pour ne pas être jalouse de lui depuis qu'il l'avait acheté, d'autant plus que j'avais au moins reçu son vieil écran. Sans lui, je ne verrais pas de graphismes du tout.

Je retournai à mon écran, émerveillée par les représentations artistiques et colorées du paysage fantastique. Des montagnes escarpées au loin, des clairières jaunes, de petits ruisseaux qui coulaient… des forêts luxuriantes. Même avec les options d'affichage au plus bas afin de pouvoir utiliser le minimum de ressources de mon ordinateur, c'était à couper le souffle. J'avais lu qu'à mesure que le temps passait, le jeu allait suivre la transformation des saisons. Il me tardait de le voir.

— C'est parti ! dis-je une fois que j'eus fini l'écran de création du personnage.

J'avais choisi une enchanteresse spirituelle elfe avec de longs cheveux noirs et des yeux d'un violet très vif. Je l'appelai Eloisa. Bien sûr, la pauvre n'avait pas le moindre bout de tissu décent pour se vêtir. Ses fesses étaient à l'air libre, pleinement exposées aux éléments et aux regards masculins, bien sûr. Je grinçai des dents en me promettant de lui trouver une armure pourrie dès que possible.

— Cette espèce de vieil elfe veut que j'aille ramasser des fleurs pour lui, grommela Heath. Quelle quête stupide !

Après avoir exploré quelques minutes, nous nous trouvâmes à l'extérieur des murailles de la ville. Et en effet, Heath avait découvert une quête auprès d'un elfe âgé vêtu d'un uniforme militaire étrange mis en valeur par un kilt.

— Ooh... c'est tellement mignon ! dis-je. Il a perdu son véritable amour et il veut se souvenir d'elle en apportant des fleurs dans un sanctuaire à son nom. Je pense que c'est vraiment romantique.

— Que sais-tu de la romance ? demanda Heath. La fille qui ne sort jamais avec qui que ce soit. La fille qui ne sort jamais tout court. Oublie la *geekette*, tu es l'*ermite*.

Je ris.

— La vie sociale, c'est tellement surestimé. En particulier quand on a un jeu de ce genre auquel on peut jouer chez soi avec son meilleur ami.

Après une heure de notre nouvelle addiction, je vis que cela n'allait faire que s'améliorer : notre plaisir à jouer ; et empirer : notre addiction. Cela dépendait du point de vue.

Le général SylvanWood – 'l'espèce de vieil elfe' – nous remercia d'avoir complété la quête. Ensuite, il fit rapidement référence à un autre personnage non joueur (PNJ) qui déclencha encore une autre chaîne de quêtes intéressante. Chaque mission nous menait de plus en plus loin dans le monde virtuel.

Oui, il y avait de quoi se fatiguer : quel jeu correct n'avait pas son lot de basses besognes pour augmenter le niveau des personnages ? Mais c'était essentiellement une histoire immersive pleine de graphismes magnifiques et de détails intrigants qui encourageaient l'exploration.

Ce jeu était comme du crack, ou pire, des métamphétamines. Et on était à fond rien qu'en courant autour de Yondareth, le monde de Dragon Epoch étant notre échappatoire la plus récente et la plus intéressante.

Il me tardait de voir qui d'autre partageait ce superbe monde virtuel. Apparemment, je n'avais pas besoin d'être une ermite, car nous rencontrâmes notre premier ami ce soir-là : une soigneuse humaine du nom de Persephone, comme la déesse des enfers. Cette rencontre se fit simplement grâce à son tag LFG, qui l'identifiait comme cherchant un groupe : 'Looking For a Group'. Nous étions justement tous les deux à la recherche de soins après nos combats.

Heath avait créé un barbare mercenaire, un énorme guerrier qui surplombait mon elfe menue et timide. Fragged était aussi grand et musclé que Heath dans la vraie vie, avec des muscles par-dessus les muscles. En ce qui me concernait, il était une machine qui absorbait les coups, j'aimais l'appeler mon bouclier de chair.

— Waouh, c'est intéressant, mais j'ai déjà quelques critiques, dit Heath. Il y a beaucoup de belles choses à regarder pour les hommes hétéros. Pas tellement d'hommes canon pour les gays.

— Ou les filles hétéros, ajoutai-je. Ne nous oublie pas !

Il rit.

— Je n'en ai pas l'intention, mais je crois que le jeu vous a oubliées. Bon sang, regarde les bonnets D sur cette maman valkyrie. N'est-ce pas douloureux de courir partout avec ce genre de décor sur le capot avant ?

Je regardai par-dessus son épaule et je vis l'avatar d'un joueur inconnu pendant que notre amie Persephone gloussait sur le chat vocal.

Je ricanai.

— Dix contre un que c'est un garçon qui joue avec. Et il a utilisé les fonctions de personnalisation pour la rendre plus pulpeuse que Dolly Parton.

— Euh... Tu veux l'inviter dans notre groupe pour le découvrir ?

Et bingo, j'avais raison. C'était un type... de moins de dix-huit ans. Je faillis tomber par terre lorsque Persephone lui demanda directement s'il était un homme et quel âge il avait. Je dus sérieusement poser la main sur mon micro parce que je riais trop fort. Même Heath eut du mal à rester sérieux en se liant d'amitié avec le jeune homme à peine pubère.

On le rejoignit encore quelques fois après cette première nuit, plaisantant toujours entre nous au sujet des mangues, melons ou pastèques ou quel que soit le fruit que nous choisissions pour les comparer ce jour-là. Heureusement que les fabricants de soutiens-gorges de Yondareth étaient suffisamment travailleurs pour inventer un soutien adéquat, même avant l'époque des armatures. De la très bonne ingénierie gnome à notre portée !

Je ne m'autorisai à me connecter qu'après avoir fait mes devoirs, ainsi que l'heure ou deux de révisions nécessaires pour l'examen. Des heures réduites à mon travail à l'hôpital à cause de différents problèmes d'emploi du temps firent que j'eus la chance de pouvoir me connecter tous les soirs pendant le bêta-test.

En dehors du fait que Persephone comprenait vraiment notre humour, on sembla bien s'entendre immédiatement. Et plus nous la rejoignions, plus nous apprenions à la connaître.

— Presque plus de mana. Nous avons besoin d'un léger break après le combat suivant, annonça-t-elle après une salle particulièrement difficile que nous avions passée dans des grottes souterraines menant jusqu'à la salle du trône du roi Minotaure.

On discuta pendant qu'elle régénérait son mana : la barre bleue qui lui permettait de lancer des sorts.

— Alors… où vivez-vous ?

Elle avait déjà compris que nous étions colocataires.

— SoCal. Et toi ? Ce doit être la côte ouest, puisque nous nous trouvons sur le même fuseau horaire.

— Colombie-Britannique, répondit Persephone.

— Waouh, une amatrice de bière et de poutine, hein ? la taquina Heath.

— La poutine, c'est dégoûtant. La bière en revanche, c'est très important, répondit-elle.

— Tu travailles ? Ou tu es à la fac ?

— Les deux. Je fais baby-sitter d'ordinateurs la nuit en tant qu'opératrice système. Le jour, je suis à la fac Simon Fraser. Le sommeil, c'est en option.

On lui donna nos informations ainsi que nos véritables prénoms. Elle nous dit qu'elle s'appelait Katya.

Je n'avais fait qu'essayer quelques jeux de MMORPG avant celui-ci *tousse* World of Warcraft, *tousse*, mais à présent j'appréciais vraiment l'attrait de jouer avec de nouvelles personnes. Avant, je m'étais vite fatiguée des joueurs désagréables qui s'amusent à rendre la vie misérable à tous les autres joueurs autour d'eux. Les conditions d'utilisation de ce jeu dictaient très clairement que ce comportement ne serait pas toléré.

Les quêtes que nous entreprîmes nous conduisirent dans des espaces plus étendus et plus dangereux qui nous menèrent à d'autres quêtes encore. En fait, le jeu semblait être constitué de quêtes après quêtes après quêtes interminables. Et j'adorais chaque minute, même quand je m'ennuyais, car la compagnie était fabuleuse. D'un autre côté, chaque jeu a ses moments ennuyeux, mais nécessaires, alors au moins ce jeu-ci avait une histoire intéressante derrière même la plus simple des quêtes. Par exemple, on nous demandait de nous rendre dans un champ et de ramasser un bouquet de jonquilles pour un gentil elfe sénile en l'honneur de son amour perdu.

Katya devint rapidement celle que l'on contactait pour travailler ensemble sur les quêtes et le levelling. Et bien que nous en étions venus à dépendre les uns des autres, il fut évident que nous avions besoin de quelqu'un qui puisse causer plus de dégâts afin de pouvoir tuer les monstres plus vite. Il s'avéra que je croisai un tel personnage, le jour où il faillit me faire tuer.

Je m'occupais de mes petites affaires, rassemblant des informations sur le jeu pour en parler éventuellement dans mon blog, une fois que l'accord de non-divulgation serait levé, bien sûr. Ce soir-là, j'étais toute seule et je testais mes aptitudes à me battre contre les mobs.

Sans mes deux compères pour m'aider, j'attaquai quelques gnolls pénibles qui gardaient l'entrée d'un monticule devant leur terrier. Avec mon niveau du moment, combattre ces deux-là était difficile, mais je poussai mes capacités d'enchanteresse au maximum de leur potentiel. Pendant que j'en ensorcelais un afin qu'il ne bouge plus, je tapai sur son compagnon qui jappait. L'homme hyène m'infligea quelques gros coups avant que je me débarrasse de lui.

Malheureusement, alors qu'il tombait à terre et que je reportais mon attention sur le gnoll qui se balançait sur ses pieds en attendant ma fureur magique, un lancier incapable apparut de nulle part pour aider à me 'sauver'.

Le truc lorsque l'on ensorcelle les mobs dans une transe, c'est que lorsqu'ils se réveillent, ils sont furax contre la personne qui les a ensorcelés. Alors bien que cet étrange petit toon avec sa longue barbe blanche commence à attaquer le gnoll pour moi avec sa lance gigantesque, l'homme hyène me poursuivit moi, à la place !

Comme j'étais une magicienne facilement écrasée, il ne me restait pas beaucoup de points de vie. Quelques coups suffisaient à me faire mal. Très mal.

Bon sang, écrivis-je tout en lançant un sort de 'mémoire embrouillée' qui allait supprimer la haine que me portait le gnoll, mais également donner tout le crédit de l'attaque au lancier. *Pourquoi attaques-tu mon gnoll ?*

Le lancier continua à frapper la créature hyène. Il répondit : *Je t'aide. J'ai vu qu'il y avait deux mobs contre toi. Je ne voulais pas que tu te fasses tuer.*

Je lançai mon plus gros sort explosif et je brûlai la moitié des points de vie du gnoll. *Je gérais. Il était ensorcelé.*

Le lancier – FallenOne d'après l'étiquette bleue au-dessus de sa tête – se retira immédiatement. *Oh merde, je suis désolé. Je croyais que tu avais des ennuis. Je n'ai pas vu que tu avais la situation sous contrôle.*

T'es vraiment un noob, répondis-je. *Ne frappe jamais un mob ensorcelé, sinon tu profites de la mort du monstre et tu pompes les points d'expérience d'un autre joueur.*

Pour ce que ça vaut, je ne suis pas certain d'avoir déjà vu une magicienne jouer de cette façon... répondit-il. *C'est une classe de perso difficile à jouer en solo.*

Je jetai mon dernier sort et le corps du gnoll tomba à terre. Pendant ce temps, FallenOne posa un genou à terre. Son message privé s'afficha sur mon écran. *Mes excuses, ma dame. Je n'essayais pas de voler ton mob. Comment puis-je me faire pardonner ?*

Je tapotai ma lèvre de l'index en réfléchissant. Était-il sincère, ou bien n'était-ce qu'un bleu préadolescent qui essayait d'entrer dans mes bonnes grâces afin que je lui jette quelques bons sorts musclés avant de reprendre sa route ?

D'un autre côté, avec cette lance, sa classe de personnage faisait beaucoup de dégâts par seconde (DPS). Cela pouvait être intéressant... à condition qu'il ne fût pas un noob idiot.

Mon groupe aurait bien besoin d'un peu de DPS, si tu n'es pas un trop grand noob, écrivis-je.

Il s'inclina très bas. *Je promets de ne plus merder.*

Je marquai une pause. Je supposai que nous pouvions le tester et voir s'il prouvait un peu sa valeur.

Joue avec nous pendant une heure. Si tu es utile, nous te garderons peut-être plus longtemps. Je me mordis la lèvre pour lutter contre un sourire diabolique. Waouh, je pouvais être vraiment affreuse quand je le voulais. Mais bon, en toute probabilité, il était possible qu'il ne se rende même pas au rendez-vous.

Demain soir, vingt et une heures HNP. Rejoins-nous aux portes de la cité et nous nous rassemblerons.

Sans hésitation, il s'inclina encore. *Je suis votre serviteur, ma dame.*

Je levai les sourcils. En tout cas, il parlait comme le voulait la période. Peut-être avait-il plus d'expérience dans les jeux de fantasy qu'il ne l'avait montré lors de cette première rencontre.

J'entamai le processus de sortie du jeu en faisant asseoir mon personnage. Il fallait environ trente secondes. Juste avant de disparaître, je lui répondis : *Nous verrons. Demain. Vingt et une heures.*

Je finis la journée par des révisions pour l'examen. Avec un peu de chance, si j'étudiais deux heures aujourd'hui, cela compenserait le fait de travailler à l'hôpital le lendemain puis de jouer avec le groupe plus tard dans la soirée.

Lorsque nous nous connectâmes à l'heure prévue, FallenOne était en ligne et il nous attendait. Surprise, même un peu impressionnée, j'expliquai rapidement ce qu'il s'était passé aux autres membres du groupe dans le chat vocal. Puis, j'invitai FallenOne à nous rejoindre.

Contrairement à Heath, Katya et moi, FallenOne n'utilisa pas la fonction de chat vocal. Il dit que c'était parce que son équipement ne fonctionnait pas.

Peut-être ne sait-il pas comment se servir correctement de la fonction. J'ai l'impression que c'est un peu un noob, dis-je dans un message privé à Heath et Katya – qui nous avait dit que nous pouvions l'appeler 'Kat'.

Ou alors il est juste timide, répondit Kat.

Ou bien c'est un étudiant pauvre avec un équipement merdique. Pourquoi voulez-vous toujours interpréter les choses, les filles ? Comme d'habitude, Heath devait nous remettre à nos places.

La beauté des MMOs, c'était que les gens les plus introvertis devenaient extravertis par nécessité.

Malgré ma rencontre initiale douteuse avec FallenOne, on finit par le trouver très utile. Il avait une bonne connaissance du jeu, ce qui était vital pour ceux parmi nous – c'est-à-dire, nous trois – qui cherchions toujours à découvrir comment fonctionnaient les choses.

Les quêtes sont à plusieurs niveaux et fermées, expliqua-t-il. *Alors il vous faut finir les quêtes de bas niveau en premier afin que les quêtes plus élevées s'ouvrent à vous. Elles sont liées. Comme un réseau.*

Cela ne faisait qu'environ dix jours que nous jouions à ce jeu, alors je fus stupéfaite. J'étais également surprise qu'il soit toujours au même niveau que nous.

— Comment se fait-il que tu en saches autant sur ce jeu ? demanda Persephone lors de notre première soirée ensemble en tant que groupe.

Je me promène, fut sa seule réponse. *Il y a eu un test alpha fermé avant ça, vous savez. Ceci est peut-être le bêta fermé, mais le bêta stress ouvre dans deux semaines seulement. Vous serez tous des experts par rapport aux gens du bêta ouvert !*

Il y eut une longue pause parmi nous.

— D'accooord. FallenOne, tu es officiellement l'homme mystère, déclara Heath.

Exactement comme j'aime, répondit Fallen.

— Je suppose donc que nous ne pourrons pas savoir ton a/s/l ? plaisanta Kat.

Il donna une réponse sarcastique : *a = assez vieux pour faire preuve de bon sens, s = oui, aussi souvent que possible, et l = ici et là.*

— Et Yondareth, bien sûr, dis-je d'un ton espiègle. Où les seins défient les lois de la gravité et les hommes sont joyeux, forts et attrayants pour tout le monde. Sauf pour ceux qui sont attirés par les hommes, dis-je en riant lorsque Heath fit la grimace.

Attends, quoi ? demanda Fallen.

Ah, bien sûr, il ne l'avait pas remarqué. Voir des femmes si peu vêtues dans un univers de fantasy était devenu la norme, à tel point que la plupart des hommes l'acceptaient sans se poser de questions. Encore un mâle ignorant à éduquer ! La Geekette se sacrifia encore une fois afin que le reste des femmes n'ait pas besoin de le faire, sauf si elles en avaient envie, bien sûr.

— Je veux juste dire qu'à mon avis les créateurs du jeu ne se rendent pas compte qu'il y a des femmes qui jouent aussi.

Je suis sûr qu'ils le savent. Pourquoi pas ? Mais bien sûr, ils vont davantage essayer de vendre le jeu aux hommes. Après tout, les statistiques sont ce qu'elles sont et la majorité des joueurs de ce type de jeu est masculine.

— Pff, ouais, dis-je. Et ça ne changera pas sauf s'ils se calment un peu sur l'armure-lingerie qui ne cache rien et les nichons gigantesques.

Je n'ai rien contre les nichons gigantesques. J'adore une belle paire de nichons.

— Dans ce cas, ils devraient nous donner quelques beaux paquets en contrepartie, dit Heath.

— Ou des abdos luisants ! ajoutai-je.

Mais, en tant que fille, ne veux-tu pas que ton personnage soit sexy dans le jeu ?

— Les filles peuvent aussi foutre des branlées, pas juste servir de régal pour les yeux, intervint Kat.

Je suis certain que les producteurs du jeu apprécieraient ce genre de retour de la part des bêta testeurs. 'Plus de régal pour les yeux pour les personnages féminins.'

— Ou encore mieux, égalité des chances dans le régal pour les yeux ! Je pense que je vais soumettre ça à la boîte à idées virtuelle, dis-je d'un ton dégoulinant de sarcasme. Dommage que ce soit immédiatement jeté avant même d'être lu.

Hmm. Le sarcasme est très fort chez celle-ci.

— Oh, Fallen, tu n'as pas idée, dit Heath. Je vis avec Sa Majesté, la monarque absolue de Tout Sarcasme. Et crois-moi, il lui en reste encore beaucoup plus.

— J'ai des exutoires lorsque le sarcasme déborde, dis-je.

Je me demande si le jeu pourra être à la hauteur de tes exigences extrêmement élevées, Eloisa.

— En effet, la plume est plus forte que l'épée, répondit Heath. Dans ce cas précis, littéralement : la plume virtuelle devient plus puissante que l'épée virtuelle de Yondareth.

Tu es écrivain ?

Je fis signe à Heath de se taire, mais il cracha le morceau bien trop tôt.

— Pire. C'est une blogueuse, cher ami.

Je lui fis un doigt au-dessus de la table que nous partagions et il me tira la langue.

Tu tiens un blog ? Sur quoi ? Le jeu vidéo ? La photo ? Le tricot ?

Heath éclata de rire et avant qu'il puisse répondre, j'intervins :

— Heath n'a pas le droit de donner plus d'informations au sujet de mon blog, sinon il encourt la peine de mort. Et *crois-moi*, je peux la rendre très pénible.

— Elle écrit sur le féminisme et les jeux vidéo. Tu vois ? Je n'ai pas peur de toi !

Heath me fit un clin d'œil.

Je couvris le micro et je me tournai vers Heath.

— Il pourrait être un de ces gamers masculins activistes. On ne sait jamais.

Heath coupa son propre micro et secoua la tête.

— Je les reconnais à des kilomètres. Ils se révèlent très rapidement. FallenOne et moi nous discutons par MPs depuis le début de la soirée. Je sais qu'il est cool.

Ah, c'est cool, ça. J'aimerais le lien. Faut que je le lise.

Heath me regarda en levant les sourcils.

— Tu vois ? Et puis, ce n'est pas comme s'il savait où nous trouver. Ce sont des personnages bêta. Nous pouvons les laisser tomber quand nous voulons et prendre de nouveaux noms. Voilà, c'est magique, aucun harceleur ne saurait où nous trouver dans le jeu.

Je m'adressai à Fallen dans mon micro.

— Les commentaires désobligeants sont interdits. Et tu ne dois pas me griller. Je ne révèle jamais mon nom de personnage ni le serveur sur lequel je joue.

Mais Heath n'avait pas tort : si Fallen faisait un mauvais coup, il était encore tôt. Peut-être était-ce un bon révélateur de la confiance que nous pouvions avoir en lui. S'il devenait quelqu'un de régulier dans notre groupe, il fallait que je sache si je pouvais lui confier des informations sensibles. Quelle meilleure façon que de le tester maintenant, quand nos personnages étaient encore jetables ?

Tu ne te fais quand même pas harceler, si ?

Je haussai les épaules.

— Parfois. Mais rien de sérieux, heureusement.

J'avais de la chance. Certaines femmes avaient été harcelées sérieusement pour avoir ouvert leur bouche dans le monde masculin du jeu vidéo. Avec même des menaces de violences et de cyberattaques. C'était affreux. J'avais eu de la chance grâce à ma plate-forme plus petite.

Heath se mit à taper furieusement sur son clavier et je supposai qu'il envoyait le lien du blog à Fallen. Enfin… je postais mes pensées sur ce blog, afin que le monde les lise. Pourquoi pas le pauvre gars timide que nous avions rejoint pour la soirée ?

Alors, depuis combien de temps sortez-vous ensemble, tous les deux ? demanda soudain Fallen.

— Lesquels deux ? demanda Heath. Nous deux ?

Heath leva la tête vers moi et je me mis à ricaner très fort.

— Ce n'est pas si drôle, dit Heath en souriant. Fallen, nous ne sortons pas ensemble. Nous sommes simplement frères et sœurs mutuellement adoptés et maintenant colocataires. J'aime les hommes. Elle, elle n'aime personne.

Je me mordis la lèvre, mais je hochai la tête, approuvant son explication.

— Ooh, peut-être que Fallen aime les hommes, lui aussi ! Dommage que tu sois pris.

Heath posa la main sur le micro et dit :

— Ce type est un facteur docile de la quarantaine qui vit dans la cave de sa mère, tu veux parier ?

Je haussai les épaules. J'espérais bien que non. FallenOne était intrigant, mais son côté secret m'inquiétait. Il y avait des chances pour que Heath soit plus près de la vérité que je ne voulais l'admettre.

Kat avait été informée de mon blog plus tôt dans la semaine et elle m'avait dit qu'elle en avait déjà lu une partie et que cela lui avait plu. Elle m'avait même demandé si j'avais besoin d'articles de la part d'invités. Étant donné son talent aux jeux, ce serait super de l'engager… gratuitement, bien sûr.

— Nous sommes quatre dans ce groupe. Nous pourrions recruter une cinquième personne et commencer une guilde, dit soudain Kat. On pourrait s'appeler les *Misfits* !

Heath fit une grimace.

— Ce n'est pas très authentique pour la période.

Je ne peux pas rejoindre une guilde, je suis désolé, répondit FallenOne. *En fait, je dois partir. Je suis épuisé au-delà de tout. Vous m'avez retenu en otage avec vos bavardages amusants. J'avais presque oublié que je dois me lever trèèèès tôt demain matin.*

Je fronçai les sourcils en regardant l'horloge. Merde, il était déjà minuit et le temps était passé sans que je m'en aperçoive. J'avais cours très tôt le lendemain matin.

— Beurk, moi aussi, je dois partir. Labo d'analyse chimique demain matin.

Tu es une chimiste ?

— Prépa médecine, répondis-je.

— Ouais, c'est une intello. Elle gaspille la majeure partie de son temps à étudier, même quand j'essaie de l'en détourner avec des jeux vidéo. C'est vraiment une fêtarde…

Je me mordis la lèvre, habituée à la description qu'il m'appliquait depuis des années. Oui, j'étais une élève brillante, et j'en étais fière. Et il fallait vraiment, *vraiment* que je le sois, étant donné mes ambitions. Certaines personnes se vantaient de descriptions physiques flatteuses. Moi, j'étais fière de mon cerveau au-dessus de la moyenne. Cela suffisait à éloigner la plupart des hommes. En général, ils étaient facilement intimidés par une femme intelligente.

— On verra si tout est pour rien quand je passerai le MCAT.

Qu'est-ce que c'est ?

— C'est le concours d'entrée en école de médecine, le 'Medical College Admissions Test'. Celui qu'il faut avoir pour faire des études de médecine. Quatre mois encore.

Je poussai un soupir tendu et nerveux, sentant à nouveau l'angoisse familière peser sur moi. Pour contrer cela, je me promis de passer mon repas de midi à étudier au lieu de regarder de vieilles rediffusions à la télé ou de me connecter au jeu.

Eh bien, vous tous, c'était sympa de vous rencontrer. Peut-être nous reverrons-nous un de ces jours.

— Tu devrais nous rejoindre une autre fois, Fallen, dit Kat. On est très amusants et on aurait bien besoin de plus de DPS de lancier.

Peut-être ! Je suis un peu un électron libre, mais je vous chercherai à l'occasion. Je vous ai tous ajoutés à ma liste d'amis.

— Pareil, répondit Heath.

Et puis il disparut.

— Eh bien, il est étrange, celui-là, dit Heath quand on se déconnecta.

Je haussai les épaules.

— Il est timide. Mais il a l'air sympa.

— On ne le reverra jamais, intervint Kat. Soit il va passer un autre bêta-test, ou bien il trouvera un nouveau personnage quand celui-ci l'ennuiera. Un des problèmes avec les MMORPG, c'est que l'on rencontre de nouvelles personnes, on se lie d'amitié, on traîne ensemble, on s'amuse et puis la personne disparaît sans laisser de trace. J'ai déjà vécu ça.

Je haussai encore les épaules.

— Ben, ce serait nul, mais je suppose que c'est ainsi…

— Allez-vous tous, moi aussi, je m'en vais. Bonne nuit ! dit Katya.

Heath leva les bras au-dessus de la tête en s'étirant.

— Bonne nuit, Kat. Il est temps que l'on s'arrête, nous aussi. Je dois me lever demain matin et aider Brian à poster une partie de ses affaires sur eBay.

Je levai les sourcils.

— Ah, alors il se prépare au déménagement ?

Il s'éclaircit la gorge, l'air gêné et selon moi, un peu coupable.

— Oui.

Je haussai les épaules et je lui fis un sourire en coin pour l'aider à détourner sa culpabilité.

— J'ai un peu de temps libre ce week-end pour chercher des appartements. J'en ai quelques-uns qui m'intéressent. Je te raconterai ça.

— Dis-le-moi, si tu veux que je t'accompagne.

— Je pense qu'il vaut mieux que tu aides Brian. Mais si jamais j'ai du mal à me décider, tu choisiras de quel côté penche la balance, d'accord ?

Il hocha la tête, n'ayant toujours pas l'air ravi. J'avais l'impression qu'il avait envie d'exercer un certain contrôle sur l'endroit où j'allais déménager. Mais il fallait qu'il accepte que j'étais une grande fille maintenant et que cette étape, je devais l'entreprendre seule.

Nous partîmes ensuite nous coucher. Et je ne pus pas m'en souvenir complètement après, mais j'aurais pu jurer avoir rêvé d'un geek gamer qui, au lieu d'être un facteur dégarni de la quarantaine, était grand, aux cheveux sombres, et canon. Avec des kilomètres de muscles et une voix sexy.

Ha. Si seulement.

Chapitre Trois :
Le mystère de FallenOne.

« QUINZE QUESTIONS : QUELLE EST TA FAÇON DE jouer ? » – posté sur le blog de *Geekette*

Il y a ce meme qui flotte partout sur les sites de jeux vidéo, et on m'a demandé de participer. Pourquoi pas ? Geekette est toujours prête à jouer le jeu (vous avez vu le jeu de mots ?).

Sans plus tarder...

Geekette répond à Quinze questions :

1. Quel est ton nom de gamer / gameuse ?

Euh. C'est Geekette. Oui ? Je ne surprends personne !

2. PC ou Console ?

PC. Je ne possède même pas de console. D'accord, mon PC est juste un cube de boulons rouillés, mais je peux jouer à mes jeux préférés en ajustant l'affichage des graphismes et les effets sonores au minimum. J'espère bientôt renouveler mon matériel, mais c'est dur financièrement ! Au moins, je peux toujours m'en servir pour mon blog, n'est-ce pas ?

3. Clavier ou manette ?

Clavier. Je ne suis pas très distinguée !

4. *Solo ou multijoueur ?*

Multijoueur, même si j'adore certains jeux en solo. Il y a quelque chose dans la camaraderie de travailler ensemble vers le même but. J'aime également rencontrer de nouvelles personnes dans les jeux. J'ai rencontré quelques amis fantastiques grâce à ma nouvelle obsession, Dragon Epoch.

5. *Quel a été le premier jeu auquel tu as joué ?*

Final Fantasy – je ne sais même plus lequel.

6. *Le jeu le plus dur que tu aies fait ?*

N'importe quel jeu de tir subjectif (FPS). Parce que je suis nulle. De toute façon, je n'ai jamais envie de tirer sur qui que ce soit. Je préfère les zapper avec des éclairs ou des boules de feu !

7. *Quel est ton jeu préféré de tous les temps ?*

Legend of Zelda ! Les jeux old-school sont cool.

8. *Quel jeu est en ce moment ton préféré ?*

Dragon Epoch est le jeu qui bouffe ma vie. J'adore chaque seconde, malgré mes petites bêtes noires !

9. *Genre préféré de jeux vidéo ?*

MMORPG, ou presque n'importe quel jeu de rôle.

10. *Personnage de jeu vidéo préféré ?*

Le choix est difficile entre Lara Croft de Tomb Raider – parce qu'elle est badass – et Alistair, de Dragon Age Origins, qui me fait rêver. Il est peut-être fait de pixels, mais Mesdames, il est parfait.

11. *Quel personnage de jeu vidéo détestes-tu le plus ?*

Wirt à la jambe de bois dans Diablo. Parce que vraiment, pourquoi, mais pourquoi continuons nous à faire confiance à ce petit crétin qui escroque les héros de Tristram depuis des années ?

12. *Quels systèmes de jeu possèdes-tu en ce moment ?*

Mon PC est tout ce dont j'ai besoin. Je suis une gameuse PC et j'en suis fière. Je laisse les jeux de console aux autres.

13. *Depuis combien de temps joues-tu aux jeux vidéo ?*

J'ai commencé en première année de lycée quand je suis restée absente une partie de l'année à cause d'une maladie. Mon meilleur ami m'a présenté le monde du jeu vidéo. Il est venu vivre avec ma famille peu de temps après et nous sommes devenus accros co-dépendants aux jeux vidéo. Nous avons essayé tout ce qu'il y avait à essayer, mais comme je l'ai dit, je préfère les RPG aux FPS, alors que mon meilleur ami n'est pas aussi exigeant. En gros, si ça a des pixels et que ça fait 'bip', il adore.

14. *Combien de temps a duré ta plus longue séance de jeux ?*

Euh... est-ce que je veux vraiment l'avouer ? J'ai déjà fait une nuit blanche, c'est-à-dire vingt-quatre heures complètes !

15. *À quel jeu as-tu joué le plus longtemps ?*

Difficile à dire... le vieux record était Final Fantasy, mais avec un peu de temps, je suis certaine que Dragon Epoch prendra le dessus. Ça devient vite une addiction. Que puis-je dire ? Je n'ai jamais vraiment cherché à connaître les heures que j'ai passées à jouer. J'ai peur de voir exactement quelle portion de ma vie a été absorbée par le jeu ! Peur, je vous dis. L'ignorance est une bénédiction !

Voilà donc mon meme. J'espère qu'il vous a plu. Comme toujours, laissez vos questions et réponses dans les commentaires, mais ne me charriez pas à ce sujet, sinon je vous supprime.

***

Un message privé de FallenOne clignota sur mon écran sous la forme d'un texte violet.

*FallenOne dit : *J'ai lu ton blog.*

Il m'avait surprise le lendemain alors que je travaillais toute seule sur le jeu. Heath était toujours avec Brian et après avoir passé quelques heures à m'entraîner au concours, j'avais besoin d'une pause. J'étais donc allée courir, puis je m'étais connectée afin de découvrir le système de création d'objets et de commerce dans le jeu.

Ce que je préférais, et de loin, c'était les quêtes et l'exploration de nouveaux territoires. Cependant, je pensais que mes lecteurs auraient des questions au sujet d'autres aspects du jeu une fois qu'il sortirait officiellement et que l'accord de non-divulgation serait levé, bien sûr.

J'allais devoir écrire comment fabriquer une armure, créer de la nourriture pour les personnages afin de leur donner la force maximale, améliorer des statistiques et les possibilités de régénération des points de vie, comment faire des sacs pour porter toutes nos merdes virtuelles pendant qu'on tue et qu'on vole des monstres, etc.

Mais je ne m'étais pas attendue à ce que FallenOne apparaisse vingt minutes après que je me sois connectée et qu'il m'envoie son message direct, sans aucun préambule.

Je fixai le curseur clignotant, soudain inexplicablement nerveuse.

*FallenOne dit : *C'est bien Mia, hein ? Ce n'est pas Heath qui utilise le personnage de Mia ou quelque chose de ce genre ? Tu es peut-être AFK ?*

Je clignai des paupières, me rendant compte que j'avais passé tant de temps à fixer l'écran sans répondre qu'il pensait maintenant que j'étais AFK : *'away from keyboard'* donc pas assise devant mon ordinateur. Je me penchai en avant et je posai les mains sur le clavier.

Vous dites à FallenOne : Tu as tout lu ? Heath t'a seulement parlé du blog hier soir !

Lui : *Je lis vite.*

Moi : *En vrai, t'es un ordinateur, hein ?*

Lui : *Les ordinateurs n'ont pas d'opinion. Quoi qu'il en soit, je pense que c'est un très bon blog. Mieux que beaucoup de blogs plus gros. Il me tarde de lire ce que tu as à dire au sujet de Dragon Epoch quand le bêta-test sera terminé.*

Moi : *Je n'ai toujours pas intégré le fait que tu aies lu tout mon contenu. Cela fait deux ans que je blogue. Ça fait beaucoup d'élucubrations à lire.*

Lui : **hausse les épaules* Ça m'a plu.*

— Masochiste, murmurai-je, pas pleinement consciente du fait que mon sourire était si grand que j'en avais mal aux joues.

Notre conversation ne dura pas beaucoup plus longtemps. Il devait aller travailler et il me fallait terminer quelques corvées avant d'aller travailler à l'hôpital. Mais il se fit un devoir de retrouver notre groupe, alors qu'il nous avait prévenus qu'il ne jouait pas régulièrement avec les mêmes personnes.

En fait, au cours des semaines qui suivirent, FallenOne et moi passâmes beaucoup de temps ensemble quand les autres n'étaient pas là. Persephone avait un emploi du temps bizarre, avec beaucoup de travail en équipe de nuit sur un énorme système informatique, et Heath sortait souvent avec Brian, sans doute pour faire du lèche-vitrine d'appartement. Quant à moi, je révisais pour le concours, je travaillais de temps en temps à l'hôpital, j'écrivais sur mon blog ou, ce que je préférais, je jouais au jeu. Cependant, je ne dormais pas beaucoup. Mon esprit ne voulait pas s'éteindre plus de quelques heures par nuit.

Je compensais par une autre addiction : Dr Pepper. Ahhh… la caféine. La meilleure invention qui soit.

Et FallenOne, mon mystérieux jeune homme – ou mon facteur de quarante ans vivant à la cave – semblait avoir les mêmes horaires en ligne que moi. Ainsi, nous commençâmes à travailler sur des quêtes secondaires qui ne nécessitaient pas d'être un groupe entier. Pendant ce temps, nous nous amusions en bavardant.

Moi : *je suis certaine à cent pour cent que le concepteur de ce jeu est un adolescent prépubère sexuellement frustré.*

Lui : (après une longue pause) *Qu'est-ce qui te fait dire ça ?*

Moi : *Il suffit de le regarder. Toutes les filles ont une poitrine *parfaite. Ferme, souple, mais pas molle. Ample. Je parie que ce type n'a même jamais *touché un sein féminin.*

Lui : *On ne sait jamais...*

Moi : *Je sais que j'ai raison.*

Lui : *Alors tu n'es pas seulement une étudiante brillante en prépa médecine, une blogueuse spirituelle sur tout ce qui concerne les jeux vidéo, mais tu es aussi une experte du sexe qui peut déduire l'expérience sexuelle de n'importe quel homme à partir de connaissances limitées ?*

Je rougis et mes joues se mirent à brûler. Si seulement il savait qu'il ne pouvait pas être plus éloigné de la vérité. Je n'avais encore jamais eu d'expérience sexuelle. Pas même du pseudo-sexe.

Moi : *Penses-tu que je révélerais tous mes talents en même temps ? Bref, j'ai quelques articles pas encore publiés au sujet de Dragon Epoch qui seront mis en ligne une fois que l'accord de non-divulgation sera retiré. Il me tarde de les publier.*

Lui : *Quel est ton verdict jusque là ?*

Moi : *C'est pas mal...*

(Après une pause)

Moi : *Je déconne ! C'est fabuleux. Je m'amuse vraiment avec ce jeu. J'attends juste que ça arrive.*

Lui : *Que quoi arrive ? Que veux-tu dire ?*

Moi : *Je suppose que j'attends que le jeu me déçoive. Ça arrive toujours. Mais cela ne fait qu'une semaine, et j'ai déjà l'impression qu'il reste beaucoup plus de Yondareth à explorer.*

Lui : *Oui, il y en a beaucoup plus.*

Moi : *Comment le sais-tu ?*

Lui : *J'ai mes sources.*

Moi : *Depuis combien de temps joues-tu aux jeux vidéo ?*

Lui : *Des années.*

Moi : *Tu es étudiant ?*

Lui : *On pourrait dire ça.*

Moi : *Et voilà, tu refais le mystérieux.*

Lui : *J'aime être mystérieux. Presque autant que tu aimes être narquoise.*

Moi : *Eh bien, ils ne devraient pas me rendre les choses si faciles. Je peux passer des jours à parler des insultes au féminisme dans ce jeu.*

Je vais peut-être continuer mon thème concernant l'armure féminine inadaptée et des garçons sexuellement frustrés.

Lui : *Et voilà, tu parles encore de sexe.*

Moi : *...*

Lui : *Bon... on va tuer des trucs, ou quoi ?*

Moi : *On doit travailler sur cette quête pour le Général Machin-Truc.*

Lui : **bâille**

Moi : *Allez, on n'est que de niveau cinq. Alors, ramassons de jolies jonquilles pour honorer son amour perdu !*

Lui : *Les créateurs de ces quêtes sont pourris.*

Moi : *C'est romantique. Général SylvanWood veut se souvenir de son amour perdu.*

Lui : **soupir**

*****

**Eloisa est entrée dans le monde de Yondareth*

FallenOne et Eloisa quittent les portes de la cité, encouragés par le Général Sylvanwood qui hoche la tête d'approbation. Il leur souhaite bonne route et les remercie de bien vouloir l'aider.

— La clairière suivante, là-bas.

Le général indique un chemin passant entre les barricades de la cité et au-delà de l'orée du bois. C'est dans cette première clairière. Elles ne poussent que là-bas.

Eloisa se tourne vers FallenOne, le lancier de niveau cinq qui ne porte qu'un pagne et possède une arme aussi longue qu'il est grand. C'est un personnage étrange, avec la tête chauve et une longue barbe blanche :

un sage qui semblerait ne pas être aussi vieux que son physique le laisserait croire...

Eloisa, en revanche, est une mage spirituelle portant des vêtements très légers de couleurs vives, des breloques raffinées et des bijoux étincelants remontant le long de ses bras. Ses oreilles sont peut-être pointues, mais elle est très différente des petits êtres qui font des gâteaux et chantent dans les arbres. Elle est plutôt une vieille âme éternellement jeune, une protectrice. Comme la légendaire Galadriel.

Ils entrent dans la forêt, affrontant des chauves-souris et des squelettes animés en chemin. Ce faisant, ils commencent à travailler ensemble. Lorsque FallenOne meurt dans la troisième bataille contre un squelette particulièrement irritant, Eloisa retourne en courant jusqu'aux portes de la cité pour rejoindre son fantôme et partir ensemble récupérer ses affaires.

— Allez, Fallen, faisons en sorte que ça ne se reproduise pas, dit Eloisa.

FallenOne soupire, la tête basse de découragement.

— J'en ai marre de mourir. Je crois que nous devrions faire la quête plus tard.

Mais Eloisa est déterminée !

— Je crois que nous avons compris, cette fois. On essaie une dernière fois ? Si les mobs sont sur le point de te tuer, je me jetterai en travers de leur chemin !

— Ça ne servirait à rien ! Ils me poursuivront de toute façon quand tu seras morte.

— Non, parce que tu peux courir vite et les éviter.

Finalement, aucun d'entre eux n'eut besoin de se sacrifier ou de mourir.

Ils apprirent à travailler ensemble. Comme Fragged était absent, ils n'avaient pas de guerrier solide qui absorbe les dégâts et puisque

Persephone n'était pas là non plus, ils ne pouvaient pas profiter de ses soins magiques.

Ils n'avaient que la lance de Fallen pour causer des dégâts et la magie d'Eloisa pour ralentir les monstres... et augmenter les capacités au combat de FallenOne !

Ils réussirent, parce qu'ils avaient découvert une façon de le faire ensemble.

Ils finirent par atteindre la clairière en un seul morceau, et ils y trouvèrent un champ de coquelicots avec seulement quelques minuscules points de fleurs d'autres couleurs : des violettes, des soucis éclatants et des pâquerettes blanches. Trouver le nombre requis de jonquilles jaunes est difficile lorsque l'on se bat contre des abeilles géantes – avec des têtes humaines, rien que ça – et que l'on est poursuivi par un jardinier enragé avec une binette.

— Tu as vu ça ? dit FallenOne. On fait vraiment une bonne équipe.

— Oui, répond Eloisa. Tope-la, lancier !

C'est ainsi que commencèrent leurs aventures en duo durant lesquelles ils passèrent du temps ensemble jusque bien trop tard dans la nuit.

***

*Vous dites à FallenOne : Où étais-tu l'autre soir ?

*FallenOne dit : J'avais un rendez-vous. Pardon.

Moi : Oh, intéressant... je ne savais pas que tu avais une petite-amie.

Ce n'était que pure conjecture de supposer qu'il était sorti avec une femme, mais ses commentaires sur son appréciation des nichons m'avaient conduit à penser qu'il était hétérosexuel... donc j'avais supposé que c'était une femme.

Lui : *Pas vraiment une petite-amie. Juste une amie.*

Moi : (étrangement soulagée) *Ah. Elle joue à DE ?*

Lui : *Non. Pas moyen.*

Moi : *Pourquoi 'pas moyen' ? Tu ne t'associerais pas avec une gameuse, ou quoi ?*

Lui : *Je m'associe bien avec toi, non ?*

Moi : *Pas pareil. Nous ne sommes pas amis IRL.*

Lui : *C'est pareil. Je te considère comme une amie.*

Moi : *Mais je parie que cette amie connaît ton prénom. Tu ne me dis jamais ton nom.*

Lui : *Tu ne l'as jamais demandé.*

Moi : *Tu connais le mien. Échange de bons procédés, tu vois...*

Lui : *Échange de quoi ?*

Moi : *Dis-moi ton nom. Ne fais pas l'idiot.*

Lui : *Je suis naturellement idiot. Je suis un mâle.*

Moi : *Ha. Ha. Tu as passé trop de temps à lire mon blog. Bon alors... crache le morceau.*

Lui : *Mon nom est FallenOne.*

Moi : *T'es nul. ../.. (c'est un majeur virtuel au cas où tu n'aurais pas compris)*

Lui : *Tu me blesses.*

Moi : *Je m'en fous.*

Lui : *C'est juste que j'aime rester mystérieux.*

Moi : *Je vois ça. Un de ces jours, je t'arracherai la réponse...*

Lui : *Il se pourrait que ça me plaise.*

Hmm. D'accord. Hétérosexuel, c'était sûr.

Attendez, flirtait-il avec moi ? Après être sorti avec une 'amie' ? Je fronçai les sourcils, perplexe. Les habitudes relationnelles des gens de mon âge – ou potentiellement de mon âge – continuaient à me laisser perplexe.

Moi : *Enfin bref, nous pourrions devenir amis IRL et ce serait bizarre de t'appeler Fallen tout le temps. Et si jamais tu passes en Californie, tu pourrais traîner avec Fragged et moi. On te ferait passer un bon moment.*

Lui : *Dans quelle partie de la Californie êtes-vous ? Le nord ? Le sud ?*

Moi : *Le sud. Pas loin de LA.*

Lui : *Ah bon, vraiment...*

Moi : *Tu sembles surpris. Où es-tu, toi ?*

Lui : *Je vais encore une fois choisir d'être mystérieux.*

Moi : *Pff.*

Lui : *En fait, je suis crevé. Il est quatre heures du matin et je m'endors.*

Il devait vraiment être fatigué, car il venait de révéler, malgré son attitude évasive d'avant, qu'il avait trois heures d'avance sur moi. Cela limitait l'endroit où il se trouvait de entre le Maine et la Floride, aussi loin à l'est que le Massachusetts et à l'ouest que l'Ohio.

Oh, merde. Ça ne limitait rien du tout...

Moi : *Tu as cours tôt, demain ?*

Lui : *Je dois quitter la maison à neuf heures. C'est pas cool.*

Moi : *Bois des tonnes de caféine. Bonne nuit !*

Lui : *Zzzzzzzzzz*

À mesure que le temps passait et que nous nous rejoignions régulièrement deux ou trois soirs par semaine, il devint de plus en plus difficile de lui soutirer des détails. Ma mission était devenue de découvrir qui était FallenOne, mais même Heath n'était d'aucune aide.

Et bien sûr, lorsque Fallen n'était pas là, nous ne manquions pas de spéculer à son sujet.

— C'est peut-être une star de cinéma, dit Katya. J'ai entendu dire qu'il y a des célébrités aimant jouer à ce genre de jeux afin de pouvoir se sociabiliser tout en restant anonymes. J'ai lu dans un article que Henry Cavill jouait à World of Warcraft quand son agent l'a appelé pour lui dire qu'il avait eu le rôle de Superman. Il a failli ne pas décrocher parce qu'il était sur un raid !

Je gloussai et le seul commentaire de Heath fut :

— Si Fallen ressemble à Henry Cavill, je suis prem's, peu importe qu'il soit hétéro.

— Sérieusement, continua Kat. Mon auteur préféré parle de WoW sur son blog, mais ne veut pas dire quel personnage elle joue ni sur quel serveur.

En face de moi, Heath haussa les épaules.

— Peut-être est-ce juste une sorte d'ermite.

— Il a une petite amie, dis-je.

— Tu déconnes ! dit Kat en hurlant presque dans le chat vocal. Les types qui jouent à ce jeu n'ont *pas* de vie sociale.

Heath poussa un soupir.

— Je t'emmerde. Moi, j'ai une vie sociale.

— Tu ne comptes pas, répondit Kat. Tu sors avec des hommes. Tu pourrais simplement rendre tes partenaires accros aux jeux vidéo afin d'avoir de la compagnie et aucun souci d'emploi du temps.

Je jetai un coup d'œil à Heath par-dessus mon écran et je me mis à rire. Rien ne pouvait être plus éloigné de la vérité en ce qui concernait Brian. Non seulement ce connard – un nom que je ne lui donnais que dans ma tête afin de ne pas blesser Heath – ne s'intéressait pas aux jeux vidéo, mais en plus il se moquait de notre passe-temps. Heath avait complètement arrêté de jouer lorsque Brian était présent, ce qui m'irritait encore plus.

— Ce n'est sans doute pas une star du cinéma, puisqu'il vit sur la côte est, intervins-je. Peut-être quelqu'un dans le sport où… hé, il est peut-être à DC et travaille pour le gouvernement ?

— C'est peut-être le président Obama. Tu crois que les services secrets le laisseraient jouer ? demanda Kat.

Heath pouffa.

— Obama ne jouerait jamais un moine à moitié nu. Je parie que le président serait plutôt une sorte de barde, étant donné les beaux discours qu'il fait.

— Je me demande ce que Michelle Obama choisirait ? dis-je. Une elfe qui déchire tout… et qui s'appellerait FLOTUS, bien sûr.

— Bon, FallenOne n'est probablement pas notre président, dit Kat. Alors qui est-il ? Quelqu'un doit déclencher une enquête sur FallenOne. Heath, es-tu l'homme de la situation ?

Heath haussa les épaules, concentré sur son écran pendant qu'il s'occupait de quelque chose dans le jeu.

— Je pense que c'est juste un type bizarre qui n'aime pas être sociable et qui ment au sujet d'avoir une petite-amie.

Je fronçai les sourcils. Je risquais de ne jamais en savoir plus, mais pour une raison ou pour une autre, cela ne me plaisait pas du tout.

Cependant, les spéculations s'arrêtèrent là et nous nous accordâmes à dire que FallenOne allait rester un mystère temporaire. C'était un bon joueur et nous appréciions tous sa compagnie. Alors qu'il était un 'électron libre', il continuait à revenir vers nous.

Notre petit groupe ne mit pas longtemps à revenir régulièrement dans le jeu. Nous avions tous un travail dans la vraie vie. Kat et moi – et sans doute FallenOne – avions également nos études. Les autres avaient des vies sociales aussi. C'était pendant ces heures-là que j'étudiais. Mais lorsqu'il était l'heure de jouer, nous nous rencontrions dans notre espace virtuel. Et on jouait. *À fond.*

Il nous restait encore beaucoup de mystères à découvrir : à Yondareth, pendant que nous faisions du levelling ensemble, et à l'extérieur, dans le monde réel. Peut-être que l'un des mystères que nous allions résoudre était l'identité de FallenOne.

Chapitre Quatre : Mia se fait un nouvel ami

*P*OGO VOUS DIT : *SALUT. T'ES MIGNONNE*
   *Vous dites : *Qu'est-ce que t'en sais ?*
   Pogo : *J'ai des yeux. Jolie armure.*
Pogo siffle Eloisa.
Eloisa lève les yeux au ciel.

J'adorais quand des gamins sans cervelle ne savaient pas faire la différence entre un avatar de fantasy et la réalité, draguant des avatars canon comme s'ils étaient réels.

*****

— Hé... bonne nouvelle. J'ai trouvé un appart, dis-je à Heath en attrapant la collection de vaisselle sale sur son bureau et en me dirigeant vers la cuisine.

Heath leva la tête de son ordinateur, où il était concentré sur son travail de web design. Il lui fallut une minute pour intégrer la nouvelle, mais il ruminait encore quand je revins après avoir posé la vaisselle dans le lave-vaisselle. J'avais même eu le temps de prendre un verre d'eau glacée que je posai sur mon bureau avant de me rasseoir.

Mais lorsque je croisai son regard, je me rendis compte qu'il ne paraissait pas aussi content et soulagé que je l'avais supposé. En fait, il semblait sceptique. En se penchant en arrière sur sa chaise, il dit :

— Où se trouve cet appartement ? Au sud de Santa Ana ? Orange ouest ?

Naturellement, il avait supposé les pires parties de la ville.

— Non, dis-je en lui tirant la langue. C'est au centre-ville d'Orange, près de l'université.

Il leva les sourcils.

— T'as gagné au loto ?

— C'est un studio au-dessus d'un garage.

— Ah. Bon, il faudra que je le voie avant de donner mon approbation.

Je levai les yeux au ciel et je croisai les bras.

— Je n'ai pas besoin de ton approbation. Je suis une adulte, tu sais.

J'avais eu vingt et un ans le mois précédent et même si j'avais l'âge légal pour boire, je n'avais pas fait de folies. D'ailleurs, je ne me sentais pas vraiment comme l'adulte que j'affirmais être.

Et puis, Heath n'avait que six mois de plus que moi. Depuis quand était-il devenu mon chef ?

Il me regardait toujours dans les yeux, impassible devant mes protestations.

— Ta mère m'a ordonné de m'occuper de toi.

Je ricanai en posant les pieds sur mon bureau, attrapant mon manuel de MCAT.

— Ce n'est pas comme si j'étais une fêtarde ou une droguée. Je suis aussi proche d'une grabataire que l'on peut l'être sans, tu sais, en être vraiment une.

Pour souligner mes paroles, j'indiquai le livre que je venais de prendre. Un livre que je pouvais presque réciter de tête, tant je l'avais étudié.

Il se mordit la lèvre inférieure, semblant ne pas avoir entendu ce que j'avais dit.

— Bon… je veux venir, de toute façon. Mais ne fais pas une grosse scène, d'accord ? Je veux juste m'assurer d'avoir la conscience tranquille.

— Tu n'as pas à te sentir coupable ! Mais d'accord…

Je soupirai. J'avais presque déjà pris ma décision, mais il valait mieux le mettre à l'aise. J'étais déterminée à déménager dès que possible, ne voulant aucune responsabilité dans la mort de leur relation, si elle devait en arriver là. En fait, déménager était peut-être ma façon de m'assurer que j'aie la conscience tranquille.

***

— Non. Pas moyen. Tu ne vas pas vivre ici.

Heath se tenait au milieu de mon futur nouveau studio. L'endroit était petit, mais assez charmant. Et au moins, c'était très propre.

L'appartement était situé au-dessus du garage d'une famille vivant dans une maison modeste juste à l'extérieur du célèbre quartier historique de la ville d'Orange. Comme les maisons alentour, celle-ci avait été construite dans les années vingt dans le style bungalow Craftsman. Elle avait été agrandie par des ajouts, y compris la pièce unique au-dessus du garage, dans laquelle j'étais bien déterminée à emménager.

— Heath, soupirai-je. Cet endroit est très bien.

— C'est trop petit.

Il jeta un coup d'œil par-dessus son épaule pour s'assurer que la propriétaire qui nous avait ouvert soit hors de portée.

— Il se trouve au-dessus d'un garage qui n'est pas isolé, ce qui le rendra brûlant en été et glacial en hiver.

— Glacial en hiver, ricanai-je. Nous sommes en Californie du Sud.

— D'accord, la température est toute relative. Mais je ne te donne pas plus de dix jours ici avec le climat sud-californien en septembre. Ce sera un four. En plus, le chauffe-eau est minuscule et il n'y a pas de pression.

Je soupirai… encore. Il ne savait peut-être pas à quel point mes revenus étaient minuscules.

— Je ne peux vraiment pas être difficile. En plus, je n'ai pas besoin d'un gros appartement : il me faut juste assez de place pour étudier, faire à manger, me doucher et dormir.

Il fronça les sourcils.

— Mais tu n'as même pas de meubles et de plats, ou quoi que ce soit d'autre.

Je fis le tour de la pièce comme pour démontrer qu'elle était assez grande pour moi.

— J'ai déjà tout ce qu'il faut pour la chambre et maman dit que je peux venir au ranch et prendre quelques meubles. Elle a une vieille causeuse et une table, si je peux emprunter un fourgon pour aller les chercher. Et de la vaisselle. Je n'ai pas besoin de grand-chose. Ce n'est pas comme si j'allais faire de grands dîners, ou même des fêtes. C'est un petit endroit qui avec un peu de chance, sera assez calme afin que je puisse étudier. Si ce n'est pas le cas, j'aurai la bibliothèque au bout de la rue.

Il secoua la tête.

— Tu sais vraiment faire la fête, poupée.

Je lui fis une grimace.

— Bref...

Il leva la main pour m'interrompre.

— D'accord, d'accord, j'ai compris. Mais promets-moi au moins de ne pas signer quoi que ce soit tout de suite ? Il se pourrait que je te trouve quelque chose de mieux.

Je ne voyais pas comment. J'avais parcouru tous les sites, y compris Craigslist, appelé des agences immobilières, vérifié à l'office des chambres universitaires, et je connaissais presque tout ce qui était compris dans mon budget dans la région, ce qui n'était pas grand-chose, car mon budget était extrêmement limité. L'alternative aurait été de faire apparaître un colocataire par magie.

J'étais certaine que si je laissais une semaine à Heath, il parviendrait à la même conclusion que moi. C'était juste qu'il se sentait coupable à cause des exigences de Brian qui voulait me faire déménager au milieu de l'année scolaire. Je n'allais pas le laisser s'en faire pour cela. Je hochai donc la tête, mais je ne promis pas de ne pas signer.

Je comptais appeler la propriétaire le soir même quand il ne serait pas là et passer le lendemain après mon premier cours pour signer les papiers. Il serait irrité en le découvrant, mais aussi soulagé. Et puis... cela lui passerait. Heath n'avait jamais été du genre rancunier.

***

Quelques jours plus tard, après avoir travaillé à l'hôpital le matin, je résistai à l'envie de faire une sieste, bien que mes paupières tombent toutes seules. Je révisais donc à mon bureau au lieu d'écouter l'appel de mon oreiller. Ce fut une invitation à m'endormir avec le nez contre mon manuel.

À la place, je fis une tasse de café, ce qui était rare dans l'après-midi et qui allait sûrement me faire veiller, et je la bus en parcourant la longue liste de définitions, utilisant mon ordinateur pour vérifier des informations au sujet de termes dont je n'étais pas sûre.

Le concours MCAT contenait une série de problèmes hypothétiques qui devait être résolue à partir de nos connaissances. Ces termes clés étaient donc essentiels et il fallait les savoir sur le bout des doigts afin de pouvoir résoudre les défis hypothétiques.

Je me faisais un devoir de répondre à au moins cinq questions par jour que je trouvais sur le net parmi les exercices. En plein milieu de mes questions, une clé tourna dans la serrure et je supposai qu'il s'agissait de Heath revenant de chez Brian après y avoir passé la nuit.

Ce fut Brian à la place… seul. Il examina la pièce, puis il se tourna vers moi sans même me saluer.

— Heath n'est pas encore rentré ?

J'écarquillai les yeux. Brian se comportait déjà comme s'il vivait ici. En même temps, je supposai que c'était déjà le cas.

— Je croyais qu'il était avec toi, répondis-je. Et euh, salut, d'ailleurs. Comment vas-tu ?

J'ajoutai cela juste pour souligner son comportement grossier.

Il m'ignora complètement, portant un carton et se rendant tout droit dans la chambre de Heath avant de revenir dans le salon les mains vides.

— Il a dû conduire sa Jeep en révision. Il l'attend sans doute encore. En fait, c'est bien parce que cela nous donne l'occasion de parler.

Il ne s'était encore jamais adressé à moi en privé et n'avait pas exprimé de désir de 'parler'. Et chaque fois qu'il s'adressait à moi, sa voix dégoulinait de condescendance et de misogynie.

Je fronçai les sourcils lorsque Brian se laissa tomber sur le canapé, me fixant de ses yeux d'un bleu glacial. Ses cheveux étaient parfaitement coiffés à la Harry Styles. En fait, il s'habillait avec soin et avec l'attention aux détails de tout homme voulant ressembler à un skateur sans jamais avoir été à moins d'un mètre d'un skateboard.

— Il faut que tu arrêtes de faire culpabiliser Heath, commença-t-il avant d'incliner la tête comme s'il faisait la leçon à un enfant.

Je reculai la tête, stupéfaite.

— Il n'y a pas de culpabilisation. J'ai trouvé un endroit. C'est lui qui émet des objections.

Il secoua la tête.

— Oui, je comprends que c'est ce que tu *dis*... mais ton discours sous-jacent est complètement différent. Heath se sent responsable de toi et il est *vraiment* temps que tu grandisses et que tu quittes le nid, petit poussin.

Mon sang se mit à bouillir et j'eus soudain l'impression que la vapeur allait s'échapper de mes oreilles. J'étais certaine que Brian allait remarquer le rouge de mes joues. *Je t'emmerde, abruti.*

— Eh bien, je suis désolée que tu ressentes cela et tu seras ravi de savoir que j'ai trouvé un appartement et que j'ai signé tous les papiers il y a plusieurs jours !

Je fermai bruyamment mes livres, mes fiches et mon cahier, les rassemblant dans mes bras, puis j'ajoutai :

— Et *toi*, tu peux arrêter les conneries. Je sais que nous ne nous aimons pas, mais tu sais quoi ? Nous aimons tous les deux Heath. Et même si je déménage bientôt, je serai *toujours* dans sa vie. Alors il vaut mieux que *tu* acceptes *ça*, petit poussin.

Je me levai et je marchai d'un pas lourd vers ma chambre, quittant Brian dont la bouche était ouverte et les sourcils très hauts sur son front. Je résistai tout juste à l'envie de claquer la porte.

Je ne lui avais encore jamais montré une telle hostilité et cela faisait bien trop longtemps que je supportais ses piques sans réagir.

C'était fini.

Avec un soupir, je me rendis compte qu'ayant craché le morceau à Brian, j'allais à présent devoir mettre Heath au courant du studio au-dessus du garage. Malgré son aversion à l'admettre, il n'avait pas réussi à me trouver un meilleur endroit, comme je m'en étais doutée.

Malgré mes meilleurs efforts, je m'endormis sur le lit en moins d'une demi-heure, ma séance de révision gâchée à cause de ce trou du cul de Brian. Lorsque je me réveillai de ma sieste, l'appartement était à nouveau vide et il faisait nuit dehors. Je n'étais pas d'humeur à retourner à mes révisions et je n'avais pas non plus envie d'aller courir. Alors pour me détendre, je me connectai au jeu.

Je n'étais pas encore pleinement connectée lorsqu'un message d'un total inconnu se mit à clignoter sur mon écran.

*RageRod vous dit : *Salut bébé.*

Beurk. Vraiment ? RageRod ? Comme dans 'bite enragée' ?

*RageRod vous dit : *Es-tu une vraie fille ?*
*Vous dites à RageRod : *Plus réelle que ta poupée gonflable, gamin.*
RageRod : *Je n'ai pas de poupée gonflable.*
Moi : *Eh bien, dans ce cas tu devrais peut-être en trouver une et arrêter de harceler tous les avatars féminins que tu vois.*
RageRod : *T'es un mec, c'est sûr. Il faut qu'il y ait plus de vraies filles dans ce jeu.*
Moi : *Parce que dans ce cas elles seraient obligées de faire attention à toi ?*
RageRod : *Tu n'es pas très sympa.*
Moi : *Peut-être devrais-tu me dénoncer auprès de ta directrice d'école primaire. Maintenant... ne me parle plus.*
Vous ignorez à présent RageRod

Un nouveau message s'afficha à mon écran quelques minutes plus tard quand j'étais à la banque du jeu. Je faillis devenir dingue, me disant que ce crétin avait créé un nouveau toon pour m'envoyer des messages. À la place, je vis avec soulagement que c'était Kat. Pile la personne qu'il me fallait pour améliorer mon humeur.

*Persephone vous dit : *Je crois que tu plais à FallenOne.*

*Vous dites à Persephone : *Quoi ?*

Elle : *Tu as très bien compris.*

Je poussai un grand soupir.

Moi : *On est de retour au lycée ? Et puis... qu'est-ce qui te fait penser ça ?*

Elle : *Parce que ça fait deux fois qu'il s'est connecté et qu'il m'a rejoint pendant quelques minutes avant de demander où tu étais. Quand j'ai dit que tu étais en cours ou occupée, il a vite inventé une excuse pour partir.*

Moi : *Je suis sûre que c'est une coïncidence.*

Elle : *D'accord. Si tu le dis. Mais il ne se connecte jamais en demandant si Fragged ou moi nous sommes là.*

Moi : *Mais nous avons déjà décidé qu'il était un peu bizarre, non ? Qui peut savoir ce qu'il se passe dans la tête d'un gamer reclus ?*

Elle : *Nous devrions appliquer la méthode scientifique à ma théorie un de ces jours, si tu veux bien.*

Moi : */hausse les épaules. Trouve une façon de le faire et je suis partante !*

Elle : *D'accord, je commencerai par l'étape un : faire une observation. Comme nous avons peu d'informations au sujet de notre mystérieux ami, je ne peux me baser que sur son comportement dans le jeu. Il se connecte et il demande régulièrement de tes nouvelles. Lorsque tu n'es pas disponible, il se déconnecte rapidement. Quand tu l'es, il reste et il joue avec toi, ou avec le groupe entier.*

Moi : *Soupir. D'accord... ta problématique ?*

Elle : *FallenOne a-t-il des sentiments pour Mia ?*

Moi : *Et ton hypothèse ?*

Elle : *FallenOne a des sentiments spéciaux pour Mia... et vice versa.*

Moi : *Maintenant, tu deviens pénible.*

Elle : *Prédiction basée sur mon hypothèse au sujet de FallenOne et Mia. D'abord c'est l'AMOUUUUR. Puis le mariage. Puis le bébé dans son landau.*

Moi :../..

Elle : *Maintenant, je dois tester mon hypothèse en posant des questions subtiles à FallenOne sur sa vie amoureuse... et s'il croit ou non à la cyber romance !*

Moi : *Bonne chance pour ça. Je ne veux pas m'en mêler.*

***

Peu de temps après, le bêta-test de résistance de Dragon Epoch fut terminé. Comme il n'y eut pas de suppression des personnages, nous eûmes le droit de continuer à jouer les mêmes que dans le bêta. L'accord de non-divulgation fut levé et j'eus le droit de poster des articles au sujet de Dragon Epoch sur mon blog.

En fait, j'étais au milieu de l'écriture d'un nouvel article lorsque je décidai de regarder les revenus publicitaires. Il était presque temps de payer les factures, et je travaillais furieusement afin de gagner assez d'argent pour que le blog se paie lui-même – c'était encore mieux s'il commençait à rapporter un peu d'argent de poche.

Je fus ainsi stupéfaite de remarquer que le crédit sur mon compte avait significativement augmenté. Cela me poussa alors à vérifier mes statistiques.

Depuis que j'avais posté du nouveau contenu au sujet de Dragon Epoch, le nombre de visites sur mon site avait été multiplié par plusieurs centaines. Ma mâchoire en tomba.

— Putain de merde !

Heath leva les yeux de son travail.

— Quoi ?

— C'est de la folie sur mon blog. Je n'ai même pas parlé de quoi que ce soit de controversé dernièrement ou qui mérite de faire l'actualité. On dirait que les articles sur Dragon Epoch attirent le plus de monde.

— Tout le monde a envie d'avoir des informations sur le nouveau jeu, dit-il en haussant les épaules. Tu reçois beaucoup de visites de Google ?

Il fit le tour du bureau pour regarder mon écran.

— Laisse-moi… bon sang, c'est un énorme bond dans tes visites ! Et très soudain, en plus. Tu vois ce changement d'un jour à l'autre ? Donne-moi une seconde pour revenir à la source et voir d'où vient tout le trafic.

Au bout de quelques minutes, il poussa un soupir et secoua la tête.

— Waouh. On dirait que quelqu'un chez Draco Multimedia a trouvé ton blog. Tu as été affichée sur leur page d'accueil.

J'écarquillai les yeux.

— Vraiment ?

— Oui, ricana-t-il. Je me demande si cela signifie qu'ils vont commencer à vêtir les pauvres femmes qui couraient toutes nues sur Yondareth jusque là.

Je me connectai à l'interface de mon blog pour regarder les commentaires. Il y en avait des douzaines. La plupart étaient attentionnés, même respectueux. Je dus bloquer quelques trolls, et j'avais à présent des réponses à donner aux nombreuses questions.

Il me fallut des heures pour tout passer en revue. Le blog venait de devenir un plus gros travail, mais avec la récompense de plus d'argent, également. Ce qui était une bonne chose, vraiment. Mais c'était encore une exigence sur mon temps libre déjà restreint.

Et je devais admettre que c'était un peu inquiétant de savoir que les employés de l'entreprise de jeux vidéo responsables de ma nouvelle obsession préférée lisaient mon blog, commentaires sarcastiques et critiques comprises.

Waouh.

C'était une sensation étrange : de valorisation, de gratification et oui, de me sentir observée. Je sentis qu'il s'agissait de mes quinze minutes de célébrité, alors je devais capitaliser dessus tant que c'était possible. En outre, j'avais besoin de l'argent pour mon déménagement alors, j'accueillis cette attention les bras ouverts.

Je jetai un coup d'œil à Heath qui avait repris son travail. Je lui avais parlé de la signature des papiers pour déménager dans le nouvel appartement, puisque j'avais déjà tout révélé à Brian. Heath avait été un peu vexé au début, mais heureusement il s'en était remis. Et je m'étais retenue de répéter les petites remarques merdiques de Brian.

Cependant, comme je n'allais avoir accès au camion de déménagement que le week-end suivant, mon plan était de bouger lentement quelques cartons de temps en temps. La propriétaire, Lupe, était assez gentille pour me permettre de le faire, bien que ma date d'emménagement ne soit officiellement que dans quelques semaines, parce que l'appartement devait être repeint et la moquette nettoyée.

Cependant, je ne pus nier la petite excitation à l'idée d'avoir mon propre appartement. Qu'il s'agisse d'un minuscule studio ou pas. Il serait à moi. Entièrement à moi.

***

Quelques jours plus tard, je transportai encore un autre carton, celui-ci rempli de livres, vers mon nouvel appartement. Je descendais les marches lorsque je faillis bousculer une jeune femme d'environ mon âge. Quand elle fut remise de sa surprise en me voyant là, elle fit un grand sourire et tendit la main.

— Bonjour ! Je m'appelle Alex. Tu dois être la nouvelle locataire.

Elle me regarda directement dans les yeux sans me dévisager des pieds à la tête comme certaines femmes de mon âge semblaient le faire en rencontrant une nouvelle personne. Leurs yeux passaient en revue chaque vêtement et accessoire, comme pour traiter ces informations dans un ordinateur super rapide, du genre qu'il y avait dans l'armure d'Iron Man. Les yeux d'Alex ne firent rien de ce genre.

Je lui serrai la main.

— Bonjour, Alex. Je m'appelle Mia.

Son sourire incroyablement large s'étira encore et elle se pencha en avant avec enthousiasme. Cela faisait très longtemps que je n'avais pas rencontré quelqu'un d'aussi ouvertement aimable.

— Je suis la fille de ta nouvelle propriétaire.

Alex était une jolie fille avec de longs cheveux bruns, une peau d'olive et des yeux immenses, presque comme dans les animés. Son maquillage était appliqué jusqu'à la perfection.

— Et tu es une fan de *Firefly* !

Sa voix monta d'une octave sur le dernier mot lorsqu'elle pointa du doigt mon tee-shirt de la série.

Je baissai la tête, me sentant soudain un peu gênée.

— Oui, ça me correspond… Mal et Inara pour toujours !

J'ai toujours aimé les femmes fortes qui résistaient à l'objet de leur attraction continue, malgré les protestations explicites de Mal concernant la profession d'Inara.

— Tope là !

Elle leva la main et je la tapai doucement.

— Tu as bon goût. Super relation ! Moi, je suis totalement à fond pour Kaylee/Simon !

Je souris. Elle me plaisait déjà. N'importe quelle fille qui zoomait immédiatement sur mes obsessions de geek avait mon respect immédiat.

— Question suivante, dit-elle en changeant de position. Qui est ton Docteur préféré ?

Je ris.

— C'est facile. Le neuvième !

Elle leva le poing au ciel.

— Wou-hou ! J'adore ! Tu viens à ma prochaine soirée de beuverie ! Je vis à Fullerton. Comme tu es ici à Orange, je suppose que tu vas à Chapman ?

Je hochai la tête.

— Oui, je suis en troisième année. Et toi ?

— Deuxième année à Cal State Disneyland.

Son sourire en coin accompagna le surnom populaire de la fac California State University Fullerton.

— Je suis ravie de te rencontrer, Mia. Je dois me dépêcher avant que ma mère sorte et me demande de faire autre chose pour elle.

Elle leva les yeux au ciel avant de continuer.

— Je serai de retour ici pour dîner la semaine prochaine. Tu auras emménagé, n'est-ce pas ?

— Une fois que l'appartement sera prêt, oui !

— D'accord, très bien, je te verrai donc dans les parages ! Prends soin de toi.

Je souris et je la vis se dépêcher vers le trottoir où sa voiture était garée. Eh bien, c'était encourageant. Je n'avais même pas encore emménagé et j'avais déjà fait une amie potentielle.

En me dirigeant vers ma voiture, je ne pus m'empêcher de me sentir reconnaissante. La propriétaire semblait gentille et sa fille aussi. Peut-être était-ce le signe de bonnes choses à venir ! Peut-être était-ce une bonne chose que je sois forcée de m'éloigner de la protection de mon grand frère adoptif et que je doive voler de mes propres ailes. Avec un peu de chance, je deviendrais bientôt un membre productif de la société. Pour l'instant, il me suffisait de réussir brillamment le MCAT.

C'était du gâteau, non ?

***

*FallenOne vous dit : *Salut, toi !*

Je regardai mes notifications avec de grands yeux. C'était la fin de la matinée et le mardi était ma journée la plus légère : je n'avais qu'un seul cours et je ne travaillais pas à l'hôpital. Je m'étais connectée pour faire des transactions bancaires virtuelles dans le jeu et pour voir s'il y avait de l'armure aux enchères que je pouvais acheter pour mon personnage.

Je remarquai avec une légère excitation que je gardai pour moi, que FallenOne s'était connecté juste après moi.

*Vous dites à FallenOne : *De retour parmi nous ! Ça fait longtemps qu'on ne t'a pas vu.*

Lui : *Des TONNES de travail. Désolé.*

Moi : *Eh bien, tu as raté la grande ouverture du jeu. Le bêta-test est terminé ! Et la vague de noobs a envahi les serveurs...*

Lui : *J'ai vu ça. Mais les gens semblent beaucoup aimer le jeu.*

Moi : *Évidemment. Ce qui est chouette, c'est que l'accord de non-divulgation a été levé, alors je peux en parler sur mon blog !*

Lui : *J'ai vu ça ! Je lis toujours ton blog.*

Moi : *Toi et beaucoup d'autres gens. Je suis submergée. Mais c'est une bonne chose, même si cela empiète sur mon temps de jeu. J'ai à peine eu le temps de faire le tour depuis l'ouverture.*

Lui : *J'ai un peu de temps ce week-end...*

Moi : *Aïe, pas moi. Désolée. Je vais chez ma mère pour le week-end. Je déménage bientôt !*

Lui : *Félicitations ! Tu emménages avec des colocataires ou avec une personne en particulier ?*

Je levai les sourcils. Était-ce sa façon de découvrir si j'avais un petit ami ? Je me mordis la lèvre en repensant aux soupçons de Katya.

Moi : *Non. Il n'y a pas de 'personne en particulier' dans ma vie. Je déménage parce que le petit-ami de Heath veut emménager avec lui.*

Lui : *Ah, d'accord. J'espère que tu auras du monde pour t'aider à déménager. Je te verrai peut-être la semaine prochaine ?*

Moi : *D'accord. Envoie-moi juste un texto quand tu es libre et je verrai si je peux me connecter. Tu sais, ce serait tellement cool si on pouvait envoyer un message à quelqu'un dans le jeu, et s'ils ne sont pas connectés, cela apparaîtrait sous la forme d'un texto sur leur téléphone.*

Lui : *C'est une bonne idée.*

Moi : *Oui, mais peut-être ne peuvent-ils pas le faire. Je suis certaine qu'ils l'auraient déjà installé si c'était possible. Je ne peux pas être la première personne à y avoir pensé.*

Lui : *Pourquoi ne pas le mettre dans la boîte à suggestions des bêta-testeurs ?*

Je souris et je ne lui dis pas l'avoir déjà essayé plusieurs fois sans aucun retour.

J'envoyai mon numéro VOIP à Fallen, cela transmettait les textos à mon nouveau portable prépayé – au cas peu probable où il serait un harceleur. Je le connaissais depuis plusieurs mois et il semblait normal, mais… on n'était jamais trop prudent en ce qui concernait internet.

Une heure plus tard, un texto de sa part apparut sur mon téléphone. C'est ainsi que nous commençâmes à nous envoyer des textos plus ou moins régulièrement. Peut-être qu'une véritable amitié pouvait se former après s'être rencontrés au hasard sur internet… on ne savait jamais.

Je dois admettre avoir rentré son numéro dans Google pour voir si je pouvais découvrir autre chose à son sujet. Mais bien sûr, c'était une impasse. L'indicatif téléphonique venait d'un endroit du Texas.

Et je n'avais pas l'impression qu'il était un cow-boy. Ni un tatou. J'étais encore une fois contrecarrée.

Chapitre Cinq :
Mauvaise nouvelle

MA MERE VIVAIT DANS UNE PETITE VILLE DE montagne juste au-dessus de Temecula, à environ deux heures de route de ma fac d'Orange. Le week-end suivant, Heath me conduisit là-bas avec un camion qu'il avait emprunté pour aller chercher quelques vieux meubles et rapporter des fournitures pour mon nouvel appartement. Finalement, je pense qu'il était soulagé que les choses se soient arrangées si vite.

Bien sûr, Brian avait été aux anges que je parte. Oui, il n'était pas du tout sensible au déchirement que ressentait Heath à ce sujet. *Trou du cul.*

Quoi qu'il en soit, dans l'intérêt de Heath, je leur souhaitais d'être bien ensemble, même si j'avais mes doutes quant à leur compatibilité. Oui, ils étaient attirés l'un par l'autre, mais ils se disputaient comme Mario et Bowser. Je ne dis rien, car Heath semblait avoir de l'espoir pour le déménagement et la relation. Pendant notre trajet, il bavarda de leur intention d'acheter un appartement à Orange Hills. C'était terrible, car je ne pus penser à rien d'autre qu'à celui qui le garderait lors de leur séparation.

— Maman ! appelai-je en entrant dans la maison.

Elle était dans la cuisine et elle passa précipitamment la double porte pour nous saluer.

— Les voilà. Mes jumeaux !

Elle nous avait donné ce surnom au lycée. Au début, j'avais détesté ça, mais maintenant je trouvais que c'était drôle. Heath et moi ne nous ressemblions pas du tout. Il était grand, solide, blanc à la peau pâle alors que j'avais des cheveux bruns, des yeux marron et que j'étais assez grande, mais fine. Et, grâce à mes origines grecques, ma peau était légèrement plus disposée à bronzer que ce que lui permettait son héritage scandinave.

Comme cela faisait presque deux mois que je n'avais pas vu ma mère, je la serrai très fort dans mes bras. Elle semblait... plus mince. Et lorsque je m'écartai et que je la regardai dans les yeux, elle sembla fatiguée. Elle avait des cernes sous les yeux et elle était un peu pâle.

Je n'avais pas non plus manqué de remarquer l'absence de voitures garées dans l'allée.

— Où sont les clients ?

— Oh, j'ai fermé les réservations pendant un moment pour me donner un petit break.

Son regard se détourna du mien.

— Le nettoyage de printemps et tout ça...

Je fronçai les sourcils, mais je n'insistai pas. Pourquoi fermer le B&B pendant la haute saison ? Et ici, le printemps était vraiment la haute saison. Le début du printemps dans le désert était à ne pas rater. De magnifiques fleurs de toutes les couleurs imaginables tapissaient le désert pendant une courte période : parfois seulement deux ou trois semaines avant que le soleil brûlant dessèche les plantes. En général, des foules entières venaient visiter la région à cette époque de l'année.

Maman prépara nos repas préférés et Heath profita de la floraison avec sa passion pour la photo. Un jour, il fit même un trajet d'une heure jusqu'au parc national d'Anza-Borrego. Ses photos s'étaient beaucoup améliorées et il avait suivi des cours pour développer son talent.

Comme d'habitude, il évita habilement de voir ses propres parents, bien que ceux-ci ne vivaient qu'à dix kilomètres de chez ma mère.

Je passai mon temps à aider ma mère à aérer les chambres et à les nettoyer en profondeur. On défit les lits et on lava tout, on dépoussiéra les plafonds et les lumières, on frotta les plinthes et on lava même les vitres.

Nous étions en train de terminer une des petites maisons, Roy Rogers, notre meilleure chambre. Elle polissait la petite table rustique installée comme bureau, pendant que j'étais assise sur le sol et que j'essuyais les plinthes.

— Tu es maintenant assez grande afin que je ne me sente pas coupable de ne pas te payer un salaire décent pour tout ce travail gratuit, plaisanta-t-elle.

Je haussai les épaules et je souris.

— C'est agréable. Ça me fait penser à autre chose.

— Autre chose que ton examen ?

Je haussai encore les épaules.

— Oui… ça… entre autres.

En fait, cela me rongeait depuis la veille. Le B&B vide, les joues creusées de maman. Il se passait quelque chose. Quelque chose qu'elle semblait me cacher.

Je me mordis l'intérieur de la joue. Les gens faisaient-ils cela ? Cachaient-ils les choses importantes – peut-être même très graves – aux membres de leur famille ?

J'allais devoir trouver un moyen de lui tirer les vers du nez. Mais fallait-il que je sois subtile et que je tourne autour du sujet ou que je pose la question directement ?

— Quelque chose dont tu veux parler ?

Elle essuya le dernier morceau de bois poli et elle s'assit pour me regarder. Je passai une dernière fois un torchon propre sur les plinthes.

J'inspirai profondément, puis je soufflai. *La question allait donc être directe...*

— Oui, en fait.

Ma mère posa son torchon et me regarda.

Je levai les sourcils.

— Je veux savoir pourquoi tu sembles si fatiguée. Et je veux savoir comment tu t'es blessée.

Elle écarquilla les yeux.

— Comment je me suis blessée ?

Je montrai le bandage qui avait glissé de son bras et qui était maintenant visible sous son tee-shirt à manches courtes. Maman pinça les lèvres.

Puis elle déglutit.

— Je ne veux pas que tu t'inquiètes pour quelque chose qui pourrait n'être rien du tout.

Je me raidis et il y eut soudain une boule de peur froide dans ma gorge.

— *Quoi ?*

Je serrai les dents lorsqu'elle ne répondit pas tout de suite.

— N'essaie pas de surmonter ça toute seule. Dis-le-moi, maman.

Elle soupira.

— Mais tu as déjà tellement de soucis, et c'est... potentiellement rien du tout.

Je croisai les bras avec raideur.

— Ce qui signifie que c'est potentiellement *quelque chose*, dis-je en grimaçant. Crache le morceau, mère.

— J'avais quelques grains de beauté sur le bras, un groupe de petites taches de naissance, en fait. Ils ont commencé à avoir une drôle de tête, alors le médecin a voulu les enlever et en faire une biopsie.

— *Quoi ?*

Je bondis sur mes pieds.

— Quel genre de biopsie ? Une ponction ? Une excision ? Est-ce que tu vois un oncologue ?

Ma mère leva la main.

— Calme-toi, Mia. Je vais bien. Ce n'est peut-être rien.

— Alors pourquoi as-tu l'air si fatiguée ? Pourquoi annuler les réservations ?

Elle serra la mâchoire, puis elle haussa les épaules.

— C'est juste un peu de stress. Rien de plus. J'ai passé quelques mauvaises semaines à m'inquiéter. Mais le médecin est très optimiste et pense que ce n'est rien.

Je fronçai les sourcils en me mordant la lèvre.

— Et si ce n'est pas rien ? J'ai travaillé avec un oncologue, tu sais, à faire des recherches cette année. Je pourrais lui en parler un peu plus, obtenir plus d'informations.

Elle fronça les sourcils, les rides s'approfondissant sur son front.

— Tu es en train de te faire peur. Cette semaine, j'ai appris à ne jamais chercher les symptômes sur Google et je ne veux pas

que tu fasses l'équivalent de l'étudiant en médecine, d'accord ?
J'aurais les résultats plus tard dans la semaine...

— Tu m'appelles à la seconde où tu les apprends.

Ce n'était pas une question.

Elle sourit.

— Bien sûr.

— Maman, tu as besoin d'un plan... au cas où le test serait positif.

Elle haussa les épaules.

— Les gens meurent-ils du cancer de la peau ?

J'avalai un énorme rocher dans ma gorge. *Oui*, voulus-je dire. *Tout le temps.* C'est insidieux et mauvais. La peau est le plus grand organe du corps – de loin – et il joue un rôle très important. À cause de cela, le cancer de la peau s'étalait très vite. Une fois qu'il y avait des métastases...

Si c'était un mélanome, que Dieu nous vienne en aide. Cela ne *pouvait* pas être un mélanome. De toutes mes forces, je souhaitai qu'il s'agisse d'une des versions les moins agressives de cancer de la peau. Mais la description des tâches de naissance sombres, le changement d'apparence, la localisation sur son bras... tout cela indiquait la forme la plus mortelle de cancer de la peau.

— Y a-t-il eu ulcération ? Saignement ? Dis-moi tout.

Elle me dit tout et je clignai des paupières et je déglutis, ignorant les larmes qui montaient et qui poussaient contre mes yeux. Je luttai pour ignorer la sensation d'avoir pris un coup de poing dans l'estomac.

Et si... et si je la perdais ? En dehors de Heath, ma mère était ma seule famille.

Je parvins tout juste à ne pas craquer pendant l'heure qui suivit, essayant d'agir naturellement pendant que nous finissions ce que nous faisions. Mais ensuite, je lui dis que j'allais faire une promenade.

Je choisis ma randonnée préférée dans les collines qui entouraient le ranch, jusqu'au point de vue où j'adorais regarder le coucher de soleil. C'était très paisible là-haut... calme. Je pouvais entendre le vent et mes propres pensées et pas grand-chose d'autre.

Je réfléchis beaucoup et les possibilités continuèrent à tourner dans ma tête, me rendant de plus en plus effrayée. J'étais si remontée que je me dirigeai tout droit vers l'étable en rentrant, afin de passer du temps avec les chevaux jusqu'à ce que Heath rentre de son excursion photographique.

Lorsqu'il finit par arriver, je lui fis signe dans l'allée et je lui dis la nouvelle dans l'étable. Il fut beaucoup plus calme que moi, mais il avait beaucoup de questions. Et il parvint à me calmer, moi aussi.

Nous allions attendre les résultats. Nous n'allions pas tirer de conclusions hâtives. Nous n'allions pas nous faire de soucis pour rien.

***

Il nous fallut une demi-journée pour déménager mes maigres possessions jusqu'au nouvel appartement. Une autre demi-journée afin que je déballe mes affaires et que je m'installe.

Le jour suivant mon déménagement, Heath partit camper dans les High Sierras avec Brian. C'était leur dernière petite escapade avant d'emménager ensemble, comme s'ils n'allaient pas être tout le temps ensemble désormais. Heath proposa de l'annuler, mais il avait eu des difficultés à convaincre Brian le métrosexuel de partir profiter de l'un des plaisirs préférés de Heath : camper, faire de la randonnée et pêcher. Je n'avais pas le cœur de lui retirer cela, alors ils partirent avec ma bénédiction.

Cela signifiait que lorsque la nouvelle arriverait… j'allais être seule. Et cette pensée sembla s'ajouter au stress que je ressentais déjà.

— Quelqu'un va venir réparer la ligne téléphonique la semaine prochaine, m'informa ma propriétaire quand je terminais de vider mon dernier carton. Il y a eu beaucoup de grésillements sur la ligne.

— Attendez, il y a un téléphone fixe ?

Soudain, je fus ravie à l'idée de ne pas avoir à dépenser toutes mes minutes prépayées de téléphone portable.

— Oui. C'est inclus dans le loyer.

Cet endroit correspondait de mieux en mieux à mon budget. Et en plus de cette bonne nouvelle, le pack internet pas cher que j'avais commandé était installé et prêt à être utilisé le lendemain.

Mais lorsque la semaine se termina, je devins de plus en plus tendue, envoyant fréquemment des textos à ma mère pour découvrir si elle avait eu des nouvelles de ses tests. Elle n'en avait pas eu.

Pendant que j'attendais, au lieu d'étudier pour mon MCAT, ce que j'aurais dû faire, je passai tout mon temps libre sur le jeu. Il se trouva que FallenOne était dans les parages, lui aussi, et il prenait tous les jours de mes nouvelles.

Après le troisième jour, il aborda le sujet.

*FallenOne vous dit : *Tu n'as pas ce concours, bientôt ?*

Mon estomac tomba dans mes talons. J'étais si préoccupée par mes inquiétudes pour maman que j'avais chassé les examens de mon esprit. Je me dis que je savais une bonne partie des bases, non ? Que mes simples talents de déduction suffisaient à résoudre les situations hypothétiques du test. De la logique et des raisonnements. Je maîtrisais ça. J'utilisais ces talents presque tous les jours.

En fait, j'utilisais ces talents en ce moment même pour justifier le fait de ne pas étudier.

*Vous dites à FallenOne : *Ouais...*
Lui : *Dois-je te dire de te déconnecter du jeu et d'étudier ?*
Moi : *Tu peux me dire ce que tu veux. Ça ne veut pas dire que je t'écouterai.*

Et je ne le fis pas. Je continuai à jouer. Cette semaine-là, j'avais besoin d'être distraite par le jeu pour tout supporter.

Parce que jeudi, ma mère appela. Et non, la nouvelle n'était pas bonne.

J'eus du mal à en croire mes oreilles, les mots 'test positif pour mélanome' résonnant à l'arrière de ma tête, dans tout mon cerveau. J'avais fait comme elle l'avait demandé et j'avais évité de chercher toutes les possibilités sur Google. Mais j'avais bien eu une discussion avec Dr Martin, le médecin dont j'étais l'assistante pour un projet de recherche. Nous avions discuté du processus de diagnostic, de ce qu'elle pouvait avoir, et des protocoles préférés de traitement, donc j'étais aux moins armée de quelques connaissances.

— Ils ne veulent pas faire de radiothérapie, mais… ils veulent que je commence la chimiothérapie. Ils sont inquiets, car les marges n'étaient pas très claires sur la biopsie.

Oh mon dieu. Je me mordis la lèvre et je me balançai d'avant en arrière sur ma chaise en écoutant sa voix calme continuer de façon monotone. Elle paraissait en fait *remarquablement* calme pour quelqu'un qui venait de recevoir cette nouvelle. Le fait que les bords ne soient pas clairs signifiait que les médecins ne savaient pas s'ils avaient tout enlevé lorsqu'ils avaient retiré les grains de beauté.

— Mia ? Tu es toujours là ? demanda-t-elle quand je luttai pour me contrôler.

— Oui, dis-je en haletant un peu.

— Dr Shuman est certain qu'avec ce traitement, ce sera favorable.

J'aurais pu jurer entendre les battements de mon cœur dans mes tympans ainsi que chacune de mes respirations.

— Mia… tout ira bien.

Je fermai les yeux et je me mordis la langue afin de ne pas prononcer les mots qui y étaient posés. Elle ne savait pas du tout que tout irait bien.

Je m'excusai de devoir raccrocher peu de temps après, utilisant l'excuse réelle qu'il ne me restait presque plus de minutes. Mais en réalité, je le fis, car ma mère n'avait pas besoin de m'entendre craquer à cause de sa nouvelle.

Oh, merde. Oh, merde. Merde. Merde. Je pouvais la perdre. C'était une vraie possibilité. Mais en faisant mon ménage normal – la vaisselle, le rangement –, je ne pleurai pas. À la place, je m'engourdis de l'intérieur.

Je finis par passer presque la nuit entière sur DE. Je fis un marathon de levelling sans me soucier de l'avance que je prenais sur mes amis. Peu de temps après avoir atteint le niveau 35, une notification familière s'afficha à l'écran.

*Votre ami, FallenOne, est en ligne.

*FallenOne vous dit : *Salut, tu es connectée bien tard... et... waouh. Félicitations pour tous les nouveaux niveaux. Tu as l'intention de nous laisser te rattraper un jour ?*

*Vous dites à FallenOne : *Pas d'humeur. Va falloir que tu ailles embêter quelqu'un d'autre.*

Lui : *...*

Moi : *Je passe une très mauvaise nuit ici.*

Lui : *Que se passe-t-il ? Puis-je t'aider ?*

Moi : *Seulement si tu as un remède miracle contre le cancer.*

Lui : *Le cancer ? D'accord, maintenant je suis inquiet. Que se passe-t-il ?*

Moi : *Une mauvaise nouvelle. Quelqu'un que j'aime a un cancer.*

Lui : *Veux-tu en parler ? Je peux t'appeler...*

Moi : *C'est gentil de ta part, mais il ne me reste plus de minutes ce mois-ci.*

Lui : *Pas de téléphone fixe ?*

Moi : *Oh, en fait si, j'en ai un dans mon nouvel appartement.*

Mes doigts traînèrent avec hésitation au-dessus du clavier. Voulais-je vraiment ouvrir cette boîte de pandore ? Il me semblait tellement plus simple et presque amusant d'avoir un ami mystérieux, quelqu'un dont je ne savais presque rien, mais qui pouvait être là pour moi. C'était un peu romantique, en réalité, l'idée que nous puissions être amis de cette façon sans qu'aucun sentiment romantique vienne bouleverser tout cela.

Cette idée me plaisait assez et j'avais des scrupules à l'abandonner – même si ce n'était qu'un appel téléphonique.

D'un autre côté, Heath était en montagne au-dessus de Yosemite, hors de portée du réseau mobile, et je n'avais envie de vider mon sac auprès de personne d'autre. Soudain, je me rendis compte que je voulais vider mon sac. J'en avais besoin.

Et puis… je n'allais pas me mentir… j'étais toujours morbidement curieuse au sujet de FallenOne. Peut-être allais-je même obtenir son vrai prénom. Après avoir découvert mon nouveau numéro de téléphone sur la feuille d'informations de Lupe, je l'envoyai par texto à Fallen.

Quelques minutes plus tard, le téléphone sonna et je décrochai d'une main tremblante.

— Allô ?

— Salut, répondit une voix grave et distinctement masculine.

Un étrange petit frisson me parcourut le dos lorsque je l'entendis pour la première fois, et je ne sus pas d'où cela me venait. Était-ce la nervosité ? *L'attirance* ? Aucune idée.

La ligne se mit immédiatement à grésiller et je me souvins de l'avertissement de Lupe, qui avait expliqué qu'elle devait être réparée.

— Pardon pour les grésillements… apparemment, la ligne mauvaise.

— Oui, elle est merdique, dit-il. Tu vas bien ?

— Euh, ouais. À peu près.

— Veux-tu en parler ?

Sa voix était un peu brouillée, mais je parvenais tout de même à le comprendre.

— Je ne sais pas. Heath n'est pas là et je n'ai personne d'autre à qui parler, mais je ne suis pas certaine d'avoir autre chose à dire en dehors de 'ce n'est pas juste et la vie est merdique'.

— C'est vrai que la vie n'est pas juste.

Si je perdais ma mère, je perdais toute la famille que j'avais sauf Heath. J'eus soudain les larmes aux yeux et pour la première fois depuis que j'avais reçu la nouvelle, elles coulèrent sur mes joues avec une telle force que je ne pus les retenir avec mes paupières. C'était comme l'ouverture d'une écluse.

Fallen me laissa sangloter sans rien dire. Je l'entendis respirer de temps en temps, mais pour l'essentiel je ne fis que me noyer dans ma propre tristesse.

— Je suis désolée, finis-je par gémir dans les grésillements du téléphone après presque dix minutes de sanglots. C'est ma mère...

— Oh, merde. Je suis désolé.

— C'est vraiment nul, putain.

— Oui, c'est nul. Elle va s'en sortir ?

Je déglutis.

— Je ne sais pas...

Les grésillements reprirent de plus belle et je peinai à entendre ce qu'il dit ensuite.

— Je ne t'entends pas, dis-je.

Les grésillements persistèrent et j'écartai le combiné de mon oreille, puis j'attendis. Et j'attendis.

Et j'attendis.

Enfin, je jetai un coup d'œil à mon écran et je vis qu'il m'avait écrit un message dans le jeu :

*FallenOne vous dit : *Ton téléphone, c'est de la merde. J'ai dû raccrocher.*

*Vous dites à FallenOne : *Je sais... désolée ! Mais merci d'avoir rappelé... je crois que j'avais besoin de parler.*

Lui : *Je pense qu'il te faut te défouler encore plus. Allons tuer des trucs. Tu te sentiras mieux.*

Moi : *Merci d'avoir rappelé. Mais je ne veux pas te retenir. Il doit être *vraiment tard là-bas.*

Lui : *Je suis content d'être là pour une amie... même une amie avec une ligne fixe pourrie.*

Je ris entre les larmes et la morve restantes. Puis nous nous dirigeâmes tout droit vers une zone de forte densité dans le jeu afin de tuer des mobs sans faire de quête. On resta campé au même endroit en attendant qu'ils apparaissent afin de pouvoir les battre. Pas besoin de tank ou de soigneur. Un travail d'équipe parfait. Et on le fit des *heures* durant. Pendant les temps morts, on bavardait.

On venait de terminer un combat particulièrement difficile et je devais attendre de récupérer du mana pour mes sorts. Eloisa mangea et but de la nourriture virtuelle pour l'aider.

Lui : *J'espère que tu as eu l'occasion de passer du temps avec ta mère. Je veux dire, je sais que tu as un emploi du temps très chargé, mais... c'est important. Juste pour qu'elle comprenne ce que tu ressens. Ne laisse aucun non-dit.*

Moi : *Nous sommes proches, mais merci pour ce rappel. Je ne laisserai pas de non-dit...*

Mes doigts hésitèrent au-dessus du clavier avant de continuer à taper.

Moi : *On dirait que tu parles d'expérience... quelqu'un que tu aimes est tombé malade ?*
Lui : *Oui. Quelqu'un que j'aimais beaucoup.*

Aimait. Au passé...
FallenOne avait donc perdu cette personne dans sa vie. Mon cœur se serra de compassion en sachant que je risquais de vivre la même chose que lui, sauf si l'univers en décidait autrement.

Moi : *Je suis désolée. J'espère que tu vas bien.*
Lui : *Je n'espère rien d'autre que ta mère aille bien. Mais... souviens-toi juste de ne rien laisser d'inexprimé, d'accord ?*
Moi : *Tu as retenu des choses que tu aurais dû dire ?*
Lui : *Oui. Et je le regrette. Chaque jour de ma vie.*

Une boule se forma dans ma gorge. Il ne donna pas de détails sur sa propre perte, il se contenta d'avoir de l'empathie et d'écouter pendant que je tapais paragraphe après paragraphe sur mes propres peurs et inquiétudes.

Avoir quelqu'un avec moi à ce moment-là m'aida tellement. Si je ne pouvais pas avoir un des fameux gros câlins de Heath, au moins pouvais-je avoir la présence virtuelle de FallenOne.

C'était surprenant de recevoir du réconfort par ce biais-là.

Il fut en ligne avec moi jusqu'à l'aube. À un moment, après que le soleil se fut levé, je me réveillai, le visage écrasé sur le bureau. Je bougeai la souris pour réveiller l'écran et je vis qu'il s'était déconnecté, mais seulement après avoir envoyé plusieurs messages sans réponse, dont le dernier était…

*FallenOne vous dit : *Je pense que tu t'es endormie. Du moins, je l'espère. Je suis sur le point de tomber moi-même, mais s'il te plaît, envoie-moi un texto quand tu te réveilles, afin que je sache que tu vas bien.*

Je me traînai jusqu'au lit et je m'endormis au bout de quelques minutes, mais avant de sentir le sommeil me prendre, je fus réchauffée par l'idée que Fallen avait veillé toute la nuit avec moi pour me tenir compagnie. Et pourtant, après tout cela, je n'avais toujours aucune idée de son nom.

Chapitre Six :
Les retombées

" *F* EMMES INVISIBLES " – *POSTE SUR LE BLOG DE* GEEKETTE

Une lettre ouverte à Draco Multimedia Entertainment... et ses dirigeants.

Messieurs,

et je vous adresse cela sans ironie, car je ne peux que supposer qu'il n'y a aucune femme à moins de cent cinquante mètres de vos bureaux. Ou s'il y en a, alors elles sont aussi invisibles que vos joueuses féminines.

'Joueuses féminines ?' demandez-vous, les sourcils grimpant de surprise sur vos fronts masculins.

Oui. Nous existons. Mais en ce qui vous concerne, nous sommes invisibles. Ou bien nous sommes des dégâts collatéraux symboliques dans votre quête de vendre votre produit aux hommes. Car si vous osez tenir compte de notre présence dans vos campagnes marketing, d'une façon ou d'une autre les garçons se sentiront aliénés par 'tous ces horribles trucs de filles'.

Mais laissez-moi vous expliquer quelque chose... nos dollars se dépensent tout aussi bien que ceux des gens portant leur appareil génital à l'extérieur.

Alors, pourquoi toutes ces belles filles court-vêtues en bikini ? Pourquoi les amazones canon avec des tonnes de peau nue exposée aux éléments ? Il n'y a pas d'équivalent parmi vos personnages masculins.

Ou s'il y en a, je dois encore le trouver. Y a-t-il des Chippendales sur Yondareth? Égalité des chances de la peau exposée, s'il vous plaît !

*Les histoires centrées sur les hommes et les quêtes orientées pour les hommes sont partout. Sauver la belle demoiselle? Gagner l'épée la plus longue et la plus grosse? *clins d'œil* Obtenir un baiser d'une jeune dame ayant gagné le concours de beauté du village? *haut-le-cœur**

Je reçois souvent des messages privés dans le jeu de la part de membres de la guilde et d'autres, me demandant si je suis vraiment une fille 'IRL'. Et bien sûr, l'obligatoire, 't'as un petit-copain?' lorsque je réponds. Car, naturellement, je suis dans le jeu pour trouver un petit-ami. Ce serait bien la seule raison pour que je m'intéresse à tout ce qui est geek, n'est-ce pas?

Que Dieu nous préserve si une fille peut être une fille ET geek. Parce que les filles geeks font simplement semblant pour attirer l'attention.

Je me rends compte qu'il s'agit d'un symptôme de problèmes beaucoup plus larges. Les gameuses ne sont pas traitées comme des égales, elles n'ont pas des personnages et des histoires parallèles à celles orientées pour les hommes. Les gameuses ne sont pas reconnues ni même vraiment appréciées dans la communauté dans son ensemble.

Mais Dragon Epoch a la possibilité de faire la part dans le renversement de cette croyance. Et j'en appelle aux voix masculines du siège social pour le faire.

Voici mon défi officiel pour les créateurs de mon jeu préféré du moment : faites mieux. Faites preuve d'imagination. Souvenez-vous que presque la moitié de vos joueurs est effectivement féminine. Et nous ne voulons plus être invisibles.

Bien cordialement,
Geekette

***

Cet article avait mis longtemps à sortir… et il était le résultat des insultes contre les femmes dont j'avais souffert dans les jeux, que ce soit sur DE ou ailleurs. Des jours plus tard, je gérais encore les retombées.

J'avais été critiquée dans les blogs gérés par des hommes et d'autres supporters avides de Dragon Epoch qui affirmaient que 'tout était dans ma tête' avec une bonne dose de 'mecsplication'. Il me fallut empêcher les commentaires sur mon article, bloquer de multiples harceleurs sur mes sites de réseaux sociaux et arrêter de regarder ma boîte mail à cause des commentaires fâchés et même de quelques menaces.

Ce n'était pas une bonne semaine pour que tout ceci se produise. Pas après la mauvaise nouvelle de ma mère et le concours toujours plus proche.

J'essayai de faire de mon mieux afin de me mettre dans le bon état d'esprit pour le concours dans les moments où j'aurais normalement travaillé sur le blog ou les réseaux sociaux. Je connaissais les cours par cœur, mais me concentrer assez longtemps pour travailler sur les problèmes hypothétiques, c'était autre chose.

Je n'étais pas aidée par mes heures à l'hôpital qui furent significativement augmentées à cause de la saison estivale qui arrivait. Même si j'étais ravie d'être détournée de ma propre déprime liée à la nouvelle de ma mère et de voir mon salaire augmenter, j'avais vraiment très peu de temps pour étudier.

Et encore moins de temps pour dormir.

Et pas du tout de temps pour jouer.

Heureusement, FallenOne resta en contact avec moi tous les jours par texto. Et il me tardait toujours de recevoir le suivant.

Hé, intervint-il à une heure pas possible. *Tu vas bien ?*

Ouais, super occupée, répondis-je.

C'est bientôt ton concours, non ? Tu es prête à être la meilleure ? J'entendis presque le sourire dans sa voix – le peu que je me souvenais de cette voix grave, fluide et oui, un peu sexy, sortant de la ligne téléphonique grésillante.

Je me contenterai de réussir de justesse. Le concours est spécifiquement conçu pour éliminer soixante-quinze pour cent de tous les candidats en médecine qui le passent.

Eh bien, c'est réjouissant. Mais bon, Heath a dit que tu étais une intello.

Heath ne sait rien. : p

Tu révises pour ce truc depuis quoi ? Deux, trois mois ?

Chaque jour depuis quatre mois et demi, oui.

Tu vas y arriver. Je vais t'encourager.

Tu vas agiter des pompons et crier des choses qui riment ?

Quelque chose du genre. Bonne chance, Mia.

Lorsque Heath revint de ses vacances, il frappa à ma porte. Le camping ne s'était pas passé comme il l'avait prévu. Brian s'était plaint pendant la majeure partie du temps, donc Heath avait décidé de passer un peu de temps sans lui en traînant dans mon 'tripot' comme il l'appelait. C'était bien de l'avoir avec moi, car j'avais besoin de réconfort.

Mais entre les heures supplémentaires à l'hôpital, les révisions frénétiques de dernière minute et les cours en eux-mêmes, je n'avais pas beaucoup de temps. Et j'étais épuisée.

Une semaine plus tard, le jour du concours arriva.

Je sortis tôt du lit, je bus de la caféine et je transportai mes cinq crayons à papier numéro 2 bien taillés et ma calculatrice scientifique.

Des heures plus tard, je sortis de la salle en ayant l'impression d'avoir été frappée par un bus. Écrasée. À plat. Brisée.

J'avais été prévenue.

Le MCAT était réputé pour foutre les gens en l'air. Beaucoup d'étudiants en sortaient en ayant l'impression d'avoir totalement échoué. En gros, c'était ainsi que je me sentais.

Mais je fus rassurée par les nombreux commentaires sur les forums du MCAT expliquant comment ils géraient la suite et l'attente des résultats de trente et un jours.

Cela allait être un enfer d'attendre ces résultats. Mais j'étais en bonne compagnie : j'avais l'impression d'avoir échoué tout en espérant avoir su de quoi je parlais. J'avais eu du mal à me concentrer sur les problèmes et mon esprit avait continué à gérer.

Mais j'avais fini tôt…

C'était bon signe, non ?

J'allais le découvrir dans trente et un jours.

Chapitre Sept :
Résultats du concours

L'ATTENTE ME TUAIT. *ME. TUAIT.*

Les jeux vidéo en ligne ne m'aidèrent pas beaucoup parce que Fallen était parti pendant trois semaines pour le voyage-mystère, Kat n'était présente que sporadiquement et Heath était dans la dernière ligne droite de l'achat de son nouvel appartement.

Oui, je travaillais beaucoup d'heures, mais je n'avais plus de cours, car c'était les vacances d'été. J'avais donc besoin de quelque chose de plus.

Cela me conduisit à traîner avec des gens de mon âge… dans la même pièce… en face à face.

Et, étonnamment, cela me plut !

— Montée des eaux ! cria presque Alex en tournant une nouvelle tuile.

— Oh, allez, Alejandra, encore ? Tu portes la poisse, soupira Jenna, la colocataire d'Alex.

Je regardai Jenna, assise en face de moi. Elle était très belle avec des cheveux blond pâle complétés par une seule mèche bleue, et des yeux bleus sereins. Elle entortilla une de ses mèches platine autour de son long doigt fin. Je l'avais seulement rencontrée la semaine précédente, quand j'étais encore traumatisée par le concours, alors nous ne nous étions pas immédiatement entendues. Elle était plus réservée que la bruyante Alejandra, mais ce soir-là je commençai à l'apprécier.

Mon regard passa de Jenna aux tuiles disposées sur la table entre nous. Alex réfléchit à la façon de jouer les cartes qu'elle avait tirées pendant que Jenna se penchait en avant en lui donnant des idées. Comme l'Île Interdite était un jeu coopératif, nous devions toutes travailler ensemble et non pas les unes contre les autres.

Jenna sembla presque oublier les deux garçons à la table, qui bavaient pratiquement sur elle. D'après les potins d'Alex, Jenna sortait avec les deux en même temps. Si c'était vrai, elle les gérait comme une pro et cela ne la faisait même pas transpirer.

Ou peut-être était-ce juste une rumeur infondée.

— Alors, Mia, fréquentes-tu quelqu'un ? demanda Alex.

Je me retins de lever les sourcils de surprise en piochant mes trois cartes Trésor et en les posant sur la table devant moi : *calice, statue, statue.*

Je jetai un regard méfiant aux garçons, que je connaissais à peine, et je dis :

— Personne en particulier.

Aucune raison de préciser le fait que je ne sortais jamais avec qui que ce soit ni de dire les raisons pour cela. Ce n'était pas l'endroit pour parler d'un ex petit-ami cauchemardesque et du terrible incident au lycée.

— Je suis moi-même entre deux copains, dit Alex avec un sourire en coin adressé à Jenna.

Elles échangèrent un regard appuyé, partageant une plaisanterie personnelle. En fait, Alex était assise entre les deux copains de Jenna. Les garçons, dont j'avais oublié les prénoms, ne semblèrent rien remarquer.

— OK, Mia, pioche tes cartes Inondation.

— Certaines personnes sont vraiment douées pour passer d'une relation à une autre avec facilité, dit Alex. Je n'en fais pas partie. J'ai besoin de temps pour récupérer entre les deux.

Elle jeta un regard appuyé à Jenna qui l'ignora de façon évidente.

— Je suppose que nous ne sommes pas toutes à la recherche de l'âme sœur.

— L'âme sœur ? dit Jenna. En réalité, tu cherches ton chevalier en armure. Tu es née environ quatre cents ans trop tard pour ça, chica.

Alex leva les yeux au ciel et dit à Jenna de jouer.

Je m'amusais beaucoup avec les filles et j'apprenais même auprès d'elles. J'apprenais que je pouvais toujours avoir plus d'amis. Bien sûr, j'avais mes propres amis virtuels en ligne et Heath, mais ils ne pouvaient pas toujours être là pour moi, et je ne pouvais pas l'exiger de leur part.

Tout le monde avait sa propre vie et j'avais la mienne, c'était ainsi.

Mais je découvrais que parfois, on pouvait se sentir très seule.

En me forçant ainsi à m'ouvrir davantage à de nouvelles amitiés, j'apprenais la valeur des nouvelles relations. De nouvelles expériences.

Je n'en étais quand même pas au point de chercher un petit-ami, peu importe ce que disait Alex. Pas besoin de faire des folies, non plus !

***

Quelques semaines plus tard, Heath vint chez moi pour se servir de mon internet, assez ironiquement. Brian et lui venaient tout juste de déménager dans leur nouveau logement, un bel appartement avec deux chambres dans les collines, et internet n'était pas encore installé. Ce soir-là serait donc un peu comme au bon vieux temps, nous allions jouer ensemble dans la même pièce.

— Tu es prête ? Je crois que nous nous sommes mis d'accord pour travailler sur la quête du sort de soin complet de Kat. On sera rejoint en ligne dans une heure.

— Oui, dis-je. Je me connecte pour voir si les résultats du concours sont affichés. Officiellement, ils ne les donnent pas avant demain, mais il paraît qu'ils sont parfois disponibles la veille, après la fermeture des bureaux.

— Eh bien, connecte-toi, alors ! Regardons ça. Tu as dit avoir eu l'impression de t'en sortir pas trop mal...

— Je n'ai aucune idée de ce que j'ai vraiment fait.

Je m'étais contentée de me rassurer encore et encore chaque fois que mon cerveau voulait hurler que j'avais échoué de façon spectaculaire.

Soudain, j'eus comme une pierre dans le ventre. Et si j'avais tout foiré ? J'avais vraiment été perturbée pendant le concours. D'un autre côté, je maîtrisais bien le vocabulaire et les connaissances de base. Pouvais-je vraiment avoir merdé si terriblement en appliquant le tout ? Ah, c'était l'effet psychologique terrible du MCAT à l'œuvre...

J'écartai le clavier.

— Attends... attends. Je ne suis pas sûre. En fait, j'aime bien ne pas savoir.

Heath approcha le clavier de moi.

— Il vaut mieux savoir. Tu es brillante à tous les tests, de toute façon. La meilleure amie que peut espérer un type pour copier au lycée.

Je hochai la tête et j'inspirai profondément, naviguant sur le site de 'l'Association of American Medical Colleges' et utilisant mes données pour me connecter. J'eus l'impression qu'il me fallut une éternité à récupérer mon score. Et lorsqu'il apparut, mon estomac se noua. Puis je rafraîchis la page, incapable de croire ce que je voyais.

— Dix-huit, parvins-je à peine à piailler.

Même moi, j'entendis l'incrédulité de ma voix tremblante.

— C'est bien ? demanda Heath, chaque muscle de son corps se tendant, comme s'il était prêt à bondir et à m'attirer dans ses bras pour un gros câlin de félicitations.

— C'est terrible, dis-je d'une voix rauque. C'est plus que terrible. C'est abyssal. C'est...

Mes paroles restèrent coincées dans ma gorge et la nausée me menaça.

— Ça ne peut pas être si terrible que ça. C'est dix-huit sur... combien ?

— Quarante-cinq. Je me trouve tout en bas du vingtième centile.

Il s'éclaircit la gorge, l'air inquiet.

— Eh bien, c'est sûrement récupérable grâce à tes notes, n'est-ce pas ? Je veux dire, tu as eu des notes excellentes dans toutes les cours. Tu n'as même jamais eu un A-.

Je secouai la tête, mes yeux s'emplissant de larmes.

— Pas même mes notes peuvent sauver ça. C'est vraiment mauvais au point de laisser tomber mon rêve de faire médecine.

J'essayai de respirer. Je n'avais pas eu confiance en moi… mais je ne savais pas à quel point j'avais été mauvaise.

Comment allais-je pouvoir le dire à ma mère ? Je me sentis encore plus mal en repensant au moment où j'avais passé le concours, le mois précédent. Comment avais-je pu me tromper à ce point ? Avoir si mal travaillé et pourtant n'avoir eu absolument aucun indice de m'être plantée ainsi. C'était vraiment coup double.

Heath se redressa, m'observant de près pendant que je clignais férocement des paupières pour retenir mes larmes. Il m'avait rarement vu pleurer et je savais que cela le perturbait beaucoup de voir à quel point j'étais proche de le faire.

— Alors tu le repasses. Tout n'est pas perdu. Tu peux repasser ce truc autant de fois que tu veux, n'est-ce pas ? Comme avec ce bac de merde ? L'oral m'avait vraiment fait chier.

J'évitai son regard pendant que chaque gramme de vie et d'excitation s'échappait de moi, tombant dans une flaque déprimée sous mon siège. Toutes ces révisions. Toutes ces heures que j'avais passées à ne pas faire quelque chose d'amusant. J'aurais pu faire n'importe quoi d'autre de préférable. Toute cette énergie mentale et émotionnelle. Je ne savais même pas si je pouvais rassembler le courage de recommencer. N'aurais-je pas simplement les mêmes résultats ?

— Oui, je suppose, chuchotai-je.

Il posa une main sur mon épaule.

— Tu sais quoi ? Nous n'allons plus y penser. On va se connecter et faire exploser des trucs ce soir.

Je m'écartai de sa main et je secouai la tête.

— Je crois que je vais juste faire une sieste.

— Mia…

Je levai une main.

— Je suis sûre que vous pouvez trouver un autre enchanteur ou enchanteresse pour la quête de groupe. S'il te plaît ? Je me sens juste… super mal et j'aimerais être seule. Peux-tu aller à Starbucks pour leur connexion internet ?

Heath me regarda longuement.

— Laisse-moi me connecter et annuler. Je vais rester avec toi pour m'assurer que tu vas bien.

Je frappai le bureau devant moi.

— Je vais bien et je ne pourrai pas dormir si tu es ici. S'il te plaît. J'ai juste besoin d'être seule. Ça ira. Je te le promets.

Les plis sur le front de Heath s'approfondirent.

— D'accord… et si j'allais au Starbucks du Circle, comme ça je pourrais repasser te voir en rentrant ?

Je haussai les épaules.

— Si ma lumière est éteinte, ne frappe pas. Je serai en train de dormir. Il est temps que je dorme. Je suis tellement épuisée. Je t'appelle demain matin.

Je détestais la façon dont ma voix tremblait.

Heath fronça tellement les sourcils qu'il risquait de former un mono-sourcil permanent, mais il finit par partir.

Et puis… et puis. Alice tomba dans le trou, le cul par-dessus la théière. Et elle n'atterrit pas au pays des merveilles. Carrément pas. À la place, elle se morfondit, elle marina dans le sel de ses propres larmes et de son échec, mijota dans son propre sang d'encre. Hantée par des *si seulement.*

Si seulement j'avais travaillé plus dur.

Si seulement j'étais restée concentrée. Quel genre de médecin aurai-je été, après tout, si je ne pouvais pas mettre mes inquiétudes personnelles de côté et faire le travail pour lequel j'étais formée ? Quel genre de médecin aurai-je été si j'étais distraite alors que des vies dépendaient de moi ?

Si seulement maman n'était pas tombée malade. Si seulement…

Si seulement je n'avais pas perdu espoir.

J'étais restée en contact avec ma mère tout ce temps, l'appelant tous les jours. Elle avait déjà fait quatre séances de chimio et je savais qu'il ne faudrait pas longtemps avant que cela commence à devenir très dur. J'avais réussi à rentrer tous les week-ends où j'avais pu rassembler l'argent pour l'essence et le temps de faire le voyage.

Chaque fois que je lui parlais, elle paraissait juste légèrement plus fatiguée. Bientôt, ses cheveux allaient tomber, si cela n'avait pas encore commencé. Je ne savais pas ce qu'elle ne me disait pas pour essayer de me protéger de la vérité. Afin de ne pas me distraire. Afin que je puisse réussir.

Je ne pouvais même pas imaginer la déception écrasante qu'elle ressentirait en entendant cette nouvelle.

Ce n'était pas seulement pour moi que j'avais échoué. J'avais échoué pour elle.

Et c'était douloureux. Très douloureux. Tellement.

Peut-être n'étais-je pas assez douée pour être médecin, finalement. Ce test était conçu pour éliminer les plus mauvais. Peut-être étais-je mauvaise.

Cette pensée me faisait mal, plus que les autres. Épuisée, je pleurai jusqu'à m'endormir.

Et comme je n'avais pas cours le lendemain, je fis la grasse matinée… enfin, je l'aurais fait si mon téléphone n'avait pas reçu un texto à huit heures.

Ça va ? C'était FallenOne.

Je clignai des paupières pour chasser le sommeil de mes yeux et j'essayai d'interpréter son message. Pourquoi m'avait-il envoyé cela ? Cherchait-il à savoir pourquoi je ne m'étais pas connectée la veille ? Heath avait-il dit quelque chose ? Que devais-je dire à FallenOne ?

Salut. Je vais bien, répondis-je.

Sa réponse revint au bout de quelques secondes. *Je ne te crois pas.*

Pourquoi... parce que je suis tellement accro que seules les pires circonstances m'empêcheraient de me connecter à DE ? Ma tendance au sarcasme ne m'avait pas quittée, même par texto et quand j'étais émotionnellement épuisée.

Quelque chose du genre.

Que vous a raconté Fragged ?

Il a dit que tu ne te sentais pas bien. Ai-je le droit de prendre des nouvelles d'une amie ?

Mes pouces traînèrent au-dessus du clavier virtuel, j'hésitai avant de taper : *Non. Je vais bien.*

Encore une fois, sa réponse arriva rapidement. *Alors c'est tout ? Juste bien ?*

Je soupirai, bien qu'il ne puisse pas m'entendre. *Tu es pénible. Tu n'as pas cours, ou autre chose ?*

Ou autre chose... mais pas avant une heure. J'ai du temps. Qu'est-ce qui t'ennuie ?

J'ai eu les résultats de mon MCAT...

Mon pouce hésita au-dessus du bouton 'envoyer'. Voulais-je vraiment lui en parler ? Étais-je prête à décharger ça sur un ami seulement virtuel ? D'un autre côté, il avait été là pour moi lorsque ma mère avait eu son diagnostic. Fallen avait veillé toute la nuit, prouvant ainsi qu'il se souciait de moi.

J'inspirai profondément, j'appuyai sur le bouton 'effacer' et je retapai le message. *Je me suis plantée au MCAT.*

Tu as déjà les résultats ?

Oui. Échec total.

Définis quand même 'plantée'. Est-ce que ça veut dire que tu n'as pas eu le score que tu espérais avoir ?

Je me mordis l'intérieur de la joue en continuant à taper, encore une fois hantée par ce qui s'était mal passé. Le stress ? Une mauvaise préparation ? Personne ne le savait… *cela signifie que je suis une ratée.*

Ah. Non. Je rejette totalement cette affirmation.

J'ai bien peur que ce soit vrai.

Non, Mia. Tu as eu un score de merde. Il se passe beaucoup de choses dans ta vie dernièrement.

J'ai bien peur que l'AAMC n'accepte pas les mots d'excuse de maman.

Ce n'est pas ce que je voulais dire. Je voulais dire que tu peux le repasser.

Tant que je ne sais pas ce qui s'est mal passé, ce serait sans doute une erreur. Mais je dois accepter le fait que – je déglutis bruyamment en tapant les mots qui suivirent – *je ne serais sans doute jamais un médecin.*

N'importe quoi. Bien sûr que tu seras médecin. Et, un très bon, en plus. Qui se soucie des autres.

Je dois découvrir si c'est vrai, ou si je suis seulement une pseudo étudiante qui ne peut pas assez se concentrer pour passer le test.

J'ai entendu dire que ce concours était très dur. Je me suis renseignée quand tu m'en as parlé la première fois. Et tu avais vraiment beaucoup de soucis. Tu peux le repasser. Je viens de trouver trois lieux différents sur Google dans la région de Los Angeles où tu peux le passer le mois prochain. Je vais t'envoyer le lien.

Je me rendis soudain compte qu'il n'essayait pas seulement de m'aider, mais qu'il était aussi vraiment adorable en essayant de me remonter le moral. Et moi, je piétinais sommairement tous ses encouragements.

Je me mordis la lèvre en réfléchissant. Il fallait sans doute que j'arrête d'être négative. Et si j'étais honnête, il me faisait me sentir un peu mieux...

Merci. Je ne crois pas le repasser tout de suite avant d'avoir formulé un plan d'attaque. Mais quand je le repasserai, je n'irais pas conduire jusqu'à Los Angeles alors qu'il est régulièrement disponible à Anaheim et Fullerton. C'est beaucoup plus près.

Quelques secondes après avoir appuyé sur 'envoyer', je me rendis compte que je venais de révéler où. Mais après m'être inquiétée pendant une fraction de seconde, je n'y pensai plus. Plus de trois millions de personnes habitaient dans le comté d'Orange. Ce n'était pas comme s'il pouvait me harceler juste d'après cette information, même s'il décidait de s'envoler vers mon coin du pays et d'essayer de me rencontrer.

Trop d'informations. Je pourrais être un tueur en série, tu sais.

Je ris à voix haute. *C'est l'impression que je commençais à avoir, mais après le résultat de mon concours, j'ai un peu envie de mourir.*

J'espère que tu plaisantes. Dis-moi que tu plaisantes, s'il te plaît.

Je souriais à présent, alors que je me sentais comme une merde. *Je plaisante.*

Je dois partir dans une minute, mais je reprendrai de tes nouvelles plus tard dans la journée. S'il te plaît, appelle-moi ou Fragged ou n'importe qui si tu te sens vraiment déprimée.

Lui reparler au téléphone ? Mon estomac eut une espèce de tremblement de papillon bizarre. J'avais espéré, depuis notre dernier appel – malgré les circonstances – qu'il essaie de me rappeler. *Tu as ma parole*, répondis-je.

Tu vas te connecter ce soir, d'ailleurs. Toi et moi on va s'amuser. Il y a cet endroit génial dans la zone de Forgotten Ridge. Une grotte cachée. Je vais te la montrer.

Je fronçai les sourcils. Une grotte cachée ? Comment était-il au courant d'une telle chose ? *Tu mens... je n'en ai jamais entendu parler.*

C'est un secret. Tu ne dois le dire à personne. Tu ne peux pas en parler dans ton blog.

Je fronçai encore plus les sourcils. *Pourquoi ?*

Sinon ce n'est plus un secret !

Si c'est tellement secret, comment l'as-tu découvert ? Et pourquoi me le dire à moi... une blogueuse ?

Je pourrais te répondre, mais il faudrait ensuite que je te tue.

*Tu es donc *bien un tueur en série.*

Je suis un tueur en série... de gobelins, de trolls et de vampires pixelisés. Et de toutes les autres merdes qu'il nous faut tuer pour gagner des niveaux.

Je soupirai et je m'adossai contre ma chaise, surprise d'avoir presque oublié de me sentir misérable au cours des dernières minutes.

Tu te connecteras, hein ?

Sinon quoi ?

Sinon je dirais à Fragged d'aller chez toi pour t'embêter.

Je me connecterai. D'ailleurs, s'il vient ici, son copain va faire une crise. Ce soir, c'est le soir où ils sortent.

Super. C'est juste toi et moi alors. Et notre petite cachette secrète.

Je faillis – faillis – taper 'une escapade romantique' avant de me raviser.

***

Fallen m'emmena comme promis à l'aventure. On se rejoignit près de la gare de transport et on grimpa à bord d'une gondole portée par les griffes d'un énorme dragon argenté. Cela fonctionnait un peu comme un ballon dirigeable de style fantastique, qui nous portait d'un bout à l'autre du continent en battant ses ailes géantes de reptile au lieu d'utiliser les lois de la thermodynamique. Dans le jeu, ces longs voyages étaient représentés par des délais en temps réel.

Ce fut durant un de ces délais, quelque part entre la Tour du Dragon de la ville ancienne et notre destination inconnue, au-dessus des montagnes de Forgotten Ridge, que Fallen m'envoya un message.

*FallenOne vous dit : *Clique sur la trappe. Maintenant !*

La trappe ? Je parcourus l'écran des yeux jusqu'à voir le fond de la gondole, où il y avait bien une petite trappe cachée dans un coin. Je fis immédiatement ce qu'il avait dit. Soudain, mon personnage tomba en chute libre à côté du sien, chute qui dans des circonstances normales nous aurait conduits à une mort certaine. Manifestement, cet endroit n'avait rien de normal.

Nous plongeâmes dans un lac de montagne isolé niché entre les sommets. Depuis le fond de la zone et à pied – ou même sur une monture – je savais que cette partie de la carte était inaccessible.

Je le savais, car j'avais essayé de grimper jusqu'au sommet des montagnes et le jeu ne l'avait pas permis. J'avais atteint le 'bord' de ce qui était accessible aux joueurs. D'une façon ou d'une autre,

FallenOne avait découvert un 'trou' dans cette barrière en se laissant tomber d'en haut... et il avait été récompensé par ce merveilleux endroit.

Le soleil se levait tout juste au-dessus de la crête escarpée, le ciel virtuel était couleur pêche et crème. Nos personnages nagèrent sur place dans le lac, l'eau ondulant autour de nous. J'aurais pu rester là pour toujours, mais FallenOne nous dirigea vers une rive en face d'une falaise.

On traversa le lac à la nage jusqu'à cette rive, où une immense cascade puissante tombait dans le lac, éclaboussant tout autour, poussant des vaguelettes vers les bords.

*FallenOne vous dit : *Quand tu nageras à travers la cascade, plonge vers le bas. Au fond du lac, tu verras une entrée : nage dedans. Tu dois le faire assez vite avant de perdre ton souffle et de te noyer. Tu es prête ?*

Une entrée cachée vers une grotte, derrière une cascade, dans un lac inaccessible aux joueurs, sauf s'ils sont au courant du trou dans la zone de survol ?

Effectivement, c'était bien caché !

Vraiment dommage que je ne puisse pas en parler dans mon blog...

Je suivis les instructions de FallenOne et je terminai dans un minuscule tunnel sous-marin au fond du lac. Nous étions presque à bout de souffle lorsque le tunnel se mit à remonter et on émergea dans une grotte féérique.

J'hallucine ! écrivis-je. *C'est incroyable...*

Une lumière diluée entrait par une source indirecte et quelque chose sur les parois de la grotte créait une lueur verte bioluminescente. Des stalagmites aux couleurs de pierres précieuses pendaient du plafond, les stalactites correspondantes s'élevant du sol. L'eau était claire comme le cristal, sa surface réfléchissant tout, et le bruit distant et mélodieux de l'eau s'égouttait avec un rythme régulier. C'était renversant.

De l'endroit où nous nous trouvions dans l'eau profonde de la grotte, on avait l'impression qu'il y avait d'autres salles menant à d'autres passages.

Moi : *Cet endroit est immense. On dirait que ça continue sans fin.*
Lui : *Tu veux l'explorer ?*
Moi : *Si je le veux ? Est-ce que les mynocks aiment ronger les câbles électriques ?*

Nous trouvâmes une salle avec des meubles d'un style rustique, façonnés à partir de bûches et couverts de peaux de bêtes. Les parois d'une autre salle étaient recouvertes d'initiales gravées. Parfois simplement deux initiales comme A.D. ou C.W. et d'autres fois trois, comme J.G.F. ou W.J.D. Il s'agissait de graffitis virtuels. Toutes les initiales étaient gravées dans des styles d'écriture différents, comme si les personnes les avaient inscrites elles-mêmes.

Qui était-ce ? Les développeurs du jeu ? Les employés de l'entreprise ayant créé DE ? La famille et les amis du développeur qui avait caché cette grotte ici ?

Comme c'était étrange… et merveilleux.

On continua notre exploration. Une partie de la grotte s'ouvrait sur une prairie cachée derrière la montagne. Elle était pleine de fleurs sauvages et un ciel bleu pur brillait au-dessus avec le soleil qui s'était levé. *Magnifique.*

Moi : *J'aimerais qu'un tel paradis existe dans le monde réel.*

Lui : *Tu te sens mieux maintenant ?*

Moi : *Oui ! Merci.*

Lui : *Avec plaisir.*

Moi : *Vas-tu me dire comment tu connais cet endroit, à présent ?*

Lui : *Disons que j'ai passé du temps à explorer et à chercher des failles.*

Moi : *QUI es-tu ? Comment peux-tu avoir le temps de faire ça ?*

J'aurais pu le soupçonner d'être un employé de l'entreprise qui concevait le jeu, sauf que je savais que l'entreprise était basée en Californie et que lui, il avait des horaires de la côte est. Peut-être avait-il un ami qui travaillait pour l'entreprise...

Connaissant FallenOne – enfin, le peu que je le connaissais – cela resterait sans doute un mystère pendant des années. Et je pouvais l'accepter ou bien essayer de lui faire cracher la vérité.

***

Il fallut environ une semaine, mais je finis par me remettre du désastre MCAT de la décennie. Non pas que la sensation cinglante de l'échec avait complètement disparu.

Je me remis sur pied essentiellement parce que Heath venait physiquement me traîner hors de chez moi, m'emmenant au cinéma, au minigolf, n'importe où. Et parce que Kat et FallenOne me harcelaient virtuellement pour que je me connecte et que je fasse des quêtes avec eux. On obtint le sort de soin complet de Kat et on passa à la quête barbare de Fragged pour qu'il apprenne des techniques cachées du Grand Ermite mercenaire qui, ironiquement, vivait à Forgotten Ridge.

FallenOne ne fit jamais allusion à la grotte cachée devant les autres, et bien que j'aurais aimé en parler, je restai muette. Ce serait donc notre petite cachette secrète, un paradis virtuel presque incroyable. Mais je n'y retournai jamais plus.

Un soir, quelques semaines plus tard, nous travaillions sur la quête incroyablement ennuyeuse de Heath avec beaucoup de commentaires désobligeants de la part de Persephone et moi.

— Arrête de te plaindre, Eloisa. Ta grande quête est la suivante. Sauf si tu veux que je grogne et gémisse tout le temps que nous travaillerons dessus, dit Heath. La vengeance est une salope.

— Tout comme toi, lui répondis-je en une fraction de seconde.

Tout le monde dans le groupe bénéficiait de la présence d'un mercenaire entraîné, car c'était lui qui se plaçait devant, criant des choses énervantes contre les monstres afin qu'ils n'attaquent que lui. Son seul travail était de se tenir devant nous comme un bouclier de viande pendant que nous nous occupions d'attaquer le monstre. À notre niveau, chaque combat était un effort commun.

— Vous savez quoi, dis-je après que nous ayons tué notre quinzième troll. Ce jeu me plaît vraiment beaucoup. Il y a quelque chose pour tout le monde et j'aime la créativité des quêtes. J'aimerais seulement qu'ils aient quelque chose pour ceux parmi nous qui ont envie de creuser plus profondément et de résoudre un mystère.

Mes pensées revenaient sans cesse à cette grotte cachée et la raison de sa présence. J'avais voulu creuser plus loin.

FallenOne envoya un message au groupe. *Que veux-tu dire ?*

— Eh bien, par exemple, j'adorerais qu'il y ait une quête secrète.

Je me redressai sur ma chaise et je regardai l'écran, tapant sur les boutons correspondants à mes sorts qui illuminèrent l'écran comme un orage.

— Comme quelque chose de caché dans le jeu en dessous des quêtes évidentes. Peut-être devrions-nous chercher des indices ou parler à des PNJ pour avoir des pistes qui nous mèneraient à des chaînes de quête secrètes. J'adore être obligée de penser de façon créative.

C'est une idée très intéressante, commenta FallenOne.

— Eh bien, un jour il y aura un jeu qui le permettra, dis-je.

Fragged se mit à rire.

— Je ne pense même pas qu'ils peuvent faire quelque chose de ce genre. Pas avec les techniques de programmation actuelles.

J'envoyai mon dernier sort d'explosion pour achever le gros monstre, puis j'indiquai que nous devions attendre la régénération de mon mana avant notre combat suivant.

— J'aurais aimé qu'ils le puissent. Dragon Epoch est tellement plus avancée que les MMO auxquels j'ai joué jusqu'à maintenant. Si quelqu'un peut faire une chose aussi cool, c'est bien les gens qui ont créé DE.

— Peut-être, répondit Fragged.

FallenOne intervint. *Ce n'est pas très compliqué à mettre en place. Un peu de codage imbriqué construit de façon créative.*

Fragged ricana.

— Ah, alors maintenant tu es un expert en programmation ?

Non pas que nous avions la moindre idée de ce que pouvait être son expertise… hormis son talent à garder des secrets.

FallenOne dit au groupe : /*hausse les épaules Ce n'est qu'une supposition. Peut-être est-ce trop compliqué. Qui sait ?*

Je soupirai.

— Ce serait dommage, car ça pourrait être très amusant. Ils pourraient donner des astuces hebdomadaires pour les joueurs intéressés. Je ne sais pas. C'était juste une idée.

Des astuces ? C'est trop facile. Il faut faire travailler les joueurs, dit Fallen.

— Enfin, ce serait comme ils voudraient, répondis-je. Ils pourraient devenir très créatifs, même le faire ouvrir sur une nouvelle zone ou une extension. Il pourrait y avoir toute une histoire derrière.

— Quoi qu'il en soit, interrompit Persephone, ne devons-nous pas chercher ce boss pour finir la quête de Fragged ?

— Il n'est pas encore apparu, dit Fragged.

Persephone soupira.

— Allons faire autre chose pendant un petit moment. Je m'ennuie.

C'était une plainte courante de la part de notre amie canadienne énergique.

— Tu es sanguinaire, l'accusa Fragged.

Ils continuèrent leur dispute amicale pendant qu'une autre conversation démarra.

*FallenOne vous dit : *Alors, parle-moi un peu plus de cette idée de quête secrète. Je trouve que c'est cool.*

Je souris, je me mordis la lèvre inférieure et je répondis.

*Vous dites à FallenOne : *Oh, c'est juste une idée en l'air. J'aimerais que le jeu insère des surprises cachées comme ça. Des 'Easter eggs', tu vois ? Juste des petites quêtes secrètes amusantes que l'on peut découvrir quand on en a assez de collectionner les langues de lézard géant pour une sorcière locale ou des dents de tigre pour le chaman de la ville...*

Lui : *Ces quêtes ne sont pas *si mauvaises...*

Moi : *Non, elles ne sont pas mauvaises, mais elles ne poussent pas vraiment à réfléchir de façon créative, tu vois ce que je veux dire ? C'est juste que DE est un jeu si énorme et ils ont montré avec la conception du jeu qu'ils sont fabuleux. Je pense que ce serait amusant s'ils pouvaient mettre ça en place. Dommage qu'ils n'aient pas une 'boîte à idées' de façon à ce que les joueurs puissent soumettre ce genre d'idées aux concepteurs.*

Lui : *Ha ha, très drôle. J'espère que tu utilises vraiment la boîte à idées au lieu d'être 'sarc-tastique'. Peut-être devraient-ils juste lire ton blog. Quelqu'un devrait leur en parler.*

Moi : *Apparemment, quelqu'un l'a déjà fait. J'ai été mise en lien sur leur page d'accueil plusieurs fois, assez bizarrement !*

Lui : *Tu sous-estimes à quel point ton blog est intéressant. Tu ne devrais pas faire ça.*

Moi : *Eh bien... merci. Je suis contente qu'il te plaise. Si je ne finis pas par devenir médecin, je pourrais peut-être découvrir comment vivre de mes super talents de blogueuse.*

— Qu'est-ce que vous foutez, tous les deux, vous fumez des joints ? cria Fragged dans le micro. On se bat, ici !

Ce fut donc terminé. On finit la quête de Fragged ce soir-là. Et plus tard, je soumis vraiment ma fichue idée de quête secrète à la boîte à idées que probablement personne ne vérifiait.

Si c'était le cas, comment savoir si l'idée allait servir ? Cela aurait été vraiment super si elle leur servait.

Chapitre Huit : Action ou vérité

L'AUTOMNE REVINT ET AVEC LUI, LE DEBUT DE MA dernière année : le dernier semestre de cours avec plusieurs disciplines des plus compliquées que j'aie pu suivre de toutes mes études. Et pour le MCAT, je passai deux bons mois à réévaluer ce qui s'était mal passé et à chercher un plan d'attaque.

Manifestement, il y avait toute une stratégie derrière ce test. Il fallait que j'apprenne cette stratégie. Et vite.

Car plus je tardais à le repasser, plus cela allait retarder mes candidatures en École de Médecine. Je risquais de perdre une année entière entre la fin de la prépa et l'école de médecine.

Je pris sur moi et je rejoignis un groupe de révisions. Ce n'était vraiment pas mon truc, pourtant c'était nécessaire.

— Nous devrions peut-être commencer par nous présenter ? intervint la blonde guillerette en s'agitant sur sa chaise dans une des salles d'études réservées de la bibliothèque de Chapman University Leatherby. Je m'appelle Alicia Smiley, je fais une majeure en chimie organique. Pas de plaisanteries sur mon nom, s'il vous plaît, merci. Je souris beaucoup, effectivement.

Elle ponctua cette affirmation par des fossettes parfaites sur chaque joue.

Le petit groupe rit de sa plaisanterie. Nous avions utilisé un forum universitaire pour nous rassembler, à partir de la date approximative du test MCAT que nous allions passer. La plupart avaient un an d'études de moins que moi, et j'avais l'intention de ne pas parler de mon échec précédent.

Celui qui se présenta ensuite, ce fut un type avec des cheveux bruns hirsutes plaqués sur son front et un pull très moche. Il se présenta doucement comme étant Clark. Je le modifiai mentalement, lui faisant porter des lunettes à la Clark Kent. Ce qui me passa ensuite dans la tête, ce fut une image de lui arrachant son pull atroce pour révéler une combinaison bleue avec un 'S' géant sur le torse. Il fallut que je me morde la lèvre pour étouffer un fou rire.

Quelques autres se présentèrent. Puis ce fut mon tour.

— Je suis Mia Strong. Majeure en biologie. Et, euh, oui, je veux juste vraiment bien me sortir de ce concours.

La pierre dans mon estomac se remit à s'agiter, comme chaque fois que je contemplais mon échec et ce qu'il causait si je ne me bottais pas les fesses pour passer ce foutu concours.

Enfin, un type a l'air vraiment jeune avec des cheveux blonds bouclés et assez beau, mais très ordinaire se pencha en avant.

— Je m'appelle Jon. Majeure en kinésiologie. J'ai récemment été transféré de Penn – c'est-à-dire, de l'université de Pennsylvanie de l'Ivy League, *pas* Penn State. Et je tuerais tous ceux qui confondent les deux. Je rigole, bien sûr.

Tout le monde eut un rire nerveux. Les gens de la côte ouest n'avaient aucune idée de la différence entre ces deux universités, en dehors du fait qu'il y en avait une prestigieuse faisant partie de l'Ivy League, et une autre qui avait une équipe de foot américain très célèbre. Cela ne nous intéressait pas beaucoup.

Harvard ou Stanford, *ça*, on comprenait. La différence entre les Penns ? Pas tellement.

Je ris avec le reste du groupe et lorsque le regard de Jon se posa sur moi, un sourire espiègle apparut. Je lui souris et quelque chose changea dans ses yeux, devint plus intense. Comme des codes passant aux phares. Je me renfrognai.

Oh oh. J'avais déjà vu ce regard, quand j'avais pris la peine de regarder assez longtemps pour le remarquer.

Je détournai immédiatement les yeux et je fis exprès d'ignorer Jon pendant le reste de la séance de révisions. Avant de partir, nous fîmes tourner une feuille avec nos numéros de téléphone et nos adresses mail, avant d'organiser le rendez-vous suivant. Miss Smiley McFossettes, comme je l'appelais désormais mentalement, allait nous envoyer un emploi du temps avec les spécifications du concours et nous allions nous revoir, prêts à nous mettre par paires afin de nous tester mutuellement.

Je pouvais le faire. J'allais y arriver. Je me chantai ces phrases en me précipitant hors de la pièce à la minute où ce fut terminé. Pour me protéger, j'appuyai mon téléphone contre mon oreille, faisant semblant de parler au cas où quelqu'un aurait pensé pouvoir s'approcher de moi après la séance.

J'avais appris beaucoup de tours de ce genre et ils fonctionnaient très bien. Certains auraient dit *trop* bien.

— Quand vas-tu enfin commencer à sortir avec quelqu'un ? m'avait récemment demandé Heath.

— Le douze du mois de Jamais, hypothétiquement.

Heath avait soupiré et levé les yeux au ciel.

— Espèce de tête de mule.

— Espèce de *déterminée*.

Je levai un sourcil en croisant les bras.

— Ma vie ne va pas dépendre des volontés d'un homme.

Heath ricana.

— Crois-moi, les volontés d'un homme peuvent être très agréables… quand tu trouves le bon.

— As-tu trouvé le bon, Heath ?

Lorsque le sourire disparut brusquement de son visage, je sus que j'avais dit ce qu'il ne fallait pas. *Oh, merde.* Cela m'arrivait tout le temps, dernièrement.

— Je veux dire, tant qu'il te rend heureux, n'est-ce pas ?

Après une pause gênée, on changea de sujet et je notai mentalement de gérer le sujet beaucoup plus subtilement dans le futur. D'un autre côté, ce genre de réactions susceptibles me servaient bien, car elles apprenaient à Heath qu'il lui fallait éviter le sujet. Et heureusement, il apprenait vite.

Ma mère, eh bien, c'était une autre histoire. Mais en général, elle n'insistait pas. Elle me regardait simplement avec des yeux tristes et je savais qu'elle pensait à ce qui m'était arrivé au lycée. Cependant, chaque fois qu'elle abordait le sujet, je parvenais à le changer. C'était ainsi.

***

Comme c'était ma dernière année à l'université, la pression était montée. Mes journées étaient réparties entre les cours, les devoirs, du travail supplémentaire pour le groupe d'études du MCAT, des recherches au labo pour – et parfois avec – mon professeur conseiller. Il y avait aussi les heures à l'hôpital, bien qu'elles aient été à nouveau réduites, maintenant que l'été était passé. Et quand j'avais le temps, l'écriture sur mon blog et les jeux vidéo. Dormir et manger se faisait quelque part entre tout cela. On rince et on recommence.

Malheureusement, notre groupe de jeux vidéo ne se rejoignait qu'une fois par semaine, mais je parvenais à faire quelques heures de plus ici et là. Et lorsque c'était le cas, je croisais fréquemment FallenOne. Je me demandais souvent si c'était par hasard ou exprès.

Mais pourquoi remettre en question une bonne chose, hein ?

Bien sûr, les soupçons de Kat tournaient également dans ma tête. FallenOne s'intéressait-il à moi ?

Je devais admettre… qu'il me plaisait bien.

*FallenOne vous dit : *J'ai réfléchi à cette histoire de quête secrète dont tu parlais il y a quelques semaines. C'est une idée très cool.*

*Vous dites à FallenOne : *Ils travaillent sans doute déjà sur quelque chose du genre. Je ne serais pas surprise.*

Lui : *Moi non plus.*

Moi : *Oui, quand ces geeks ne sont pas obsédés par les corps des femmes, ils sont assez intelligents.*

Lui : *Alors comme ça, tu penses, que nous autres geeks nous passons notre temps à être obsédés par les femmes ?*

Moi : *Ai-je tort ?*

Lui : *Mais en quoi est-ce différent des autres hommes ?*

Moi : *Tu n'as pas tort. C'est sans doute pareil. Sauf si tu es Heath.*

***

Il ne me fallut que deux autres séances de révision afin que Jon me demande de sortir avec lui. C'était juste pour un café après et aussi pour 'réviser un peu plus'. En outre, il l'avait proposé après que nous soyons tombés ensemble par hasard – du moins, je l'espérais – lors de la deuxième séance où nous avions révisé en binômes. Il s'était ensuite délibérément assis à côté de moi lors de la troisième.

Je détestais devoir rejeter quelqu'un. Particulièrement quelqu'un d'aussi gentil que Jon. Et au fond de moi, je me demandai : serait-ce vraiment si désagréable de sortir boire un café avec lui ?

Mais le café allait conduire à quelques verres. Et les verres pouvaient conduire à sortir en boîte, ou ce que faisaient les gens normaux de mon âge. Et cela conduirait peut-être à 'passer chez moi' après. Et puis… et puis. C'était la partie qui me faisait toujours tout arrêter.

— Je suis désolée. Je suis super occupée. Je rejoins quelqu'un dans une heure.

— D'accord… il laissa sa voix traîner, peut-être pour que je développe.

Lorsque je ne dis rien, il changea de tactique.

— Ah. Je suppose que j'aurais dû te demander si tu as un petit-ami.

— Je n'en ai pas…

Son visage s'illumina de façon visible. J'aurais peut-être dû mentir ?

— *Mais* je prends mes études très au sérieux. J'ai une bourse, ce qui nécessite que j'obtienne des notes parfaites. Je ne fais pas grand-chose, y compris sortir.

Il leva les sourcils.

— Ah bon ? À cause de ta religion ?

C'était une question logique. Après tout, l'université de Chapman était liée à l'église et il y avait un certain nombre d'étudiants qui étaient là pour cette raison. Mais pas moi. J'étais là grâce à la belle bourse complète qu'ils m'avaient proposée quand j'avais terminé le lycée.

Encore une fois, j'aurais pu mentir, mais je choisis de ne pas le faire.

— Pas particulièrement, non. C'est juste un choix personnel.

Jon cligna des paupières, perplexe, et je rassemblai mes affaires, prête à me débarrasser de lui. Il me suivit quand je me précipitai hors de la bibliothèque comme si j'avais des choses à faire, des gens à voir. J'avais effectivement beaucoup de choses à faire ce jour-là. Bon, peut-être pas *beaucoup*, mais il y avait un projet à terminer et la lessive à faire quelque part au milieu.

Le 'choix personnel' ne devait pas être une excuse valable, car Jon fit une remarque aimable en disant que je m'épuisais. Moi, tout aussi aimablement, je plaisantai sur le fait qu'il y avait plusieurs membres convoités de notre groupe – Smiley McFossettes, par exemple – qui avaient semblé s'intéresser à lui.

Jon ne fut pas dissuadé, d'après l'air déterminé dans ses yeux.

Malgré tout, je fus capable de le détourner de son objectif et de continuer ma journée. Malheureusement, en un sens, ma soirée allait répéter la chose.

Pendant que je jouais avec mes amis, je faisais des pauses pour descendre en courant déplacer les vêtements du lave-linge au sèche-linge. La preuve que je ne mentais pas !

Ce soir-là, ce fut le tour de FallenOne, alors nous travaillâmes sur sa quête de l'arme épique, le Bâton de Grande Puissance. Parmi les ingrédients, il fallait une plume spéciale d'une créature très rare. Le Flamand Rose Superflu apparaissait dans le Lagon Perdu. Mais il nous fallut traverser des hordes d'hippopotames hostiles, d'alligators enragés et d'autruches aggro par milliers, tuant encore et encore afin que le Flamand apparaisse. Il nous fallut des *heures*.

De longues heures ennuyeuses. Au point que nous commençâmes à sortir les boissons caféinées et à devenir un peu bêtes, plaisantant et riant à la moindre chose.

Fallen avait depuis longtemps proposé de laisser tomber, mais nous n'en avions pas l'intention. Nous étions les enfoirés grincheux les plus têtus du serveur et nous n'allions pas céder.

Nous allions arracher cette plume rare de ce putain de flamand rose même si c'était la dernière chose que nous faisions !

C'était une soirée chaude de septembre, le pire mois de chaleur en Californie du Sud. Mon appartement – même si c'était une trouvaille fabuleuse – n'avait pas d'air conditionné, je devais donc dépendre des ventilateurs de fenêtre pour me soulager un peu. Cela ne faisait que souffler de l'air chaud partout sur moi.

Bien sûr, les fenêtres ouvertes signifiaient que j'avais une ligne directe vers les cris et les hurlements de mes voisins, qui appréciaient le sexe bruyant à n'importe quelle température. Qu'il fasse chaud, froid, sec. Qu'il pleuve ou qu'il fasse soleil. Ces deux-là baisaient comme des chiens perpétuellement en chaleur.

— Bon sang, ce n'est pas vrai. Les voisins recommencent, dis-je enfin après le quatrième 'Oh oui !'

Kat soupira profondément.

— J'aimerais tellement être en train de baiser. Je suis jalouse.

— Qui ne l'est pas ? répondit Heath.

— Ça ne veut pas dire que j'apprécie d'entendre mes voisins le faire en continu. Bon sang. Quelqu'un doit leur faire jouer aux jeux vidéo.

— Oui, parce qu'attendre l'apparition d'une créature rare est *tellement* plus amusant que les orgasmes, répondit Heath.

— Peut-être devrions-nous faire quelque chose pour passer le temps pendant que nous faisons cette quête merdique ? Manifestement pas aussi agréable que ce que font les voisins de Mia… mais que pensez-vous d'un jeu ? Action ou vérité ? demanda Persephone.

— Qu'est-ce que tu vas bien pouvoir nous donner comme gage ? Traverser le marais tout nu sans armure ? Vous voulez bien refuser ça ? répondit Heath.

— Oh, allez, gémit Kat. Je commence. Quel est l'endroit le plus fou où vous avez couché ? Vérité, vous devez répondre. Action, vous devez combattre le monstre suivant en solo sans armes pendant que nous regardons tous en rigolant.

— C'est facile, répondit Heath. Sous les gradins au lycée pendant un match de basket.

— Quoi ? m'exclamai-je. Heath ? Même pas vrai.

Il rit.

— Et pourtant, c'est vrai.

Je ricanai.

— Avec qui ?

— Ah, ah, ah ! On ne triche pas, gronda Kat. Ce n'est pas à ton tour de poser la question. Fallen, que choisis-tu ? Tu réponds à la question ou tu laisses tomber tes nunchakus et tu attaques le monstre avec les poings ?

Comme d'habitude, Fallen répondit seulement par texte. Mais comme il tapait vite, il était facile pour lui de suivre la conversation.

Bon allez. Pourquoi pas ? Vérité. Moi aussi, ça date du lycée. Je travaillais au bureau de mon oncle quand j'étais en terminale et cette fille qui travaillait là-bas aussi m'a fait une proposition intéressante.

Nous l'avons fait sur la table de conférences après les heures de bureau quand il n'y avait plus personne.

— Oh la la ! rugit Heath en riant. Le tien est beaucoup mieux que le mien.

Carrément pas, il n'y avait pas une foule pour le mien ! rétorqua Fallen.

— Non, pourtant je parie que la conférence suivante a dû être… intéressante. Particulièrement avec ton oncle assis là.

*Non, je ne faisais que bouger des cartons et m'occuper du courrier pour ce boulot. Je n'ai jamais eu à m'asseoir aux réunions. *Elle, oui, par contre, alors je suppose que c'était bizarre pour elle LOL.*

— Ah. Je suis certaine que ces conférences spéciales ont été menées avec doigté, dit Kat.

Cela ne s'est produit qu'une fois. C'était un peu plus conventionnel ensuite.

Lorsque les plaisanteries se calmèrent, Katya se remit à parler.

— D'accord, Mia. Crache le morceau… ou bien préfères-tu attaquer en solo sans magie ?

— Sans magie ? Attendez !

Je paniquai, devant réarranger mon plan, qui avait été de choisir 'action' et de brûler mon monstre avec mon plus gros sort explosif. Je l'avais gardé parce que le temps de rafraîchissement du sort était tel que je ne pouvais le lancer qu'une fois toutes les vingt minutes.

— Tu as dit pas d'arme. Je n'utiliserai pas ma baguette.

— La magie est ton arme. Étant donné l'apparition de ces monstres, je dirais que ton petit corps mou devrait durer un ou deux coups avant de te faire achever.

— Crache le morceau, Mia, dit Heath.

*Fragged vous dit : *De toute façon, tu n'as pas vraiment grand-chose à raconter, n'est-ce pas ?*

*Vous dites à Fragged : *Merci pour ton soutien ! Je m'en souviendrai.*

Je me souvins également que je n'avais pas à avoir honte.

— Très bien. Vérité. Je n'ai pas d'endroit bizarre.

— Alors tu l'as seulement fait dans un lit ? demanda Kat, incrédule.

— Je ne l'ai jamais fait, répondis-je en croisant les bras, même si je savais qu'ils ne pouvaient pas me voir.

FallenOne commenta : *Attends, quoi ?*

— Pas moyen, dit Kat. Je ne te crois pas.

— Heath peut l'attester. Je ne sors pas. Je ne couche pas...

— C'est à cause de ta religion ? demanda Kat.

Waouh, c'était la deuxième fois que l'on me posait cette question dans la journée.

— Non. C'est juste que je n'en ai jamais eu envie.

Ce n'était pas tout à fait vrai. J'avais seulement eu une mauvaise expérience... une expérience dont je n'avais *aucune* envie de parler. Je ne développai donc pas.

— Je confirme, intervint Heath. C'est une vierge... d'après ce que je sais. Je veux dire, nous sommes amis depuis que nous avons treize ans. D'un autre côté, elle ne savait rien sur mon escapade au match de basket – auquel elle a même assisté, je crois. Alors ma confirmation vaut ce qu'elle vaut. Mais je suis témoin du fait qu'elle ne sort avec personne.

Et pourtant tu te moques de tous les informaticiens concevant les jeux qui d'après toi n'arrivent pas à coucher ? demanda Fallen.

— Il y a une différence entre le vouloir et ne pas y arriver, et ne pas le vouloir pour commencer. Mais surtout, je plaisante, en général. C'est juste que ça m'énerve qu'ils pensent devoir montrer toute cette chair féminine.

Kat demanda :

— Es-tu prude, Mia ? Ou bien est-ce que tu te réserves pour le mariage ?

Je poussai un soupir en m'affalant contre le dossier de ma chaise. Encore ces étiquettes. Pourquoi devait-il toujours y avoir des étiquettes pour le statut sexuel d'une femme ? *Prude. Allumeuse. Pétasse.* Elles décrivaient toute la palette des niveaux d'accès au corps féminin par n'importe quel homme.

— 'Prude', c'est un mot assez grossier. Et je n'ai pas l'intention de me marier, donc cela élimine le fait que je veuille me préserver pour quelque chose qui n'aura jamais lieu. Mais pourquoi essayer de m'étiqueter d'après mon statut sexuel ? Pourquoi faut-il toujours qu'il y ait des étiquettes au lieu de respecter les choix personnels ?

Il y eut une pause et je sus qu'ils réfléchissaient tous à ce que je venais de dire. Enfin, Kat s'éclaircit la gorge.

— Oui, tu as raison. 'Prude' c'est aussi terrible que 'pétasse'. Je ne voulais pas l'utiliser de cette façon et je suis désolée. Peut-être peux-tu récupérer le mot et le rendre tien. Comme… je sais que je suis une pétasse et je n'en ai pas honte.

— Peut-être, mais le mot prude a une telle connotation négative. Par exemple, si tu ne veux pas coucher, c'est que tu ne dois pas aimer ça. Comment pourrais-je savoir si cela me plaît ou pas ? Je n'ai jamais essayé !

Bonne remarque, acquiesça FallenOne.

— Je vais donc peut-être choisir une nouvelle étiquette pour moi. Je suis 'joyeusement célibataire'.

— Il y a des avantages à choisir de ne pas s'encombrer de toutes les casseroles que le sexe peut créer, dit Kat d'une voix beaucoup plus sérieuse. J'étais beaucoup trop jeune quand j'ai commencé.

— Moi aussi, ajouta Heath.

Je secouai la tête.

— Sérieusement, *quand* as-tu fait tout cela ? Je n'en avais aucune idée.

Le rire ironique de Heath résonna dans mon casque.

— Quand tu es un ado homo, tu deviens un expert pour garder les secrets – du moins jusqu'à ce que tu sortes du placard. Ensuite, tu es prêt à le crier sur tous les toits !

— Et à marcher nu dans les parades de la Gay Pride ? demanda Kat.

Heath rit.

— Ou juste à rester sur le bord et en profiter à fond !

— Eh bien, vous connaissez maintenant mon sordide secret, dis-je.

Ça n'a rien de sordide ou de honteux. En fait, c'est plutôt merveilleux. Tant mieux pour toi, Mia, intervint FallenOne.

Je souris et je poussai un soupir de soulagement. Je ne regrettais plus ma candeur. Pas un seul 'tu ne sais pas ce que tu rates' auquel je m'attendais. Bien…

J'étais donc toujours vierge… et alors ? Peut-être allais-je mourir en vieille vierge, ou peut-être essaierais-je une fois pour voir de quoi tout le monde parlait. Mais quoi que je finisse par décider, la décision était la mienne.

Chapitre Neuf : L'intention de mal se comporter

MALGRE MON TEMPS LIBRE QUI SE RETRECISSAIT, JE faisais l'effort de rentrer chez moi voir maman au moins une fois par quinzaine, même si ce n'était que pour une journée. Cependant, mon emploi du temps n'était parfois pas compatible. Il m'arriva plusieurs fois d'échanger en faisant des heures de nuit le jeudi, pour me rendre directement en classe le vendredi, puis faire une sieste de quelques heures avant de prendre la route.

Comme ma mère vivait dans un coin reculé qui n'était accessible ni par train ni par bus, conduire était la seule option. Cependant, je parvenais quand même à réviser, même pendant le trajet. Une personne de mon groupe d'études m'avait conseillé un podcast gratuit de stratégie MCAT et je l'écoutais en conduisant pour absorber des conseils sur ce fichu concours.

Un samedi matin par un temps magnifique, on se rendit au marché fermier d'Idyllwild pour aller chercher des produits frais. Ma mère voulait me montrer comment faire la vieille recette de famille du baklava et elle affirmait que seuls les meilleurs ingrédients faisaient l'affaire.

Je ne pus me résoudre à lui demander si c'était une sorte de transmission frénétique de tout le savoir qu'elle avait hérité. Sa mère lui avait appris comment faire ce même dessert, alors j'essayais de considérer que c'était un rite de passage naturel, car j'étais la femme suivante dans la lignée. Pourtant mes mains tremblèrent lorsque je hachais les noix et les pistaches en suivant ses instructions. Était-ce la dernière fois qu'elle pourrait me le montrer ? Si elle ne guérissait pas ?

— Il faut que tu arrêtes de me lancer tes regards, je commence à me sentir gênée, dit-elle sans me regarder.

D'un air coupable, je reportai mon attention sur la planche à découper.

— Quels regards ? Je ne sais pas de quoi tu parles. Tu es très bien.

Elle me fit un sourire pincé.

— Oui, je suis très bien, même si je le dis moi-même. Et je pense que j'aurais pu te tromper… peut-être même ne jamais te dire ce qu'il se passait. Je crois qu'une grippe affreuse aurait pu expliquer quelques mauvaises journées, et tu n'en aurais rien su.

Je fronçai les sourcils et je posai soigneusement le couteau.

— Que veux-tu dire par 'me tromper' ? Tu parles de ne pas me dire que tu étais malade ?

Elle haussa les épaules.

— J'aurais pu attendre d'aller mieux avant de cracher le morceau. Je n'aime pas que tu t'inquiètes. Que tu te fatigues à venir aussi souvent que tu l'as fait. Même si… je dois dire que j'adore te voir aussi souvent.

Je lui fis une grimace.

— Comme si tu aurais pu me cacher ça.

Elle se mordit la lèvre inférieure et ses yeux exprimaient quelque chose. De la culpabilité, peut-être ? Y avait-il quelque chose qu'elle ne me disait pas ? De légers soupçons qui me rongeaient depuis le début du week-end refirent surface.

— Tu vas bien, n'est-ce pas ? Le médecin dit que tu vas mieux ?

Sa lèvre inférieure s'échappa de ses dents et elle s'approcha de moi, posant la main sur ma joue.

— Oui, je te le promets. Tu en sais autant que moi.

Je poussai un soupir quand elle indiqua la planche à découper.

— Il faut que ce soit beaucoup plus fin si tu veux que le baklava vaille quelque chose.

J'attrapai le couteau en grommelant et je retournai à ma tâche, essayant de faire de mon mieux pour ne pas jeter des coups d'œil inquiets dans sa direction.

Cela continua jusqu'à ce qu'il soit l'heure de partir le dimanche après-midi. En sortant, je regardai discrètement le bureau de ma mère en lui faisant la bise sur sa joue toute sèche. Ma mère avait commencé à porter des foulards pour cacher sa tête chauve et elle mettait un chapeau de cow-boy en paille avec de grandes lunettes de soleil. Une allure qui se situait quelque part entre une ancienne starlette de Hollywood et une cow-girl qui n'était plus de première jeunesse.

Cependant, lors de mon trajet de retour, les soupçons qui me rongeaient finirent par me frapper sur la tête comme une batte de base-ball. Sur le bureau de ma mère, j'avais vu de nombreuses factures entassées sans avoir été ouvertes. Je savais qu'il s'agissait de factures, car il y avait de petites enveloppes à fenêtre, de plus, elle jetait immédiatement les publicités quand elle les recevait. Si elle avait gardé et empilé ces enveloppes, c'est qu'elles étaient importantes.

Je notai mentalement d'aborder le sujet avec elle lors de notre appel téléphonique suivant. Elle avait dû temporairement fermer le B&B pour gérer sa crise de santé. Et j'en avais été contente, car cela diminuait sa charge de travail pendant qu'elle guérissait. Mais sans argent qui entrait… comment faisait-elle pour payer ses factures normales et en plus, ses factures médicales ?

Ces inquiétudes se mêlèrent à d'autres… je m'inquiétais pour elle, toute seule là-haut. J'étais son seul soutien. Il fallait que je garde un œil sur elle.

En continuant ma route, je pensai à la semaine à venir, submergée par la lassitude à l'idée de recommencer le cycle vicieux encore une fois. D'autres jours de cours, de devoirs, de recherches médicales méticuleuses, de travail à l'hôpital, de révisions pour le MCAT…

J'avais l'impression d'être dans une roue pour hamster sans fin, et je me faisais broyer lentement mais sûrement.

Il me tardait, avec toute l'énergie qui me restait, d'être à notre soirée jeux vidéo hebdomadaire. Heureusement que j'avais mes amis en ligne.

Pourtant, même l'immersion dans mon jeu préféré avec certaines de mes personnes préférées ne suffit pas à chasser complètement toutes mes inquiétudes.

Le parfait exemple, c'est que nous nous battions dans une immense grotte gelée remplie de Géants des Glaces. Ils cherchaient à nous écraser et faisaient tomber de gros rochers sur nous pendant que nous attaquions leurs chevilles et que nous les faisions lentement tomber. En général, j'adorais me battre contre les géants, car je pouvais utiliser ma magie pour les ensorceler et les pousser à se battre pour moi. Si le sort fonctionnait, un géant sous mon contrôle se retournait contre ses collègues géants et agissait comme mon gigantesque assassin domestique. Pour moi, combattre les géants était un vrai plaisir.

Pas cette fois. D'habitude, je pouvais en occuper trois si j'en endormais un et que j'ensorcelais un autre pour combattre le troisième pendant que les membres de mon groupe attaquaient le quatrième sans obstacle.

Sauf que je me plantai dans l'ordre de ce que je devais faire, et le géant que j'essayais d'ensorceler se mit à me tabasser. Une fois que je ne pus plus occuper les trois géants supplémentaires, ils se jetèrent sur les membres de mon groupe, les transformant en guacamole.

C'était la vie. Nous fûmes supprimés.

Ensuite, on réapparut sous la forme de fantômes.

Dans mon casque, j'entendais Heath taper furieusement sur son clavier, comme s'il envoyait des messages aux autres qu'il ne voulait pas que je voie.

— Bon, c'est la troisième fois que l'on meurt dans les Cavernes de Glace des Mammouths. Je ne le sens pas ce soir. Vous voulez faire quelque chose de plus facile ? Nous pourrons revenir ici la semaine prochaine.

— Je suis d'accord, acquiesça Kat sans la moindre objection.

Sans parler de mes erreurs. Sans reproches. J'adorais mes amis.

*FallenOne vous dit : *Tu es bien silencieuse, ces temps-ci.*

Même si j'étais préoccupée, je ressentais toujours une petite excitation chaque fois que FallenOne m'envoyait un message privé. Je me penchai en avant pour répondre.

*Vous dites à FallenOne : *Pardon. Soucieuse.*

Lui : *Comment va ta mère ?*

Moi : *Elle guérit. Je crois. On ne le saura que quand elle ira faire un scan dans quelques mois.*

Lui : *Je suis sûr qu'elle va s'en sortir.*

Moi : *Mon professeur de recherche essaie aussi de me rassurer. C'est un oncologue, alors je suppose qu'il sait de quoi il parle. Cependant, c'est une chose de le savoir dans la tête et une autre chose de ressentir cette peur dans son cœur, tu vois ce que je veux dire ?*

Lui : *Oui. Carrément. Je comprends.*

Moi : *J'ai décidé que je veux devenir oncologue. On a vraiment besoin de casser la gueule au cancer.*

Lui : *C'est génial... pas seulement parce que tu as décidé de choisir ça en l'honneur de ta mère, mais le fait de savoir ce que tu veux devenir alors que tu es si jeune. Tu as quoi, vingt ans ? Vingt et un ?*

Moi : *Tu essaies de me poser des questions personnelles tout en ne me disant rien de toi-même ? Je demande ton a/s/l et tu te contentes de répondre que tu es un mec. Je ne sais même pas si ça, c'est vrai.*

Sauf que je le savais. J'avais entendu sa voix au téléphone. Pendant quelques minutes brouillées, en tout cas. Quelques minutes qui avaient piqué ma curiosité. Mais il n'avait jamais proposé de me rappeler et ma fierté avait sans doute été trop heurtée pour lui demander un autre coup de téléphone. Je voulais qu'il le propose. Mais j'avais l'impression, étant donné sa réticence à divulguer des informations à son sujet, que Fallen évitait soigneusement le sujet d'un autre appel.

Je m'appuyai contre le dossier de la chaise et j'attendis, ignorant le combat à l'écran pendant que je fixais le curseur clignotant dans la boîte de dialogue, en me demandant ce qu'il allait répondre. Allait-il enfin tout révéler, ou bien allait-il se défiler, comme d'habitude ? Je devais admettre que j'étais extrêmement curieuse à son sujet et que je le devenais de plus en plus à mesure que le temps passait, ce qui signifiait seulement qu'il devenait beaucoup plus radin avec ses informations. Et bien sûr, je commençais à me demander s'il jouait à un petit jeu dans le jeu.

Lui : *Je pratique la cyber sécurité. *Cyber sécurité stricte.*

Moi : *Alors tu as peur que j'aille te trouver, te harceler et faire bouillir ton lapin domestique ?*

Lui : *Jamais eu de lapin domestique, heureusement. Et l'anonymat est un cadeau. Il est difficile à abandonner – parfois, si difficile que c'est presque impossible, même quand on le veut. Je suppose que c'est un peu comme de s'enterrer dans un petit trou chaleureux et de ne pas vouloir en sortir.*

Moi : *Maintenant, on dirait que c'est TOI, le lapin.*

Lui : *Je suis désolé, je ne veux pas être difficile. Je pense simplement que c'est mieux ainsi.*

J'eus un rictus en lisant cette phrase. Cela signifiait qu'il était marié ou qu'il avait une copine. C'était *sûr* qu'il avait au moins une copine. Peut-être avait-il minimisé de façon typiquement masculine quand il avait dit que son rendez-vous était 'juste une amie'. Impossible à savoir. *Et pourquoi m'en souciais-je ?*

Il était juste un ami, non ? Comme Heath ? Et Kat ? Et ce que j'espérais qu'Alex et Jenna deviennent un jour ? Quelqu'un sur qui je pouvais compter et qui pouvait compter sur moi en retour.

Mais comment pouvais-je devenir une amie proche de quelqu'un dont je ne savais presque rien ? Était-ce possible ? Et voulais-je vraiment un tel ami ?

On se fit encore une fois supprimer et Heath nous souhaita bonne nuit avec un soupir frustré. Je courbai le dos, sachant que j'avais déçu tout le monde. Katya s'excusa peu de temps après et il ne resta plus que Fallen et moi. On travailla sur des *quotidiennes*, des quêtes que l'on pouvait recommencer et qui offraient de l'expérience et quelques autres bénéfices.

Cela nous permit également de continuer notre conversation.

Moi : *Si l'anonymat est un cadeau, je devrais peut-être le pratiquer également.*

Lui : *Pas de problème. Je peux respecter ça.*

Moi : *Tu ne peux pas vraiment faire autrement...*

Je tapai des doigts sur ma souris en attendant sa répartie. Elle ne vint jamais. Il changea de sujet à la place !

Lui : *Alors, laisse-moi te poser cette question... pourquoi veux-tu devenir médecin ?*

Moi : *Oh, ce n'était pas un changement de sujet très subtil.*

Lui : *Pardon. Je pensais juste que nous avions dit tout ce qui était nécessaire sur le sujet. Pas toi ?*

Moi : *Hmm. Je suppose. Mais nous sommes revenus à des questions personnelles.*

Lui : *Pas des questions permettant de nous identifier...*

Moi : *D'accord... j'ai toujours voulu être médecin pour aider les gens.*

Lui : *C'est cool. J'admire ça.*

Moi : *Et toi ? Sais-tu ce que tu veux faire ?*

Ou peut-être faisait-il déjà ce qu'il voulait faire. Cette question supposait qu'il était toujours assez jeune pour décider de son avenir. Peut-être qu'être facteur habitant dans la cave à quarante ans était le rêve de sa vie !

Lui : *Plus ou moins. Je suis d'accord avec toi. Moi aussi, je veux aider les gens, mais d'une façon différente. En les divertissant. Ou en leur donnant un moyen de s'évader.*

Mon Dieu, j'espérais vraiment qu'il veuille devenir acteur et pas une espèce de gigolo, ce que ses mots m'évoquaient. Mais bon, les gigolos gagnaient beaucoup d'argent... c'était à lui de voir. Je ne pus m'empêcher de glousser à cette idée : *FallenOne, Gigolo de Fac.*

Lui : *Il se fait tard... je devrais sans doute partir. Et toi aussi. Après tout, tu dois changer le monde, non ?*

Moi : *C'est tout moi, la changeuse de monde !*

Lui : *Dis-moi que tu vas te réinscrire au concours le mois prochain.*

Moi : *Je vais y réfléchir.*

Cette même petite routine sembla se répéter à la fin de toutes nos sessions de jeu : Fallen insistait afin que je repasse le test et moi je le repoussais parce que j'avais peur.

C'était attendrissant. Et... adorable. Et frustrant, car il gardait tout pour lui. Katya m'avait dit qu'elle pensait qu'il finirait par changer. Qu'il était juste timide. Mais je trouvais que ma supposition était sans doute plus juste...

Il cachait un gros secret. Je ne savais pas ce que c'était, mais réfléchir au mystère me fatiguait, pour être honnête.

J'avais besoin d'amis. Des amis qui ne se retenaient pas. Des amis sur lesquels je pouvais compter dans le monde réel pour me soutenir. Je me promis de traîner plus avec Alex et Jenna – quand j'en avais le temps – et de dire 'oui' à ce qu'elles allaient proposer.

Je priais juste pour qu'il ne s'agisse pas de bêtises insensées d'étudiantes, ou de la fête d'une fraternité...

****

Quelques semaines plus tard, j'eus une rare soirée de libre. Et heureusement, ce ne fut pas la fête d'une fraternité. Au lieu de jouer aux jeux vidéo, je traînai avec Jenna et Alex dans leur appartement hors campus à Fullerton.

Il était tard. Très, très tard. J'aurais dû rentrer chez moi, mais j'étais assise dans leur salon sombre devant leur vieille télé : une grosse télé à tube cathodique dont Alex avait hérité quand sa mère était passée à un écran plat. Le bol de pop-corn s'était depuis longtemps transformé en une coupelle graisseuse de beurre fondu refroidi, de sel et d'un million de grains de maïs qui n'avaient pas éclaté.

À travers les trous de mon pull – tout en cachant le fait que j'essayais de me cacher –, je regardai l'épisode 'Pilleurs d'épaves' de *Firefly* avec Alex et Jenna. L'équipage de *Serenity* avait découvert un vaisseau abandonné flottant dans l'espace sans survivants connus. Et, ne sachant rien de ce qui était arrivé sur le vaisseau, ils l'avaient fouillé à la recherche de butin et en espérant découvrir ce qu'il s'était passé.

J'avais déjà vu l'épisode avant, plusieurs fois. En tant que fan dévouée de *Firefly*, je pouvais choisir parmi environ une douzaine d'épisodes de la série télé courte, mais adorée. J'avais peut-être vu celui-ci une douzaine de fois, mais je me faisais avoir *à chaque fois*.

— Oh merde, je déteste tout ce qui a un rapport avec les Ravageurs, souffla Alex. Ils me font trop peur.

Elle posa un gros coussin devant son visage, puis elle le contourna de temps en temps pour regarder l'écran.

La seule parmi nous qui ne semblait pas affectée par la tension à l'écran était Jenna, assise les jambes croisées, les coudes posés sur ses genoux, le menton dans ses mains, en fixant l'écran.

— Ils vont t'attraper, Alex ! Les pirates cannibales de l'espace vont se faufiler dans ta chambre cette nuit !

— La ferme, Jenna.

Jenna se contenta de ricaner, puis elle répéta la citation célèbre de Zoë au sujet des terribles Ravageurs.

— Ils nous violeront tous, mangeront notre chair et coudront notre peau sur leurs vêtements. Et si on a beaucoup, beaucoup de chance, ils le feront dans cet ordre.

Je frissonnai lorsqu'à l'écran, Jayne fut frappé par-derrière. Il se mit à tirer en tournant vivement sur lui-même. Alex et moi sursautâmes toutes les deux quand il fut touché pendant que Jenna continuait à sourire comme si elle regardait un leprechaun chevaucher une licorne par-dessus un arc-en-ciel. Franchement, soit cette fille avait vu cet épisode huit mille fois – ce qui était possible – ou bien elle avait des nerfs en titane, peut-être les deux.

Soudain, nous fûmes surprises par quatre silhouettes qui entrèrent en trombe dans l'appartement sombre en poussant des cris gutturaux. On bondit toutes sur nos pieds et on courut jusqu'à la cuisine pendant que les types nous poursuivaient, les visages cachés par des masques d'horreur d'Halloween. J'avais le cœur battant, l'adrénaline au maximum. Agitant les bras au hasard, Alex poussa des cris aigus. Plus elle criait, plus on entendait un rire profond et dur venir des envahisseurs masqués. Même Jenna avait poussé un cri quand ils étaient entrés la première fois. Mais maintenant, elle se tenait les bras croisés dans la cuisine.

— D'accord, les crétins, finit-elle par dire. Très drôle.

— On t'a fait crier, Jen. Ça fait une fois parmi les cent que l'on te doit encore.

— Va te faire, Orin, dit-elle avec mépris en donnant un coup de pied dans la direction de son entrejambe.

S'il avait été plus près, c'est lui qui aurait poussé un cri aigu. Alors qu'il se trouvait déjà à un mètre d'elle, il fit un pas en arrière en arrachant son masque.

— Enfoiré ! hurla à nouveau Alex. Je vais me venger.

— Hé, ça, c'était pour le bombardement à paillettes ! Maintenant, nous sommes quittes, répondit l'un d'eux.

Alex m'avait parlé de cette plaisanterie. Les filles avaient rempli un carton et l'avaient étiqueté 'pâtisseries' alors que c'était un paquet de paillettes prêt à exploser grâce à des ballons.

— Nous trouvons encore des paillettes partout. C'était vraiment méchant.

— Pleurnichard, répondit Jenna. Peut-être que si vous nettoyiez de temps en temps votre tanière dégoûtante, il n'y aurait plus de paillettes.

— Pourquoi ne la nettoies-tu pas ? N'est-ce pas ce que les femmes sont censées faire, de toute façon ?

Ils furent assez sages pour le dire en courant hors de l'appartement. Jenna les poursuivit jusqu'à l'escalier, en gloussant tout le long et ils se mirent à courir visiblement plus vite. C'était intelligent. Elle leur aurait botté le cul, littéralement, si elle les avait rattrapés.

Elle revint en haletant, alors qu'Alex et moi ramassions le bol renversé de maïs qu'Alex avait lancé aux intrus quand ils avaient passé la porte.

— D'accord, nous commençons nos plans de vengeance ce soir, marmonna Jenna en serrant les dents.

— Tu n'as pas peur que ça ne fasse qu'envenimer le conflit ?

Je ramassai les miettes de pop-corn sur le vieux tapis à poil long et je les regardai tour à tour.

— Une fille ne peut pas se laisser faire, marmonna Alex avant de quitter la pièce et de revenir très vite avec l'aspirateur. Sinon, ils vont continuer à nous terroriser. En parlant de ça, verrouille la porte au cas où ils décideraient de revenir. Il nous faut un mot de passe ou quelque chose.

— Ouais, j'en ai un. *Interdit aux super-crétins*, grommela Jenna.

— C'est trop évident, objectai-je en secouant la tête.

Je jetai un coup d'œil à la télé où Mal Reynolds faisait face au commandant de l'Alliance.

— Il faudrait en faire un club réservé aux filles. Interdit aux garçons. Comme à l'école primaire.

— Heath pourrait être un membre honoraire ! intervint Alex.

Heath avait rencontré les filles quelques semaines auparavant, et tout le monde s'était bien entendu.

— Notre mot de passe devrait faire peur à tous les hommes, dit Jenna avec une lueur dans les yeux.

— Je l'ai ! dit Alex. Notre mot de passe est : *J'ai l'intention de mal me comporter*. Et en ce qui concerne ces garçons, c'est vraiment la vérité !

— Même si Orin veut sortir avec toi, Alex, dit Jenna en ricanant. Il laisserait totalement tomber cette vendetta si tu arrêtais aussi.

— Certainement pas ! siffla-t-elle.

Jenna s'approcha de nous et elle nous tendit les mains.

— Avons-nous tout dit ? Notre club, nous n'allons même pas le nommer. Nous l'appellerons le Club Qui Ne Sera Pas Nommé. Girl power !

Je posai ma main sur celle de Jenna et Alex posa la sienne sur la mienne.

— Nous avons l'intention de mal nous comporter !

— Nous pourrons peut-être autoriser des types mignons en tant que membres temporaires ? Mais il faut qu'ils soient extrêmement canon, dit Alex en se mordillant la lèvre d'un air pensif.

— Jack Eversea pourra être notre mascotte ! gloussa Jenna. Il me fait rêver.

Jack était son béguin célèbre du jour.

— D'accord, des exceptions pour les types canon. Particulièrement les bruns, dit Alex en hochant la tête.

— Je préfère les blonds et les roux, intervins-je en me demandant bizarrement de quelle couleur étaient les cheveux de

FallenOne, puis en me rappelant rapidement que je ne devais même plus penser à lui de cette façon.

Les deux filles froncèrent les sourcils. Il fallait toujours que je sois la voix de la discorde, hein ? Typique…

Peu de temps après, nous commencèrent nos plans infâmes pour faire monter d'un cran le cycle de blagues contre les garçons de l'immeuble.

Hé, je vivais à onze kilomètres de l'immeuble, alors je ne craignais pas leurs représailles. Je participai donc joyeusement et c'était amusant de traîner avec les filles. C'était *réel*.

À ce moment de ma vie, le *réel* était exactement ce dont j'avais besoin.

Chapitre Dix :
JF cherche JHC

— OUI. COMME ÇA ! OHHH, BEBE !

Les voisins d'en face avaient recommencé. *Encore.*

J'avais la fenêtre ouverte à cause de la chaleur, ce qui signifiait que malgré la distance, j'entendais qu'il était dans la position parfaite pour la 'baiser comme une bête'.

Ils baisaient tout le temps. Tout. Le. Temps. On aurait cru que c'était vraiment la meilleure chose à faire. Ou bien qu'il fallait en profiter, car ce ne serait plus à la mode le lendemain.

Merde. Il leur fallait un passe-temps ou quelque chose.

— Oui. Mon Dieu, oui ! Oui ! Oh mon Dieu.

D'après ce que je savais, ils n'allaient même pas à l'église le dimanche, bien que leurs nombreuses exclamations semblaient proclamer une croyance profonde en un esprit supérieur.

Révisions ou pas, il fallait vraiment que je sorte de cet appartement et que je m'éloigne pendant quelques heures du sex-a-thon.

J'envoyai un texto à Heath pour lui demander s'il voulait manger avec moi. Tant que l'on choisissait un endroit pas trop cher avec de l'air conditionné, j'allais être heureuse comme un poisson dans l'eau.

Il passa me prendre une demi-heure plus tard, juste au moment où l'odeur de la fumée de cigarette commençait à monter depuis la fenêtre des voisins. Ils allaient recommencer plus tard dans la soirée, c'était certain.

On s'installa à la sandwicherie au bout de la rue : impossible de se rafraîchir dans l'air conditionné, mais au moins on pouvait poser nos corps tout collants devant un ventilateur géant à forte puissance.

Je tripotai les miettes grasses et trop salées de mes frites.

— Ça va ? demanda Heath.

— Mm, marmonnai-je distraitement.

Heath mordit dans son sandwich italien extra large aux oignons et me fixa d'un air circonspect. Il attendit, sachant très bien que j'allais finir par lâcher le morceau. Ils n'eurent pas besoin d'attendre longtemps.

Je laissai tomber le dernier morceau de nourriture sur mon assiette.

— Pourquoi tout le monde fait-il tout un plat du sexe, hein ?

Je pris conscience de l'avoir dit légèrement trop fort lorsque les têtes de la table à côté de nous se tournèrent dans ma direction. Je poussai un soupir frustré, mon visage se mettant à brûler.

En m'éclaircissant la gorge, je déglutis et j'ignorai leurs regards jusqu'à ce qu'ils retournent à leur conversation en cours. Heath me regarda bouche bée.

Je lui fis une grimace.

— T'attrapes les mouches ?

Il leva les yeux au ciel.

— Je n'arrive pas à croire que tu viennes de me demander ça. Tes voisins s'y sont remis ?

Je poussai un soupir.

— Ils ne font rien d'autre. Ils ont besoin d'une télé.

Heath eut un sourire espiègle.

— Il n'y a rien à la télé qui soit aussi amusant que ce qu'ils font.

— Mais est-ce qu'ils ont besoin de le faire savoir au monde entier ? Je veux dire, cette femme est… bruyamment émue… par ses orgasmes.

Encore une fois, le son de ma voix devait être élevé, car les mêmes têtes se tournèrent. Je fronçai les sourcils en les regardant dans les yeux.

— Oh, c'est bon, occupez-vous de votre nourriture et de votre propre conversation ! aboyai-je et ils écarquillèrent les yeux.

Heath était tout rouge et il avait du mal à respirer à force de rire.

Une fois que le groupe s'était remis à parler – sans doute de moi –, je me tournai vers Heath. Je mis les mains de chaque côté de mon visage et je pointai les majeurs vers lui tout en lui tirant la langue. Cela eut pour effet de le faire rire davantage. Et au bout de quelques minutes, après l'avoir regardé lutter pour respirer, je dus admettre que c'était contagieux. Moi aussi, je me mis à rire.

Cette situation était vraiment ridicule. Il se racla la gorge et s'essuya les yeux.

— Soit tu dois imiter Meg Ryan et faire une scène à tes voisins comme dans le film *Quand Harry rencontre Sally*, ou alors tu dois télécharger un bon porno bruyant et le mettre en route à fond la prochaine fois.

Je levai les yeux au ciel.

— Je suis certaine que ça ne ferait que les exciter.

Il haussa les épaules en essuyant les larmes de ses yeux.

— Probablement.

Je poussai un soupir frustré.

— Je ne comprends pas.

— Oh, tu comprendras un jour. Si tu prends la peine de sortir avec quelqu'un, bien sûr.

— J'ai bien conscience que les orgasmes sont agréables.

— Les orgasmes venant du sexe avec une autre personne sont encore meilleurs, rétorqua-t-il.

Je m'occupai en balayant les miettes de mon set de table.

— Je n'ai pas besoin de sortir avec quelqu'un pour coucher avec lui.

Cette fois au moins, je m'étais souvenue de parler à voix basse.

Heath écarquilla les yeux, mordit dans son sandwich et mâcha d'un air pensif.

— C'est vrai. Mais tu ne sors pas du tout, donc tu ne peux rencontrer personne, même si ce n'est que pour coucher. Et comme tu es terriblement mal à l'aise en société…

Je lui jetai un regard noir.

— Bon sang, Heath. Tu es très fort pour me donner confiance en moi. Je suis mal à l'aise et socialement handicapée. Mais je ne suis pas moche.

Il leva les sourcils.

— Tu n'es *certainement* pas moche. Au contraire, même. Les hommes te regardent tout le temps quand nous sortons ensemble. *Mais* tu ne t'en rends absolument pas compte, ce qui est à la fois attendrissant et un peu pathétique.

Je fis une grimace pour cacher le moment gênant, mais je ne pris pas la peine de corriger son affirmation. Ignorer les regards, les flirts et les avances était un *choix*.

— Pas quand tu fais cette tête, en revanche.

Je ramassai la croûte de mon pain et la lui jetai. Elle rebondit sur son épaule massive et elle atterrit sur la table. Il la ramassa et la jeta sur mon assiette en carton.

— Je dis juste que si tu veux l'opportunité… d'explorer… tu dois te rendre disponible.

J'entrelaçai mes doigts et je me tins droite, imitant une étudiante exagérément attentive, ouvrant grand les yeux et clignant des paupières d'un air innocent.

— Dois-je faire paraître une petite annonce sur Craigslist ? JF cherche JHC pour sexe torride et défloration virginale ?

Le front de Heath se plissa.

— JHC ?

— Jeune Homme Canon.

Il ricana.

— Ne va pas sur Craigslist. Tu risques d'y croiser des tarés. Je te l'interdis.

Je me mordis la lèvre.

— Une de ces applis où on fait défiler à gauche ou droite, alors ?

Heath pinça les lèvres, pensif.

— Fais-toi des amis. Fais la fête. Arrête de passer tous les soirs à jouer aux jeux vidéo avec Fallen, Kat et moi. Ou les idiots immatures avec lesquels Jenna et Alex flirtent tout le temps. Eux non plus, ils ne te mèneront à rien.

Un groupe de lycéens chahuteurs passa près de notre table, heurtant le dos de Heath. Il leur jeta un regard noir et ils reculèrent tous immédiatement, les mains levées.

— Ah bon, tu veux que j'arrête de jouer aux jeux vidéo avec toi ?

Il se tourna vers moi en levant les yeux au ciel.

— Non, je n'ai pas dit ça. J'ai dit qu'il fallait que tu arrêtes de jouer avec nous pendant ta seule soirée de libre. Sors et profite de tes années de fac, surtout maintenant qu'elles sont presque terminées. Il ne te reste plus qu'un an.

Je secouai vivement la tête en serrant plus fort mes mains ensemble.

— Je ne veux pas faire le truc social. Je ne veux pas passer du temps avec un type qui me dira ce que je dois faire. Ou pire : quelqu'un qui voudra me changer pour correspondre à l'image de ce qu'il veut que je sois.

Je ne regardai pas Heath dans les yeux en lui disant cela. De bien des façons, je décrivais *son* petit-ami. Si possible, il ne saurait jamais à quel point Brian me déplaisait.

Je n'avais vraiment aucune intention d'imiter leur type de relation. Je ne voulais *aucune* relation romantique. Je n'en voyais pas le besoin. Je n'avais *jamais* eu besoin de dépendre d'un homme, même depuis ma naissance, et cela ne serait jamais le cas.

Mais le sexe... le sexe pouvait être bien. Je ne pouvais pas le savoir sans essayer, n'est-ce pas ?

Il me fallait juste dépasser l'obstacle pénible de la virginité. Aucun type acceptant de coucher juste pour un soir n'allait vouloir s'en charger. Non ?

— Et qu'en est-il de ce Jon dans ton groupe d'études ? Il m'a semblé gentil quand je l'ai rencontré.

Je haussai les épaules. Jon était beau, mais... Il ne me faisait rien. Il y avait quelque chose chez lui qui me repoussait. Peut-être était-il trop empressé.

— Tu lui plais. Ce n'est pas un mystère, dit Heath avec un sourire en coin quand il avala sa dernière frite. Tu sais, qui que ce soit, pas besoin d'avoir un engagement sur le long terme. Tu es amie avec ce type. Pourquoi ne pas te contenter de faire un arrangement entre amis ?

Je me frottai la joue, mes yeux se perdant dans le vide pendant que j'y réfléchissais. Ce n'était pas vraiment une mauvaise idée. Jon était assez gentil. Il était malin, attirant, bien qu'un peu collant. Je ne voulais pas qu'il traîne tout le temps en temps comme petit-ami, mais après avoir repassé le MCAT, il ne serait plus dans mon groupe. Et nous ne suivrions pas non plus les mêmes cours, puisqu'il avait fait un an de moins.

Je contemplai cette possibilité. Il allait sans doute me redemander de sortir. Il avait été persistant jusque là. Mais… pouvais-je aller jusqu'au bout avec lui ? Et si je le faisais, s'en irait-il ensuite ?

Je poussai un soupir.

— Il doit bien y avoir une façon plus facile de le faire.

Heath se mit à rire.

— T'inquiète pas, Mia. Si tu arrêtes d'être aussi… froide et indisponible, cela arrivera sans doute tout seul. Mais ne fais rien de stupide, d'accord ?

Je levai un sourcil.

— M'as-tu déjà vu faire quoi que ce soit de spontané et potentiellement autodestructeur ?

Son sourire s'estompa.

— Il y a toujours une première fois… alors, essaie d'être aussi raisonnable que d'habitude. Je suis certain que tu seras vite déflorée. Ne t'attends simplement pas à ce que ce soit la meilleure expérience de ta vie. Et ne pense pas que ce sera l'amour de ta vie. Et puis, ne laisse pas tomber le sexe parce que cette première fois s'avère merdique.

Je secouai la tête en grimaçant.

— Waouh, présenté de cette façon, qu'est-ce que j'attends ? Retiens-moi avant que je trouve un beau mec à qui offrir ma virginité !

Heureusement, j'avais pensé à parler à voix basse. Juste au cas où, je jetai un coup d'œil vers la table à côté de nous et je fus soulagée de voir qu'elle était vide.

Heath me raccompagna chez moi et on traîna un peu avant qu'il déclare qu'il faisait bien trop chaud. Moins de vingt minutes après son départ, les voisins recommencèrent à baiser bruyamment.

***

Ma mère cachait quelque chose. Cela me travaillait depuis le jour où j'avais vu ce regard. Quand elle avait laissé entendre qu'elle m'aurait caché son cancer afin que je ne m'inquiète pas.

Bien sûr, je lui cachais des choses, moi aussi.

Mon échec au MCAT, pour commencer. Et le fait que j'avais décidé de jouer au détective amateur la prochaine fois que je retournerai au ranch.

Elle me surprit à son bureau, fouillant dans ses factures.

— Que fais-tu avec mes papiers privés ?

Elle venait de passer le coin et elle me trouva couverte d'enveloppes. Son visage rougit immédiatement.

On se regarda dans les yeux pendant un long moment gênant.

Maman n'avait pas l'air en forme ce week-end-là et elle n'avait pas semblé ravie de ma visite-surprise. Peut-être avait-elle voulu passer le week-end seule ou au lit. Elle avait dormi plus tard que d'habitude et j'en avais profité ce matin-là pour fouiller dans son courrier : essentiellement les factures habituelles, et beaucoup de frais médicaux en plus.

Sous son léger rougissement, son visage semblait cireux avec ce jaunissement pas naturel d'une personne ayant traversé un traitement médical éprouvant. En outre, ses joues étaient creusées.

— Je, euh, je rangeais un peu.

J'étais prise la main dans le sac et je commençai moi aussi à rougir.

— Ça n'a pas besoin d'être rangé ! aboya-t-elle. Pourquoi fouilles-tu dans mes affaires ?

Je me levai lentement et j'avalai une boule dans ma gorge.

— Je, euh, je n'essayais pas de fouiller.

Un mensonge éhonté. Je détournai mon regard du sien.

Les lèvres pincées, elle se pencha et attrapa vivement son courrier qu'elle rangea dans une enveloppe en papier Kraft géante.

Je croisai les bras sur ma poitrine.

— Maman. As-tu des problèmes financiers ?

Elle poussa un soupir.

— Mia, tu dois arrêter de t'occuper des affaires de tout le monde et faire ta propre vie.

Elle tourna les talons, passa le coin et disparut dans sa chambre.

Je restai là, bouche bée. Soudain, je sentis des larmes cuisantes et douloureuses. Ma propre mère pensait que j'étais une ratée qui n'avait pas de vie.

C'était comme un coup de poing dans le ventre.

Je sortis de la maison et je me rendis à l'étable pour passer du temps avec les chevaux. Je ne savais pas du tout ce que maman faisait dans la maison. Manifestement, elle se sentait très mal ce week-end et une grande partie de son attitude venait de là.

Mais le reste ?

Ses factures étaient-elles la source du stress qu'elle essayait de me cacher ?

Pourquoi les gens qui s'aimaient essayaient-ils tout le temps de se cacher des choses ?

Si maman était en difficulté financière, le stress la rendait-il plus malade ? Elle semblait vraiment pire ce week-end. Et elle avait terminé la chimio des semaines plus tôt…

Plus tard, je lui achetai de la nourriture qu'elle aimait quand elle ne se sentait pas bien. Quand je revins des courses, la porte de sa chambre était fermée, la lumière éteinte.

Je supposai qu'elle faisait la sieste.

Je lui laissai un long mot avec des excuses et une explication foireuse disant que je devais rentrer réviser.

Je partis alors, avec plus de questions et beaucoup plus d'inquiétudes qu'à mon arrivée.

Chapitre Onze :
Elle met *quoi* aux enchères ?

J E RETOURNAI ASSEZ TÔT DANS L'APRÈS-MIDI DU SAMEDI, CE qui me permit l'occasion rare de passer du temps à me détendre seule sur DE. Je ruminais encore le comportement tranchant de ma mère, particulièrement son affirmation que je n'avais pas de vie.

Et au lieu d'essayer de découvrir comment sortir et avoir une vie, je pansai mes blessures à la maison un samedi soir en jouant aux jeux vidéo. Toute seule.

Heureusement, je ne restai pas seule longtemps. FallenOne se connecta environ une heure après moi. Lui non plus ne devait rien avoir de mieux à faire de son week-end.

Cependant, les deux personnes manquantes de notre groupe n'avaient pas hésité à nous informer plus tôt qu'elles allaient passer du bon temps. Heath et Kat avaient des vies sociales – et des vies sexuelles en plus !

Je me demandais ce qu'il s'était passé pour que Fallen traîne avec moi. Il fréquentait quelqu'un assez régulièrement. Jusqu'à récemment, il avait nonchalamment mentionné sortir avec 'une amie' et comme d'habitude, il était resté mystérieux à ce sujet. Seul l'accord au féminin indiquait qu'il s'agissait d'une femme.

Ou peut-être parce qu'il était à l'heure de l'Est, était-il déjà sorti et revenu de son rendez-vous avant de jouer avec nous... allez savoir.

*Vous dites à FallenOne : *Alors, pourquoi ne sors-tu pas ce soir, toi aussi, me laissant faire mes quêtes quotidiennes toute seule ?*

*FallenOne vous dit : */hausse les épaules. Sais pas.*

Moi : *C'est fini avec ton " amie " ?*

Lui : *Tu es curieuse. Et pourquoi mettre amie entre guillemets ?*

Moi : *Je suppose que c'est juste ma façon de désigner une amie avec laquelle on couche.*

Lui : *Eh bien, nous avons travaillé ensemble. Elle est récemment passée à autre chose. Je ne la vois pas beaucoup, et franchement, nous n'avons jamais beaucoup traîné ensemble...*

Moi : *Vous vous fréquentiez juste pour coucher ?*

Lui : *Pas *juste pour coucher, non... mais... souvent.*

Moi : *Hmmm.*

Lui : *Quoi, hmmm ? Je suppose que tu désapprouves ?*

Moi : *Moi ? Non... je me demande juste comment une telle chose peut arriver... la situation dans laquelle les amis couchent ensemble. Alors il y a quelqu'un avec qui tu traînes en tant qu'ami et vous décidez simplement de commencer à coucher ensemble ? Est-ce que ça se passe tout seul ou bien en parlez-vous avant... ?*

Lui : *Tu réfléchis trop.*

Moi : *Je réfléchis *toujours trop. Je suis la reine de la réflexion superflue.*

Lui : *Je vois ça. Comment se fait-il que tu t'intéresses à tout ça ?*

Moi : *Je sais pas. Je crois qu'il est temps de... d'avancer et de vivre de nouvelles choses. Mais je ne m'intéresse pas du tout aux relations ou aux rendez-vous galants. Tu sembles avoir réglé ça de façon pratique, alors j'essayais juste de comprendre comment tu faisais.*

Lui : Je suis certain que tu trouveras un moyen avec un peu de toute cette intelligence.

Je vis qu'il écrivait, mais je ne recevais rien. C'était comme s'il écrivait et qu'il effaçait les lignes, plus d'une fois. Enfin, un message finit par passer.

Lui : Mais tu sais, pourquoi te presser, hein ? Tu as le concours et l'école de médecine et tout ça...

Moi : L'urgence, c'est que je ne veux pas être une vierge octogénaire, merci...

Lui : Eh bien, tu as encore du temps avant de devenir octogénaire.

Moi : Enfin, bref. Allons tuer des trucs.

Lui : Comme tu viens de tuer cette conversation ? D'accord, très bien. Que penses-tu d'essayer cette nouvelle quête de feu d'artifice ? Il paraît que les gens s'amusent beaucoup avec.

Moi : Faire exploser des choses, c'est presque aussi bien que de tuer des monstres. Je suis partante.

***

**Eloisa est entrée dans le monde de Yondareth*

FallenOne et Eloisa gravissent le cratère d'un volcan fumant, évitant des puits de lave tout en récoltant des poches de soufre pour leur concoction diabolique.

Hassim, celui qui leur a donné la quête, leur a fourni un contenant spécial pour leur récolte ainsi qu'une liste des ingrédients dont ils auront besoin pour l'aider dans ses créations magiques – et explosives. Quand ce sera terminé, il leur faudra s'aventurer dans les grottes les plus profondes et les plus sombres de Yondareth pour récolter du salpêtre...

— J'espère que cette quête en vaut la peine, murmure Eloisa à FallenOne en se pinçant le nez pour bloquer l'odeur d'œuf pourri du soufre.

Elle parvient malgré tout à enfoncer sa louche dans une poche de la substance jaune cachée sous un rocher et elle la fait tomber dans son contenant en argile qu'elle rebouche bien.

— Hassim fait des feux d'artifice magnifiques, répond FallenOne en hochant la tête. Je suis certain que ce sera beau à voir.

Après plusieurs jours de longue marche difficile à travers le pays, les deux aventuriers arrivent dans le camp d'une mine de nains où ils proposent de travailler à réparer les voies des chariots de la mine en échange de morceaux de cuivre brut. Le métal est un ingrédient vital pour produire les étincelles bleues du Jeu d'artifice, parmi les nombreuses couleurs du spectacle.

C'est une longue quête incessante et enfin, lorsque tous les ingrédients nécessaires sont rassemblés, ils retournent voir Hassim. Le chimiste des spectacles exotiques va les assembler et former ses célèbres créations avant le Grand Festival Mondial des Gnomes.

FallenOne et Eloisa sont très excités et il leur tarde de participer.

— Nous allons récupérer nos propres feux d'artifice que nous pourrons faire exploser quand nous le voulons, mais il me tarde aussi de préparer le spectacle pour le Festival.

FallenOne caresse sa barbe blanche d'un air pensif, le regard rêveur, comme s'il imaginait déjà le spectacle.

Eloisa est toutefois restée silencieuse depuis qu'ils ont apporté leurs ingrédients à Hassim. Pendant que les deux aventuriers attendent qu'il assemble ses fusées de feu, on leur a demandé de déboiser une zone, de construire une plate-forme et, une fois que les fusées seront prêtes, de les installer comme il faut. Elle commence à penser que c'est beaucoup de travail pour très peu de récompense.

À mesure que les tâches se sont accumulées, Eloisa s'est de moins en moins amusée.

— C'est beaucoup de travail pour rien, d'après moi, dit-elle en faisant la moue.

FallenOne se redresse après son travail harassant, ayant assemblé la plate-forme et préparé les supports des fusées.

— Nous avons presque terminé. Tu verras ! Quand le soleil se couchera, ce sera quelque chose à voir, et nous serons de grands héros pour avoir apporté la magie spéciale des créations d'Hassim aux habitants de cette région.

Mais il reste encore d'autres tâches à accomplir. Hassim est très exigeant quant à la disposition des fusées, qui doivent être arrangées selon un schéma bien particulier, tout comme la poudre noire qui sert de détonateur.

Les joues d'Eloisa deviennent rouges de frustration et même d'un peu de colère. Elle arrive au bout de sa patience. Et elle n'a aucune patience pour les imbéciles.

Elle va se défendre.

Elle attrape la majorité des fusées et le baril de poudre noire avant que FallenOne se rende compte de ce qu'elle fait. Les traînant sur la plate-forme, elle fait un grand tas d'explosifs.

— Hassim ne nous a pas dit de le faire de cette façon ! proteste Fallen quand il la rattrape enfin, toujours un peu stupéfait qu'elle puisse bouger si vite.

— Je m'en fiche, rétorque Eloisa. Il n'aura pas mieux !

Elle débouche alors le tonneau de poudre noire et elle se met à l'étaler sur le sol sous la forme de dessins complexes. Elle écrit également des mots dans une langue étrangère mystérieuse que FallenOne n'a encore jamais vue.

Il la regarde, écarquillant les yeux en voyant les images que semblent former les traits de poudre.

— Ce n'est pas... tu ne peux pas... quoi... ?

— Regarde, dit sèchement Eloisa en jetant le baril de poudre vide et en sortant sa pierre à feu. Je te conseille de t'écarter.

Avec de grands yeux et la mâchoire tombant à terre, FallenOne obéit en reculant autant qu'il le peut tout en restant assez près pour voir ce qui est sur le point de se passer dans ce minuscule hameau malheureux à la lisière de la forêt.

Quand elle est prête, Eloisa met le feu à l'extrémité de la longue traînée de poudre noire, qui mène directement au gigantesque tas de feux d'artifice, qui exploseront quand la flamme les atteindra.

— C'est la dernière fois que je fais un travail aussi idiot pour un foutu feu d'artifice réutilisable qui restera dans mon sac à dos et qui prendra de la place jusqu'à ce que je décide de le détruire !

FallenOne peut seulement secouer la tête pendant que le feu suit la traînée de poudre noire, serpentant autour des formes complexes et des lettres de l'alphabet étrange, s'approchant de plus en plus de la pile d'explosifs au centre de la plate-forme.

— Je vais leur donner un spectacle qu'ils n'oublieront jamais ! crie Eloisa avec joie.

***

Je regardai le spectacle à l'écran, le poing serré contre ma bouche en retenant un gloussement. Je sentis l'irritation de Fallen de l'endroit où je me trouvais.

La poudre s'enflamma et les schémas s'illuminèrent. Je ne savais pas du tout ce qui passait par la tête de Fallen pendant qu'il était témoin de ma rébellion, mais je trouvais cela vraiment très drôle.

Les flammes firent le tour de deux cercles géants, s'étirant en un rayon de lumière allongé. Des étoiles blanches s'échappèrent par le haut. Des lumières étincelèrent, créant des dessins et des mots.

'*Je t'emmerde, Hassim*' en était un. '*Draco, t'es pourri*' un autre. Et d'autres petits messages amusants de ce genre.

FallenOne resta remarquablement silencieux jusqu'à ce que la traînée de flammes conduise au grand final : une pile énorme de feux d'artifice qui explosèrent tous à la fois, brûlant presque mes rétines avec la quantité de lumière détestable à l'écran.

Tout le village – s'il avait existé en dehors du domaine des pixels et des bytes – aurait été démoli.

Je gloussai comme une enfant en regardant mes dégâts : le cratère fumant géant dans la clairière, les environs noircis. Un quart d'heure plus tard seulement, tout allait revenir à la normale pour les villageois PNJ et les joueurs qui s'aventureraient ici avec leur propre quête à compléter.

Mais j'avais sans doute torpillé mes arrières, si l'on peut dire.

Cette pensée me fit rire encore plus fort.

*FallenOne vous dit : *Bordel de merde, Mia, VRAIMENT ?*

*Eloisa dit à FallenOne : *C'est drôle ! La quête d'Hassim c'était *vraiment des conneries ennuyeuses. Tu n'es pas d'accord ?*

Lui : *Ce n'était pas *si ennuyeux.*

Moi : *C'était carrément chiant. Ce jeu est rempli de quêtes où il faut travailler comme ça. J'en avais assez.*

Lui : *Oh allez, c'était une quête intéressante. Et une belle récompense ! Non pas que TU étais là pour la recevoir.*

Moi : *C'est toi qui le dis. Je me suis rebellée.*

Lui : *J'ai remarqué. Une vraie rebelle.*

Moi : *J'aime bien changer de temps en temps, que veux-tu que je te dise ?*

Lui : *Je suppose qu'il y aura bientôt un compte rendu détaillé de cette chaîne de quêtes sur ton blog ?*

Moi : *Bien sûr, j'ai fait des captures d'écran et tout.*

Lui : *Waouh. Tu sors l'arme nucléaire.*

Moi : *Ben. Si je pratiquais la terre brûlée, tu le saurais. Ça, ce n'est rien. Ils s'en remettront. Peut-être arrêteront-ils de faire autant de quêtes avec tant de petites tâches. C'est gagnant-gagnant pour nous autres joueurs.*

Lui : *Essaies-tu de dresser les créateurs du jeu avec ton blog sarcastique ?*

Moi : *Je propose simplement un autre point de vue.*

Lui : *Ouais, c'est sûr.*

Je pensais que FallenOne aurait ri un peu plus, ou au moins écrit un médiocre 'ha ha'. Mon humour était peut-être trop immature pour lui.

Ou peut-être, juste peut-être, fallait-il que je sorte de chez moi pour avoir une vie. Je me mordis la lèvre en essayant d'écraser la pointe de désespoir qui menaçait de s'épanouir en quelque chose de plus sérieux. Peut-être même en dépression.

Parfois, une fille avait besoin de s'échapper de ses inquiétudes et de ses peurs. Quelque chose de sûr et non de destructeur.

Et c'était exactement ce que le jeu me fournissait.

Une fois de retour en ville, on rassembla nos objets pour les offrir à la donneuse de quêtes pour obtenir une autre quête. Cette fois, c'était une brute du nom de Dirty Deena qui avait pillé une armurerie et était prête à nous donner – surprise ! – de nouveaux plastrons brillants en échange des objets dont elle avait besoin.

On lui donna nos coquillages durement acquis, nos doublons incrustés de mollusques et les voiles déchirées récupérées sur une épave. Dirty Deena rit et chanta et fit une danse de pirate. FallenOne, en tant que lancier, reçut un plastron en cuir poli et clouté qui brillait au soleil. Je lui transmis rapidement mon enthousiasme par le chat, sifflant et applaudissant et l'encourageant pendant qu'il enfilait la chose. Il était MAGNIFIQUE.

Moi : *Montre-moi les stats du plastron ! Je veux voir à quel point il est bien.*

Lui : *Le tien aura exactement les mêmes caractéristiques !*

Je jetai donc un coup d'œil à ma propre récompense. Une véritable amélioration du plastron que je portais depuis les trois derniers niveaux. Mais à quoi ressemblait le graphisme ?

Je retirai mon vieux plastron de la case 'torse' de mon écran de personnage et je l'équipai. Puis je retournai à l'écran principal pour voir ce que donnait le graphisme sur l'avatar de mon personnage.

Bruit de trombones déprimés. *Wah wah waaaaaah.*

Ce n'était rien de plus qu'un haut de bikini brillant, parfaitement taillé pour exposer la forte poitrine d'Eloisa.

RAGE de la joueuse.

Moi : *W.T.F !*

Lui : *Ça, euh, te va bien.*

Moi : *La ferme, lancier. Sinon j'attrape cette lance et je te l'enfonce là où le soleil ne brille jamais.*

Lui : *Hou, susceptible.*

Moi : *Tu le serais aussi si tout Yondareth conspirait à te forcer à partir au combat sans rien de plus qu'un pagne à armure. Tu n'aimerais pas ça, hein ?*

Lui : *Eh bien, non. Mais vois le bon côté des choses.*

Moi : *Le bon côté ? Il y a un bon côté ?*

Lui : *Ouais, nos plastrons ont exactement les mêmes caractéristiques. Même classe d'armure, mêmes points de dégâts. Même protection, pourtant le tien pèse beaucoup moins lourd.*

Moi : *C'est parce que ce sont DEUX MICROSCOPIQUES TRIANGLES DE PAPIER ALUMINUM.*

Lui : *Mais il y a bien un côté positif...*

Moi : *Ouais, tu m'as convaincue. Maintenant, je suis ravie de montrer mon décolleté virtuel à tout Yondareth. N'importe quoi.*

Lui : *Tu ne vas pas quitter le jeu de rage, hein ?*

Moi : *J'ai le doigt sur le bouton 'quitter' pendant que j'écris !*

Lui : *Respire profondément, Mia. Ne le fais pas. Tu sais que tu adores Dragon Epoch.*

Moi : *Je l'aimerais plus s'ils se souvenaient que toutes les femmes n'ont pas envie de montrer leurs atouts au monde.*

Lui : *Peut-être sont-ils en train d'instaurer des changements pendant que nous parlons. Peut-être donneront-ils à chaque femme le choix du type d'armure qu'elle souhaite porter...*

Moi : *Je ne peux pas être la seule fille à me plaindre de ça. Je sais que Kat n'aime pas tellement ça non plus.*

Lui : *Ils prennent à cœur tout notre feed-back.*

Moi : *Vas-y, continue à croire ça. Les filles veulent juste avoir l'air d'être des dures, tu vois ? Plus Jeanne d'Arc et moins princesse Leia dans son bikini doré d'esclave.*

Lui : *Mais Leia a tué Jabba pendant qu'elle portait ce bikini doré. C'était une dure ET elle était terriblement sexy.*

Moi : *Soupir. C'était peut-être un mauvais exemple.*

Lui : *Il se pourrait très bien qu'il y ait du changement.*

Moi : *Ou, ce qui est plus probable... la quête suivante donnera un mini-short moulant en métal assorti à ce haut de bikini !*

Lui : */soupir*

Fallen continua à m'écouter râler. D'abord dans le chat, puis lorsque j'en eus assez d'écrire, j'allumai mon casque et je recommençai dans le micro. Une fois que je me fus calmée, nous retournâmes à la grand-place de la ville, où il nous fallait faire quelques tâches pour nous préparer à notre grande quête suivante avec le groupe. Là, nous allions vendre notre bazar et acheter de la nourriture et des fournitures, puis mettre les objets restants à la banque afin de ne pas avoir à les porter tout le temps.

Cependant, en route vers la banque de Cormir City, je remarquai un rassemblement étonnant. Un avatar féminin – une elfe sexy avec des kilomètres de cheveux blonds jusqu'à ses chevilles et vêtue de la plus minuscule armure brillante, tours des seins incrustés de pierres précieuses et tout – se tenait sur une plate-forme entourée par un certain nombre d'autres personnages.

Le dialogue dans le chat général donnait l'impression qu'il s'agissait d'une vente aux enchères. Et d'après l'installation, l'objet des enchères semblait être l'avatar de l'elfe lui-même.

FallenOne sembla tout aussi perplexe que moi lorsque je lui envoyai un message en lui demandant ce qu'il se passait, au nom de Yondareth.

Lui : *Aucune idée. On dirait que les gens enchérissent pour avoir un peu de temps en tête-à-tête avec l'elfe, qui s'appelle LadyHaHa.*
Moi : *Un tête-à-tête ? Pour quoi faire ?*
Lui : *Euhhh...*

Je continuai à suivre les événements pendant quelques minutes alors que Fallen m'envoya des émoticônes où il secouait la tête et feignait son incrédulité. Enfin, l'innocente petite vierge – c'est-à-dire, moi – comprit.

La fille elfe vendait du cybertemps aux enchères. Comme pour le cybersexe. Les gens proposaient de payer pour avoir un chat virtuel sexuel avec cette elfe 'canon', dont les seins bonnet G n'étaient même pas réels. Bon sang, ce n'était sans doute même pas joué par une femme dans la vie réelle.

Moi : *Hein ? J'hallucine.*
Lui : *Oui. Moi qui croyais avoir tout vu au cours de mes années de jeux vidéo... je suis sans voix.*
Moi : *Tu es toujours sans voix. Tu n'écris que dans le chat.*
Lui : *Très drôle.*

On plaisanta ainsi pendant un peu plus longtemps, mais Fallen me fit bientôt savoir qu'il devait se déconnecter. Je restai à regarder cette vente aux enchères merdique jusqu'au bout. Enfin, un gagnant fut déclaré, la somme fut échangée et les deux participants disparurent dans une chambre privée quelque part au sous-sol d'une auberge pour s'envoyer des émoticônes sexuelles.

Waouh. La plus vieille profession existait même sur Yondareth. Était-ce dérangeant ou ingénieux ? Cela devait dépendre... de tant de choses. Tout d'abord du consentement et de l'âge.

Je haussai les épaules en fronçant les sourcils et je pris note d'enquêter sur ce phénomène lorsque j'aurais plus de temps, peut-être pour créer un article sur mon blog. Tant de choses entraient en jeu et le problème pouvait devenir très complexe, particulièrement pour les créateurs du jeu.

Au cours des jours qui suivirent, je dus admettre que cette elfe me donna vraiment de quoi réfléchir. Si elle était majeure et que l'autre participant était majeur et qu'elle avait besoin d'or... alors, pourquoi pas ?

Y avait-il vraiment quelqu'un qui en souffrait ?

***

Notre groupe s'arrêta de jouer pendant les vacances de Noël. Je rentrai au ranch, où internet était trop médiocre pour les jeux vidéo de toute façon. Heath alla passer du temps avec la famille de Brian en Californie du Nord, et Kat travailla deux fois plus que d'habitude. Fallen faisait ce que Fallen faisait, sans nous en parler, comme d'habitude.

Quand je rentrai à la maison, on ne dit pas un mot de notre petite dispute. Je fus reçue les bras ouverts, avec un câlin et un baiser. Et merci aux divinités, je fus reçue par une mère plus vigoureuse bien que notablement plus maigre.

Mais... je ne fus pas dissuadée de mon enquête sur son mystère financier. Sauf que cette fois, j'attendis qu'elle quitte la maison pour faire quelques courses avant de commencer à fouiller.

Son bureau était complètement rangé. C'était très suspect.

Il n'était *jamais* aussi vide, sauf si elle le rangeait exprès pour m'empêcher de trouver le contenu.

Je ne me laissai pas décourager et je me dirigeai tout droit vers ses livres de comptes. Comme je l'aidais à faire sa comptabilité quand j'étais ado, je savais exactement quoi chercher.

J'ouvris le cahier à la page qui listait ses factures à payer et ma mâchoire tomba. Comment pouvait-elle avoir pris autant de retard ?

Je réfléchis à toute vitesse en parcourant la colonne du solde. Ma mère n'était toujours pas assez en forme pour rouvrir l'auberge, et même si elle l'était, la haute saison ne commençait qu'à la moitié du printemps.

Son solde bancaire était négatif.

Je partis à la recherche de ses bordereaux de paiement. Au bout d'environ cinq minutes, je les trouvai dans le tiroir du bas de sa table de nuit. Je sortis une poignée d'avis de retard de paiement du crédit et un tas inimaginable de factures médicales.

Des factures pour le traitement de sa chimio... pour ses médicaments sur ordonnance... pour les traitements hospitaliers. Elle n'avait pas eu d'assurance pour les couvrir.

Les mains tremblantes et l'estomac dans les talons, je sus ce que je devais faire.

Contrairement à ma mère, il me restait encore de l'argent mis de côté. Il n'y avait que quelques milliers que j'avais économisés de l'argent de ma bourse en vivant chichement, car j'espérais lentement créer de petites économies pour commencer l'École de Médecine.

Ce fut cet argent que je déposai à sa banque le jour même. Quand il arriva sur son compte une semaine plus tard, je sortis ses factures et son livre de comptes – pendant qu'elle donnait de l'eau et à manger aux chevaux, bien sûr – et j'envoyai les factures avec le paiement avant qu'elle puisse protester.

De cette façon, ce serait déjà fait au moment où je lui avouais, et elle ne pouvait défaire ce qui avait été fait.

Je fus capable de couvrir presque tous les paiements en attente.

Sauf le crédit. Je ne savais pas du tout à quel point elle était en retard, et je ne pouvais pas faire de miracles avec mes petites économies. J'allais devoir trouver comment régler le reste plus tard.

Cependant, je ne savais pas encore ce que cela signifiait pour l'École de Médecine. Si je parvenais un jour à passer le concours.

Mais j'allais sûrement trouver un moyen.

Quelques minutes avant de l'embrasser pour dire au revoir, je dis à ma mère ce que j'avais fait.

— Maman, euh, regarde ton livre de comptes avant de payer quoi que ce soit, d'accord ? Et s'il te plaît, ne sois pas fâchée.

Elle me regarda comme si je venais de parler en russe avant de comprendre lentement.

— Mia… qu'as-tu fait ?

Je souris.

— Tu ne peux plus le défaire. Alors, te fâcher contre moi n'arrangera rien du tout.

Elle pâlit.

— Mia…

— Au revoir, maman. Bonne année.

Je montai dans la voiture et je fermai la portière.

— Espèce de sale tête de mule, marmonna-t-elle.

Je descendis ma vitre.

— J'ai entendu ! Et si je suis têtue, c'est parce que je l'ai hérité de toi.

Elle me regarda partir avec de l'inquiétude et de la culpabilité dans les yeux. Je ne savais pas si cette culpabilité venait du fait qu'elle m'avait caché son secret ou du fait qu'elle avait eu besoin de sa fille pour se sortir du pétrin. Cela n'avait pas d'importance.

Je fis du mieux que je pouvais pour ignorer ce regard coupable. Peut-être savait-elle toujours quelque chose que je ne savais pas. Peut-être cachait-elle autre chose.

Peut-être, juste peut-être, ce poids sombre que je portais en moi depuis les derniers mois – depuis l'*année* passée, en fait – allait-il devenir plus lourd au lieu de plus léger…

Chapitre Douze :
Ohé, le manifeste !

" LE JEU DE ROLE EROTIQUE, OU ERP POUR 'EROTIC ROLE Play, doit-il rester ou disparaître ? " – posté sur le blog de Geekette

'Should it stay or should it go?'

(Devrait-il rester ou devrait-il s'en aller?)

S'il reste, il y aura des ennuis…

Bon, je ne vais pas citer de vieilles chansons des années quatre-vingt aujourd'hui.

À la place, j'aimerais parler de la chose la plus étrange que j'ai rencontrée sur la grand-place de Dragon Epoch. Une – ahem – joueuse de rôle érotique professionnelle.

Oui, vous avez bien lu. Une professionnelle qui pratique le jeu de rôle érotique.

C'est bien ça : elle fera plaisir à votre avatar pour la bonne quantité d'or virtuel. Elle vous écrira des choses salaces sur le chat si vous la payez pour son temps.

La plus vieille profession a une place dans Dragon Epoch. Ce type de comportement va-t-il à l'encontre des conditions générales d'utilisation du jeu? Vous savez, ce pavé qui se déroule sur votre écran et pour lequel vous cliquez 'J'accepte' chaque fois qu'il y a une

modification – mais sans jamais le lire ? Nous savons tous que vous vous contentez de mentir et de dire que vous l'avez lu.

Eh bien, je me suis sacrifiée et je l'ai lu afin que vous n'ayez pas besoin de le faire. Les conditions générales de Draco n'interdisent pas explicitement le jeu de rôle coquin, mais bien sûr, il dicte l'utilisation appropriée des ressources du jeu, en particulier en présence de mineurs. Parce qu'il y a beaucoup de moins de 18 ans qui jouent à ce jeu – et bon sang, la plupart sont pénibles –, l'âge de la personne derrière l'avatar doit vraiment être pris en compte.

Personnellement, je pense que tant que les participants sont des adultes consentants et qu'ils prennent la peine de vérifier à la fois l'âge et le consentement, qui suis-je pour m'opposer à ce qu'il se passe dans un chat privé ?

La prostitution est illégale dans de nombreux pays. Son équivalent devrait-il être rendu illégal à Yondareth ? Je pense qu'il faut qu'il y ait un débat sain apportant des arguments des deux côtés du problème. Intervenez et partagez votre opinion dans les commentaires.

***

Brian et Heath rompirent. Comme ça. Sans le moindre avertissement.

Enfin, en dehors du fait que leur relation était merdique, il n'y eut pas de grosse dispute ni d'explosion qui mena à la rupture.

Un week-end, Heath était venu à Anza avec moi pour aider ma mère à faire quelques réparations au ranch, et quand il rentra, son appartement avait été vidé. Cette petite merde de Brian n'avait même pas laissé un mot. Il avait juste pris ses affaires – et plus – et il était parti comme le gros gamin lâche qu'il était.

Et Heath fut dévasté.

Voilà donc Mia avec sa pelle et sa balayette pour venir ramasser les morceaux brisés. J'avais toujours été nulle pour le ménage.

Je lui dis d'apporter son ordinateur portable, des vêtements et son sac de couchage chez moi. Je ne pouvais pas bien garder un œil sur lui là où il se trouvait. Quand il hésita, j'insistai. En fait, je me rendis chez lui et je fis moi-même son sac.

Les épaules courbées, il se résigna à son sort. Il allait rester sous ma surveillance jusqu'à ce que je sache qu'il allait bien.

On passa une grande partie de cette semaine à jouer aux jeux vidéo, entre mes cours, mon travail et les révisions pour mes examens de fin d'année. Plus que quelques semaines avant mon dernier semestre de fac sans cours. Cependant, je devais toujours confronter la question de ce que j'allais faire au sujet de l'École de Médecine.

Le baby-sitting du cœur brisé de Heath servit à me distraire parfaitement de mes propres problèmes.

— Devine ce que j'ai lu sur les forums de Dragon Epoch ce matin ? demanda-t-il vers la fin de la semaine.

— Est-ce que tu trollais les forums au lieu de travailler ?

Il me fit un sourire gêné.

— C'est mon client le plus compréhensif et le plus patient. Il va attendre. Un petit peu, au moins.

J'inspirai profondément et je levai les sourcils sans répondre. Il semblait de bien meilleure humeur ce jour-là et je ne voulais rien dire pour gâcher cela.

— Alors, tu n'as pas deviné… et tu ne le feras sans doute pas, alors je vais simplement te le dire.

Je hochai la tête.

— Je t'en prie.

— Il y a eu un mot mystérieux sur les forums ce matin fournissant des informations au sujet d'une 'quête secrète' qui serait installée dans le jeu.

Je le regardai fixement sans comprendre.

— Une quête secrète ? Que veux-tu dire ?

— Eh bien, personne ne le sait vraiment. C'est juste que nous sommes censés parler à tous les PNJ et qu'il y aura une histoire impliquant la princesse Alloreah'ala – ou quelle que soit la façon de le prononcer. Une espèce de mystère pour lequel il faudra trouver des indices.

Quelque chose au sujet de cette information me parlait. Je fronçai les sourcils en me souvenant d'une conversation que j'avais eue avec mon groupe de jeux vidéo plusieurs mois auparavant...

J'adorerais qu'il y ait une quête secrète... Comme quelque chose de caché dans le jeu en dessous des quêtes évidentes. Peut-être devrions-nous chercher des indices ou parler à des PNJ pour avoir des pistes qui nous mèneraient à des chaînes de quête secrètes.

Ce que Heath venait de décrire ressemblait exactement à ce dont j'avais parlé !

Comme c'était étrange.

Ils avaient finalement accepté une de mes suggestions...

Ou peut-être l'avait-il suggérée, *lui* ?

Peut-être travaillait-il là-bas, finalement. Ou connaissait-il quelqu'un qui y travaillait. La même personne qui lui donnait toutes ces informations internes, comme cet endroit secret, impossible à trouver, où il m'avait emmenée.

Quand j'y pensai vraiment, j'étais simplement contente de voir que mon idée était devenue réalité, du moins, réalité virtuelle. Peu importe comment.

Les possibilités étaient excitantes ! Il me tardait de voir ce que le jeu avait fait avec l'idée, s'il s'agissait bien de plus qu'une simple rumeur.

Après cela, je parcourus les forums à la recherche d'informations sur la quête, écoutant toutes les remarques indiquant qu'il s'agissait de plus qu'une rumeur. Cela pouvait être de la réalité virtuelle, ou bien juste une annonce publicitaire. Je n'allais pas bloquer là-dessus avant d'en être certaine.

Malheureusement, FallenOne fut très rarement en ligne au cours des semaines qui suivirent, alors je ne pus pas le harceler pour obtenir des informations. Mais il ne pouvait pas rester loin pour toujours !

***

À cause de mon compte bancaire à présent presque vide et mon absence de réserves financières, je demandai et j'obtins plus d'heures à l'hôpital. *Bien.*

Même si j'étais parfois irritée par le travail fastidieux, le salaire plus important allait aider à compenser ce que j'avais payé pour les factures de ma mère. Contrairement à mes premières années de fac, je n'allais pas pouvoir financer l'École de Médecine avec des bourses académiques.

Et il restait toujours la question du crédit immobilier de ma mère... tous ces avis de retard me troublaient. Je ne savais pas combien de temps cela allait continuer ni comment ma mère pourrait rassembler l'argent pour couvrir ce qu'elle devait.

Pour cette raison, l'augmentation de mes heures était une bonne chose. Cela signifiait également plus de responsabilités à l'hôpital, ainsi qu'un bon aperçu de ce que pouvait donner le travail dans le domaine médical.

C'était intéressant et ennuyeux, long et excitant. Je me promis de me souvenir de ces expériences quand – si j'allais jusque là – j'allais devenir médecin. Bien que les tâches d'une aide-soignante étaient nécessaires et vitales au fonctionnement de l'hôpital, elles étaient profondément épuisantes. Et frustrantes. Une fois médecin, j'avais l'intention de faire de mon mieux pour avoir de l'empathie et de la reconnaissance envers ceux qui travaillaient dans des métiers souvent ingrats.

— Je suis ici pour un test sanguin, comme le médecin l'a demandé, dit une patiente âgée assise à mon bureau quand j'arrivai un matin.

— D'accord, madame, répondis-je. Pouvez-vous me dire quel médecin l'a demandé ?

Elle me regarda comme si je venais de lui enfoncer le doigt entre les côtes, écarquillant les yeux.

— Oh, je ne sais pas, ma chère. Il était grand. Et mince.

Un grand homme mince. Je ne connaissais pas la majorité des médecins qui travaillaient dans ce département, mais cette description correspondait à environ la moitié de ceux que je connaissais.

— Euh, et quel type de bilan sanguin ?

Elle me fixa avec des yeux vides. J'attendis. Et j'attendis. Quand je n'eus aucune réponse à ma question, je réajustai ma tablette contre ma hanche.

— Comment vous appelez-vous, madame ?

— Johnson, répondit-elle. Elizabeth Johnson.

Oh merde. Elle n'aurait pas pu avoir un nom plus courant.

Je tapai son nom dans l'ordinateur. Quatre Elizabeth Johnson apparurent. Cependant, il me restait encore un moyen de trouver celle qu'il me fallait.

— Quelle est votre date de naissance, madame ?

Son front âgé se plissa.

— C'est une question assez grossière, n'est-ce pas ? Pour une dame de mon âge.

J'eus du mal à ne pas lever les yeux au ciel.

— Euh. J'ai besoin de vous trouver dans le système.

Elle me regarda d'un air suspicieux.

— Hmm. Eh bien, je suis née un treize juin.

— L'année ?

Elle leva les sourcils.

— Cela ne vous suffit pas ?

Je regardai les quatre Elizabeth Johnson. Aucune d'entre elles n'avait pour anniversaire le treize juin.

— Euh. Êtes-vous sûre d'être au bon endroit ?

Elle rougit sous son maquillage épais.

— Enfin, bien sûr ! Je ne suis pas *sénile*.

Je clignai des paupières.

— Je suis désolée, madame. Ce n'est pas ce que je voulais sous-entendre. Mais… vous n'apparaissez pas dans le système sous le nom d'Elizabeth Johnson, et afin de vous trouver par votre date de naissance, j'ai également besoin de l'année.

Ceci continua pendant dix minutes avant que je puisse la convaincre de me donner sa 'véritable' année de naissance, pas celle – cinq ans plus tard – qu'elle donnait habituellement. Je découvris donc qu'elle était enregistrée sous le nom de famille de son deuxième mari.

Ohlala.

Une fois que j'eus localisé le bon compte, je vis qu'elle avait eu sept médecins différents, et aucune demande de test sanguin. Je le sus, car je dus appeler chacun de leurs bureaux pour poser la question.

Oh, mon Dieu, épargne-moi de la folie !

En retournant à la maison un soir après un moment particulièrement difficile aux urgences avec un homme ivre qui avait vomi partout entre deux insultes qu'il me jetait, je pris la douche la plus chaude possible. Bien sûr, chez moi, cela ne dura que trois minutes à cause de la situation de mon chauffe-eau. Mais dans ce temps bref, je sanglotai plus fort que je ne l'avais jamais fait. Il fallait juste que ça sorte.

Puis je me connectai.

Et même si j'étais principalement là pour me détendre, je dus admettre être un peu déçue qu'aucun de mes amis ne soit en ligne. Je vérifiai. Cela faisait plus d'une semaine que FallenOne ne s'était pas connecté ! Mon cœur se serra un peu...

Il m'avait vraiment tardé de discuter avec lui, mais je n'avais pas non plus eu de textos. Je ramassai mon téléphone portable, mais je me ravisai quand je me rendis compte de l'heure qu'il était sur la côte Est.

Je notai mentalement de lui envoyer un texto le lendemain matin pour voir comment il allait...

Il s'avéra que je n'en eus pas besoin. Vingt-cinq minutes plus tard, un message privé de Fallen s'afficha par magie à l'écran. J'essayai de ne pas examiner de trop près le petit frisson d'excitation qui me parcourut lorsque je vis que c'était lui.

*FallenOne vous dit : *Hé. Comment ça va au travail ? Ils te font travailler beaucoup plus que d'habitude.*

*Vous dites à FallenOne : *Pff. Je suis tout le temps fatiguée.*
Lui : *Pourquoi fais-tu autant d'heures ?*
Moi : *Juste envie d'argent, je suppose...*

J'avais décidé de ne pas détailler nos soucis financiers avec qui que ce soit. Je n'avais même pas encore révélé la chose à Heath. Peut-être allais-je le faire, un jour. Mais je devais d'abord régler le problème. La réponse à mes ennuis financiers ne viendrait pas de ce travail. J'avais fait des calculs et malgré le fait que j'avais réussi à vivre avec mon salaire et le revenu du blog, il n'y avait pas grand-chose pour renflouer mes économies.

Les larmes me montèrent aux yeux et je m'ordonnai d'arrêter ces bêtises. Je m'étais seulement autorisé ce bref effondrement d'émotions dans la douche.

Moi : *Je me sens un peu déprimée, ce soir.*
Lui : *Je suis désolé. Puis-je faire quoi que ce soit pour te remonter le moral ?*
Moi : *Je ne sais pas... le pourrais-tu ? As-tu des infos sur cette quête secrète dont tout le monde parle ?*
Lui : *J'ai bien peur que non. Un peu de carnage de pixels ?*
Moi : *C'est tentant... mais non...*
Lui : *Je suis désolé. Tu veux en parler ?*
Moi : *Je ne suis pas sûre d'avoir l'énergie pour ça. Ça t'arrive parfois, ces moments dans la vie ou les choses ne se passent pas comme tu t'y attendais ?*
Lui : *Est-ce que c'est encore au sujet du concours ? Est-ce que tu te tortures pour ça ?*
Moi : *Ce n'est pas seulement le concours.*

Lui : *Tu devrais juste le repasser, tu sais. Passe-le et passe-le et repasse-le. L'échec est simplement une façon d'apprendre. Et à chaque tentative, tu apprendras plus et tu t'en sortiras mieux.*

Moi : *Je me sens trop nulle pour l'envisager. Mais vraiment, c'est plus que juste ce fichu concours. Il n'est qu'une infime partie de mes inquiétudes...*

Lui : *Je suis là pour toi. Je suis ton ami. S'il te plaît, fais-le-moi savoir si je peux faire quoi que ce soit pour t'aider.*

Moi : *Je le ferai. Je te le promets. Je sais que je viens de me connecter, mais en fait, je suis vraiment épuisée. Je crois que je vais plutôt aller me coucher.*

Lui : *D'accord. Mais contacte-moi demain, s'il te plaît ? Je ne veux pas m'inquiéter pour toi toute la journée.*

Moi : *D'accord. Promis. :)*

Lui : *Bonne nuit.*

Moi : *Au revoir.*

Je somnolai avant que ma tête touche l'oreiller, mais mes pensées fusaient dans tous les sens alors que je m'endormais. Bizarrement, la dernière chose à laquelle je pensai, ce fut cette scène étrange dans DE où l'elfe en lingerie d'armure brillante se tenait sur la plate-forme de la grand-place, se vendant aux enchères au plus offrant.

Si seulement c'était aussi facile dans la vie réelle...

Je me réveillai avec une idée entièrement formée dans la tête, prête à être réalisée. Je courus à l'ordinateur, j'ouvris le logiciel de traitement de texte et je me mis à écrire furieusement.

Oh, c'était une idée folle. Complètement tarée. Je n'allais pas pouvoir aller jusqu'au bout. *Jamais* je ne pourrais le faire. Mais c'était tellement insensé et je ne pouvais pas ne pas l'écrire. J'écrivis juste ça comme ça... n'est-ce pas ?

Tout à fait. Et j'écrivis donc aussi vite que mes doigts me le permirent.

Je pense choquer la plupart d'entre vous en affirmant qu'à l'âge presque impensable de vingt-deux ans, je possède toujours un hymen intact. Non, je ne répondrai pas aux questions demandant pourquoi. Oui, je suis hétérosexuelle. NON, je ne veux pas sortir avec toi...

Et je continuai à taper au clavier, ne sachant même pas quand j'allais montrer ceci à une autre personne. Mais je ne pus pas m'arrêter. Je ne pus pas m'arrêter.

Chapitre Treize : WTF ? Qu'est-ce que je viens de lire ?

À : Heath, Persephone (Katya), FallenOne

De : Mia

Re : Une idée folle

Bon, sur un coup de tête, j'ai écrit un 'manifeste'. Je ne suis pas encore certaine de ce que cela signifie ni ce que je vais en faire. Mais je serais honorée que vous le lisiez et que vous me disiez ce que vous en pensez.

Bises,

Mia

Pièce jointe : Manifeste d'une vierge.doc

***

JE ME RENDIS A MON GROUPE DE REVISIONS.

Jon me demanda de sortir avec lui. *Encore.*

Je dus trouver une excuse minable sur le moment. *Encore.*

Cela devenait pénible. Je me promis de faire une séance de brainstorming avec Alex et Jenna pour créer une liste d'excuses qui me serviraient à l'avenir. Il allait finir par comprendre que je n'étais pas intéressée... *non ?*

Et le fait que ce soit lui qui me soulage de ma virginité... j'avais décidé que non.

Non pas que j'avais envie de la vendre aux enchères, non plus. J'attendais d'abord les réactions des autres.

Quand je retournai à mon appartement, le téléphone sonnait pendant que je montais les marches quatre à quatre. C'était la ligne fixe, car, comme toujours, il ne me restait pas beaucoup de minutes ni beaucoup d'argent, alors j'avais demandé aux gens de m'appeler sur la ligne fixe.

J'atteignis le téléphone juste au moment où la personne à l'autre bout raccrochait sans laisser de message.

Merde.

Je devinai que c'était sans doute Heath, alors j'attendis de me poser avant de le rappeler.

Tout d'abord, je vérifiai ma boîte mail et je découvris un rappel du rattrapage MCAT. Sans hésiter plus de cinq secondes, je suivis le lien, je me connectai au site et je repoussai ma date de concours de trois mois. J'avais déjà fait cela deux fois, car ils permettaient une latitude de trente et un jours ou plus avant le test pour décaler la date.

Ceci commençait à devenir un petit jeu malsain d'Évite la Date du Concours, pas moins intense qu'un jeu de chat perché à la récréation de l'école primaire. Lorsque la tension dans ma poitrine diminua, je sus, comme je l'avais su les deux fois précédentes, que j'avais bien fait.

Bien sûr, je me condamnais presque certainement à rater une année avant de pouvoir commencer l'École de Médecine. Ma peur m'avait fait attendre trop longtemps et je m'étais poussée hors du créneau pour m'inscrire l'année suivante. J'avalai une boule dans ma gorge et je rangeai mon lourd fardeau avec le reste de l'inquiétude, de l'angoisse et de la culpabilité qui m'écrasaient dernièrement.

Sans une autre pensée, je déroulai ma liste de mails et je regardai s'il y avait des réponses à mon manifeste. En effet, des mails de Persephone et de FallenOne m'attendaient.

À : Mia
De : FallenOne
Re : Une #%@$ & d'idée

Qu'est-ce que je viens de lire, putain ???
Non, sérieusement. WTF ?

D'accooord. Apparemment, Fallen n'était pas partant. Ou bien il le prenait comme une plaisanterie.

Je l'avais envoyé à moitié pour rire, alors... c'était compréhensible. Je répondis rapidement, en espérant obtenir des clarifications plus tard.

Je descendis jusqu'à la réponse de Kat.

À : Mia
De : Katya Ellison
Re : Une idée géniale

C'était super. Vas-tu le faire ? C'est un peu effrayant, mais aussi super excitant, et... pour être franche, je suis un peu jalouse de ne pas avoir essayé de profiter financièrement de la perte de ma virginité ! T'es trop intelligente.

Alors... vas-tu le faire ?

Ça, c'était mieux... j'avais donc un oui et un non, encore que ce dernier était peut-être une plaisanterie. Et Heath, le joker. Il était temps de découvrir ce qu'il pensait.

Je décrochai le combiné et je l'appelai.

— Salut, poupée, répondit-il, bien plus en forme qu'il ne l'avait été au cours des trois dernières semaines depuis le départ de Brian. Heath commençait enfin à guérir... même si j'avais pris de ses nouvelles chaque jour.

— Salut ! piaillai-je. Comment vas-tu aujourd'hui ?

— Je suis épuisé. J'avais une date limite pour ce projet. Je viens de poster la dernière partie du travail il y a une heure. Maintenant, je suis assis devant la télé et je végète sans réfléchir.

Je marquai une pause.

— Ah d'accord, alors tu ne viens pas d'essayer de m'appeler ?

— Non, pourquoi ?

— Je rentrais du groupe de révisions et je n'ai pas décroché à temps. Pas de message.

Il y eut un bruissement, comme s'il réajustait sa position sur son canapé en cuir bruyant.

— Tu sais que je laisse toujours un message. Même si je déteste ça.

— C'est vrai. Alors, je suppose que tu n'as pas regardé tes mails ?

Je tripotai le fil de mon téléphone, me sentant soudain nerveuse sans vraiment comprendre pourquoi.

— Non. Je n'ai fait rien d'autre que travailler sur cette mise à jour du site. Pourquoi, j'ai raté quelque chose ?

— Euh, j'ai envoyé quelque chose à Kat, Fallen et toi pour avoir votre opinion. Les deux autres m'ont répondu, plus ou moins, et je me demandais ce que tu en pensais.

— Une seconde. J'ouvre mon portable…

Je m'éclaircis la gorge, souhaitant soudain raccrocher pendant qu'il lisait. Voulais-je vraiment entendre sa réaction en temps réel ?

— Je vais…

— C'est une blague, hein ? Le Manifeste d'une Vierge ?

— Je l'ai écrit pour rigoler.

— D'accord.

Il marqua une pause et je supposai qu'il lisait encore. Je m'agitai sur ma chaise, mal à l'aise.

— C'est un traité intéressant, Mia. À quoi sert-il ? Es-tu en train de défendre ton droit de rester vierge sans jugement, ou bien essaies-tu de dire que tu veux profiter du fait d'être encore vierge ?

Je clignai des paupières.

— Je, euh, la deuxième idée, en fait.

Une longue pause.

— Je suis perdu. Peux-tu recommencer du début ?

— Il y a quelques semaines, Fallen et moi étions ensemble dans le jeu parce que tu étais… sorti, tout comme Kat…

Il valait mieux ne pas lui rappeler qu'il était avec son ex.

— Nous avons travaillé sur cette quête crétine des feux d'artifice et je me sentais énervée. Quand nous sommes revenus en ville, une femme se tenait sur une scène de la grand-place et elle se vendait aux enchères pour du cybersexe.

Il rit.

— Ouais, je l'ai déjà croisée. Elle m'a fait une proposition une fois. J'ai dû la rejeter gentiment et lui dire que je n'étais pas intéressé. Je vais supposer qu'elle t'a inspirée pour écrire sur le thème des enchères de cybersexe dans ton blog ?

— Elle m'a effectivement inspirée, mais pas seulement pour mon blog.

Il rit.

— Tu ne vas quand même pas te mettre toi-même aux enchères…

J'hésitai, espérant qu'il parvienne à la bonne conclusion, craignant l'appréhension que j'entendais déjà dans sa voix.

Après une minute de gêne, il brisa le silence.

— C'est hilarant, Mia. Tu m'as bien eu. Tu m'as fait trop peur pendant une minute.

Je déglutis.

— Je, euh… je ne plaisantais pas.

Silence.

Plus de silence.

Je ne l'entendais même pas respirer. Rien.

— De toutes les conneries débiles que j'ai entendues – et j'en ai entendu beaucoup, étant donné avec qui j'avais une relation – , je n'ai jamais entendu quelque chose d'aussi ridicule. S'il te plaît, dis-moi que c'est une blague.

Je soupirai, tentée de faire passer la chose pour une plaisanterie. Je n'étais même pas obligée de me tenir à cette idée, non ? Tout cela, c'était… théorique. Je testais, me dis-je. Mais quelque chose au fond de moi me dit de ne pas céder.

— Je viens de te dire que non, répondis-je doucement.

Une autre longue période de silence. J'attrapai un stylo et je me mis à griffonner sur le dos d'une enveloppe. Des boucles et des carrés tous connectés. Mon stylo repassa plusieurs fois sur les mêmes lignes, creusant de profonds sillons dans le papier.

— Je sais que nous venons de parler de te faire dépuceler, mais ça, ce n'est pas ce que je voulais dire. Tu m'as aussi demandé si tu étais connue pour avoir fait quelque chose de stupide, et jusqu'à maintenant, j'aurais dit non. Merde. C'est de la folie. Pourquoi envisager de faire une chose pareille ?

Je m'agitai sur ma chaise.

— Je crois que je l'ai assez clairement expliqué dans le manifeste.

— N'importe quoi. C'est une histoire d'argent. Dis-moi ce qu'il se passe.

— L'argent, c'est un bonus, oui. J'aimerais avoir une façon de payer l'École de Médecine et, euh, d'autres choses.

— Quelles autres choses ?

Je lui expliquai brièvement les factures de ma mère et les rappels du crédit immobilier. Il inspira et rétorqua tout de suite :

— Pourquoi ne me l'as-tu pas dit ? J'aurais pu t'aider…

— Tu avais tes propres problèmes à ce moment-là, répondis-je en faisant référence à sa rupture. Et j'avais tout sous contrôle, autant que possible.

— Je ne comprends pas du tout. Tu as une période difficile avec l'échec au concours et la maladie de ta mère, et maintenant les problèmes financiers. Je comprends. Mais c'est tout ce que c'est : une période difficile. Et elle va passer.

— Peut-être ai-je envie de faire quelque chose d'actif au lieu d'attendre pendant que la vie jette des obstacles devant moi.

Ma voix trembla lorsque je sentis ma détermination grandir.

— Peut-être ai-je envie de surmonter...

— Comment pourrais-tu même le faire ? Au cas où tu aurais besoin d'un rappel, la prostitution est illégale dans ce pays.

Je regardai le morceau de mur blanc devant moi sans le voir.

— Pas partout dans ce pays. Il y a des bordels légaux et sécurisés dans le Nevada. Je pourrais en contacter un et leur demander de l'aide.

Il poussa ce qui ressemblait à un grognement de frustration.

— Je peux pas, avec ces conneries, Mia.

Mon estomac se noua. L'approbation de Heath était si importante pour moi que je faillis tout arrêter. *Presque...*

— J'adorerais avoir ton soutien, mais je continuerai sans lui, si nécessaire.

— Tu veux que je t'*aide* à te vendre aux enchères à un inconnu ? Tu te rends compte que c'est pour du sexe avec quelqu'un, n'est-ce pas ?

Je levai les yeux au ciel, ne prenant pas la peine de répondre à cette stupidité. Les cercles et les carrés s'étaient transformés en x colériques, si profondément entaillés dans le papier qu'ils marquaient également la couche au-dessous.

— Je ne peux pas te forcer à m'aider si tu ne le veux pas...

Ma voix trembla, mais une nouvelle possibilité émergeait. *Pouvais-je le faire ?*

Heath marmonna quelque chose d'incohérent, sans doute rempli de gros mots, puis il dit :

— Je suis épuisé et je n'arrive pas à réfléchir, et je ne peux pas bien intégrer tout ceci. Je veux te rencontrer à ce sujet demain.

— D'accord. Je suis là et je suis disponible pour ça.

— Promets-moi de ne rien faire en attendant que nous nous parlions.

Je haussai les épaules, tout en sachant qu'il ne pouvait pas me voir.

— Si nous nous voyons demain, il n'y a pas grand-chose que je pourrai faire de toute façon.

— Tu ne contactes pas les bordels ou quoi que ce soit. Tu réfléchis vingt-quatre heures. S'il te plaît, c'est tout ce que je demande.

— Tout ce que tu demandes avant de travailler à me faire changer d'avis ?

Il poussa un soupir impatient.

— Promets-le-moi, c'est tout.

— D'accord, je te le promets.

Nous raccrochâmes et je m'enfouis immédiatement le visage entre les mains, en me frottant les yeux. Même si je ne l'avais pas laissé paraître à Heath, j'étais toujours indécise. J'adorais l'idée des enchères, mais je détestais sa réalité. J'adorais le fait de m'affirmer tout en détestant le fait de devoir m'engager pour au moins une nuit de travail sexuel afin de l'accomplir.

Tout ceci était sans doute théorique. Cela n'aboutirait à rien. Je n'avais pas le cran d'aller jusqu'au bout.

Si ?

Troublée, je fis ce que je préférais : je passai un short et des chaussures pour courir puis, au lieu de sortir, je démarrai l'ordinateur et je me connectai au jeu.

Je ne savais pas pourquoi je m'attendais à ce que Fallen soit connecté. Il l'était rarement durant la journée. Mais les quelques dernières fois que je m'étais connectée, peu importe l'heure du jour ou de la nuit, il s'était connecté peu de temps après. C'était presque comme s'il avait découvert le rythme de mes connexions et qu'il savait à quel moment me chercher.

Et je ne voulus pas admettre à moi-même que je me connectais pour le trouver. Ou que j'attendais qu'il me trouve.

Au bout d'environ une heure de jeu en solo, une notification éclaira la boîte de dialogue de mon écran. Je fus très déçue lorsque je vis que c'était Katya, pas Fallen.

Elle m'envoya immédiatement un message.

*Persephone vous dit : *Salut ! Allume ton chat vocal !*

Je cliquai sur le menu des paramètres, car cela faisait un moment que je n'avais pas allumé le chat vocal. Dernièrement, cela avait eu tendance à ralentir mon jeu, alors je n'avais pas utilisé cette fonction autant qu'avant.

— Raconte ! Ce Manifeste d'une Vierge, c'était pour de vrai ?

Je tripotai le casque, l'ajustant de façon à ce que les enceintes couvrent mes oreilles.

— Oui... oui, dis-je en essayant de cacher le doute dans ma voix.

— Waouh, t'es couillue, copine. Je suis impressionnée.

— Merci. Je suis ravie que quelqu'un approuve.

— Ah bon ? Heath a-t-il dit quelque chose ? Les hommes sont bizarres avec ce genre de choses.

— Oui, soupirai-je. Ils ne le prennent pas bien.

— *Ils* ? Qui d'autre ? *Fallen* ?

Je m'agitai sur ma chaise, attrapant le jouet d'un Happy Meal Star Wars que j'avais depuis des lustres.

— Oui, il m'a envoyé une réponse très sèche. J'ai répondu en lui disant que ce n'était pas une plaisanterie, et il n'a pas réagi depuis.

— Ça ne fait que quelques heures, non ? Je ne m'inquiéterais pas. Il a un emploi du temps bizarre, tu te souviens ?

Je jetai mon enveloppe couverte d'encre à la poubelle.

— Oui. Je suppose.

— Et puis, ça lui fait sûrement mal au cul, puisqu'il s'intéresse à toi.

Je fronçai les sourcils.

— De quoi parles-tu ?

— Oh, allez, ne fais pas la pudique. Je sais que toi aussi tu as dû le remarquer. Tu te souviens de notre méthode scientifique ?

Je ricanai.

— On s'amusait. Il ne s'intéresse pas à moi !

Je m'agitai à nouveau et j'essayai d'ignorer cette impression que j'avais lorsque je le cherchais et qu'il apparaissait. Un béguin de ce genre ne menait nulle part, alors il valait mieux le supprimer tout de suite.

— Comment est-ce possible ? Nous ne nous sommes jamais vus en personne… nous n'avons même pas eu une conversation décente au téléphone.

— L'amour a ses raisons… dit-elle en chantonnant.

L'amour… n'importe quoi.

Je ricanai encore.

— Tu es folle.

— Beaucoup de gens trouvent l'amour en ligne. Et des tonnes de gens se lient à travers des jeux en ligne comme DE. Ce n'est pas impossible, Mia.

— Mais pour qu'il s'agisse d'amour, il faut que ce soit réciproque. Et ce n'est pas le cas.

— En es-tu *certaine*? Cela fait longtemps que je te soupçonne d'avoir un petit béguin, toi aussi.

Je rougis terriblement et je fus ravie qu'il ne s'agisse pas d'un chat vidéo à cause de la chaleur qui irradiait de mon visage et de ma poitrine. Une chaleur due à la gêne, mais aussi parce que j'étais obligée de reconnaître ce qu'elle disait.

— Je crois que tu hallucines et que tu projettes des choses sur les autres, aboyai-je.

Elle poussa un long soupir.

— Si tu le dis. Allons tuer des choses... peut-être auras-tu réglé toutes tes enchères après avoir commis un massacre virtuel.

— C'est toujours bon pour l'esprit créatif, répondis-je en riant.

C'est donc ce que l'on fit. Au lieu de faire des quêtes, on se positionna dans un coin peuplé d'un donjon et on attendit des respawns, les tuant encore et encore.

Fallen ne se connecta pas ce soir-là et cela causa une sensation de déception et de tension en plus de tout le reste. Les soupçons de Katya m'effrayaient et m'enthousiasmaient en même temps. Mais qu'est-ce que tout ceci voulait dire sur le long terme? Et comment quelque chose de valable pouvait-il naître entre nous alors qu'il me cachait constamment des choses? FallenOne ne pouvait jamais être plus pour moi qu'un bon ami en ligne. Dans quelques années, nous serions sans doute des étrangers l'un pour l'autre.

Malgré tout, après tout ce massacre et ces bavardages avec Katya, je ne savais toujours pas quoi décider au sujet de ce manifeste.

***

Pour la première fois depuis longtemps, je luttai contre une insomnie. Et quand je finis par m'endormir, je fis des rêves toutes les minutes, qui me réveillaient et m'épuisaient. Ils apparaissaient de façon persistante, comme des respawns dans le jeu, m'assaillant encore et encore.

Dans un de ces rêves, j'étais au ranch à Anza… sauf qu'il était désert. J'étais entièrement seule. Ma mère, toutes les aides du ranch, même les chevaux avaient disparu. C'était comme si j'étais la dernière personne sur Terre. J'errais dans ce lieu en l'appelant, en appelant n'importe qui, sans réponse. Le vent et les échos de mes cris me parvenaient sans autre réaction.

Ensuite, je fus assise à un bureau dans une classe lumineuse, un test vierge devant moi. Mais je ne pouvais pas le lire ni comprendre quoi que ce soit. Le papier était couvert de symboles incompréhensibles – ou peut-être d'une langue étrangère que je ne pouvais reconnaître. J'avais plusieurs crayons parfaitement alignés sur mon bureau, avec des pointes parfaitement taillées, prêts à être utilisés. Mais avec chaque minute qui passait et que je regardais ce test, il devenait de plus en plus difficile à comprendre. C'était ma dernière chance au concours MCAT et j'étais totalement perdue.

Je me réveillai un bout de souffle.

Et avec une nouvelle conviction. Je détestais cette sensation d'impuissance. J'allais être proactive. Il était temps de prendre le contrôle.

Pas en repassant ce fichu test, cependant. Je n'étais pas tout à fait prête pour *ça*.

Plus tard dans l'après-midi, Heath apparut sur le seuil de ma porte, les beaux traits de son visage figés dans un air solennel, un sac d'ordinateur portable sur l'épaule, la bandoulière faisant le tour de son torse massif. Sans un mot, je fis un pas de côté et je le laissai entrer.

Il s'installa prudemment sur mon vieux canapé grinçant et je m'installais sur le pouf. Puis, je lui proposai une bouteille d'eau fraîche qu'il déboucha et dont il but rapidement la moitié.

— J'ai vraiment, *vraiment* besoin de savoir, que tu ne me joues pas une farce avec ces conneries fut sa façon de commencer.

Je levai les sourcils et je me mordis la lèvre.

— Je ne suis pas si cruelle.

Heath défit son sac et sortit son appareil en l'ouvrant d'un geste brusque et déterminé.

— J'ai réfléchi à une liste d'alternatives à cette connasse de vente aux enchères.

Ma colère monta et je croisai les bras.

— Je suis une connasse, maintenant ?

— Pas toi. La vente aux enchères. Écoute-moi.

Il indiqua la liste. Waouh… il avait vraiment réfléchi, hein ?

— Premièrement, tu as terminé tes cours, alors tu peux obtenir un boulot mieux rémunéré que celui que tu as à l'hôpital.

Je fronçai les sourcils.

— Mais celui de l'hôpital n'est pas seulement une histoire de salaire. C'est pour m'aider à préparer mon CV pour l'École de Médecine. J'ai besoin de ce boulot pour mon CV.

— D'accord, alors tu peux trouver un deuxième travail.

Je hochai la tête.

— Très bien. Dans un club de strip-tease, peut-être ? Il paraît qu'ils paient bien. Mais je suis une danseuse merdique.

— Alors tu pourrais faire le service chez Hooters.

Je regardai ma poitrine minuscule.

— Il n'y a qu'un homo qui pourrait me suggérer que j'ai assez d'atouts pour travailler chez Hooters.

Alors un travail normal de serveuse. Ou une réceptionniste. Ou n'importe quoi qui ne t'oblige pas à te coucher sur le dos et à écarter les jambes.

Je lui jetai un regard noir.

— Suivant ?

— Tu pourrais vendre tes objets de valeur.

Je me mis à rire si fort que cela m'empêcha de respirer. Mon vieux tas de ferraille motorisé m'obtiendrait peut-être mille ou deux mille dollars, mais c'était tout. Et il savait très bien que je n'avais pas d'objets de valeur. Pas de bijoux, pas d'objets électroniques coûteux. Rien.

— D'accord, d'accord. J'espérais juste que tu avais un vieil objet de famille par exemple.

— Oui, les millions en obligations de mon bon à rien de donneur de sperme biologique. Mais je gardais ça pour une occasion spéciale.

Heath leva les yeux au ciel et se remit à lire sur son ordinateur.

— Il existe des crédits.

Je levai les mains.

— J'en dois déjà plusieurs milliers. Arrête-toi, s'il te plaît. Tu ne m'aides pas. Tu crois que je n'ai pas déjà réfléchi à tout ça ? Comment pourrais-je gagner assez d'argent en très peu de temps pour aider le problème du crédit immobilier de maman ?

Il secoua la tête.

— Tu ne sais même pas combien d'argent elle doit.

— Plusieurs milliers. J'en suis certaine. Maintenant, arrête la condescendance.

Il rougit.

— Je n'essayais pas de…

Il ferma les yeux et il inspira profondément.

— Je sais que tu as de bonnes intentions, commençai-je.

Il grinça des dents.

— Toi aussi, tu peux arrêter d'être condescendante. J'essaie simplement de te faire entendre raison et de te montrer que cette voie drastique et destructrice n'est pas la seule option.

Je serrai les bras autour de moi comme si j'essayais d'invoquer plus de force, mais je restai silencieuse.

Heath secoua la tête et il bougea en faisant grincer le canapé.

— Je ne peux pas te dire à quel point je suis sérieux. Quand on ne parlait que de la perte de ta virginité, c'était une discussion sans conséquence. Maintenant, tu veux la monétiser ? Et pour quelle raison ? Si ta mère découvrait ce que tu faisais pour l'aider, elle piquerait une crise.

Je me penchai en avant en lançant des éclairs avec les yeux.

— Elle ne va pas le découvrir, n'est-ce pas ?

Heath grimaça.

— Pas par moi. Mais Mia, c'est de la folie. Vraiment, je dois dire que c'est de la folie. S'il te plaît, réfléchis à tout ça et…

Je tapai du pied.

— J'y ai réfléchi. *Constamment.* Alors, n'essaie pas de me faire ta petite 'mecsplication'.

Il rit et il leva les yeux au ciel, jetant la tête en arrière d'exaspération.

— Ce n'est pas une mecsplication. Bon sang. Je veux juste… je veux ce qu'il y a de mieux pour toi. Je veux que tu aies une meilleure expérience pour ta première fois que ce que tu as prévu. Un inconnu louche dans une chambre d'hôtel quelque part, franchement ?

— Eh bien, tu m'as dit que la première fois n'était pas si fabuleuse, de toute façon. Pourquoi ne pas le faire avec une longue liste de règles et de précisions ? C'est *mon* corps et *je* contrôle ce qui lui arrive.

Heath s'immobilisa subitement avant de pousser un long soupir. Il redressa la tête en me regardant dans les yeux.

— Alors c'est pour ça ? Pour avoir le contrôle de la situation ? À cause de ce que Zach t'a fait au lycée ?

Je croisai à nouveau les bras.

— Le contrôle, c'est très important pour moi. Particulièrement après cette année, après avoir presque perdu maman. Et échoué au MCAT. Ce n'est pas juste à cause de ce qui est arrivé au lycée. C'est pour tout le reste.

Heath hocha la tête, la bouche légèrement ouverte.

— Mais ce n'est pas simplement le contrôle sur cette nuit. Tu veux tout contrôler. Comment cela se passe. Quand cela se passe. Ce qu'il se passe après…

Sa voix s'estompa.

Je soutins son regard et je hochai lentement la tête. Tout ceci me semblait parfaitement évident, mais il venait juste d'avoir une sorte d'éclair de compréhension.

— Je crois que je comprends maintenant… l'histoire de contrôle.

Il continua à me regarder fixement.

J'inspirai profondément.

— Pas besoin de me psychanalyser. Tu n'es pas mon psy.

— Tu devrais peut-être discuter avec le tien.

Je haussai les épaules.

— C'est peut-être ce que je ferai… quand j'y retournerai la prochaine fois.

Je n'avais aucune intention de le faire, mais si Heath se sentait mieux en le pensant, pourquoi ne pas ajouter cela à mes arguments ?

— En fin de compte, il s'agit de mon corps. Ma décision. Je le ferai avec ou sans ton aide, Heath.

Il hocha la tête.

— D'accoooord… mais si tu veux mon aide, tu dois me convaincre que tu le fais pour les bonnes raisons.

Je me mordis la lèvre.

— Et que sont les bonnes raisons, Heath ? Quelles que soient les raisons que j'ai, cela devrait être les bonnes raisons pour moi.

Son visage s'assombrit.

— Je suis désolé. Ce que j'ai dit était arrogant, n'est-ce pas ? Comme si j'étais en mesure de déterminer ce qui était le mieux pour toi. C'est juste… c'est juste que je ne veux pas que tu souffres, Mia.

Je me levai et je me glissai sur le canapé à côté de lui, sur la petite place qui restait entre sa grande carcasse et le sac de son ordinateur.

— Je sais que tu ne voulais pas paraître arrogant. Mais oui, tu sais que je suis une grande fille.

Il secoua la tête en se penchant en avant.

— Mia. Il faut que tu sois sûre de toi. Et tu dois faire attention. On parle de quelque chose de très grave.

Je ris en tremblant un peu.

— Je sais. Et moi aussi, ça me fait mourir de peur.

Et c'était vrai… mon cœur battait dans ma carotide, j'avais du mal à déglutir. Cet instant – ce clignement de paupières au cours duquel ma détermination prit forme – était absolument terrifiant.

Et… *libérateur*.

— Il y a si peu de choses que je peux faire pour elle. Si peu en mon pouvoir pour l'aider. Mais je peux faire *ça*. Heath… *s'il te plaît…*

Heath ferma les yeux et se pinça l'arête du nez.

— Je vais t'aider, dans ce cas. Mais seulement si tu me laisses tout contrôler.

Et il pensait que j'avais des problèmes avec le contrôle ? Je levai les sourcils.

— Seulement si ça signifie que tu ne vas pas tout annuler.

Il secoua la tête.

— Non. Je ne ferai pas ça. Au final, c'est toi qui diras si la chose se fait ou pas. Mais… je veux pouvoir avoir mon mot à dire sur les détails. Comment tu t'y prends. Comment tu te protèges. Le jargon légal. J'ai un ami avocat qui peut nous aider, je crois.

Je hochai la tête.

— Je peux faire ça. Je peux…

Ma voix s'estompa, soudain étranglée d'émotion.

— Heath… merci.

— Ne me remercie pas encore. Nous ne savons pas du tout comment toute cette merde va finir.

Il se pencha en avant et il me fit un de ses câlins géants.

— Tu sais que je ferais n'importe quoi pour toi et je vais faire tout ce qui est en mon pouvoir pour te protéger.

— Je sais. Merci. Et je vais faire tout ce qui est en mon pouvoir pour ne pas avoir besoin de cette protection.

— Quel que soit le pervers qui gagne ces enchères et qui couche avec toi…

— Essayons de ne pas y penser de cette façon, dis-je contre son épaule. Peut-être est-ce quelqu'un de gentil qui veut s'assurer que ma première fois soit bonne.

— Et tu crois que moi, je suis idéaliste ?

— Enfin, qui qu'il soit, je penserai à lui comme un moyen de sécuriser mon avenir et de prouver mon nouveau paradigme.

J'essayai d'ignorer la boule dans ma gorge.

— Tout se passera bien, Heath, dis-je avant de m'interrompre brutalement lorsque ma voix se mit à trembler.

Il me serra plus fort, mais il ne dit rien. Je fermai les yeux et je posai ma tête sur son épaule.

J'espérais seulement que qui que soit ce type, il ne laisse qu'une marque quelconque et insipide sur mon passé. Qu'il ne crée pas d'impression durable. Ce serait une nuit dans ma vie et rien d'autre ne changerait, si ce n'était la taille de mon compte bancaire et mon statut de vierge.

C'était aussi simple que cela.

***

— D'accord, tourne-toi de l'autre côté et, euh, penche-toi contre les rochers.

Heath tenait l'appareil photo devant lui, fixant le viseur à l'arrière tout en appuyant sur le bouton.

Une semaine s'était écoulée depuis notre conversation dans mon appartement. Heath avait le mérite de ne pas avoir essayé encore une fois de me faire changer d'avis.

Je suivis ses instructions, essayant d'ignorer les curieux qui me regardaient en passant. Je portais un bikini jaune et noir à pois, le vent de la plage agitant mes cheveux dans tous les sens. Je les enlevai de mes cheveux et je basculai mes hanches vers la droite, me sentant à la fois ridicule et courageuse.

Arg. Je ne portais jamais de bikinis. Ce n'était pas parce que je n'aimais pas mon apparence. Je m'étais toujours bien sentie dans ma peau, enfin, en dehors de ma poitrine inexistante.

Mais l'*ironie* de la chose. L'ironie terrible de prendre la pose dans un bikini en tissu dans la vraie vie pour cette vente aux enchères alors que je passais tellement de temps à rager contre les bikinis métalliques habillant si souvent les avatars féminins…

Pour être honnête, je me sentais hypocrite.

J'étais complètement dépassée. J'avais déjà mentalement accepté le fait que j'allais coucher avec un inconnu qui allait payer le privilège de me déflorer. Ça, je l'avais accepté. Mais le fait de prendre une pose sexy en bikini, de me dégrader sur la jetée de Corona del Mar, cela frôlait la limite à toute cette combine illicite, c'était la goutte d'eau.

J'avais la gorge serrée tout le temps, et bizarrement, je me sentis détachée de mon environnement lorsque Heath m'ordonna de faire la moue pour l'appareil photo. Si je n'avais pas été pas dans cette étrange fugue en dehors de ma propre réalité, je me serais moquée de lui.

Cela venait de devenir réel.

Plus tard dans la journée, Heath m'envoya des photos. Elles n'étaient pas mauvaises, coupées de façon à cacher mon identité.

Je préparai l'article. Tout d'abord, je listai le Manifeste d'une Vierge avec les photos et un lien vers le site des enchères. Ce lien menait à un autre serveur et un lieu situé à l'extérieur du pays, ainsi que Heath l'avait mis en place. Je m'étais donné trois semaines pour les enchères et j'espérais que cela minimiserait l'attention des médias ayant vent de l'affaire. Avec un peu de chance, le marché aurait lieu peu de temps après.

Je programmai l'article de façon à ce qu'il soit mis en ligne tôt le lendemain matin pendant que j'étais encore travail, espérant avoir mis en place suffisamment de garde-fous pour protéger mon anonymat.

Et… je restai loin des réseaux sociaux ce jour-là. Je partis travailler, puis au groupe de révisions et je n'ouvris même pas mon navigateur quand je rentrai à la maison.

J'évitai également les mails.

À la place, je me connectai sur DE et je regardai ma liste d'amis. Personne n'était en ligne. Je fis quelques quêtes mineures et bien sûr, une demi-heure plus tard, mon écran de notifications s'éclaira.

*Votre ami, FallenOne, est en ligne.

Mon écran clignota immédiatement avec un nouveau message privé de Fallen.

*FallenOne vous dit : *Tu vas vraiment laisser un inconnu te baiser pour du fric ?*

Ma mâchoire tomba et je reculai la tête de l'écran. Waouh. Il n'avait pas l'intention de mâcher ses mots, hein ? Il y allait sans retenue. Cela ne lui ressemblait pas du tout. Je serrai la mâchoire et je posai les mains sur le clavier pour écrire ma réponse.

*Vous dites à FallenOne : *C'est une façon un peu crue de présenter la chose. C'est au sujet de mon nouveau paradigme. C'est un acte féministe.*

Lui : *C'est de la prostitution. Tu te transformes volontairement en pute ordinaire.*

Moi : *Une fois. Et tout sera parfaitement légal.*

Lui : *On s'en fout des détails légaux. Ce que tu fais, c'est destructeur. Pour TOI. Pour ton avenir.*

Moi : *C'est MON corps.*

Lui : *C'est aussi ce que disent tous les drogués, les alcooliques, les anorexiques.*

Moi : *As-tu envie d'avoir une conversation adulte sur ce thème, ou bien vas-tu te contenter de m'insulter ?*

Lui : *Si je pensais que tu allais m'écouter, j'écrirais toute la nuit.*

Moi : *D'accord. Eh bien, je t'écoute.*

Lui : *Mia, as-tu considéré comment ceci va affecter ton avenir ? Et si tu rencontrais quelqu'un dont tu tombais amoureuse... diras-tu à ton futur mari que tu as été prostituée pour une nuit ?*

Moi : *Diras-tu à ta future femme que tu as baisé cette fille sur la table de conférences au bureau de ton oncle ? Quelle est la différence ? Que savent vraiment les gens et que veulent-ils savoir des anciens partenaires de leurs amants ?*

Lui : *Ce n'est pas la même chose. Pas du tout.*

Moi : *Et si tu tombais amoureux d'une femme et que tu étais sur le point de l'épouser, cela ferait-il une différence pour toi qu'elle te dise avoir vendu du sexe contre de l'argent dans le passé ? Est-ce que tu romprais avec elle à cause de ça ?*

On continua de cette façon pendant des heures. J'avais mal aux doigts et il continuait à taper au clavier. Parfois de longs traités de plusieurs paragraphes au sujet de la nature destructrice du travail sexuel et comment ces actes niaient vraiment le message féministe que j'essayais de faire passer sur mon blog, même si j'essayais de le cacher avec mon 'manifeste idiot'.

Fallen devint de plus en plus frustré et de plus en plus insultant à mesure que le temps passait. Quand j'eus les yeux larmoyants et irrités d'avoir trop bâillé, je sus qu'il fallait que je me couche. Mais je ne voulais pas être la première à abandonner cette conversation.

Et pour Fallen, je vis qu'il était *très* important que je change d'avis.

Cependant, il refusa de me dire pourquoi c'était si important pour lui. Oui, il était évident qu'il avait une opinion très marquée sur la chose, mais apparemment il ne ressentait rien d'aussi fort à mon sujet. Il me cachait toujours des choses. Alors, je n'étais clairement pas assez importante...

Lui : *En fait, tu t'endommages volontairement.*

Moi : *Excuse-moi. Mais je ne vois pas du tout les choses de cette façon. Tu ne peux pas me juger ainsi. Tu es comme Malcolm Reynolds et son manque de respect hypocrite pour Inara.*

Lui : *Ce n'est pas Firefly, Mia. C'est la vraie vie, pas la télé.*

Comme je m'y étais attendue, il avait parfaitement compris la référence.

Moi : *C'est un exemple.*

Lui : *En outre, Mal respecte tout à fait Inara. Ce qu'il déteste, c'est sa profession. Et tu n'es pas une " compagne officielle " comme l'est Inara. C'est quelque chose qui n'existe même pas dans notre monde.*

Firefly est le fruit de l'imagination de Joss Whedon. Le fait que tu écartes les jambes pour un pervers, ça ne l'est pas.

Moi : *Arrête de me parler comme si j'étais un enfant.*

Lui : *J'essaie simplement de te raisonner.*

Moi : *La façon dont je perds ma virginité, c'est mon affaire.*

Lui : *Et, bien sûr, l'affaire du pervers dégoûtant qui t'achète.*

Moi : *Je ne vais pas supporter tes conneries plus longtemps. Va les débiter ailleurs.*

Lui : *Eh bien, je ne te retiens pas. Je suis certain que tu veux t'occuper de tes enchères. Que le meilleur dépravé gagne.*

*FallenOne s'est déconnecté de Dragon Epoch

Je restai assise à fixer l'écran, stupéfaite, remarquant le nœud que j'avais à l'estomac. Mes yeux se mirent à piquer.

Juste un petit peu…

Peut-être… peut-être ne le verrais-je plus jamais en ligne.

Et peut-être que cette vente aux enchères était une erreur. Mais c'était la mienne.

Peut-être avait-il raison de dire que les ramifications de cette unique nuit allaient influencer tout le reste de ma vie. Qui pouvait dire ce que l'avenir me réservait ?

J'étais à un tournant de ma vie… sans savoir où cela me conduirait. Et je me préparai à faire mon choix, le cœur battant, et une peur froide dans la gorge.

J'espérais que mon chemin n'allait pas s'effriter sous mes pieds et me conduire au désastre…

L'histoire de Mia continue dans *À n'importe quel prix*…

Au sujet de l'auteure

Brenna Aubrey est une auteure Best sellers USA TODAY d'histoires d'amour contemporaines qui se concentrent sur la culture geek.

Elle a depuis toujours cherché le réconfort dans de bons livres et les longues histoires compliquées qu'elle tisse dans sa tête. Brenna est une fille de la ville avec le cœur d'une amoureuse de la nature. Elle se retrouve donc dans des espaces verts dès qu'elle le peut. Elle est aussi une maman, professeur, fille geek, francophile, une joueuse de jeux vidéo décomplexée et une lectrice compulsive.

Elle réside actuellement sur la côte ouest avec son mari, deux enfants, deux adorables chiots golden retriever, un oiseau et quelques poissons.